Sam Hayes grew up in the Midlands, and has lived in Australia and America. She lives in a three-hundred-year-old farmhouse in a Leicestershire village with her husband and three children.

For more information about Sam Hayes, visit her website
www.samhayes.co.uk

BLOOD
SAM TIES
HAYES

headline

First published in 2007
by HEADLINE PUBLISHING GROUP

First published in paperback in 2007
by HEADLINE PUBLISHING GROUP

4

ISBN 978 0 7553 4080 4 (A-format)
ISBN 978 0 7553 3733 0 (B-format)

Typeset in Plantin Light by Avon DataSet Ltd,
Bidford-on-Avon, Warwickshire

Printed and bound in Great Britain by
Mackays of Chatham plc, Chatham, Kent

HEADLINE PUBLISHING GROUP
An Hachette Livre UK Company
338 Euston Road
London NW1 3BH

www.headline.co.uk

For Terry, Ben, Polly and Lucy, with love.
Keep on holding hands.

ACKNOWLEDGEMENTS

When I started writing this book it was just me. Now lots of other people are involved, directly and indirectly, and I'd like to thank them most sincerely for making my book a book.

Chris d'Lacey, superstar children's author, King of Dragons, wonderful friend and best email writer ever – thank you for introductions, for kicking the ball off, for sticking your neck out, for showing me Leicester cafés and inspiring my daughters with your books. Merel Reinink, my cool, calm and totally awesome agent. Thank you for believing in me, for taking risks, for dealing with everything so superbly, for friendship. Without you I'd be spinning in circles. Sherise Hobbs, my editor at Headline, heartfelt thanks for making me feel so welcome, for enlightened editing and more passion and belief in my work than I could ever have hoped for. I truly count myself lucky to be working with you and your dedicated team. And special thanks also to talented and insightful designer Richard Green, who has created the perfect cover for this book. And I'd like to thank everyone at Headline from copyeditors to editorial assistants and beyond. I am stunned by your slickness.

I'd also like to say a special thank you to Emma Dean, beautiful singer and songwriter from Brisbane (www. emmadean.com), who doesn't even know that her special music has saved me many times and inspired me to keep writing – oh, and she happens to be my niece. Thanks, Em. You deserve massive success.

Grateful thanks to Angela Witcher, Jennifer Clugston and Dan Leigh for prompt and helpful technical advice on DNA and genetics issues.

Thanks and love in abundance to my own blood ties – my husband Terry and my three children, Ben, Polly and Lucy, for loving the chaos and never letting me give up; my parents, Avril and Graham, for always having faith; Joe and Heidi for inspirational chats outside the back door; and Edward and Emily for their fun.

I'd also like to thank Neil Ayres, a very talented writer, for his e-friendship; Benny Rossi, a truly wonderful woman who is always there when I turn; Stephen Gallagher, who gets more charming each year; and Sandra, for helping dreams come true.

ONE

My milk started leaking about thirty seconds after I realised my baby was stolen. Stupidly, I remember worrying that my blouse would be stained with crisp white circles for the afternoon's duty visit to the in-laws. I'd only stopped at the supermarket to pick up a cake, the kind that looks home-made, in the hope I might con Sheila into thinking it had recently slid steaming from my oven. I'd even got a plate and a doily to put it on. But when I got back to the car – I'd left it for two minutes, *two minutes*, because the drive had finally put my screaming Natasha to sleep – the car seat in the back was empty. Just a warm indentation where she'd been and an oval of clotted baby sick on the padded cover.

I dropped the cake on the frosted ground and searched the car. Stupid things occurred to me. Had I taken her into the supermarket and left her behind in a trolley? Or perhaps a kind old lady had taken a shine to her rosy cheeks and pouting top lip. Was my baby so precocious that when I found her everyone would marvel at how an eight-week-old infant had got up and walked? Was it possible that Andy had come looking for me, seen my car parked and woken her up for a cuddle? He was allowed. He was her father.

I'm sure I locked the car.

I bumped my head on the roof as I got out, finally

acknowledging that Natasha wasn't in there. Precious seconds. Then my milk started leaking; that burning breast-orgasm when you just have to feed your baby. Except I'd lost mine.

The winter dazzle of a low sun bothered my view as I searched for Natasha's face bobbing over Andy's shoulder. I wanted that waterfall of relief as I realised my baby was safe. I wanted to know that what I thought had happened to her hadn't, that my skewed reality wasn't real at all. Surprisingly, there weren't many people around, only an old couple fumbling groceries into their car.

'Andy,' I shouted, but it came out as if I had bronchitis. My throat was all stuck together with thick spit and it burned as I panted in the freezing air. I forced myself to focus on every corner of the car park but my eyesight flared and my ears whooshed every time I turned my head. That's when I turned into an animal.

'*Tasha!*' This time my scream came out. A wilderness growl. My feet were apart, fists clenched, shoulders hunched. My neck stiffened and my head lurched forward as I began to run between the cars, screaming my baby's name. I hurtled up to the old couple, who raised their hands in defence, terrified, I now realise, that I was going to mug them.

'Have you seen my baby?' I don't think they understood my puffing animal-English; didn't answer if they did. I moved on, instinctively aware that every second counted. I screamed Natasha's name until my voice caved in. I pinballed off cars until I slipped on the ice and fell down onto the ground.

Then a hand rested on my shoulder, and just as I looked up, just as I focused on the luminous plastic jacket above me, I heard a baby wail.

I leapt to my feet and stood on tiptoe, straining my ears. There was a dog yapping, perhaps left too long in a car, the hum and whine of a forklift as it scooped up palettes of groceries from the back of a delivery truck, the rattle of shopping trolleys as a teenage boy collected them in an out-of-control train from around the frozen car park. My senses were on fire.

Then the baby cry again.

Beneath the layers of clatter, I heard a baby wailing, screaming, shrieking for its mother. A baby just like Natasha. It was a circle of pure sound that ripped the inside of my already sore head to shreds. The cry, the wailing, the incessant howling of my baby. I didn't know which way to turn.

I stepped on a bumper and up onto the bonnet of a blue Ford estate, quite a new model, and I was worried that it would dent. It's all so clear. I even remember the gloves on the dashboard, the Christmas tree air freshener hanging from the rear-view mirror. Then I climbed onto the roof and saw the whole car park and beyond from the top of that car. The slippery metal gave a little under my weight.

'Miss,' said the man in the yellow jacket. 'Calm down, miss.' His eyes were black and wide and I knew he thought I was a madwoman.

'Be quiet,' I begged, desperate to hear the cry again. It had come from the high street end of the car park. I squinted against the shield of sun and after what seemed like ages but was only really a second or two, I saw a figure running.

I saw someone running through the supermarket car park carrying a baby.

'Natasha!' I yelled again, stupidly, as if she would be able to answer. I jumped directly off the car roof, my left ankle crumbling beneath me, and ran towards the high street. I'm quite tall, but not as tall as being on the top of a car, so following the running person over the heads of all the Saturday shoppers proved nearly impossible. But I was a monster-mother with distilled panic in my eyes and I battled towards the road to get a clear view up and down the street.

I stood, breathless, my leaky breasts heaving up and down beneath my winter coat, sweat prickling the skin on my back. I scanned up and down the high street, and the shops that I'd visited nearly every week of my life suddenly dissolved into discoloured, alien places. The whole town, from that moment on, became completely foreign. I was a lost tourist who didn't speak the language.

The sight of the same running figure, scarved and hatted-up against January, disappearing down Holt's Alley – a gloved hand cradling the tiny head of a screaming baby – sent me darting between honking cars and down the narrow passage. Looking back, I was about fifteen or twenty seconds behind. Looking back, I didn't know what I was doing.

Holt's Alley always smelled of hot chips, beer and piss. There was usually a cluster of teenagers lurking at the far end and 4 January 1992 was no exception. Once or twice, when the gluttonous hunger pangs of pregnancy had got the better of me on a shopping excursion, I furtively ducked down the alley and slid into Al's Chippy. The resident group of teenagers always had a smart heckle or two, usually about getting fat or didn't I know that eating too many deep-fried sausages got you up the duff. I would smile politely, not wanting to rile the pack, and go into Al's to gorge myself, feeling as guilty as a pregnant mother caught smoking. It was only chips. But as I'd done everything right for that baby, *nearly* everything, I figured that hot chips and the smell of piss as I passed by wouldn't hurt.

I barged into the group of lolling adolescents, knocking a can of Pepsi from one of them.

'*Oi*—'

'Have any of you seen a baby? Someone running?' I spat as I spoke, panting, not caring. 'Just now. Someone running down here?' I leaned forward, hands on the knees of my elastic-waisted black velveteen trousers, the only half-smart thing I could fit into for my afternoon with Sheila.

'Nope.'

'*Please*. My baby's been taken.'

They were all spots and bravado. I don't blame them. One of them at least made a statement a couple of weeks later, after seeing the police posters. I ran on. Street after street.

The running figure had disappeared. Natasha, too.

On the walk back to the car park, I convinced myself Natasha would be safely strapped in her car seat. I'd obviously missed her in a new-mother panic. Baby blindness, a syndrome I'd not heard of before. Then I found a white baby bootee lying in the middle of the road. It looked hand-knitted. I picked it up.

'It could be Tash's bootee,' I said to myself, thinking of all the knitting Sheila had done for my baby. I took it as a good omen that I had found an item of baby clothing. Someone had sent me a sign, except I was too stupid to realise exactly what the sign meant.

Dear Natasha,

Happy birthday, sweetheart. My little Tash is a teenager . . .

I can't write that to her. It sounds as if she's still a baby. I screw up the letter and begin again. To me, she still is a baby.

Dear Tash (*informal, sounds better*),

It's hard to know where to begin after all these years. You're probably wondering why I haven't written to you before now. The truth is, I was too scared. Even hearing the name Natasha on TV crumples me. You see, I still love you just as much as when I had you for those few short weeks. Loving something you can't have, well, it hurts and . . .

I screw this one up too. It's rubbish. She'll laugh.

I started to run again, back from Holt's Alley, but with my stomach lurching as if I'd drunk a gallon of fresh orange juice and milk, I had to be patient with my aching post-partum body.

When I got back to the car, Natasha wasn't there. She was gone. Still gone. The man in the yellow jacket wasn't there either and neither were the old couple. I longed for someone familiar, a hand of kindness, a voice crooning that everything would be OK. My car door was still open, scraping against the paintwork of the car beside it, and the cake was lying on the ground where I'd dropped it.

Suddenly, I was thinking clearly, as if the sprint through town had given me some sense. I would go back into the supermarket to get help and telephone Andy; he might still be at work.

The plan had been to meet him at his parents' house, Sheila and Don's, but that would have to be delayed now. Sheila would be cross and mutter about ruined food. The supermarket manager would probably give me a cup of tea – just what I needed in my new, colourless, light-flared world where there was no sound or feeling or time or any possibility of a normal life ever again.

I picked up the cake, brushed it off and wondered
shop might think I had stolen it because it wasn't in a c
bag. I went into the supermarket, convinced I would soon
wake up. I needed people. Thoroughly kind people.

Dear Natasha (*formal again. It's been a while, after all*),

I want you to know that I have thought about you
every day for thirteen years. Each time I remember you
I have to imagine someone a little older, a little taller,
and now more womanly as the years slip by. I look at
photographs of myself as a child to see what you might
have become. Everyone said you were my double, those
dimples, those lashes. Are your eyes still blue? Have you
started your periods? Are you dead and rotting?

I screw that one up too. It's raining outside; pearly-sleeting,
actually. Four o'clock and already the street lights are on,
making the pavement peachy-grey, the leafless trees spring-
like and more alive than they should be on a dull November
afternoon.

I've switched on the electric fire, put the telly on – a slushy,
feel-good show where happy families win fridges and cars.
I've made a cup of tea, which later will be chased by a bottle
of gin or vodka, whatever's on special at Spar, and sit curled
up under a fleece blanket, with a writing pad and fountain
pen. I am also holding Natasha's bootee, the one that was
dropped on the high street, the one that was handed back to
me in a Ziploc bag when the police gave up looking for her.

I do this every Saturday in January, the month she went,
and every 6 November, Natasha's birthday. Otherwise, apart
from this, I try to be normal. You'd never know that I once had
a baby.

Dear Natasha Jane Varney (*full name now because honestly, would she know it otherwise?*),

It is with pleasure that I write to you with news of your mother, Mrs Cheryl Susan Varney. She is alive and well and wishes you were too. She prays that both your souls will be saved. She is filled with sadness and regrets that she never got to push you on a swing or give you a birthday party or cook you sausages and beans . . .

This won't do either. I make a ball of it and lob it into the waste bin. It's the ad break on TV. I don't like commercials. They don't advertise products but rather the life we should be living. Who says we should have a shower in a glass-fronted bathroom overlooking a milk-sand beach, the sun shining always and if we'd only use new improved Spiffo Shampoo, then our hair would be long and glossy like the naked waif of a model on telly?

Maybe I should buy some Spiffo, just in case my dank, mildewy bathroom might spin like a top and reappear on a Bermudan beach when I squirt the stuff on my head. Maybe it will wash away my life and I can have Natasha back. Another chance.

The thing is, I know the car door was locked.

While the adverts are on, I rummage through the kitchen cupboards in search of alcohol because my inability to write a nice letter to my daughter has upset me. Other mothers get to write to their daughters.

All I can find is cooking sherry. I sneak back to the living room on tiptoes, concealing the sticky bottle under my pilled cardigan, and swig furtively, making sure I face the window so that someone sees me.

I have this thing with myself that I'm being watched all the time. There are several reasons why this is so. Possibly it's God, because he feels sorry for me, tucking me under his wing with the other forgotten, worthless creatures of the world. Or it might be my guardian angel and if this is the case, then I reckon it's Natasha because this person seems to know me pretty well. Or, and this is most likely the truth, it could be because I'm a bit strained at present and not really on top of things. Some would call it guilt. I call it my life.

So I face the window when I swig the sherry in the hope that someone will see me. It makes me feel a little less mad about being watched.

There. A woman walking her dog through the murky dusk. She stared right into my cosy little house and clocked me slugging. I rarely close my curtains, so passers-by can get a glimpse of my life and give me a guess at theirs. I have regulars, each with their own time slot and reason for walking past my squashed-in terrace. Some have names, characters and lives that I have invented for them. My own library of unknown friends.

Marjory comes by early in the morning to get the paper. She once tried to jog and wore a pink velour tracksuit but walked on the way home, sweating and red-cheeked. There are the school kids at eight twenty-five and three fifty each day during term time. Now that Natasha would be at secondary school, I'm not so keen to watch the teenagers skulk by my gate. They leave their mark though; Coke cans and crisp packets and cigarette butts sown in my pillowcase-sized front garden. I usually tap on the window and smile and nod at Frederick when he passes on the way to buy his tongue. He has tongue sandwiches for lunch every day. He's a client but hasn't been for a few months. His wife died four years ago and he hears knocking inside his house.

*

When I got back inside the supermarket, I wasn't sure whether to queue up at one of the busy checkouts or go straight to the customer services desk, which also had a long line of Saturday shoppers. I chose the express till as everyone had ten items or less, except the woman in front of me who had a small trolley clearly containing more than ten things.

The whole world had gone through a high-temperature coloureds wash and come out dingy grey. And everything was flat, like a child's cardboard puppet theatre. If I blew hard, I reckon the shop would have toppled over.

My state of severe, sun-flared panic had gone now and all I wanted was for someone to look after me. I didn't care who and I knew that by reaching the head of the queue and telling the checkout girl that my baby was missing, I would get the sympathy and kindness I needed. I shuffled forward, clutching the chocolate cake, my thumbs sinking through the cellophane. I put it down on the conveyor belt so it wouldn't get even more mangled. I still wanted to impress Sheila with my home baking.

The woman in front of me finally paid for her groceries and took forever to pack her bags and slot the remains of her pension into her faux crocodile purse. The details, the obscure but exact minutiae overloaded my senses, perhaps to knock out reality. I didn't realise it then but had I been revved up to red alert, I might have been able to fire up enough people to begin an immediate search. Looking back, Natasha couldn't have been far away. Looking back, I didn't handle it very well.

My body ached as I shuffled forward, approaching the apathetic, spotty checkout girl with her hands poised to receive my cake.

'I don't have any shopping actually. I was just wondering if anyone could—' Too late. She scanned my cake.

'Two ninety-nine, please. I'll getchanother 'cos this one's squished.' She bent forward to a microphone, closing her eyes as she spoke as if she was singing karaoke. 'Sandra to checkout three, please. Checkout three. Customer waiting.'

'But I've already . . .' I couldn't be bothered to explain. I fumbled with my purse, which didn't seem like my purse any more, and the hands messing with the buckle on my handbag plainly weren't familiar. Neither was the voice that came out of my mouth. I wasn't Cheryl any more.

Trembling, I handed the girl my debit card. I'd used up my cash paying for the cake the first time.

'Check and sign, please.'

Sandra delivered my replacement cake. The first thing I noticed was the use-by date. This cake was a day older than the original cake I'd chosen.

I remember thinking: if I'm bothered by such a triviality then surely my baby can't have been taken. If Natasha was really missing then I wouldn't be standing in a shop, paying for a cake that I'd already bought. I'd be screaming, calling the police, crying, wailing, floundering hysterically between customers, begging them to help me search.

I signed the debit card slip and started laughing. It was a laugh of relief, a massive release of emotion that of course Natasha hadn't been taken. I'd left her in the car. I was on the way to Sheila and Don's where I was meeting Andy, and we were going to spend the afternoon talking about babies, drinking tea and eating chocolate cake, which I was now purchasing.

Sheila was good at telling me about babies. She'd had three and knew all the ropes. She knitted, goodness knows she knitted, and she provided me with a hundred useful tips each time I visited on how to keep a happy baby, as if Natasha was an exotic pet.

'When baby's finished feeding, slip your little finger in the corner of her mouth to release the suction. Sore nipples for you otherwise,' Sheila had said when I was getting to grips with breastfeeding my baby. 'At change time, let baby kick free for half an hour. No nappy rash for our little pumpkin! And winter or summer, a nap in the garden makes for healthy babies. Mind you fit a cat net, though.' The woman was a baby helpline and I never called her up.

'You were just wondering if anyone could what?' Checkout girl was grinning at me now, not so bad after all. 'You didn't finish what you were saying.'

'Oh, nothing.' I smiled, bagging my cake. I left the cardboard shop, my pace quickening as I approached the door, passing through a rush of warm overhead air before I dived into the car park cold. I ran to my Renault.

Stupid me. Mad me. Irresponsible, messed-up, nervous first-time-mother me. How could I have thought my baby was lost? Obviously my senses had been playing tricks. The health visitor warned me about not getting enough sleep. Natasha was a little madam at night. She cried right through, making sure she took snatches of beauty sleep during the day and, by playing such a game, she had bled me of my ability to reason and see straight. I just hoped I didn't look too fraught when I arrived at Sheila and Don's.

But when I got to the car, it was empty.

Natasha had been taken. No doubt.

I peed myself and screamed before dropping to the ground.

★

Dear Natasha,

When you were eight weeks old, you were taken from me. I was stupid and left you in the car when I went into a shop. We were on our way to Nanna Sheila's house, to meet Daddy and to eat cake. I tried to find you but only found your bootee dropped in the road. The police came and for months they searched and checked all their known criminals and put posters up and did an appeal on the telly and then they stopped looking. They shifted your file onto a less hopeful pile, gave me back your bootee and said that they were doing all they could.

I want you to know, Natasha, that I've never stopped loving you. I never will. Some days I believe that you're alive and happy and living with a kind family who love you as their own, coping with your teenage tantrums and boyfriends with motorbikes, and fighting with you because you want your belly button pierced. Other days, the truth hits me as painfully as the moment I realised you had slipped from my life.

I wonder about your last view of the world. Did you stare into your killer's face as you were smothered? Did you gaze up with the same adoration and trust that you bestowed upon me as you lay heavy in my arms while I fed you? Were you allowed to fall into a sleep of starvation and pass away from lack of nourishment? Did you slip away peacefully or did you leave this world after only eight weeks vowing vengeance?

Wherever you are, dead or alive, I sense you. I feel you. I want you back.

You are a special girl, Natasha. I love you and I am sorry.

Mummy

I know I won't find her today, which is reason enough to drink the rest of the cooking sherry. I pass out for the evening and miss my favourite quiz show.

TWO

Robert glanced at his wife as they waited for the results. He willed her to turn his way so that he could give her a reassuring smile, a touch on her small hand, anything to dissolve the nervousness that seeped from her.

But Erin didn't turn his way. Instead, she focused her attention on the headmistress and drove a brittle stare at the archetypical principal of the private college. Erin sat stiff-boned, her hands clasped across her grey flannel suit, her blonde hair tamed for the morning, wholly prepared for disappointment.

While the headmistress riffled through papers and reports, Robert allowed himself a brief look at his wife's legs. She had them crossed neatly, somewhat primly, he thought, for a woman who was more comfortable in jeans and boots. It was all a show, he knew, to impress the woman behind the desk. Like a good omen, he caught a glimpse of Erin's lacy stocking top. He knew everything was going to be fine.

'Quite frankly, Mr and Mrs Knight, I wish there were more girls like Ruby.' Miss Aucott took off her glasses and stared down the long oak-panelled library, squinting at the grand piano. Robert had almost forgotten that Ruby was present, even though her music still reverberated in the vast room like a thousand butterflies set free.

'Come and sit with us, Ruby.' Miss Aucott smiled, her face creasing into a network of powdered wrinkles.

The girl slid off the piano stool and began the long walk to Miss Aucott's desk. Robert noticed his wife's shoulders drop an inch or two as the tension unravelled from knotted muscle. He wanted to punch the air, hug Ruby, pull Erin close but he couldn't. Not until the headmistress actually said the words, that Ruby was officially *in*.

He watched his stepdaughter walk awkwardly across the polished parquet floor, one of her crêpe-soled shoes squeaking every other step. For everything she's been through, he thought, let this be all right.

Ruby sat on the edge of her chair. Away from the piano, she could be mistaken for any other teenager with her self-conscious posture and the softly glazed skin of her nose and forehead touched with only a couple of tiny spots. Robert watched fondly as she settled herself next to Erin.

He was so proud of the courage she had displayed, the control she had mustered, in spite of everything, just for this morning. Ruby had neatened her mass of black hair and, like her mother, was wearing smart clothes. But the pair of them, apart from the similar dull suits they wore, had surprisingly few common traits. Robert permitted himself an internal grin as with renewed hope that everything would be OK, he gestured to Ruby that she should tuck an escaped strand of hair behind her ear. He wanted nothing more than for his family to be happy.

'Ruby, there's a place here for you at Greywood College. It's unusual for us to take pupils mid-term but in this case I shall agree.' Miss Aucott's voice contained a tinge of triumph, as if she had discovered something rare. She put on her glasses again and began to read from the file. 'Over ninety-seven per cent on all three tests, young lady. Quite an achievement.'

Ruby blushed and lowered her head. Robert noticed the flickering smile whip across her lips, he saw her chest lift slightly as she drew breath in relief and he noticed her eyes, too, the colour deepening for just a moment. He wanted to reach and pull her into his arms, which at thirteen she was still willing to allow.

'But it's your music that we really want.' Miss Aucott leaned forward across the rosewood desk and settled herself on folded hands. Her voice was quieter now, as if she was concerned she might scare away the very thing she wished to secure for her college. As if Ruby was an exquisite, wild creature that needed trapping and taming. 'Many of our young ladies are talented.' She broke off, her voice faltering, like her scholarly veneer was lifting, as though her usual doggedness had been steamed clean off by Ruby's piano recital.

'We know that Ruby's special,' Erin interrupted. 'Not just because of her music . . .' She checked herself and reached out for Ruby's hand. 'Just special.'

Robert shot her a look, tantamount to drawing a sharp line across his neck, and nodded, signalling Miss Aucott to continue.

'You'll be in a class of eight other girls, Ruby, all musically gifted. We like to arrange the groups according to their talents. Lessons begin at eight thirty and finish at four.' Miss Aucott drew breath, removed her glasses again. 'You've had the tour, seen our prospectus. Do you have any questions?'

Robert expected a barrage of motherly interrogation from Erin but all she did was shrug.

'It all seems perfect,' she finally said. 'Greywood is just what Ruby needs. It's going to be a fresh start for her.'

'Yes,' Miss Aucott said, her voice dragging like a sudden limp. Robert's heart quickened as the headmistress once again replaced her spectacles and leafed through the file. 'I have the report from your current comprehensive school. Your mother is right, Ruby. Judging by what's written here, a fresh start is certainly in order. Are you willing to give Greywood one hundred per cent?'

'With my heart and soul, miss,' Ruby said, some of the zest bleeding from her dark eyes. 'What happens to me at my other school isn't my fault,' she continued, a pleading tone to her voice. The muscles under her eyes flickered, an indication of how much could come tumbling out, ruin everything.

Robert willed Ruby to stop. If she chose, Miss Aucott could delve further into events and reconsider her offer of a place at Greywood. Instead, she reached out a hand and took hold of the child's fingers.

Ruby smiled, that unruly strand of ebony falling across her face again, her cheeks flushing, perhaps from embarrassment, perhaps from relief. She swallowed audibly and moved closer as Miss Aucott beckoned her in.

'Greywood will become your life,' the headmistress whispered. 'You won't have a moment to get into trouble.'

Robert wanted to intervene, to protect Ruby. In his head, as if he was defending in court, he presented the evidence to prove that she hadn't done anything wrong. He was ready to lay blame on the guilty parties and even opened his mouth to speak but Erin shot him a look that mirrored the one he had just given her. Reluctantly, he remained silent and monitored Ruby instead, fearful of her reaction. Her cheeks were on fire now, her black eyes smouldering. But that rosebud smile sweetened everything.

'I'll be good,' Ruby promised. Robert and Erin exhaled.

'That's settled then. We shall see you next Monday, Ruby.' Miss Aucott turned to Erin, startling her as she spoke. 'That gives you nearly a week to sort out uniform, Mrs Knight. We're going to need the enrolment forms completed and returned along with copies of Ruby's vaccination record and birth certificate. Perhaps you could see that the school secretary receives these before your daughter starts.' Finally, Miss Aucott turned to Robert. 'We shall be sending you a pro-rata invoice for what's left of the term, Mr Knight. Likewise, if you could see that we receive payment promptly.'

'Of course.' Robert took the cue to stand and shake hands. Things were winding up. 'Ruby won't let you down.' He held on to Miss Aucott's bony hand for a beat too long but when it was offered to his wife he saw that, without prompting, she wasn't going to take it. 'Erin?' he said. 'It's time to leave.'

But Erin remained motionless, her face drained of its usual colour, her pale eyes suddenly translucent with a skim of tears collecting on their surface. Robert didn't think he'd seen her so ashen since he'd surprised her with tickets for a honeymoon in Barbados. Sadly, Erin's pathological fear of flying had prevented the holiday.

'Are you ready, Erin?' To break his wife's sudden trance, shock at the good news, whatever it was, Robert placed a hand on her shoulder. 'Time to leave, love.'

Erin jerked, as if she had woken from a bad dream. 'Sorry,' she managed. 'I was just . . .' She stood, ignoring Miss Aucott's outstretched hand, and walked briskly to the door.

With a frown tugging his brow, Robert Knight led his family out of Greywood College in the belief that Ruby would be returning there on Monday in full uniform, a bag on her shoulder, her hair brushed neatly back and ready for a fresh stepped out of the marble-tiled entrance hall into the afternoon, a discernible dome of summer pollution hanging over the city, and stopped for a moment to admire the two most beautiful things in his life.

'You were fantastic,' he said, embracing Ruby. 'Let's go and get a cold drink to celebrate.' His grin, typically reluctant, somehow morphed his lawyer's impassive expression into a mask of pride and relief. But Robert's sudden enthusiasm wasn't transmitted to his wife. Erin didn't respond to his hug, neither did she seem particularly bothered that their news had been good. Better than good. Their daughter had been offered a place at one of the most desirable private schools in London. She had been saved. Erin, to Robert's bewilderment, seemed untouched by events. He released her rigid body from his embrace and lifted her chin with his finger.

'I have a headache, Robert. I need a strong drink.' Erin squinted in the afternoon sun, raising her hand to her brow. 'There's a bar over there.' Before Robert could reply, she darted between cars, towing Ruby by the hand.

'That's going to do your head a lot of good.' Robert didn't attempt to shout after her. He doubted, in her current mood, she would listen. Instead, he impulsively purchased a bunch of flowers from a street stall, removed his pale grey jacket and headed for the bar. He was completely unable to help the grin that took over his face and felt relieved that no one he knew was there to witness it.

He entered the bar with a patina of sweat coating his face and neck. The cloying, exhaust-sodden air outside was replaced by crisp air conditioning hung with a trace of beer and smoke. He took his jacket off his shoulder and laid it over a stool, placing the flowers carefully on top. Erin and Ruby were already seated in a quiet booth. He ordered the drinks and studied his family, struck as he often was by their sudden presence in his life. Where had they come from?

Ruby was animated, her movements jerky, as if her spirit had just doubled in size. Her soul seemed to be bursting from her skin, fuelled, Robert knew, by the prospect of starting at Greywood. He refused, however, to allow the small wave of guilt that occasionally rose in his craw to swell out of proportion. It would be too easy to blame himself, he thought, for not having sent her to a school like Greywood sooner, what with her exceptional musical talent and difficulties at her current school. A simple reminder that she wasn't his real daughter, not his flesh and blood anyway, vindicated his hands-off approach thus far. After just six months as acting parent and only eight weeks as her official stepfather, he didn't yet feel he had the right, or the experience, to interfere in the way Erin handled her daughter.

Robert gave the barman a twenty and caught sight of Ruby in the mirrored wall behind the optics. Already, she was becoming more than flesh and blood and genes to him. She was special, skilfully doing what kids do best: wrapping emotional roots around a willing heart. Ruby was desperate for a father.

Robert pocketed his change and carried the drinks to the table, with the flowers stuffed under his arm.

'For a clever girl,' he said, holding out the flowers to his grinning stepdaughter. Then, 'To Ruby and her future.' His raised voice caused a few heads to turn their way as he passed Ruby a fruit juice cocktail and chinked her glass. He saluted Erin but she didn't return the gesture. Instead, she knocked back her drink in two slugs and excused herself, sliding out of the booth.

Robert watched his wife order two more shots of Jack

Daniels. She drank as if she was finishing a cup of lukewarm coffee, one foot resting on the bar rail, her fingers nervously pushing through her blonde hair.

Bemused by his wife's behaviour, he refused to allow it to dampen Ruby's success. He held her hand across the table and played with her fingers as, amongst the child's excited talk about Greywood College, he tried to guess what was troubling his wife. As she prepared to down yet another shot, he put Ruby's chatter on hold and went to the bar, coiled his arms around Erin's waist and whispered in her ear. Erin swallowed the drink anyway and twisted her face round to her husband.

'Fuck it,' she said blandly.

Robert recoiled at her whisky-mashed breath.

'Fuck everything.' She stared hard into her husband's eyes. 'Sometimes, just sometimes, I'd like the brick wall not to be there.' Erin pulled out of Robert's grip and called across the bar. 'Ruby, we're leaving.'

Robert caught up with and guided Erin as they walked along the pavement, trying to find a cab. It was Ruby who finally managed to secure one in the late afternoon rush. The child climbed in last, silently, gripping her flowers, half staring at her mother and half staring somewhere obscure. Somewhere only she knew. That place, Robert often wondered, where he thought she would rather be.

THREE

Snow is falling. Only four days until Christmas. Perhaps it's Jesus inside me. I'll call him Noel. I turn onto my side because I don't like the pulsing feeling of the baby pressing on my aorta. I learned that in biology. Aorta. The main vessel to carry oxygenated blood from the heart. Perhaps I was away on the day we were taught the facts of life. I'm not sure if this means that I'm good at reproduction, because I'm doing it, or I'm bad because I'm doing it. He's kicking. I pull up my sweater and see the taut, almost see-through skin on my belly dancing, rippling from baby. I love him.

Snow is collecting on the windowpanes. It's dark outside. I am standing up now, elbows leaning on the sill, nose fogging the glass, eyes in a spin as the fat icy chips fall to the ground, hypnotising me. The baby is dizzy too, because I stood up quickly, and punches my belly. It hurts.

Then the knock on my door. Two raps. I'll wait a moment before answering, to make sure she's gone. Or it could be him. Yes, it's Friday, bridge night, so she'll be out. I open the door and see the tray on the landing carpet. It's chops again, and mash and carrots and just a drizzle of gravy, as if I got the scrapings from the meat tray.

'Dinner, Noel,' I say, trying out the name. I carry the tray into my room and we sit on my bed and I feed myself chops.

It's tricky because there's no room on my knee to balance the tray so I put it on the bed and lean over, hoping I won't spill any down my sweater. But I do. Gravy on Noel and, as I wipe it off, he kicks again.

I've been in this room for nearly three months. They put a television in here for me, which was a nice thought, and I have my books. Mother brings me flowers once a week, usually on a Friday, and if I'm lucky and good, I'll get a walk around the garden. Mother and Father don't know it, but when they both go out I slip downstairs and steal some treats. Last week I pocketed an entire box of Milk Tray and fed myself soft, lint-covered chocolates with a glint in one eye and fear keeping watch in the other.

Of course, I've considered climbing out of the window and dropping into the front garden to run away, but that would hurt Noel and, besides, where would I go?

In two weeks I'll have a baby. It seems as if my future ends there, as if my life beyond that point hasn't been written yet. I don't know what babies are like. I've never held one before. Mother gave me a book about giving birth and a scant collection of old-fashioned baby clothes from a charity shop. They smell musty and faintly of sick.

Breathing is important, it says in the book, so sometimes I practise that. There's a whole chapter on pain relief but I doubt I'll get more than an aspirin. I'm giving birth at home. Mother will be beside me, annoying my forehead with a wet flannel, and Father will pace the landing, desperate not to see his howling daughter with her legs spread. I don't really want to do it, but honestly, do I have any choice?

I put the empty tray back on the landing and rearrange the pillows on my bed. Getting comfortable is nearly imposs-ible. I settle down to watch some television and Noel starts kicking again, as if he wants to get out now.

'Was it the chops, chickie?' I say and give him a good rubbing, which seems to settle him. I will be a good mother, even though I'm only fifteen.

FOUR

Robert dropped onto the calico-covered sofa. He let his head fall back onto the soft cushion as he covered his eyes with his hands. He wanted to moan but didn't. Instead, a memory tumbled uninvited into his head.

'I'm sure of only two things, Robert. Your paranoia and my stupidity.' Jenna had then stumbled, found her car keys and slammed the front door. Her car had revved off into the night.

Now, still contained in his mind, Robert let out a tormented noise that left his body from somewhere deep within his soul; a desperate growl followed by a barrage of verbal abuse aimed at his wife. None of it was real.

'You're having me on, right?' He shocked himself with his calmness. A perk of his job. He stared at Erin with a disbelieving expression before allowing his head to drop back onto the cushion again. He could see that his wife was serious.

'We shouldn't be teaching her to run away from her problems.' Erin swallowed so hard that Robert noticed the lump in her throat.

Slowly, he stretched out his tall body and stood up. He wasn't dressed yet, wearing only boxers beneath a robe that hung open at the waist. His hair, thick and dark and usually encouraged into a style that was intended not to look like a style, formed unruly tufts above his forehead. The rest was clipped neatly and brushed his collar.

Robert scoured his face with his palms, pulling the skin under his eyes taut, massaging his temples. He hadn't slept well for several days, mostly because of the Bowman case. Ripping two innocent children from their mother was getting to him.

'But she's starting tomorrow. What the hell are you thinking of?' Robert stood next to his wife. He looked down at the crown of her head and while part of him wanted to slide his fingers through her fine hair, the welling anger made him want to pick her up and lock her in a cupboard until Ruby had graduated from Greywood College.

'I've paid the bloody fees and she's got the uniform.' Robert prowled around Erin, his slow paces more threatening than words.

She had first whispered her intentions to him at six that morning. He thought it was a dream as Erin's sleep-stained lips teased him awake, bribing him into consciousness with words that would cripple their daughter when she was told.

'Ruby's not going to Greywood,' Erin had said. 'I can't allow it.'

A bad dream, that was all. Robert slept on but two hours later the words returned, ricocheting around his head. This time he knew they were for real. He was awake. Erin was leaning over him, the T-shirt in which she slept crawling up her waist, her warm skin smelling of sleep.

'I can't let her run away from her problems.'

'I don't see we have much choice,' Robert replied, stretching, still confident, despite his half-conscious state, that he would be able to talk Erin round.

'I've made up my mind,' she said. 'I'm going to tell Ruby later.' She looked away, so Robert couldn't read her heavy eyes.

But Robert wasn't able to change Erin's mind and his demands for convincing reasons for her sudden about-turn weren't effective either. All she offered were flimsy moral motives, that running away just wasn't right.

Since they'd met six months previously, Robert had become painfully aware of the misery Ruby suffered at school. It had begun as simple name-calling, jeering and play-ground pranks but quickly progressed to unkind phone calls and stolen property. Complaints to the head of the school were dismissed as an overreaction by Ruby, already labelled as one of their more unusual students because of her exceptional musical talent, or half-heartedly investigated but then dropped when Ruby refused to name individuals.

Robert went into the kitchen and poured himself a strong coffee. He stared back at his wife through the double doors. She was standing on the rug, arms dangling by her sides, like a lone sapling on a small island. She slowly raised her bowed head and made eye contact with him. Her mouth opened but closed again and her shoulders dropped several inches before she slumped down on the rug and sobbed.

Robert had never wanted her more. He returned to the living room, put his mug on the table beside her and cradled her narrow back in his arms. He scooped her up and half carried, half dragged her to the sofa. Stroking her hair, he saw the agony on her face.

'I won't allow you to do this,' he said. '*Let* her run away from it all. Wouldn't you want to, if it was you?' He wanted to shove Erin away for what she was doing but at the same time needed to engulf her, make it all better by gently kissing her neck, sliding his hands over her small body, by carrying her back to their bed. Instead, he did nothing.

'Yes, I *would* run away. That's why I won't allow Ruby to.' Erin stretched her baggy T-shirt sleeve and smeared it across her wet cheeks. 'It doesn't pay in the long run. Believe me, I know.'

For a moment, Robert sensed that she was speaking from experience, but if Erin had endured similar torment at school, then surely she wouldn't be insisting that Ruby suffer it too. He didn't understand.

'Reconsider,' he ordered. 'Don't tell her yet. You might feel different later.'

'I won't.' Erin stood up. 'I've decided. Ruby can't possibly go to Greywood College.'

During the moment that Erin hesitated in front of Robert, almost as if she wanted him to force her to change her mind, Robert lost sight of a tiny part of his new wife. The little figure that stood stiffly, with its back to him, draped in his old T-shirt, legs slightly apart, wasn't completely the person he remembered marrying eight weeks ago. Feeling cheated, Robert ignored Erin's defiant stance and went to dress.

The ball was a bullet, non-returnable. It skimmed Den's glasses, causing him to drop his racquet and rub the bridge of his nose. He squinted, examining the lenses.

'Take them off then,' Robert snapped. He served again. It ricocheted violently. He volleyed and took a shot in the shoulder. Removing another ball from his pocket, he did the same again, then again and again until he had run out of balls and strength. Den retreated to the edge of the court and wiped his glasses on his shirt, trying to focus on his friend's unusual behaviour.

'Anger management?' Den suggested when Robert finally ceased fire. 'Or perhaps you didn't get it last night. Either way, pal, count me out if you're going to play like that again.'

Robert took off his sports shirt and wiped it across his sweating face and neck. Taking it out on the squash ball hadn't helped. He cursed silently for having spent the last forty-five minutes soloing, hammering back his own shots as if Den wasn't there. He usually valued their time together at the weekend.

'I'll buy you a beer and you can tell me about it.' Den gathered up his belongings and opened the court door for Robert, who was putting his shirt back on. 'That's if it's safe to be with you.'

Robert walked out of the court, expressionless, his jaw clenched as tightly as his fist round his racquet and his dark eyes unblinking, unfocused.

In the locker room Robert didn't speak. He dropped his belongings onto the bench before stepping into a scalding shower. He knew that Den was watching him, trying to understand his behaviour, but to tell him, to explain what Erin was doing, would give the situation even more reality and that he couldn't stomach.

Robert hadn't seen Ruby before he left home. He'd grabbed his sports bag and keys and gone out earlier than was necessary to get to his regular Sunday morning squash session with Den. He drove badly, narrowly missing several joggers and a red light and ended up parked in a bus stop, pondering his wife's strange behaviour until it was time to go to the club.

As the engine hummed and the radio babbled quietly, Robert imagined Ruby's young face, warm and puckered from sleep, her pink flowery nightdress faded from the wash.

She'd pad barefoot into the kitchen, drink juice from the carton and pour herself a bowl of chocolate cereal, which she would eat in front of the television. She'd pull her legs up underneath her, her thick black hair bunched in a messy ponytail, her eyes ringed with the experimental make-up she hadn't bothered to remove the night before. She'd channel-hop, think about her future, beginning tomorrow, then smile as a warm, safe feeling – the first in years – began to seep through her entire soul.

Then her mother would tell her she wasn't going to Greywood College after all and she must return to her old school the next day, the school at which she had suffered so much torment. Ruby would stop, spoon of cereal midway to her mouth, perhaps smile at the joke and say, 'Nice one, Mum,' but then she'd notice the serious expression on her mother's face, the worry lines creeping out from her eyes, around her mouth, and wonder if it was indeed a joke. When Erin said it again, Ruby would put down her cereal and walk up to her mother and say, 'Mum?' in a voice that didn't quite belong to her. She would snort, half defiance, half disbelief, and then it would begin. The screaming.

'Ruby's not going to Greywood,' Robert yelled out of the shower to Den. Robert was covered in soap when the shower curtain was snapped open.

'You said what?' Den was drying his ears. Robert rinsed and covered himself with a towel.

'Greywood's off.' Robert whipped a smile over his strained face. The two men dressed in silence, Den knowing better than to press further until they both had a drink beside them. Ten minutes later they took a table in the club bar.

'Ruby get cold feet?' Den glanced around, nodded to a couple of people. That was the thing with Den; his full attention was scarce. Robert needed someone he could really talk to. Talk *with*.

'We decided that running away was cowardly. We're going to see her head teacher again. See if we can't get some ass kicked.' Robert took half a pint in three gulps.

'You won't.' Den scanned the room again. A couple of attractive young women, early twenties, skimmed past, their short skirts at nose level. 'You get that?' Den breathed in deeply. 'Beautiful.'

'Erin will. She'll kick ass.' Robert quickly ran his hands over his tired face but it was enough for Den. He saw.

'What you really mean is that *Erin* has said Ruby can't go to her new school.' It was an easy puzzle to solve. They had been close since law school, knew every nuance. 'What's she afraid of? You're paying the bloody fees.'

Robert sighed. He had to continue. 'We're not so sure about a private education. We don't want her to turn out, you know, superior.' He clapped his hands together, like a visible punctuation mark, and downed his pint. 'Another?'

But Den was already standing. He collected the glasses and walked to the bar.

On the other hand, Robert thought, could he bear it if Ruby turned out inferior?

He could sit with Den all afternoon if he wanted, unload his concerns with the aid of several pints, go over old times, new times, discuss cases from work. He let out a silent belch and fell back in the leather armchair. Guilt smothered him. He wanted to be there for Ruby as Erin broke the news, but staying out with Den and creeping back into the house when it was all over was, Robert admitted, his cowardly way of playing at parenting. When the damage was done, he would begin the repair work.

He considered taking Ruby into the office with him the next morning, perhaps for a few days, to give her time to recover, maybe find her a private tutor. She could help Tanya with the filing. He'd give her some cash and she could go shopping. To begin with, Erin need never know. He couldn't allow Ruby to go back to the comprehensive school.

Den returned with fresh drinks. 'How's our friend Jed Bowman?' he asked, a grin rising above the rim of the glass, breaking his tanned face into a network of lines. Perfectly styled grey-black hair complemented Den's smooth, lady-kill look, as did his designer dress sense. Den was a successful man-about-town, always open to offers, always willing to make them.

'Not giving up,' Robert replied. 'And don't change the subject.' Robert didn't want to talk about the Bowman case. He couldn't face shattering more lives.

Den picked up the menu and scanned the sandwiches on offer. 'Hungry?'

'Depends. Are we in for the kill?' Robert was feeling more relaxed. Being with Den was like being underground – safe but airless. And as the senior partner at Mason & Knight, he was always in control, both in and out of the office.

Den glanced at his watch. 'I'm glad to get out for a bit to be honest. Tula's got her girls round.'

Robert winced at the thought. Tula Mason and her group of girls were a tidal wave of forty-somethings desperately seeking physical perfection. He had once made the mistake of stepping inside while dropping off Erin – much younger and therefore not in need of the enhancements on offer – at one of Tula's gatherings. Even before drinks and canapés were offered, botox and collagen treatments were pressed upon him. He had grinned as he left Erin in Tula's clutches, admiring how young his wife looked at thirty-four. She could easily pass for late twenties.

'In for the kill, then.' Robert smirked.

During the time they had been at the squash club, the fine weather had been occluded by a miserable front of tepid rain. So far, June had been unusually dry and warm but, as if to match Robert's current mood, the sky was now a muddy, swirling milk. Den and Robert shared a taxi and sat in silence watching fat bulbs of rain pelt the windows. It had all been said at the club.

Robert got out of the cab first, light-headed and slightly nauseated from afternoon drinking, and walked unsteadily up the rain-glazed front steps of his house. He had left his car at the sports club and given the doorman twenty pounds and the keys to return it later. One of the perks of belonging to such an exclusive club; one of the perks of being partner to Dennis Mason.

He stood in the dim hallway of his house. It was a Victorian townhouse and while it still managed an impressive entrance, most of the rooms were in need of decoration. Until Erin and Ruby moved in six months ago he hadn't bothered much with interior design. But gradually it was becoming a family home, which, after everything, was all Robert had ever wanted.

His mind shifted to Jenna, catching him off guard. He could see her standing at the top of the stairs with a white towel slung low round her back, her cheeks glowing pink, a welcoming smile dividing her face. Jenna alive. The pair of them happy. Then she was gone, the recollection stuffed back into the bundle of pain he kept locked away. Jenna had no place in his thoughts now, so why did she insist on seeping into his new life?

He dumped his sports bag on the hall floor and shook his wet hair; shook the image from his head. He was being stupid. Jenna had never even lived in this house and certainly didn't belong here now.

Then he became aware of a sound – a low-pitched drone, repeating over and over like an animal in pain. It was barely audible but filled the entire house, making its source difficult to pinpoint. Robert went into the kitchen and was met by dirty plates littering the worktops and a basket of fresh washing giving off a sweet smell. The radio was on, quietly humming, explaining the strange noise. He flicked it off. The drone continued.

'Erin?' he called out. Nothing. He poured a glass of water and walked from the kitchen to the living room. It was empty. He thought perhaps it was the chill from his damp clothes or the beer after exercise making him feel strange and unreal, causing him to hear noises that weren't there.

Robert went upstairs to change. The drone grew stronger, making his bones vibrate. It was coming from Ruby's room. He knocked once and went straight in.

It took a moment for his eyes to adjust. The curtains were closed and the light was off but when his pupils dilated and he forced his beer-skewed vision to straighten, Robert saw Ruby trembling in the corner. She was completely naked and chanting in a growl that electrified the stale air. Ruby's only source of modesty was her hair, which dropped down over her shoulders and chest in sweaty black streaks. Her entire body was quivering, as if the resonance spewing from her parted lips tore at every cell. Ruby was completely unaware of his presence.

'Rube?' Robert approached, not comfortable with her nakedness. 'Ruby, stop.' Robert stretched out his arms but then diverted and reached for her robe hanging on the back of the door. He offered it to her but she didn't move. Just the chanting, the energy coming out.

Robert draped the robe around her shoulders but it fell off. As he bent down to retrieve it, he saw goose bumps on her pale skin. He could smell something, a metallic tang rising from between her legs. Then Robert saw the blood. Mirroring the pattern of her black hair on white skin, dark red river stains mapped the insides of her thighs.

'Ruby, you're bleeding,' Robert said, kneeling now, staring up at her. The girl's eyeballs appeared hard on the surface, as if made of glass, and her pupils had grown to the full width of her eyes. He didn't care any more that she was naked, that her legs were crusted with blood. Robert scooped her up and placed her on the bed. Still paralysed, she continued to chant, her eyes fixed on something beyond the ceiling. That place she always wanted to be.

FIVE

Robert sat alone all evening with a client's file propped open beside him and his laptop balanced on his legs. He attempted work but was unable to think of anything except his distressed stepdaughter and, of course, Erin – the woman responsible for her state.

The light from the silent television speckled the walls, casting shadows as the scenes changed. Robert stared and waited; stared at the tired magnolia paint of the living room, occasionally at the gut-wrenching letters that might have been written in blood by his client's wife, and waited with decreasing patience for Erin to return.

When he'd called her mobile, he was diverted to her voicemail. She wasn't at any of her friends' houses and if she'd gone to her shop, then she wasn't answering the phone. When finally able to speak, Ruby couldn't give any clues as to her mother's whereabouts.

As the rain continued into the evening, leaving the sky rancid and spent, the girl gradually descended back into a state that resembled normality. Robert had sat with her for ages, rubbing her tense back, warming her stiff body, wrapping her in blankets and holding a mug of sweet tea to her mouth. He didn't ask what was wrong. He knew.

Later, Robert pulled his legs up onto the sofa. He was

exhausted – from the violent one-sided game of squash earlier, from drinking all afternoon, from Erin's sudden about-turn but mostly from guilt. He should have been there for Ruby.

He kicked off his shoes and dragged a fur throw across his unusually tired body. He was a fit man, proud of the way his muscles responded quickly to workouts or lengthy sessions in the pool despite being only two years off forty. And he enjoyed Erin's approving gaze as he undressed at night. But today, ravaged by his wife's extreme behaviour, Robert felt ten years older.

He again imagined Ruby's face as her mother told her she would not be going to Greywood College. Nothing could have prepared him for the state in which he found his step-daughter. He loved Ruby as much as he loved her mother, sometimes more. Now more. Not being her father but having to be one was the hardest thing he knew. If she was entirely his, he would have stopped this nonsense long ago. Erin wouldn't have had a choice. Robert wondered if he would ever feel like a proper father, have any right to ownership.

He must have fallen asleep, but only lightly because as soon as he heard the front-door latch click he was sitting upright, mussing his hair, gathering his thoughts. Erin stood between the hall and living room and, even in the half-light, Robert could see that she was drenched. She turned on the light, revealing that she was gripping a collection of flowers by the stalks, upside down, their colourful heads hanging down to her knees.

'For Ruby,' she said. Her voice was flat as she raised the sodden bunch.

'That'll make everything better,' Robert replied, standing up. He strode into the kitchen and slammed the lid of the kettle onto the worktop. 'Coffee? Reckon that'll make everything all right too?' Erin followed him into the room; he could smell the rain in her hair as she approached him from behind. He inhaled a whiff of the summer blooms.

'I didn't tell her,' Erin said.

Robert turned round slowly, a jar of coffee in his hand. He stared at his wife. Her usually blonde hair had turned verdigris in the rain and her mascara formed dark crescents under her eyes. She had been crying. He spooned coffee granules into mugs, sloshing on half-boiled water.

'I didn't tell her because she already knew,' Erin finished.

Robert sat across the kitchen table from Erin. Her head was supported in her hands, her feet wrapped awkwardly around the chair legs. He noticed the shiver in her shoulders, how she tried to suppress it. He swallowed away the knot of hope that brewed in his throat; hope that was quickly dashed as Erin continued.

'She overheard us talking this morning.' She sighed and picked at a chip on her mug. 'It's been a hard day for her.'

Robert snorted and shook his head. 'Did you even know that she started her periods today?'

Erin covered her face. 'I wasn't here for her.'

Robert could have said the same thing but kept hold of the point he had scored. Besides, he sensed there was something heavy within Erin that she needed to unload, although he didn't like trusting instincts alone. He was a lawyer, after all, trained to make the truth shine from basic facts.

Erin was his wife. They had sworn trust and honesty at their April wedding. She was sensible Erin, hard-working Erin, practical Erin. Why was she doing this to their daughter? For Ruby, the most important thing in her life was her music and that, coupled with escaping her idiot peers, meant going to

Greywood College. The piano was as integral to her as the colour of her hair or the way her eyes turned up at the corners. Now her mother had ensured that the promised hot-housing of her talents would come to nothing. Robert couldn't bear the waste.

Erin sighed, her head briefly collapsing. 'She came to me this morning and said, "I know you won't allow me to go to Greywood." Simple as that. I was going to discuss it with her but she seemed fine. She even went out to the shop for me. I didn't know that she'd started . . .' Erin emitted a little sob of guilt. Whatever happened now, their daughter had entered a new phase of life.

Anger welled within Robert as he watched his wife tidy the kitchen, as if she didn't want to hear about Ruby, that folding the washing was more important than her daughter's happiness. There was something final about the way she smoothed the piles of towels, and the meticulous and inappropriate sock-pairing was ridiculous when her troubled daughter was whimpering upstairs.

At one thirty Robert led his wife to bed. He went to the bathroom and then to check that Ruby was sleeping soundly. She lay on her side, clutching a grubby rabbit for comfort, wheezing softly through her dreams. Robert wished he could see into her head, guide her through her nightmares and make all her wishes come true. He blew her a silent kiss and went to join Erin in bed. He slept fitfully and all too soon he noticed pink and orange lines spread across the sky from the east. His chest tightened as he realised that it was Monday morning.

'Tell me you won't send her back there today.' Robert wiped his hands across his face. He wasn't the type to plead. Other measures were needed. He rolled over to face Erin. 'Ruby can come to the office with me. Anything.'

Surprisingly, Erin nodded. 'I'll telephone Greywood and let them know the situation.'

'I'll take care of that. I can call from the office.' He didn't need to insist. Erin would gladly allow him to telephone the headmistress and explain their 'difficult' situation.

Before rising, he stared at the ceiling. Was this the first flicker of fatherhood? he wondered. His first taste of parental control? Then he looked across at Erin, who was sliding a cream satin robe over her shoulders, and thought: is this the first flicker of doubt?

Half an hour later, Robert and Erin were in the kitchen preparing for the day ahead. Ruby entered, fully dressed in her old school uniform, an unlikely smile widening her face. She had applied make-up, mascara and lipgloss, and her hair was swept back into a long ponytail tied with a blue scarf.

'Morning,' she said. She dropped her bag of books on the floor and swung the refrigerator door open, removing juice and eggs. 'I'm starving,' she continued. 'I don't need a lift today. I'm early enough to catch the bus.'

For a moment, Robert thought the smile was artificial. Had there been hesitation? Was that swallow concealing pure fear, the flicker of her eyelids chasing away welling tears? He stood and approached her, wanting nothing more than to absorb her, to save her from what the day held.

Ruby ducked aside as his outstretched arms tried to ensnare her. She took a frying pan from the cupboard and broke three eggs, dropping them into the pan from a height. Robert snorted, trying to retrieve his pride, trying to fight the ridiculous feelings of rejection that had been slung at him by this teenage girl.

Ruby threw the cracked egg shells into the waste bin and Robert considered: maybe she *wanted* to go back to her old school. Perhaps Erin was right, that running away would only create more problems in the future. What did he know? He'd never been a father before and, in his experience, facing his fears had only awarded them strength and the power to destroy what he cherished most.

Robert turned and leaned against the sink, sighing, staring out into the garden. He wanted time to think about Ruby, to figure out how he could change Erin's mind but his thoughts kept returning to Jenna, as if they were magnetised and he was charged with the opposite pole. She was as fragile as a chiffon scarf caught on a branch but Robert couldn't shift the image of Jenna in his garden – her hair blowing in the breeze, her smile as wide as the horizon as she walked under the willow tree.

What do you want? The words rattled inside his head as he watched her bend and pull roots from the soil. *You don't live here*, he said silently.

He hated Jenna for doing this to him. More so, he hated himself for letting her. Had his grieving gone horribly wrong? Had the natural process of coming to terms with loss gone awry from guilt?

Morning business and bustle continued in the kitchen as if nothing was wrong. The kettle steamed, Robert leafed through the newspaper and the post rattled onto the doormat. Ruby cooked her breakfast, cursing as she burst an egg yolk, and Erin said nothing at all. She simply stood, as if she had been caught off guard in a snapshot – mouth slightly open, eyelids drooping – and stared at her daughter as she scoffed the food. Robert could almost see the guilt dripping from Erin. This is the moment, he thought, that you could make everything all right. But Erin did nothing.

Robert blew out, a sigh combined with a moan, encapsulating his weariness. 'I'm going to shower,' he said. 'Then I've got work to do.' As he took the stairs two at a time, an image bled into his mind, only fleetingly, but it made him trip on the top step and grab the banister. As if unwanted thoughts of his ex-wife weren't enough to unsettle his usually slick veneer, Robert bore mental witness to two children, sobbing, as they were torn from their mother. The Bowman case.

Robert first-geared it through heavy traffic, drumming his fingers on the steering wheel. Ruby sat beside him, perfectly still, completely composed.

'Your mother's going to be furious,' he said but the side-ways glance of approval that Ruby shot him, her brilliant eyes charged with mischief and delight, convinced him that he was doing the right thing. Ruby nodded calmly, a faint smile tugging at the corner of her mouth.

Since she had got up that morning, Ruby had insisted on returning to the comprehensive school as her mother had in-structed and she was even willing to take the bus, a sure-fire route to twenty minutes of verbal abuse from other school kids, followed by a day of boredom while young teachers struggled to cope with the unruly classes. After much persua-sion from Robert, she finally agreed to ride to school with him if he promised to drop her around the corner. Arriving in a brand-new convertible Mercedes would mean a kicking the first time she set foot in the loos.

The thought of snarling dogs waiting for Ruby at the school gates was motivation enough for Robert to follow his impulses and secretly load the boot of his car with arm-fuls of uniform and sports kit and anything else he could think of that a young girl would need on her first day at a new school.

Robert drove his foot onto the brake. 'Christ,' he said. 'Near miss.'

'You can't have an accident to stop me going. Mum says we mustn't run away any more.' Ruby winked. Robert was relieved that she still had a sense of humour.

'But you don't believe that, do you?' He reached out and stroked Ruby's hand. He wanted her to trust him, to believe that he was doing the right thing. The traffic began to move again. 'I'll take the rap for this, when she finds out what we've done.'

Ruby swallowed and nodded. 'She's going to flip. Really flip. When Mum says no, she means no. Good reason or not.'

That's the thing, Robert thought, although he kept quiet. There *is* no good reason. He pulled over into a petrol station. 'You'd better go and change then. Don't want to be late on your first day.' They exchanged grins, one small step closer to becoming father-daughter.

Robert escorted Ruby to the ladies' toilets with a bag of brand-new uniform. While he waited, he filled up the car and bought a new torch because they were on special offer. He eyed the dismal selection of overpriced chrysanthemums that were wilting in dry buckets. Erin's shop was a shrine to healthy, fresh, unique and fashionable cut flowers. None of this unimaginative rubbish. He trailed his fingers through the thin, colourless petals and then Ruby emerged from the toilets looking every part the new girl.

'Come here,' Robert laughed. 'The tag's still on your collar.' He pulled the label off the grey and green blazer and brushed lint off her shoulder. 'Bloody fantastic,' he said and glared at the shop attendant as she stared at them while chewing gum with an open mouth.

'Dad.' Ruby giggled. 'Don't swear.'

Robert felt a surge of warmth in his heart whenever she called him Dad, which was rare. Mostly it was Robert. If only he could get through to his wife in the same way.

Robert ushered Ruby into the car and drove her through the traffic to Greywood College. Before he escorted her inside the imposing building, he said, 'I've got a big surprise for you and your mum tonight. Something that'll put a smile on your faces.' He'd do whatever it took.

'Oh Da-*ad*,' she said, grinning. She slammed the car door and skipped up the steps of the grand entrance. Robert watched her go, digging his fingernails into his leg, trying to counter the pressure in his throat, wondering exactly how he would tell his wife that he had overruled her. And now he would have to come up with a surprise.

SIX

It's strange but I don't know how I got pregnant. No, really. You can ask, but I shan't say. Of course, I know what's *meant* to happen when you want a baby although I won't be telling tales of a boy ever putting his thing inside of me. Mother thinks it was Jimmy, the not very smart kid who lives at the end of our street. Father blames all the boys at my school and wrote to the newspaper damning every male teenager in our neighbourhood.

The first I knew of it was when my school skirt wouldn't reach round my waist, when my belly had become so sore and stretched I thought I was becoming a fat person. Mother warned me about being one of those, saying greed was a sin, and took me to Dr Brigson to fetch some diet pills. I went along silently, knowingly, hoping they wouldn't prise the truth out of me.

Dr Brigson made me get on his examining couch – without changing the paper cover, I might add, which was all damp and crumpled from the last person. He lifted my sweater and pushed his fingers into my belly so deep that I wanted to cry out. But I daren't make a fuss. He'd have probably walloped me. He asked me some questions that I wouldn't answer then he sent me out of his poky, smelly room and whispered to my mother that I was going to have a baby. She slapped me when we got home. My father didn't look at me for a month.

It's Christmas Eve today. All the snow has melted. Some kids from school are hanging out on the pavement below my window. I can see them, their faces all lit up and glowing orange from the flickering street lights. They've been going from house to house, singing carols, jangling their collection box, tickles in their tummies because it's Christmas Eve. My tummy churns but not because it's Christmas.

Our house is next in line for carols but they won't come here. They won't dare do the Wystrach house but are happy to loiter outside, perhaps to catch a glimpse of me at my window. They want a peek at the girl who got pregnant. The girl who caused the biggest scandal of the decade at Biggin End High. The Year 10 girl who screwed around.

I draw the curtains to shut them out, to obliterate their happy Christmas, and lie down on my bed to sleep. It helps pass the time.

Sometimes I dream of how it happened and I wake up panting with a lake of cold sweat on my chest. If I've got any treats under the bed, stuff that I've smuggled, like Horlicks or sometimes icing sugar, I'll take comfort in that, perhaps by dipping my finger into the malty powder and sucking it off. Then I'll have nice dreams, such as the Easter parade at school – the posters made by the junior classes, the bonnets, the tissue-paper chicks, the misshapen chocolate eggs from domestic science class. The school hall filled with the joy of spring, a celebration of new life.

It might have happened then. I was on the lucky egg stall – a cardboard tray filled with fresh eggs nestling in straw, a couple of them with a happy face drawn underneath. 'Find the lucky egg,' I called. 'Only ten pence a go.' The prize was a knitted chick in a basket surrounded by sweets. Afterwards, when the teachers were clearing up, when everyone had gone home, a few of us – including Jimmy with his lopsided walk and gormless grin which sometimes caused him to drool – crept into the boiler room. We knew where the caretaker stashed his drink.

Or it could have been at the PTA disco. Mr Driver liked the look of me, kept asking me if I had a boyfriend yet. Said a pretty girl like me must have a queue of boys wanting to kiss me. 'Have you kissed a boy yet?' he said, a bead of saliva at the side of his mouth. I didn't care for that feeling low down, like I'd sat in hot cherry pie. I slipped away from him but wore his stare for the rest of the disco.

And I dream of toilet seats, or breast-stroking too close to a boy's winkle in the pool, or that God has chosen me and mysteriously impregnated me. Maybe aliens from another planet gave me Noel, or Chip, our Labrador, over-amorous, swung his wayward thing too close to my pants. I wish it was any one of those things although it doesn't matter now. It's too late for me. I'll just keep on pretending I don't know.

SEVEN

Robert dialled Louisa's number three times and each time he snapped his phone shut before it connected.

. . . Don't lose touch, Rob. If ever you need anything . . .

Her parting words still rang in his head clearly, even though it had been nearly a year since he had last seen her. Yesterday, when he and Den were forcing their way through a few pints at the club, Den had mentioned that she was back in the country for her cousin's wedding, among other things, and the thought of Louisa's practical manner and crystal-clear, honest voice had set Robert thinking. Perhaps she could help.

'Hello.' Same clear tone. Same Louisa. 'Hello?'

Robert hung up. Anyway, it was poor reception in the underground car park and she'd probably be far too busy to see him. He took the elevator up to the fourth floor to the offices of Mason & Knight, cradling the handset in his palm as if it was the only link to all things sane. If nothing else, Louisa had always splashed generous helpings of rationale and common sense into his life. She'd taught him to love and trust; taught him to take life each day and worry about tomorrow's problems when they came. All very sweet, he thought, turning the phone off and slipping it into his inside pocket. All very Louisa.

Robert reckoned he had fifteen minutes before Jed Bowman showed up for his court brief, if he even bothered to get out of bed. Explaining to the six-foot, anger-fuelled thug that it might not all go his way at the initial hearing was not an appealing task. Not today, anyway. The hearing wasn't until next week but Robert wanted to get things straight with Jed, ease him into the idea that he mustn't swear or smoke in court and that he had to wear a suit. He wanted to clarify the case, to make sure that Jed understood exactly what he was attempting to do: to gain custody of his children from his alleged drug-addict wife, not simply to get one over on her.

The thought of Bowman in a suit made Robert laugh out loud as the elevator pinged its arrival at his floor. He pictured the grimy, nicotine-stained hands protruding from too-short, frayed sleeves, his outdated, narrow tie knotted halfway down his chest. But the lazy no-hoper had been awarded legal aid and it was Robert's duty to fight his case. These days he always got the bottom of the pile at the two-man firm.

Robert smelled Jed Bowman before he saw him. Tanya, receptionist at Mason & Knight, jerked her head towards the window and pulled a face, alerting him to the large figure pacing back and forth, a silhouette of dishevelment against the blue sky. The tang of stale clothes, beer and cigarette smoke surrounded Jed in a filthy atmosphere. When he heard Robert's voice, he turned and scowled.

''Bout bloody time,' he said, dropping his dog-end into a half-finished cup of tea. 'You're not the only one who's busy, you know.'

'My apologies,' Robert replied, ever courteous, ever professional but inwardly cursing the man's ridiculous time-keeping. 'Come into my office.'

'I ain't got long, you know. I have to be back at the site.' Jed left a trail of pale mud – cement? – as he walked into Robert's office. He reeked of hatred.

'Site? Have you got a job then?' It could all change if Jed had steady work, stability and a show of commitment. It would help his case immensely.

'Not exactly,' Jed said quickly. His stubby fingers scratched at his half-grown beard, as if he'd revealed too much.

'Of course you haven't.' Working for cash, Robert thought, and still claiming benefit and legal aid. Not an ounce of him wanted to get his life in order, to help those kids, to make the court think he was a man of character and devoted to his family. All Jed wanted was to cripple his wife, the woman he had found in bed with his brother. Robert had heard it many times before, each telling of the sordid tale twisted with rage. Jed Bowman was an angry man.

'When did you last see your children, Jed?' Robert slipped his briefcase under his leather-topped desk, removed his jacket and was reminded briefly of Louisa as he felt the weight of his phone in his pocket. He would get rid of Bowman and call her again.

'Weeks ago. She won't let me near them.' Jed removed a packet of cigarettes from his dirty shirt pocket.

'It's a non-smoking office. This won't take long. Can you wait?'

Jed grimaced. 'If I have to. I just want to get me kids out of that house. She's got a man there now with a poncy car and proper job.'

'You know for sure?'

'That's what me neighbours said. Me old neighbours,' he corrected.

Robert was surprised at the way Jed Bowman's face began to slide off the jutting bones beneath. Folds of hair-spattered, sunburnt skin slumped around his forehead and neck, giving him the appearance of an ageing bulldog that had lost its fight.

'I loved her, you know. Truly I did.'

Robert, compelled by a feeling he couldn't quite put a label on, opened a cupboard in his desk and removed a cut-glass ashtray that hadn't been used since he quit the habit himself when he'd married Erin. He couldn't understand why his need for nicotine hadn't returned tenfold after the weekend's events, and seeing Jed's face regain some elasticity as he spotted the ashtray almost made Robert reach out and cadge one off his client.

Or was it because of Louisa's voice? Still the same clear bell.

Robert went through the file with his client although he wasn't sure that Jed completely understood the implications if he lost. His witnesses at best were unreliable and all but one had histories of alcohol abuse and drug addiction. Proving that Mary Bowman was an unfit mother for Jed's two children while their father himself associated with similarly socially challenged individuals would really test his persuasive skills as a lawyer.

At best, the children would be taken into care. At worst, well, Robert's gut told him it would be a life with their father, although he hadn't met Mary Bowman to measure how her parenting skills stacked up. So far he'd only had Jed's word maligning the woman.

'Nice suit and a bit of a shave, then. Nine o'clock sharp.' Robert stood, leaned over his desk through a haze of blue smoke and was about to offer his hand – more out of habit than anything else – but withdrew when he saw the filth on his client's fingers and nails.

'I'll have to borrow one.' And Jed left Mason & Knight obviously disgruntled by the prospect of procuring a suit.

Robert got in the way of his compulsion to pick up the phone again by talking through some files with Tanya until she reminded him that they had already taken care of these matters last week. Then he interrupted a telephone conference in Den's office. Finally, he returned to his own smoke-tainted office and poured himself a coffee. He switched on his mobile phone and it alerted him to one new voicemail.

'Robert, I can't believe it! Your number came up although I think reception must have been bad because I couldn't hear you. Anyway, how are you? It's been too long. Did you know that I'm back in England for a while? Look, call me back and we should arrange something. That is, if you want to. Maybe you don't, or can't or wouldn't anyway even if you could. You know. Hey, just call me.'

That was Louisa. Crystal clear.

He pressed a button to return the call and burnt his lips on his coffee just as she answered.

'Rob?'

'It is,' he said, unable to help the grin despite his stinging lip. 'That wouldn't be Miss Forrest, would it?' Then he realised his mistake.

'Uh-uh. Wrong number, I'm afraid.'

'How is married life then, Mrs . . .' he swallowed, not wanting to say the name. 'Mrs van Holten?'

'Oh, well, since you ask, my dear Mr Knight, married life is simply wonderful.' Then the giggle, bringing back a thousand years of memories. Not the giggle of a silly teen or frivolous female in her twenties, but the gentle, persuasive laugh of a woman who knew what she wanted in life. Whether she'd got it or not, Robert wasn't sure. 'And might I ask the same question of you?'

'My life is simply wonderful, also, Mrs van . . . van Holten. Just as you promised it would be.' Robert recalled a skim of pain on Louisa's face, hidden skilfully under a perfect smile, when he'd introduced her to Erin.

'Really? I'm so thrilled, Rob. You deserve it. After everything.' A virtually inaudible sigh, perhaps even static on the line.

'You too.' Robert was suddenly aware that their brief conversation was in danger of becoming maudlin, which might have the effect of bringing it to a premature close. 'Are you in London?' He held his breath, knowing the odds were slim.

'Sadly, no, otherwise I'd be knocking on your door and taking you out for lunch.'

Robert closed his eyes for a beat, thankful Louisa couldn't see.

'I'm in Somerset at the weekend for a cousin's wedding and then another few days travelling the country catching up with ageing relatives.' She sounded weary, he thought. Tired of something.

'When are you going back to Amsterdam?' Den had already told Robert she was in England for several weeks at least. Apparently he'd heard through an associate who'd used her on occasion, or was currently using her. Robert wasn't sure. He'd drunk five pints, after all.

'You know me. I couldn't resist the opportunity to pick up on a bit of work while I was here. I've a couple of jobs to do for a Dutch agency so, who knows, it might be a week but could be four.'

'We should catch up.' Robert held his breath, thought of Erin, wished he'd never called.

'Of course we should. What are you doing this weekend?'

Robert didn't reply immediately. Louisa had already said she was attending a wedding in Somerset. Was she inviting him along? Erin and Ruby too? He smiled at the thought. A few days away could be just what they all needed.

'Nothing much although that depends largely on Erin. She's quite likely to organise a dinner party on a whim.' Robert laughed to add substance to his lie. Erin was currently far too preoccupied to play hostess. 'What did you have in mind?'

'Why don't you bundle your family into the car and come up to the country for the weekend? Willem's flying over for the wedding so we could all, well, meet.'

'And stuff,' Robert added, knowing that Louisa was thinking it too.

The idea was left hanging on Robert's promise to call back once he had spoken to Erin. He hoped his wife would go for the idea. She'd only met Louisa once before their wedding, before Louisa left the country to marry a Dutchman. True, he'd been close to Louisa, she to him, but old flame was not on the list. Besides, the trip filled a needy gap – a break in the country could be the surprise he had promised Ruby and might also sweeten the news that he had to deliver to Erin – that he had taken Ruby to Greywood College.

Erin came downstairs, having showered and changed, and breezed into the kitchen like a fresh bloom. Despite her bright appearance she was shattered and made a point of regaling Robert with tales of her exhausting day at the shop. Robert handed her a glass of chilled white. The evening was muggy and airless, unusually so for early June.

'And she didn't turn up until eleven today. I told her, I

bloody told her, you're fired, young lady.' Erin took her drink and grinned at Robert. 'You're wonderful,' she said. 'What's all this for?' She eyed the array of ingredients on the worktop, breathed in heavily as unusual smells permeated the kitchen.

'No special occasion. I just fancied cooking.' Robert wrapped his arms around her, drank in the perfume of her shampoo and crushed her clean body against his day-old shirt. True, he hardly ever cooked and it was a riskily flagrant attempt at getting in her good books before he broke the news. Risky also in that it might not turn out right. He'd got Tanya to search for a recipe on the internet and sent her out to buy the ingredients.

'Ruby seems unusually chirpy. And thanks for letting her come back to your office after school. It makes a change from hanging about at my shop.'

'No bother,' Robert replied, staring at Erin briefly, wondering if this was the moment to tell her. He chucked a pile of chopped chicken into a searing wok and filled the kitchen with smoke.

'She's doing her homework, can you believe.' Erin pulled away from Robert and noticed the crease on his brow. 'Is something wrong? You don't seem very pleased that Ruby didn't get bullied today.'

'Of course I am.' Robert placed the spatula on the counter, turned down the gas and faced his wife. He planted heavy hands on her shoulders, thought how frail she seemed, and opened his mouth to speak. 'There's something—'

'Dad, I need help on a project. The other girls have been doing it for weeks and Miss Draper says I should try to catch up before the end of term and—'

'Your mother and I were just talking, Ruby. I'll come upstairs and help you in a minute.'

Ruby looked at her mother then at Robert. It dawned slowly, and her cheeks reddened. 'Oh,' she said and retreated from the room.

'Who's Miss Draper?' Erin slipped out of her husband's grip. 'And what project does Ruby have to catch up on?' She took a large sip of wine. 'Rob?'

Robert turned off the gas completely, accepting that the chicken would ruin, and pulled out a chair for Erin at the kitchen table. She sat, not taking her eyes off him, and he sat too, avoiding her gaze, focusing instead on her slim fingers fidgeting nervously.

'I took Ruby to Greywood College today, Erin. There was no way she could go back to her old school.' Finally, he looked up. He saw the thin thread of mistrust strung between them, that familiar web of doubt, sparkling tantalisingly. Only this time he was the one who had shot out the yarn.

'You did what?' Erin stood and went to lean on the sink, staring out at their small patch of garden, at the willow tree under which they'd once made love and been excited by the risk of being seen.

'I know Ruby's technically your daughter but when we married you automatically passed some parental respons-ibility onto me. We're a family now and what I think is best for Ruby—'

'So what you say goes, right?' Erin spun round. Her eyes hardened and became paler, if that was possible, and her usually full lips tightened into a thin line. 'Without a thought about what really matters.'

'What matters is Ruby's happiness. When I picked her up earlier, she was glowing.' Robert didn't particularly want to cook and didn't feel much like eating, but to curtail a major outburst, he returned to the chicken, lit the gas and added the sauce he'd prepared. He doubted if anyone apart from Ruby would eat now.

Erin left the room just as Ruby returned. She looked at Robert questioningly.

'Your mother's not very happy about it, love,' Robert said and offered a little of the sauce for Ruby to taste.

'Hot but good,' she said flatly. 'Will I have to go back to my old school?'

'Not a chance. Don't you worry about that.' Robert stared out of the window briefly, as if to catch sight of his wife's previous thoughts. The willow tree made his heart skittle as he remembered Erin's willing body, how eager she was. All he wanted was to be allowed to love her like the pounding in his chest told him. 'Anyway, I have a surprise for you both.'

Ruby immediately brightened and ran to fetch her mother.

The chicken was passable although rather spicy for such a muggy evening. A plain salad would have been better. Hungry from an exhilarating day, Ruby ate everything but Erin pushed her food around the plate, spreading it out like a child would to make it look as if she'd tried.

Conversation was limited and when Ruby mentioned her new school, Robert shot her a look that told her to save it for later. Erin was still tetchy about her bad day at work and grumbled briefly about untrustworthy employees. She was building up the business; the previous owner had not had a clue about running a florist's shop. Robert had bought the place as a wedding present for Erin, convinced that she could make a go of it. She was driven, knew everything there was to know about the flower trade, and the shop, although small, was in a prime high street location.

'I told her a thousand times but she obviously didn't want

to work.' Erin was thinking out loud. 'I'll have to advertise for someone else.' She leaned forward, head in hands. 'I can't believe I fired her.'

Robert reached across to rub her shoulders. 'Maybe you should call her and ask her to come back. At least just for this Saturday.' He looked at Ruby. 'I reckon your mum needs a break.'

'What on earth are you talking about, Robert?' Erin stood up, still mad from being overruled, and began to clear the plates but Robert stopped her.

'Sit. How about a weekend in a romantic country hotel? There's a pool and spa, riding, golf, tennis and after all that you can indulge in massages and all sorts of other beauty stuff.' Louisa had given Robert the name of the hotel where the wedding was taking place and he'd already looked at their website and called to check availability. 'And I promised Ruby a surprise earlier. I thought a weekend away would be good for us all.'

Erin's face revealed little emotion as she absorbed the news. The way she sat, perfectly still, hands clasped on the table, gave away nothing of what she was thinking. Ruby lunged for Robert and hugged him. At least he knew he had scored a hit with one member of his family.

'Can I go riding, Dad?'

She had said *Dad* again. It warmed him from the inside out. Robert nodded and squeezed Ruby's hand, noticing how icy cold it was, despite the lingering heat of the day.

'Why don't you run and get those letters from school. You said some were important.'

Ruby nodded and went to fetch her school bag.

'I'm not happy with it, Rob.' Erin stared into her husband's eyes. 'Not happy at all.'

The eye contact was a start, he thought. A breakthrough. 'It's only a weekend away.'

'Not the weekend. That will be . . .' she paused and reached for Robert's hand. 'That was a nice thought. I meant that I'm not happy about Greywood. About running away,' she added to remind Robert of her reason.

Ruby quickly returned with a pile of papers and Robert shuffled through them. 'You need a secretary for all these, Rube. Let's hope it's just because you're new at the school.' He skimmed the letters. 'These are for you to take care of, Erin. You need to send a copy of Ruby's birth certificate and her vaccination record. I'll handle the one with the large cheque.' Robert grinned, already committed to the huge expense of private education.

'I thought you'd already paid the fees.'

'I have. This is for the Vienna trip in August. The school's had it planned for a few months but because Ruby's new, we have to get all the forms back quickly in order for her to go.' Robert knew that if Ruby was going to make the most of life at Greywood, she would be expected to take part in everything on offer.

'*Vienna?*' The word was gossamer-thin. Erin's eyes narrowed in disbelief.

Ruby hopped from one foot to the other, barely able to contain her excitement. 'We're going to the Vienna Conservatory to learn stuff from their teachers and I'll get to play the piano at the Opera House. We're going to watch loads of stuff too and there'll be a disco and—'

'Vienna? That's in Austria.' Erin's voice, although barely audible, interrupted her excited daughter.

'I'll get to go on a plane, Mum. At last!'

Erin sat perfectly still, her rigid self-control allowing

nothing apart from slight shock, which was natural, to show. Only a tremor in her jaw offered any indication of her feelings.

'It'll do Ruby no end of good and give us the chance to get away for a few days ourselves.' Robert placed a hand on her leg but she flinched. 'Christ, I thought you'd be pleased, not turn into a corpse.'

He stood and cleared the plates, baffled by Erin's recent behaviour. It was completely out of character. A week for their daughter in a cultural hot-house, knowing Erin as he did, should have sent her cart-wheeling around the kitchen. One of the things Robert admired most about his wife was the way she had always put her daughter first and respected her needs.

He clattered plates into the dishwasher, making a point of being heavy-handed.

'It's not that I'm not pleased . . .' Erin trailed off, an expression of agony on her face. 'It's just . . .' she bowed her head, '. . . it's just that she *can't* go.'

'Nonsense,' Robert replied, deciding not to have any of this. Ruby was going on the school trip to Vienna if he had to escort her himself. 'At her age, Ruby does have a say in matters, you know. You don't own the girl.' He noticed Erin's skin twitch, her eyes glass over. He carried on. 'And don't forget to fill in those other forms and return the certificates to the head teacher's secretary. It's important.'

Robert dried his hands, the temporary distraction of doing the dishes having cooled him somewhat. If Erin had misgivings about the Vienna trip, he would have to understand and cajole her into what he believed was right for Ruby. He reckoned the weekend in Somerset would help. He just wasn't sure when to mention Louisa.

EIGHT

The M3 was a breeze and the A303 to Martock was similarly quiet. Robert, who transformed into a beast when stuck in traffic, was in an excellent mood, despite the strange news he'd received from Tanya that morning. Erin's hair rippled in the wind, her rigid smile a battle against the rush of air. Robert had considered putting the top up but both Erin and Ruby were happy to be whipped about. Just getting out of London seemed to be lifting everyone's spirits.

'Before you ask, Rube, about another forty minutes.' Robert grinned in the rear-view mirror. He'd wrapped up most of his pressing work by mid-afternoon and was in time to fetch Ruby from school at the end of her first week. They'd driven to Fresh As A Daisy, Erin's flower shop, and Robert reassured her once more that Tanya was perfectly capable of running the shop for a day.

'Are you sure Tanya's trustworthy?' Erin asked again as they turned off the main road and headed down a country lane. She smoothed down her hair and wrapped a cerise scarf around her head, not wanting to look a total mess when they arrived.

'Tanya's been with me for years. She's well trained.' Robert flashed a grin at his wife, taking his eyes off the narrow country lanes for as long as he dared. 'Just relax and enjoy the weekend.' He briefly gripped the wheel tighter than necessary, not because of the sharp corners or narrow road but because he couldn't prevent Tanya's strange words from earlier seeping into his mind. Convinced there must be a rational explanation, he was determined not to let it ruin the weekend. He decided not to confront Erin until they were back home.

The Maples Country House Hotel stood squarely next to the church and caught the rays of the descending sun. The western corner of the building appeared tangerine as the typical ginger stone of the area was illuminated, the shadows from the surrounding trees casting a moving lacy dance across the façade.

'Very nice,' Erin said cautiously, eyeing the building and the scattering of guests that were converging on the drive. 'I imagine Louisa will be really pleased to see you.'

Robert sighed at the slightly bitter inflection in Erin's words. 'She's here for her cousin's wedding predominantly. And we're here to relax.' He got out and shut the car door. Before he went to the boot for their luggage, he rested his hands on Erin's shoulders and he planted a tender kiss on her mouth. The last thing he wanted was for Erin to feel threatened. 'Catching up with Louisa will be pleasant, yes. I doubt her husband, Willem what's-his-name, will have any problem with our meeting.'

'Then why say his name so . . .' Erin squinted up at him, her eyes narrowed to slits from the low sun, '. . . so sourly?'

No more sourly than you mentioned Louisa, Robert thought but decided not to say. The weekend couldn't be ruined from the outset.

'Oh Dad, it looks perfect,' Ruby exclaimed, squeezing out from the rear of the car. 'And look. Horses.' She pointed to a pair of piebald animals clopping lazily through the village. 'Let's find our rooms!'

No, the weekend couldn't be ruined, Robert thought as he watched Ruby's slightly gangly limbs flapping towards the hotel entrance. She was becoming a woman but hadn't quite forgotten how to be a little girl. He hauled their two bags from the car and walked briskly after her.

Checking in was a slow process although Robert didn't mind the wait. The hotel was obviously full due to the wedding party and he realised he'd been lucky to secure two rooms at short notice. He scanned the reception area, pretending – to himself mostly – that he was admiring the collection of hunting scenes and countryside paintings and antiques that furnished the hall, when really he was searching for Louisa's face among the wedding guests. He had always told her how her face stood out from others, something about her intense jade eyes and auburn hair. Quite a hindrance, he'd thought, to draw such attention to oneself in her line of work.

Then, fleetingly, he thought he saw Louisa disappear into the ladies' across the hallway. Just a knot of red above a long, pale neck and the unmistakable height, the graceful stride.

'What are you staring at?' Erin glanced along Robert's line of vision and shrugged. 'Look, it's our turn.' She nudged Robert's arm and eased him forward to the desk. With Erin at his side, her arm wrapped round his waist, he didn't like to ask for Louisa's room number.

Check-in complete, Robert guided his family to the small lift, his eyes darting to the ladies' room several times. The lift door opened and they stood back while an elderly couple wrangled a huge suitcase out of the tiny compartment. Then Ruby skipped into the lift and pressed the button to hold the doors. Erin joined her and lastly, with the two weekend bags, Robert slid inside.

'Robert?' There was no mistaking the voice. He stuck a foot between the closing doors as she approached. The smile, way too wide for her face, reached him first, followed by her lovely green eyes, now framed by black businesslike glasses.

'I thought it was you,' Robert said, unable to help a broad smile in return. His body became wedged between the doors, causing them to open and close with a clunky sigh. 'They're nice,' he added, having no hands free to indicate that he meant her glasses.

'Dad, you're breaking the lift.'

They stared at each other silently for a time-warped couple of seconds. Robert didn't know whether to step out of the lift or offer a hasty 'I'll catch up with you later'. Louisa solved the dilemma.

'A few of us are meeting in the bar at seven for drinks. You're welcome to join us.' Louisa cast her eyes around the lift to include Erin and Ruby, although she didn't verbally acknowledge either.

'Seven then,' Robert said, breathing deeply and removing his foot. The doors wheezed shut.

The hotel bedrooms were small but very comfortably furnished in a country style that Erin adored. She curled up carefully on the bed, not wanting to disturb the pristine counterpane, but then couldn't resist stretching out to rid herself of the week's stress.

'I'll run you a hot bath,' Robert said. 'And there's chilled wine in the fridge.' It was nearly half past six. If Erin took a long bath, a really long one and then spent a while dressing . . . Robert popped the cork. He just wanted a few minutes alone with Louisa, to ask her advice, then he hoped his family would join them. He wanted to show them off.

'Are we really going to meet Louisa and her crowd at seven? I was hoping for a quiet meal in the hotel restaurant. We could order room service for Ruby and it looks like there are enough movie channels to keep her entertained.' Erin sat up on the bed.

'It's just drinks. We can make it short and then go for a meal. I doubt you'll keep Ruby in her room, though.' Robert handed Erin a glass of wine and ushered her through to the bathroom.

For the first ten minutes, he took guesses at which one of the half-dozen or so men surrounding Louisa was Willem, her husband. Robert stood in a classic waiting-at-the-bar pose, holding but not drinking a single malt, idly watching a band set up their equipment in the bar area. He was not close enough to Louisa to give the impression of standing in line for her company, but not so remote as to distance himself from the party.

'Rob.' It wasn't a direct cry for help – Louisa wasn't the kind of woman who would need assistance in extricating herself from a group, admirers or not.

'Hey,' he replied casually, smiling, but made no move towards Louisa. He noticed the slight roll of her eyes as she pulled out of the group that surrounded her. Clearly her husband wasn't among them. Robert wondered who, if left long enough, would have moved in for the kill.

'Drowning?' Robert suggested.

'I can swim. They'll scatter when their wives come down.' She allowed a grin to light up her face and Robert noticed tiny lines at the corner of her eyes, perhaps always there but magnified by her new glasses. She thrust her empty tumbler at Robert's chest. 'I'm thirsty,' she complained. 'And I hate weddings.'

Robert would gladly have offered his drink to Louisa – anything to help him spend the fifteen minutes he reckoned he had alone with her more productively than waiting at the bar for a drink.

'But you had one recently,' he said, and turned to try to catch the barman's attention.

By the time Robert had paid for her drink, Louisa was sitting at a small, highly polished table, on an equally shiny leather sofa. He lowered himself onto the squeaky chair beside her. Louisa fingered a strand of hair on her cheek.

'Had what recently?'

'A wedding,' Robert said.

'You too.' They both laughed. 'I still hate them.' She sighed and wound the strand of hair round her finger. 'They're a ceremony of possession rather than passion. That's my view, for what it's worth.'

'Problems?' Robert wanted to reach out and touch her shoulder. He hated the thread of regret in her voice. She nodded in reply. He would have left it there, he thought, had Louisa not pressed on. He recalled each of them on the telephone, breezing about their happy marriages.

'How about you? Are you wallowing in marital bliss?' Her eyes met his.

'Things are great,' he said, puzzled why the admission should make him feel he had just lied. 'It's hard taking on a ready-made family, though. Someone else's kid.'

'Is the father around much?' Louisa's voice rang clear; soothed his slightly aching head.

'That's the thing. No father. Ruby's a good girl although

she's had her share of problems at school. But don't get me started on all that.' Robert grinned, inwardly kicking himself for not continuing. Now was the time to ask her advice, to tell her what Tanya had said. He could count on Louisa's honesty.

'It was never meant to be, was it?' Louisa looked away, as if she instantly regretted the words.

'No.' He laughed as he replied. It was a cover for his shock although it took him a moment to realise what she meant. He took a large sip of his drink.

'You married, me married, you married again and now me. Plain bad timing, huh?' She reached out to touch Robert's hand but he withdrew. Upsetting Erin wasn't on his agenda. Any feelings he once had for Louisa had been firmly packed away.

'For one who hates weddings, you've had your share.' Robert took more of his whisky.

'I wouldn't have hated ours.' Another bold remark, rendering them both silent.

Robert didn't want it to be like this and was about to talk about Ruby again but Louisa stiffened. 'Willem,' she said brightly and stood, instantly divorcing the moment with Robert. 'This is my old friend, Rob Knight. He's a lawyer. I used to do the investigations for his firm.'

Willem, younger than Robert had imagined, stepped forward and offered his hand. 'Good to meet you,' he said, obviously without threat or care that his beautiful wife had been having a drink with a man he didn't know. Willem's voice was gravelled with accent, pleasantly so, and Robert couldn't immediately see anything in particular to dislike about the man.

'They're waiting in the lobby for us. We have to go.'

Louisa turned to Robert. 'We're dining with my cousin and

her husband-to-be. I'm her maid of honour and she wants to go over a few things with me.'

'You can tell her all about the delights of married life.' Robert's tone gave away none of the meaning that he knew Louisa would pick up on, especially to a foreigner who wouldn't completely understand the nuances of English. 'Perhaps I'll see you in the morning then. I'll be up early for a jog.' Robert remembered Louisa's virtual addiction to a morning run.

Louisa smiled, and then, quite unlike the woman he once knew, she allowed herself to be led away by the elbow.

Perhaps it was the second double Scotch that he'd drunk while waiting for Erin and Ruby to join him, or perhaps it would have happened anyway – a small cyst, innocuous at first, rapidly reaching out its fingers into a full-blown tumour. Either way, Robert regretted mentioning Tanya's news at dinner on the first night of their weekend break.

'Ruby doesn't seem to exist.' Robert slugged a large mouthful of wine. He couldn't help the occasional glance out of the restaurant to see if Louisa and her party had reconvened in the bar. He pushed his plate further onto the table.

'Yeah, she's gone to the toilet,' Erin replied while picking apart a fillet of salmon. Then she suddenly looked up and laid down her cutlery, struck by Robert's choice of words. 'You mean like Santa Claus or the Tooth Fairy?' The attempt to make light of the sudden heavy atmosphere was futile.

'No, not like either of those. I mean like . . .' he paused – another glance to the bar, another sip, 'I mean like Tanya not finding any record of Ruby's birth at the register office.'

There was a pause, nothing too conspicuous or stuffed with particular panic. 'And you expect me to relax tomorrow while this girl's in charge of my shop?' Erin began to dissect the pink fish again although she didn't eat any of it.

'She's quite capable of selling flowers for a day.'

'But not so capable when it comes to locating simple documents, even though such jobs must take up most of her day-to-day work in your office.' Erin smiled at her daughter as she slid back into her seat.

'Can I have pudding?' Ruby asked Robert, instinctively knowing she would have a better chance with him.

'Sure,' he said, shrugging. Then, 'It's not Tanya's mistake.' His quieter voice and refusal to look at his wife indicated that they should not argue about this in Ruby's presence. 'Like I said, the register office has no record.' Robert couldn't help himself.

Ruby wasn't stupid. 'Is this for my passport so that I can go to Vienna?' She jiggled on the seat, reaching for the dessert menu.

Robert nodded. 'Don't worry, I'll sort it.'

'Yeah, he's got his ace secretary on the case, hon.' Erin wiped her mouth neatly, stood and excused herself. 'You can tell her not to bother, Rob. Ruby's not going to Vienna.'

Robert watched his wife stride from the restaurant; he couldn't bring himself to look at Ruby and see the heart-sinking disappointment on her face.

'How about a double chocolate sundae?' he asked, knowing it wouldn't even make a small dent in Ruby's disappointment.

Erin was propped up in bed reading a book. The room smelled vaguely of face creams and herbal tea. Robert dropped his key and wallet on the dressing table and kicked off his shoes. 'She's in bed,' he said.

Erin placed the book face down beside her. Robert glanced at the red embossed cover of the standard hotel-issue bible. 'Good read?'

'Engrossing. You should try it sometime.' Erin flicked off her bedside lamp and slithered beneath the duvet even though it was warm and humid in the room.

'I said she's in bed, if you're interested.' Robert removed his shirt and went into the bathroom. He cleaned his teeth and splashed cold water on his face. In the mirror, he noted how his features had tightened, perhaps from the cold water or perhaps because of the elastic thread of doubt that pulled under his skin.

'Thanks,' was her muffled reply. Robert didn't understand. She always kissed Ruby goodnight. He walked up to the bed and whipped back the duvet to expose his wife's foetal position. He saw the muscles tense around her bones, even through the soft fabric of her summer pyjamas.

'What are you trying to do to the girl?' he demanded. 'She's just had her first week at a new school, no thanks to you, and now you're on a crash course to mess up her chances by telling her she can't go to Vienna.' Robert turned away. His palms itched. 'You know I'll pay for the trip, if that's what you're worried about.'

There was a heavy silence, disturbed only by the humdrum of chatter in the bar at the other end of the hotel. The warm night air hung between Robert and Erin like thick winter padding. Robert sighed and sat down on the bed. He tried to pull the duvet up over her again but she kicked it off. She seemed to be refracted several degrees askew of the real world.

'Would you like a reminder of what this is all about?' Robert rummaged in his bag and retrieved his iPod. He had put it in the bag as a credible aid to his planned morning run;

a scheme he hardly dared admit to himself. A day hadn't gone by in Louisa's life, he didn't think, when she hadn't run before breakfast. He toggled through the digital menu and pushed the headphones into Erin's ears. Her mouth and eyes wavered, indicating that she was suddenly drenched in Ruby's piano music.

Robert knew that particular piece perfectly. Ruby had called it 'Flight'. She had told him it was about running away and abandoning everything at a moment's notice, as if life was expendable, she had said. Robert would never forget the honesty in Ruby's face as she proudly told him of her composition. The music was rare, like her.

Now, he watched Erin listening as she lay on the bed, a tear collecting in the corner of her eye. He knew that Erin remembered Ruby composing it, her spine arced for hours at a time, head bent protectively over the baby grand that they had somehow squeezed into his dining room. The result was a collection of songs that Robert had mixed and recorded. He'd made Ruby feel special, like a professional.

It had been a condition of Erin finally moving in with Robert that the piano be allowed too; the three of them, a package. Robert had agreed without hesitation. He adored Ruby's music and, between them, mother and daughter had brought the human equivalent of spring to his life.

'So.' Robert turned down the volume. 'Does that refresh your memory? Now do you recall why we were so keen for her to go to Greywood?'

Erin nodded, strangely seeming smaller, fragile like a summer moth caught up in a light, wanting to pull away but unable, seeming trapped but nervously, stupidly, intrigued.

'I just don't understand about the birth certificate. Or lack of,' he added gently, stroking her head.

Erin sat up. A tear bulged from her left eye, which she wiped on the sheet. 'Someone's made a mistake.' She offered a small smile – a sugar-wafer smile doused with doubt. She unfolded herself from the bed and padded into the bathroom, half closing the door before she sat down. 'Obviously something's gone wrong somewhere,' she called out.

Not wanting to interrupt her, Robert stood outside the bathroom, stiff in the doorway like an uncertain builder's prop. 'You're right.' He sighed. Upsetting Erin had not been his intention. 'Something's gone wrong. Somewhere.' And, with his face relaxing from the doubt, he reached forward and pulled the door quietly closed.

Even at seven in the morning the air was humid and hung with the sickly sweet scent of dew-misted roses and honey-suckle that had just finished flowering. As their feet pounded the lane in a syncopated rhythm, Robert couldn't help a couple of glances at the gems of sweat collecting on Louisa's neck.

'Been a while, huh?' she laughed. Robert grinned back as best he could. She didn't even seem to be out of breath and they'd been running for fifteen minutes. He grimaced. He could still be in bed, curled around Erin.

'I play squash most Sundays. Go to the gym when I can.' Robert tried to stop, lean his hands on his knees, but Louisa pressed on in a steady stride, her slim legs falling perfectly in line in an economical style. She looked back and grinned – a flash of white against the clean blue sky.

'And how is our Den?' Then, 'Oh do come on. You won't make it to forty if you're that unfit.' Louisa jogged back and hooked her arm beneath Robert's, sliding it up into his armpit where the beginning of a healthy sweat was erupting. She heaved him forward and they laughed, each knowing Robert would never go the distance.

'Den's, well, Den,' Robert said, breaking into a run again. 'Business is good.'

'And who's doing your snooping now?' Louisa adjusted the waistband of her grey jogging bottoms.

'Brian Hook. He has the finesse of a clown at a funeral.' Robert reached out and touched Louisa's elbow as it pumped back and forward. 'It's a shame you don't still work for us.'

As the pair passed the last row of ginger stone cottages and the road into the countryside narrowed, it was necessary for them to run in single file and stay close to the verge as there were some sharp bends up ahead.

'Shall we take in the scenery?' Robert stopped at a gateway and raised a hand to Louisa as she turned. 'We can't talk like this,' he called, his voice replaced by shallow gasps.

'I thought the idea was to run.' She joined him at the wooden five-bar gate and they stared, side by side, out across the patchwork of green and gold fields. For a moment, neither of them said anything. They simply allowed their breathing and heart rates to return to normal while the rising sun dried their perspiration. The moment was so rare, that it was enough just to be. In Robert's mind, there was too much that needed to be said. He didn't know where to begin; wondered perhaps if he had got it all wrong. Complications that would spoil the simplicity of the moment.

'Are you and Erin really happy?' Louisa eventually asked, shifting round so that she was facing Robert squarely. 'You didn't convince me last night.' Her breathing was steady now, just a faint sheen on her cheeks and breastbone. Robert suspected her question was a link into what she really wanted to discuss. Her own marriage.

'Erin and I are good together.' Robert noticed a slight cramp in his stomach muscles. 'We adore each other. And Ruby's a lovely girl. She's an exceptional pianist.'

'But are you truly *happy*?'

Strong fingers of pain inserted themselves between Robert's ribs with every inhalation. 'Sure.'

'Why don't I believe you?' Louisa kicked her running shoe against the gate and shielded her eyes from the dazzle behind Robert.

Robert shrugged. 'Like everyone, we have our share of problems.' When Louisa didn't say anything, he continued. 'It's not like you go into a marriage, especially second time round, as if you're diving headlong into a crystal pool.'

'No,' Louisa replied thoughtfully. Then, laughing, 'More like muddy waters.'

'Exactly. You soon find out what's lurking at the bottom. And if you don't but happen to snag your toe on something, then that's when you start to question what's waiting beneath you.' Robert drummed a distracted beat on the gate before blurting it out. 'Something's not right with Erin, Lou. She's acting weird. Like she's hiding something.'

A pause, enough time for a formation of ducks to pass overhead. A van rumbled past, leaving a tang of exhaust in the air.

'Not again, Rob.' Louisa sighed. 'God, no. Not again.'

'Pfah.' Robert pushed hard on the old gate, dislodging Louisa's foot, and waved one arm in the air. 'Is that what you think? You think I haven't learned?'

'No, it's just that—'

'There's something I never told you about after Jenna's death.' Robert's usually deep voice thinned to a whisper.

To allow him time, Louisa said nothing. She knew this was way harder than a five-mile run.

'It was on her phone. A message from a man. He said how he couldn't wait for their next afternoon in a hotel.'

Louisa reached out and touched his arm. 'Did it make you feel any better?'

'What, that I was right about her affair? That I was right to hound her day and night, to have her followed, to become obsessive and intercept her post, her email, her messages . . .' Robert became breathless again. 'You mean, did it make me feel any better about being an insanely jealous, paranoid husband who sent her mad in the end, who forced her out of our home after we'd rowed, who caused her to get in her car after she'd drunk a bottle of wine, who sent her driving far away, anywhere, as fast as she could to get away from me?'

Louisa's skin prickled with goose bumps even though the day was set to be as hot as the previous one. She'd heard the story a thousand times before and it never got any easier.

Jenna crumpled over the wheel . . . Jenna's neck meticulously snapped . . . Her spirit flown from her grey-white body . . . Only one small patch of blood on her right temple . . .

'I keep thinking I see her,' Robert admitted in a voice that was suddenly as collected as if he were speaking in court. 'At the top of the stairs. By the tree in the garden. She still seems so real.' He stared at Louisa, waiting for her reaction.

'It's not been much over a year, Rob. You moved too fast, in my opinion.' Louisa lifted the hem of her running top and dabbed at her neck. 'You have to expect ghosts to clash with reality.'

'Moved too fast, in your opinion? That's good, Louisa. That's really good.' Robert kicked the gate, walked away, walked back again. 'My wife gets killed last April. Two months before that you've gone and bloody married William what's-his-name who you only met at a Christmas party a few weeks before—'

'Willem,' she interrupted. Her voice cut like a whip snapping at his ear. 'My husband's name is Willem van Holten. And yes, we met at a Christmas party, yes we were married eight weeks later, yes in another two months Jenna was dead . . .' Louisa paused, breathed deeply. 'And yes, it's a fact that you and I are never going to be given a bloody chance to get it together because one of us is always married.' Then, like a racehorse kicking turf at the start line, Louisa sprinted away from Robert, knowing that he wouldn't even try to keep up.

Robert stared out across the countryside for another twenty minutes before walking back to Martock. Never going to get it together, he thought, and wondered exactly what it was that had made Louisa, usually serene as a Buddhist monk, act the way she had.

Erin and Ruby were in the dining room, Ruby taking advantage of the full English breakfast buffet while Erin sipped pensively on a black coffee. Ruby's reaction to Robert's approach alerted Erin although she didn't look up from staring at the starched linen tablecloth.

'Hi.' Robert kissed the top of his wife's head. He had taken a quick shower and changed into jeans and a green striped shirt. His dark hair was still damp and glistened in the subdued ceiling lighting. 'Not eating?' he asked. He thought they could take a drive out to Sherborne Castle. He didn't want to be around when Louisa's cousin's wedding got underway. He didn't think he could bear to see her dressed in a maid of honour's outfit, even if she wasn't quite the bride. He pulled out a chair and sat between mother and daughter.

'Good run?' Erin's tone was as bitter as her coffee.

'Yeah, thanks.' Robert unfolded his napkin and the waitress took his order.

'You went with Louisa.'

'Dad, can we go to that castle you mentioned?' A piece of Ruby's sausage skidded onto the table as she cut it.

'You could have asked me to go with you.' Erin shielded her cup as the waitress offered her more coffee.

'I didn't think you liked running.'

'Do *you*?' Erin stood and walked briskly out of the dining room.

'Of course we can go to the castle, Ruby,' Robert said and as he was stirring his tea, he caught sight of Louisa and Erin passing each other in the foyer. Neither of them acknowledged the other.

NINE

I wake to find that I'm wet. My sheets, my legs, my fleece pyjamas are all soaked with something that smells of warm, wet animal. Mother will be angry that I made such a mess. I haven't peed the bed for several years now. I put on the bedside lamp and see that it's not just wee on the bed. There's blood too and as I walk to fetch my dressing gown, I find that I'm still peeing. With each step I take, hot liquid spills down my legs and I try to stop it but I can't.

I whimper, knowing I'll get a good slapping for this mess. I pull down my pyjama trousers and see that they're sodden and streaked with red. I take them off and hide them under the bed. I get the bucket and squat over it. At this rate, it'll be full in a few minutes. They didn't empty it yesterday and I wonder if I should tip it out of the window.

I look at my clock. It's twenty to midnight. Nearly the New Year. Mother told me that tonight they're going to a party at Uncle Gustaw and Aunt Anna's house. They'll be having delicious little savoury *pierogies*, *cwibak* loaf and *piernik* honey cake, and the children will be allowed sips of sweet *miod pitny* from tiny ceramic fish-shaped vials that smell of dust from Aunt Anna's woodwormy sideboard. Uncle Gustaw will blow the bugle at midnight, like last year, like he has done every other New Year's Eve I can remember.

Mother watched for the glint in my eyes as she told me of their festive plans, held her breath for any sign that revealed my longing to come too. I couldn't help it, thinking of them all together, laughing, dancing, singing, eating and drinking in the New Year, my cousins frolicking as a noisy pack, playing pranks, stealing the alcohol. I tried not to look at the pleasure on Mother's face, that tightening of the lips, the narrowing of her dismal watery eyes when it dawned on me that I wasn't even invited, apart from being too shamed to attend.

It didn't occur to Mother that perhaps I didn't *want* to go to the celebrations, that I was too scared. My poker, dough-faced, bloodless expression aside, trying so hard not to let her think I was disappointed, a worry spillage was set free.

What if *he* came looking for me?

In the early hours, my parents will be walking home, holding hands, rosy-cheeked, chilled, feeling sick, feeling young, exhausted but warm on the inside. The entire Wystrach family, my uncles and their wives and sisters, cousins, aunts, mothers and my *babka* will see in the New Year in their own way; under tight surveillance from Mother and her sister-in-law, Aunt Anna. It is the only night of the year when they all let down their hair.

I double up in pain and fall onto my bed. It hurts. I have a cramp in my guts, perhaps because of bad food, perhaps because of no food. I push my face into the pillow and bite and the pain drops away as suddenly as it came. When I stand up, I am shivering and more hot pee trickles down my legs. I wrap my dressing gown around my shoulders and get back into bed. Everything will seem different in the morning, that's what Mother always used to say when she liked me. I fall asleep.

I was dreaming of Christmas Day, that they let me have

extra food and put a cracker on my dinner tray. Who was I supposed to pull it with? In my dream, the cracker turned into a long carving knife and when they came to get the tray, I slipped it into each of their bellies, the flesh bursting precisely because the cracker knife was so sharp. The pain in my belly makes me stretch out and yell. I grip the bedhead behind me, my fists whitening around the metal bars. I scream again. It's a scream that comes from a place so deep inside, I don't even recognise that it's me.

I try to stand up but fall off the mattress and bang my head. That pain doesn't matter. It's the pain across my front, whipping round to my back and speeding up and down my spine that I can't bear. In between the streaks of agony, it dawns on me that the baby is coming. Where is Mother? I call out her name, while I am able, while there is no pain.

I pull a pillow off the bed and doze fitfully on the floor. I can see some of my old toys under the bed – dolly Patricia, a grubby pink rabbit, a pile of Enid Blyton books and that game of Snakes and Ladders that *he* gave me two birthdays ago. It was a sign, he said, that we had good games. He'd wrapped it in tin foil and the ribbon was from a chocolate box and now he tells me to just forget. What, that he gave me Snakes and Ladders? No, the other stuff, he says and laughs at me.

I draw my legs up but that doesn't help. My face shatters as another wave of pain helter-skelters around my entire belly.
'*Mother . . .*'

Somehow I get to my feet. I lean forward, resting my hands on the end of my bed, and rock from side to side each time the pain comes. I screw up my eyes and pant out gallons of air, which makes me feel dizzy and convinced the world is upside down. I'm sick. Water vomit erupts onto my quilt. I fall to my knees, too weak to stand.

'Someone help me! *Mother* . . .'

I sleep again, with my forehead resting on the floorboards and my domed belly stuck between my knees. I dream of *him* and when I wake, because the pain has started again, I'm sweating and scared and panting because the dream was so real and I thought that he was in here with me. I look around. He's not.

Suddenly, I want to push. I'm like a dog, holding my breath and bearing down, lifting out of myself because I'm on fire down there and I'm screaming and screaming and drowning because there's no breath in me and still no one comes to make all this better. I am completely alone in the house.

I drop down with my forehead on the floor again. I will do this.

There's the Snakes and Ladders box again, unopened, mint condition. I slide my hand under the bed, through the dust, and pull the box towards me. A game for two or more players. I lift off the lid and take out the board. Yellow ladders, green and red snakes. There's a little plastic bag of counters and two dice. I snap open the bag, roll a die and move a counter five places but then the pain comes again and I rear up and grip the metal bed frame and wail like a wolf and strain and push and those hot irons stabbing through me are going to kill me, I know.

I've landed on a ladder which takes me directly to square thirty-four. Hurray! A six this time. Then a three and another ladder and I'm reminded of *him* by the face of the little snake that, if I had rolled a two, I would have landed on. Oily, leathery face with eyelids too flared for his black bead eyes, like our heavy living-room curtains. Simply too big.

Pain again and I chip a tooth as I wrap my lips around the bed frame, trying to cool down because everything about me is burning up. I'm a space capsule re-entering the atmosphere. I put another counter at the start, for *him*, so that I can pretend he's playing too. I want to beat him. Using both dice, to hurry things up, I frantically roll and roll, taking turns, me then him, climbing up, sliding down, on and on to the top. Even with my head start, he's catching up. I can see his bald, moley scalp getting closer as he steps methodically up each rung. I'm only one level above him now and – I fold with pain – if he reached up a hand, he could probably grab my ankle as I cower on square fifty-seven.

I plunge a fist between my legs. Something's there, bulging, like a disc of wet animal. I burst out in shrieks of laughter, which turns into exotic wails coming from a part of me I didn't know existed. The urge to push is all-consuming. If I don't, I think I'll die. I'm burning, burning. I scream for my *babka*. She will help. She doesn't even know I'm having a baby. Three thirty-six, the clock says. Where *is* everyone? I pant gently; have a break; roll the dice. He's gaining on me, no doubt about it. Only three squares behind.

Instinctively, I reach for the pillow that is already lying on the floor. I drag the quilt off my bed and make a nest. It's my only hope. There are little animal noises, me I think, and a warm milky smell bubbling from inside me. This is it. I'm on my back, half sitting, half lying, propped on elbows, legs as wide as they can go. It's bursting out of me. The world goes black and quiet for a moment – the eye of the storm – before I'm stretched to infinity with a pain that now, compared to my game of Snakes and Ladders with *him*, seems bearable.

The large, masterful figure looms over me, watching, laughing, spit collecting in the corners of his wide, hungry mouth as I split myself in two, his shiny boot nudging my hip, his hands creeping where they shouldn't. The head's out. No pain for a moment, just me with two faces, one of them squirming, squinting between my thighs, the other thrown back, flushed, exhausted.

It makes a noise. A squeak. I heard it and felt the tiny vibrations shiver up its body inside me. Then, with one final griping pain, the rest of it suddenly comes out in a rush and slithers in mucus and blood onto the quilt. I grab my baby roughly so that *he* can't get a hold of it first. I press it to me, without even bothering to look at its unfolding body, urgently hiding it from the figure that is kneeling beside me now, easing me back onto the quilt, his thin lips searching for mine, his smooth, moisturised hands creeping around my deflated belly.

I press the baby's mouth to my nipple and realise, as its grey legs pound the unfamiliar space in anger, that I have a baby girl, born on the first day of the New Year.

Something else glides out of me, warm and thick and smelling of raw liver. I leave it lying between my legs and, with his finger pressed on his mouth to silence me forever, the figure vanishes, leaving behind the faint tang of pipe tar on my lips.

I wrap myself round my baby to keep her warm, praying that he won't come back. I'm shaking. The quilt is soaking but I pull it up over my shoulders anyway. I'm too tired to move and as I'm falling asleep I realise that because of Uncle Gustaw, my daughter must be my cousin too.

TEN

Robert had instructed Jed Bowman to come back in half an hour. The client wasn't pleased, his already ruddy cheeks flushing, his cold eyes darting over Robert as if sizing up which bit to thump. Robert clicked the reception door locked as Jed left so that he and Tanya wouldn't be disturbed. Den was out at a meeting all morning and Alison, his PA, was off sick so it was just the two of them.

'Right, pick up the phone.' Robert felt a pang of guilt as he addressed Tanya like an impatient teacher would address a disobedient child. However competently she'd managed Fresh As A Daisy for Erin on Saturday, she'd be clearing her desk by the end of the week if she didn't get hold of Ruby's birth certificate. He stood over her as she dialled the number.

'Put it on speaker phone.'

'Good morning, Northampton Register Office. How can I help you?

'Hi,' Tanya replied. 'I'm calling about an application for a copy of a birth certificate.'

'Hold, please, while I transfer you.'

'They're always busy,' Tanya protested, covering the mouthpiece with her hand as her boss stood glaring down at her. His dark hair, stiffened shoulders and deep chest barricaded by crossed arms told Tanya that he wasn't budging until she got answers. Having worked as Robert's assistant for many years, she'd always thought him a reasonable man.

An electronic voice told them they were number five in the queue. While he waited, Robert re-read the letter from the General Register Office: '. . . unable to issue a copy birth certificate from the information given . . . no record found for Ruby Alice Lucas . . . DOB 1/1/92 . . .' The details were correct. No doubt. He wondered if Ruby had another middle name that he didn't know about, that never got used, or if Ruby was indeed a nickname. He would ask Erin. He needed facts.

As they moved forward in the automated queue, Robert considered that Erin might have given Ruby her maiden name after the split from Ruby's father – a defiant act of completely cutting herself off from the man she didn't love any more. He could imagine Erin doing such a thing in a fit of pride and independence. If that was the case, if Ruby's birth had originally been registered under her father's name, when her parents were happily married, then of course no record would be found. Robert released the tight embrace of his arms a little, relaxing as he realised a rational explanation was entirely possible.

Although Erin never spoke of Ruby's father, understandably, and he wasn't keen to hear details, Robert had always assumed that the name Lucas came from her previous marriage. It hadn't seemed important before and delving too deep into another person's affairs, he knew from bitter experience, only ever resulted in trouble. Thus far, his relationship and marriage to Erin had encapsulated the thinnest of details, deliberately skimming the surface for fear of crushing something delicate and irreplaceable beneath. Robert chose to ignore the feelings of frustration this tactic of self-preservation had produced.

'Superintendent Registrar's office. Can I help you?'

Tanya opened her mouth to speak but Robert lunged for the telephone and picked up the handset. He didn't trust the woman not to make a mess of things again. Time was running out.

'Hi . . . yeah . . . I made an express application for a copy of my stepdaughter's birth certificate about a week ago and got a letter back saying that you couldn't find it. I was just wondering if you'd be able to check again for me. Obviously my daughter exists. I saw her just this morning.' Robert tried to inject a little humour into the request, keen to keep the woman on his side, knowing how she could make things difficult.

'Have you got a reference number on the letter?'

Robert read out the number carefully and waited, listening to the woman's breathing as she tapped at the keyboard.

'No, sorry. It says that no records were—'

'Yes, I know that. I have the letter here. I just want to know *why* no records were found.'

Robert, perched on the corner of Tanya's desk, recited details about Ruby – when she had been born, full name, how her mother had split from her father, but the woman interrupted, uninterested in what Robert had to say. There was a queue of callers racking up.

'You've supplied appropriate details on your application form. The only explanation is that either the child's name is wrong or, more likely, that the birth wasn't registered at this particular office. Other than that, I can't give specific details as to why we're not coming up with anything. It might be worth checking with Mum again, too. Just to confirm you've remembered all the details correctly.'

'I think I know my own stepdaughter's correct name,' he

replied sourly. 'Can't someone run a search for all entries for that particular birth date?'

'I'm sorry, sir. We simply don't have the staff or the time to pursue such matters. If we had to—'

'Thanks for your help.' Robert replaced the handset abruptly, biting his lips in thought. He knew he wouldn't get anything else out of the woman. He poured himself a coffee from the machine, almost forgetting to ask Tanya if she wanted one. She nodded when he held up a cup and for a while they drank in silence, each considering the outcome of the phone call.

It occurred to Robert, as he sipped the scalding coffee, that he must have made a mistake about Ruby's birthday. He knew Erin would react, the way women do, when he confessed to getting Ruby's year or even day of birth wrong – rather like forgetting an anniversary and cobbling together a hasty surprise, blaming it on the tardy jeweller or incompetent travel agent.

'First of January, nineteen ninety-two,' he pondered out loud. 'Thirty-first of December, ninety-one.' Definitely the first one, he thought. Definitely January. But maybe nineteen ninety-one?

His excuse to Erin would be that he was a father by default. It was Erin he'd loved first. Ruby came as part of the package, he accepted, but adopting a teenager was something he'd never bargained on. It was a hard task, a thankless one sometimes, but he was committed to them both forever. He dialled Erin's number.

'Fresh As A Daisy. Erin speaking.'

Robert felt himself unfurl inside when he heard his wife's voice. It was natural, he told himself, for suspicion to reign, even dimly, after what he'd been through with Jenna. Louisa had been right, although he'd not wanted to admit it. He *had* moved too fast, although if he hadn't made a move on Erin, if he hadn't gone back for his umbrella . . .

'Hi, babe. It's me. Can you talk?'

'Yes, the shop's clear at the moment. What's up?'

'Just run by Ruby's year and place of birth again. The birth certificate people are having trouble finding her entry and she needs a passport to go to Vienna.' Robert opened Tanya's desk drawer and took out a pen. He pressed the phone to his shoulder and waited to write. 'Erin?'

'Not that again, Rob. I thought we decided we weren't going to bother with the school trip.'

Robert glanced at Tanya and smiled. He hadn't meant to be so hard on her. She was a loyal employee and always willing to please. She returned his grin and began tapping away at her computer.

'Bother?' he replied in a low voice although he would have preferred to raise the volume. 'How can you not want to bother with anything to do with your own daughter?'

'Exactly,' she said swiftly. '*My* daughter.'

Robert sighed. He wasn't going into battle in front of Tanya. 'Can you at least confirm that her birth was registered in the name of Lucas at Northampton Register Office? You said she was born there, right? School trip or not, she needs a passport. Unless you're planning on not having a holiday ever again.'

'Robert, I've got to go. There's a customer. Bye.' Erin gave a little kiss before the line went dead.

Jed Bowman didn't return to Mason & Knight. Robert spent the time he had allotted to the case reading over the sordid file. It was dragging on. He should have had this all wrapped up by now. It was textbook stuff, albeit in reverse to the usual glut of custody cases.

Man wants sole residency rights of his two children. Wife is an alcoholic, a drug addict and clearly mistreats the children, who haven't even been consulted about what they want. Man now has home of own and is in employment. End of story.

'Yes, end of story, all right,' Robert said to himself, leaning back. 'If it wasn't for bloody Jed Bowman.' He felt stupid when he saw Tanya standing in the doorway.

'There's someone here to see you, Mr Knight. Mary Bowman.'

Robert slid swiftly from behind his desk and shut the door. 'Mary Bowman, as in Jed's soon-to-be ex?'

'The very one.' Tanya looked rather proud. She enjoyed a fuss.

'Did she say what she wanted?'

'Just that she had to see you. Shall I show her in?'

Robert hesitated. Den wasn't back from his meeting yet and if Tanya wanted to keep her job then she knew to keep quiet. Robert was fully aware of the ethics involved, especially without Jed present. But off the record, as a compassionate human being who sensed that something was very amiss, where children and their future happiness were at stake, Robert was compelled to hear what Mary Bowman had to say. Fleetingly, he thought of Ruby.

'Bring her in.'

Mary was small. Five foot three at most. She was wearing an old-fashioned beige and blue crimplene dress. Robert recalled his mother in something similar, which added about twenty years, Robert reckoned, to her three and a half decades.

Mary's small face was mostly obscured by a pair of large black sunglasses, also outdated in style, and a frame of mousy, shoulder-length hair of no particular cut. She had obviously tried to dress up for the occasion but the overall effect was that of a woman who had little money, little self-esteem and no confidence. From first impressions, Robert was surprised that she'd even made it to the offices of Mason & Knight. Mary Bowman resembled a woman clinging to life with the tip of one finger.

Robert took the woman's hand as she offered it, noticing the lack of rings, the lack of warmth, the slight tremor. He sent Tanya out of the room, sensing she would have gladly stayed. 'Please, sit.'

Mary Bowman solemnly positioned herself in the leather client's chair and only when Robert pulled out his chair from behind the desk and located himself right in front of her did she slowly lift her head and remove her sunglasses. Her movements were laboured as if her limbs were filled with wet concrete and her gaze was distant, her expression hollow. Her entire face conveyed to Robert everything he needed to know about Bowman versus Bowman. Mary's nose was comprehensively broken – a swollen and split welt saddling the bridge – and her eyes were like two rotting plums set into tender flesh, badly concealed beneath the wrong-coloured foundation.

Robert breathed in, partly to stifle the exclamation he felt he was about to make and partly because he couldn't help it. He'd practised family law since qualifying, represented some desperate cases in his time, but seeing Mary Bowman present herself to him as if she were a piece of evidence threw up serious personal doubts about representing Jed Bowman. And he knew it wasn't just because Mason & Knight took legal aid cases either. Robert had untangled similarly nauseating cases where his clients drove eighty thousand pound cars and still pulped their wives. The strange thing was, it had never bothered him before.

'How can I help?' Robert realised how stupid he sounded. How could anyone help this woman?

'I've come to tell you that I give up.' Mary Bowman folded her hands neatly in her lap, as if to punctuate her statement. She picked at a nail. 'I don't want my children. I am an unfit mother.' She gestured to her face, her hand accidentally bumping her lips and smudging a streak of pale pink lipstick across her already patterned cheek.

Robert was stunned. This was not what he had expected. True, it would make his life considerably easier and get the file off his desk, but he knew, after having seen Mary Bowman and her wrecked face, that that would be like sending Ruby back to her old school.

'That's something the court will decide,' he said. 'Your solicitor will present your case in the best possible way and the children's welfare officer will do the same. The judge will determine, after all the facts have been weighed up, what's best for your children. As your husband's representative, I have a duty to . . .' Robert hesitated. His obligation to Jed Bowman suddenly blurred as he was confronted by the plainest evidence of the case so far.

Faced with his client's wife, the respondent, in his own personal space, his twelve-foot-square office for which he had chosen the slate-grey carpet, the mahogany desk, the watercolours hanging on the oak-panelled walls, immediately flooded the case with a third dimension. A human aspect that he didn't think he'd now be able to ignore. Robert breathed in deeply, continuing, '. . . a duty to present your husband's case to the court. And because there is evidence of the children's neglect and your actions, adultery included—'

'Now you have proof of Jed's actions.' Mary pulled back her hair and tilted her face to the window. The damage was comprehensive. 'I give up because Jed has made it impossible for me to continue. Even if I do get the kids back, he'll never leave me alone. Not any of your stupid orders will keep him away from me. Not now I've been with his brother. That got to him more than anything.' She turned back to Robert. 'That really messed with his brain.' She took a packet of Royals from her purse and lit one without asking Robert if he minded. 'My husband will always own me, whatever the judge decides. I hope you sleep well at night.'

'Now wait up a minute.' Battered wife or not, Robert refused to have his professionalism questioned, however hard the truth stuck in his heart. 'Whatever history you and Jed have together is your business. If Jed chooses to knock you about every day for the rest of your life, that isn't my concern.' Robert felt his mouth turn sour. Old coffee, the cigarette smoke, guilt – whatever it was, swallowing didn't make it go away. 'What makes this my business is that your husband has instructed me to file for divorce on his behalf and the residency of your children is in dispute. Two helpless kids who, if given the choice, would rather not have their dad knock their mum about or learn that their mum's been at it with their uncle. That's not to mention the drugs and the alcohol and the kids rarely attending school . . .' Robert stopped himself. He wasn't in court now. Mary was damaged enough.

Mary snorted and blew out a plume of smoke. 'Is that what he told you? That I'm an alcoholic and do drugs?'

Robert walked to the window and hoisted the sash open.

The room suddenly filled with city street noise and the smell of car exhaust fumes riding on the warm updraught of humid air. He stared down at the steady stream of shoppers, women with prams, office workers, cars, taxis – all allowed to go about their own business without being intimidated or bullied. Ruby and Jenna, each hounded in their own way, flashed through his head until the guilt that welled in his gullet forced him to turn back to Mary.

Robert marched across the office and pulled his chair even closer to Mary's. He sat, hitching up his tailored suit trousers, and took her hands in his. Sirens screamed in his head. He heard Den's raised voice when he found out how stupid his partner had been. He saw himself packing up his belongings, vacating his office – the prestigious office suite that he and Den had sweated blood to be able to afford. Then he saw Ruby, miserable in her old school, relentlessly bullied by the young Jed Bowmans of the world. She had been a victim, like Mary, until he had taken control and sent her to a new school. Then there was Jenna, plagued by his own insecurities until something gave and the truth came out. That his suspicions had been correct was of no importance any more. Jenna had been sentenced to death before she had even been tried and it was entirely his fault. He had wrongly assumed the role of uninformed judge. Robert shook his head to rid himself of thoughts that had no place in his consciousness at a time like this.

'Tell me everything, Mary. From the beginning.'

Mary bowed her head. Before she began, she asked for a glass of water.

ELEVEN

Robert left the office early. His ability to concentrate on work had diminished since Mary Bowman had left several hours ago. Her presence in his office had stirred up silt at the bottom of his personal river that he was trying to forget.

Squinting as he drove out of the underground car park, Robert fished in the glove compartment for his sunglasses before pulling out through the traffic onto the opposite side of the road. The muggy afternoon air did nothing to warm his spirits, rather caused a patina of sweat to form on his face and forearms that were still cool from the air-conditioned office. As he sat in standstill traffic he flicked through several radio stations but none of the music suited his mood. He pressed the automatic roof switch and brought down the top on his Mercedes. He wanted to shut out the entire world.

'Home,' he snapped at his handset. The number rang out. Erin had forgotten to set the answer machine. But it confirmed that the house was empty and encouraged Robert to press on with what he had specifically left the office early for – aside from wanting to avoid Den for fear his wily partner would sniff out that the enemy had been visiting.

Robert couldn't deny the misgivings he had about Ruby's birth certificate. The feelings of doubt, the ones he fought hard to keep submerged, might have sunk to the bottom of the river again, given time. But, coupled with the disturbing visit from Mary and Erin's reluctance to even consider a passport for Ruby, Robert was challenging those bubbling emotions, poking a stick at them to see how they reacted. He certainly couldn't ignore that Erin had been against Ruby's school trip since she'd first heard about it. Did that mean she was worried for Ruby's safety, that she thought thirteen too young an age to travel abroad without a parent? Was she burdening her with her fear of flying? Or was it more technical than that?

Perhaps Erin was afraid of the unhappy memories she would stir if she had to apply for Ruby's birth certificate in her ex-partner's name. It could be that Ruby never knew her father – she never mentioned him, after all – and didn't even realise that her official surname wasn't actually Lucas. The possible explanations for Erin's behaviour were numerous although one thing was certain. Robert needed to know the truth, partly because the truth usually evaded him when it came to relationships but mostly because he didn't want to ruin another marriage through paranoia. Finding out clean facts now would prevent the bubbling pot of suspicion boiling over. How to get the truth, gently, without disturbing the waters, was another matter entirely.

At ten past three, Robert pulled up outside their home. The four-storey townhouse looked slightly grey and shabby in the sunlight, with black paint peeling off the window frames in places and the once-cream stonework faded and stained by the overflow from old, leaky guttering.

Robert checked his watch again as he locked the Mercedes. Ruby would arrive home in about half an hour, cheerily dumping her school bag in the doorway before raiding the refrigerator and retreating to her room to concentrate on homework or shutting herself away to play the piano. Now that she had settled in to Greywood College, they had enrolled her in the school's minibus service, which dropped off a number of pupils in their area. He didn't expect Erin back from the shop before six. Either way, he would have to be careful.

'Ruby? Erin?' he called out just to make sure, pulling the front door key from the lock and leaning his briefcase against the wall. The heady aroma of the freesias on the marble-topped hall table made him pause for a moment. He remembered Erin lovingly arranging them that morning. She was passionate about flowers, especially simple country blooms in whites and creams. Her popular shop was a credit to her and had become everything he expected she would make of it. Erin was a hard worker, determined in everything she did. He was surprised, when he'd asked not long after they met, that she hadn't gone to university or trained in one of the professions. If they had a disagreement, he always teased her that she would have made an indomitable lawyer.

Despite the unusual hour, Robert opened the drinks cabinet in the dining room and poured himself a generous single malt. The extra guilt from drinking alone in the afternoon was far outweighed by the unwelcome sense of betrayal that sat heavily in his throat and chest, making him overly aware of every thump of his heart beneath his ribs.

'For heaven's sake, man,' he said to himself. 'It's only a drink. And it's not like she's having a bloody affair.' Robert knocked back the whisky and poured another before venturing upstairs.

He hesitated and stared at the tumbler, turning it slowly in his hands. The cut crystal set had been a wedding present from Jenna's parents and, to match the memory, as he passed the bay window he thought he caught sight of Jenna, her face a disapproving wash of watercolours. He stopped to take a closer look but there was nothing there, just the brilliant fan of rays spilling into the room. He shrugged, cursed his mind for playing tricks, and went directly upstairs. He didn't have time for ghosts from the past, whatever they were trying to tell him.

He began with Erin's computer, wiggling the mouse impatiently as he waited for it to boot up. The top floor of the house had been part of the recent redecoration plan and the two attic rooms had been made into studies. One was for Erin so she didn't have to stay at the shop to attend to all the business paperwork, and the other was for Robert, who often brought files home to work on after hours.

'Finally,' Robert sighed, glancing at his watch. Immediately, he dived right into the computer's hard drive, checking to see what files and software Erin possessed. He browsed through meticulously organised folders and accounting records, unsure exactly what he was searching for, although he was convinced he would know it when he saw it.

He opened Outlook Express and organised all her emails into order, so he could tell if she had been communicating with one particular person more than another. Every time a man's name appeared on the list, Robert scanned the messages. Mostly, he read about wholesale flower orders or complaints about why a delivery hadn't arrived on time. There were messages to and from Erin's shop landlord about a rent increase and mother-daughter giggles between Erin and Ruby. One message thread in particular, initiated by Ruby, spoke so highly of Robert and what a loving father he was, it nearly exploded the guilt lodged in his craw. But this had to be done, for Ruby. For his marriage.

Erin's emails proved to be particularly uninteresting. But

they made Robert realise just how hard his wife worked to run the flower shop single-handed. It was a massive undertaking for one woman although he could see she managed the business efficiently, just as he expected. But admiration did nothing to stop Robert. He dug further into the computer, trawling obsessively through every file, whether it was a system file, a program file, a document created by Erin or her internet surfing history. He sipped on his whisky and loosened his tie. It was hot at the top of the house so he took a moment to open the skylight.

He froze. Someone was coming upstairs. Robert glanced at his watch. In panic, he pulled the computer plugs from their socket and Erin's computer immediately sighed and the screen went blank. Ruby came into the room.

'Oh.' She stood in the doorway. 'I thought you were Mum. I heard someone up here.' She frowned, shocked to see Robert in her mother's study. Her reaction was a diluted version of how Erin would have behaved.

'Just me, I'm afraid.' Robert exhaled and smelled the sweet whisky on his breath. Explaining away his presence to Ruby would be easy, perhaps even useful.

'What are you doing?' Ruby's tone was still confrontational, Robert thought, as if Erin was speaking through her daughter. He didn't want her telling her mother about this.

'I'm looking for your birth certificate.' Quick thinking was Robert's job. 'I need it to be able to get you a passport. You want to go on the school trip to Vienna, don't you?'

'Do I ever!' Ruby's expression relaxed, budding with innocence again.

'Have you ever had a passport, Ruby?' Robert stood and walked over to his stepdaughter to give her a gentle hug.

'I dunno.' She shrugged. 'I've never been on an aeroplane.'

'You're home early.' Robert tried not to show his frustration at being interrupted.

'The tennis tournament was cancelled. The other school couldn't make it so we were allowed to come home early to study for the end of term exams. The minibus dropped me off.' She shifted from one foot to the other.

Robert realised that she thought she was in for a ticking-off for perhaps taking public transport or even walking. Instinctively, he knew she would be more amenable to helping him if he let it pass. 'Do you know where your birth certificate is, Ruby?'

'I've never seen it but I know Mum keeps stuff like that hidden in here.' Ruby surprised Robert by approaching Erin's desk, which looked like a French antique writing desk but was in fact designed to take a computer as well. Ruby completely removed the centre drawer and knelt down, reaching right to the back of the space. She fumbled about for a moment and then proudly removed a battered black tin cash box and placed it on the circular rug that partly obscured the painted floorboards. Ruby then retrieved a small key from underneath the rug and unlocked the tin. 'You won't tell Mum, will you?' She glanced up, her forehead wrinkling, before lifting the lid and frowning. 'I saw her take the box out once and put something away in it. She didn't know I was watching and might be cross if she thought I was spying.' Robert noticed a little nerve spasm beneath her left eye. 'But I've never looked. I'd never pry.'

Robert crouched down beside his stepdaughter. His gaze was fixed on the tin as if she had just unearthed a pharaoh's tomb. He patted her back. 'Don't worry, Ruby. It'll be our secret, eh?'

'See? I was right. There are all sorts of papers in here and look, Mum's got a passport, so I should be allowed to have one.' Ruby pouted briefly and then waved the passport above her head. Her mother was being so unfair not allowing her to go on the school trip.

'Well, this is a start.' Trying not to sound too eager, Robert took hold of the passport and opened it to the photograph page. He noticed that it had not long expired.

Quickly flipping through the pages, Robert saw that it had hardly been used. Only a couple of faded stamps proved a long-forgotten journey to Spain and Greece. Most likely holidays, he thought, turning back to the picture of Erin as a younger woman. He studied it for a moment, his heart pulling a lopsided smile across his otherwise anxious expression. She had been a rather mousy young thing in what he guessed to be her early or mid-twenties with a sullen look about her, as if having to pose for a picture was a terrible inconvenience.

The Erin he knew had never worn her hair long or with a fringe and she regularly went to the salon to maintain its cropped layered style and ash-blonde tint. The plump cheeks and heavy make-up were obviously a trait of his wife's past too, as nowadays she was about a stone or so lighter than this picture suggested and her face was usually free from cosmetics.

Then, with a conviction to remain reasonable, Robert thought of his own passport photograph and how dissimilar that was to his current appearance. He laughed and snapped the passport shut and placed it back inside the tin. It was of no use. 'What else have we got in here?' He tried to appear casual about flicking through the contents but apart from worrying that Ruby would be loyal to her mother and disclose his search, he was also concerned that Erin herself would return and catch him in the act. When he didn't come across

Ruby's birth certificate amongst the papers and letters, Robert decided that it would be best to conduct investigations another time, when he had the house to himself.

Conduct investigations, he muttered incredulously in his head. He was reminded of Louisa and their early-morning run out of Martock last weekend. He wondered whether to call her, to apologise, but what good would that do? Theirs wasn't the kind of relationship where regret and apology had a place. From one point of contact to the next, anything tense or questionable that had gone before was always forgotten. A clean slate each time. He wondered if Louisa could help obtain a birth certificate for Ruby. She was a private investigator, after all. She had contacts.

Robert watched as Ruby locked the box, replaced the key under the rug and carefully slipped the tin back into the void behind the desk's drawer. He didn't like himself for planning to sneak back later to take a proper look at the contents, even though he had satisfied himself that there was no birth certificate for Ruby and the remaining documents were obviously personal, judging by their covert location.

'How about a cold drink and a pastry down at Luigi's? My treat.' Robert stared at the ceiling, disgusted with himself.

Ruby grinned and Robert guided her down the stairs and out into the street. Luigi's was only a block away. She had homework but it could wait.

Robert found them a table on the street and ordered strawberry smoothies and Danish pastries. He was overly aware that he reeked of whisky although Ruby didn't appear to have noticed.

The sun, still intense even through the layer of visible pollution, baked the guilt deeper into Robert's consciousness and gave him a glaring headache right across his forehead.

Knowing that he would be prying through Erin's personal papers at the first opportunity tasted too much like how it had all begun last time. If he were to confide his feelings to Louisa, well, he wasn't sure their friendship would hold out. Robert blinked heavily and sipped his strawberry smoothie.

'Guess what?' Ruby said, perched on the edge of the metal bistro chair. She stirred her straw through her drink, staring down coyly.

'What?' Robert grinned into the glare, the pain in his head cutting through his temples.

'A boy at school fancies me. He's asked me out.'

Robert knew that those words were as hard for her to say as him confessing to Erin that he'd been prying on her computer.

'That's nice, love. What's his name?' He tried to appear casual although he suspected that it would end in heartbreak in a couple of months. Briefly recalling his own awkward teenage romances, he touched her hand. The contact caused him to wonder who her father was, what he would think of this adolescent development.

'He's called Art,' she said. 'He's two years above me and plays in a rock band.' Ruby slurped her smoothie, noisily draining the tall glass. 'Art's on a scholarship because he's really clever. His dad wouldn't be able to afford Greywood otherwise.'

Robert noticed her cheeks flush with colour. This is healthy, he told himself. This is fine. He struggled to keep back the barrage of warnings about staying out late and walking alone at night and kissing and things way worse than that. But hearing Ruby tell him that someone actually *liked* her was precious enough to make him contain his fatherly instincts. Besides, Erin could talk to her about boys and going on dates and all the cautions that would stem from that discussion. So instead of deflating Ruby's enthusiasm for the boy, Robert asked more about Art.

'That's a funny name, Art. Where does he come from?'

'It's not funny. He told me it means stone. It's Gaelic.' The bright sun was swallowed up in Ruby's fathomless eyes and absorbed by her long dark hair which flowed over her shoulders. She collected flakes of Danish pastry on the tip of her moist finger before scattering them on the pavement. A couple of pigeons hopped over and fought for the crumbs.

When several more birds gathered, Robert shooed them away with his foot. He dabbed at his forehead with a paper napkin. His head still thumped just beneath his skull, and the sun wasn't helping. He opened the parasol over their table.

'Which part of London is he from?'

'They're originally from Wales.'

'That's nice. By the sea or in the countryside?' Robert was about to drop the subject of Art. Ruby wasn't giving much away, least of all where he lived.

'They used to be travellers but settled down when Art got the music scholarship. His dad thinks he'll be famous.'

Robert accidentally sent his plate and knife clattering to the pavement as he raised his hand to wipe the sweat from his face again. Pigeons flapped away from the tables and Robert felt the blood drain from his head. Nausea and a sense of not being quite real replaced the pain and a voice banged about between his ears, insisting that traveller was OK, hippy was fine, gypsies were great.

'Travellers, huh?' Robert tried to sound cool about it.

'Yeah, like caravans and trailers except they've left those in Wales while Art studies. They're living in a squat at the moment.'

'Squat?' Robert's mouth went dry. He needed a glass of iced water.

'Art says it's really nice. They've got electricity now and everything. He's asked me round for the summer solstice. They're having a party.'

'Party?' Robert waved at the waitress, used sign language to get the bill and pay, and then escorted Ruby home. He was only half listening as his stepdaughter babbled on about Art. He had heard about as much as he could bear already.

Erin was avoiding him. The only sign that his wife was actually home was her electric-blue Mazda parked in the street and the collection of orange gerberas dumped on the hall table. Robert had called out a greeting from the living room when he heard the front door bang shut but perhaps over the volume of Ruby's resounding new composition, it had gone unnoticed.

He clicked the dining-room door shut, muting Ruby's music enough to hear the bath running upstairs, and climbed the stairs wearily. He stopped in their bedroom doorway to see a pile of discarded clothes on the floor. He inhaled a dose of his wife's end-of-day scent before deciding not to bother her in the bathroom but carry on up to the solitude of his study.

The air thickened as he went up the flight of stairs to the attic rooms. It was always hot up there in summer. Robert paused on the small landing between his study and his wife's. He stared into Erin's work space, noticing that she had already been up and dropped her briefcase beside her desk. She had also booted up her computer, probably in readiness for a couple of hours' work after dinner. He wondered if she had noticed that anything was disturbed. He nodded, thankful he'd remembered to plug her computer back into the power outlet.

Robert sighed, suddenly realising how long it was since they had spent an evening alone without worrying about deadlines or paperwork or Ruby's troubles at school. They'd only been married a couple of months and already life had disintegrated into routine and responsibility.

Robert reluctantly thought of Jenna. They'd never had enough time for things to turn stale. It was all over way before that. Briefly, he considered that perhaps solid routine actually gave rise to a familiar kind of trust and had his marriage to Jenna been allowed to drizzle into the mundane, then she might not have died.

He tried to shut out the feelings but like sunlight creeping under a door, he was filled with the same suspicion that had caused the initial thread of paranoia when he was married to Jenna. It wasn't anything tangible yet and, really, wasn't anything his already stimulated immune system shouldn't be able to handle. But a series of doubts, little nagging pointers were leading him to believe that Erin was hiding something. It was the lack of transparency that drove him wild.

Robert went into his study, stretching up to open the skylight. It was stifling. A couple of angry wasps shot out above the rooftops as he secured the window open. He fell back into his chair, unable to think about doing any work until he could iron out the messy thoughts in his head.

'Ask her,' he said quietly. 'Just damn well ask her.' Robert banged his fist down on the edge of his desk, causing his keyboard to rattle. With Jenna, he had dissected their relationship into a million irreparable pieces so that had she survived the crash, their marriage would have been taken to the wreckers anyway.

Maybe it was his job that made him wary, mistrustful and suspicious. Surely he had met enough dubious characters in his work to know if his wife, who was dissimilar in every way to the unsavoury clients he usually dealt with, wasn't being entirely honest. It should be easy. He knew he should treat Erin on an innocent until proven guilty basis – if it wasn't for that *feeling* he had that all was not right. He didn't like these hunches but he wasn't comfortable ignoring them either. He decided to call Louisa before the evening was over.

Robert reached into the filing cabinet for his emergency bottle of Scotch.

For the first time ever, he felt as if his career and home life were blending at the edges. He had always been adept at separating the two, even though he often brought files home. It was the emotion that was leaking – suspicion, fear and a natural instinct to mistrust. The promise he'd made to himself, to handle his second marriage with dignity and respect, was already losing its significance. And the ethical rules by which he conducted his business life, on which Mason & Knight had built their reputation, appeared tarnished now in the light of Mary Bowman's story. A small part of Robert's life was beginning to sag and he didn't like it one bit. It reminded him too much of last time.

Erin, having finished her bath, called out that she was going down to the local shop to pick up a few provisions. They still hadn't seen each other face to face since she arrived home. Ruby's music fluttered its way to the top of the house. She was composing a song for Art and was obviously lost in her task.

Robert's stomach lurched when he remembered Ruby's news. How would he break it to Erin that her daughter wanted to go to a party in a squat? She was so protective of Ruby, he didn't think she'd allow it. Then his belly flipped even more when it occurred to him that he now had an opportunity to look in Erin's secret box. He'd have to hurry. The shop was only a short walk away.

Robert's head still buzzed and banged from the heat and guilt as he rose from his chair, not to mention the second dose of Scotch that swilled inside him, curdling the strawberry smoothie on which it sat. As he went into Erin's study, he reassured himself by promising that it was just this once; that today was an anomaly, a blip in an otherwise spotless relationship, that there was a reasonable explanation for Ruby's untraceable birth certificate. Somehow, these thoughts made it acceptable.

Robert took a quick glance behind him and knelt down to remove the cash box from the secret compartment underneath Erin's desk. Again, that spillage of feelings, from work to home, from past to present. Detaching himself from grim clients and their low acts, ironing out their guilt with the weight of heavy circumstance and persuasive talk was second nature in the office and court. Convincing himself that it was reasonable to pry through his wife's personal belongings, truly believing that if he found any evidence – of what? – it would make everything all right, should have been impossible.

Instead, he moved swiftly, dimly aware that the anxiety he was experiencing was more a marker indicating that it was happening again, like the way saliva pools on the tongue before vomiting. The droplets of sweat on his face weren't due to the shame he would suffer if Erin ever found out he'd been snooping but rather a sign that his rational side was fighting his instincts.

Robert felt for the tin and pulled it out, just as Ruby had done a few hours earlier. He paused, listening for anything other than Ruby's piano music. He reached for the key that Ruby had replaced under the small rug and inserted it into the metal box. His heart beat in time with the vibrant tune that Ruby was composing.

He opened the box and lifted out the entire pile of papers carefully. He had to make sure that he replaced everything in exactly the same order. Briefly, he visualised Erin. She would have reached the shop by now, would perhaps be choosing a bottle of wine or searching for black olives or a bag of lettuce. About another ten or twelve minutes, he reckoned.

The box contained old birthday cards, a couple of folded piano examination certificates with Ruby's name neatly written in black ink, some photographs of Ruby on a pebbled beach when, he guessed, she was about three years old – there was no mistaking her chocolate-sauce eyes and dimpled chin.

Robert flicked through several school reports, an unfinished letter that Erin had begun writing over a decade ago according to the date, which began, strangely, *Dear Erin* . . . Robert assumed that she must have been writing to herself as a cathartic exercise because at first glance he could see it was filled with painful words, although most of the handwriting was impossible to read and barely made any sense. And, finally, he separated a thick bundle of letters bound up with purple ribbon. In the short time he had, Robert didn't know what to look at first. He opened a birthday card.

'To my dear little Ruby on your fifth birthday. Love you forever. Mummy xxx.'

Robert smiled, opened another. This time it was Ruby's seventh birthday card, again signed 'Mummy'.

'No daddy?' Robert shrugged and slotted the cards inside each other again as he had found them. They were inconsequential. Everyone kept their kids' birthday cards. He couldn't remember exactly when Erin said she had split from Ruby's father, not that it mattered – he didn't *want* to dwell on such facts – but he was beginning to suspect that Ruby was very young when the separation happened.

He shuffled through the letters instead. Most of them had been sent to Erin at her previous address in London, where she'd been living when he'd first met her, but half a dozen or so, he noticed, were addressed to Fresh As A Daisy. Some were brief notes on postcards and others were several pages long, neatly folded into small envelopes. All the correspondence was scrawled in red or green Biro from someone who signed themselves floridly as 'BK'. The writing was barely decipherable and on the first letter Robert removed from its envelope, the script cascaded across a printed letterhead.

He studied the address – King's Flowers, Market Street, Brighton. The knot of guilt in his throat didn't deter him from reading what BK had to say.

My darling Erin,

Missing you madly. Everyone's asking where you've run to. So pleased to hear it's working out in the big city this time. Watch out for all those nasty men. You don't have me to protect you now, you know. Possibly coming to town in a month or two. Will call you before. Get the bed ready, darling.

Flowers all wilting since you've been gone.

Love forever,

B.K. xxx

Robert felt his stomach knot as he read that someone loved Erin forever. That was his job now, wasn't it? He replaced the letter carefully and scanned another. Again, talk of coming to stay, how much Erin was missed in Brighton, several mentions of Ruby and what a credit to her mother she was. One letter was signed 'Uncle Baxter'.

If he was Erin's uncle then Robert could hardly accuse Erin of having an affair with him. But strange, he thought, that she'd never mentioned an uncle before. Having discovered early in their relationship that Erin's parents were dead, that she had no brothers or sisters, that her parents had left behind no other living relatives, Robert had never bothered to question Erin further about family. She simply didn't have any. She and Ruby were the family, a neat little package. Uncle, he therefore assumed, must be in the familiar form rather than blood sense of the word.

There were two letters in the bundle that Erin herself had penned in reply to Baxter and evidently never posted. She talked of her new life in London, about how guilty she'd felt for leaving Brighton after the fire and that it was one of the hardest things she'd ever done, about how Ruby had started a new school and how grateful she was to him for everything he'd done for her. She wrote how good it was to see him last weekend and how she had found a new job that allowed her to specialise in wedding flowers. Robert recognised this as the shop where she was working when they had met.

Fleetingly, the first image he'd ever had of Erin flashed through his head but anger and guilt made quick work of sweeping that aside. Rifling through his wife's personal belongings, discovering that she could be having an affair was not the time to cherish happy memories.

Robert put the letter down and stared at the ceiling, trying desperately to fight the prickling in his eyes. He hadn't even known that Erin had once lived in Brighton and she'd certainly never mentioned a previous lover there or anything about a fire. She had always implied that there had been no other relationships since her separation, although it struck Robert that that was the version he preferred to believe – a convenient, no-risk synopsis that posed zero threat.

Could his scant knowledge of his wife's life, perhaps construed by her as lack of interest and therefore leading to an affair, be a direct result of him not being able to bear the pain of acknowledging previous lovers? It was Jenna's first love that had driven the fatal wedge through his first marriage, after all. And he really knew surprisingly little about Erin's past – a protection mechanism, he decided, that would have to be changed.

Then, as he swiftly scanned the other papers, stopping briefly to decipher the peculiar letter that began 'Dear Erin' although the writing was too scratchy to unravel in the short amount of time he had left, the truth occurred to Robert like a slow sunrise.

Of course Erin had never sketched Baxter King into her former life. He was no former lover. He was a current lover. It was obvious that she was still seeing him.

Before raw emotion gripped him completely, Robert's composed lawyer side kicked in, taking control of his flailing senses, preventing him from ripping up the letters, yelling out in anger and marching down to the shop to confront Erin immediately.

Robert coolly read through some more letters. Reciprocal email addresses were mentioned and Erin talked of visiting an internet café to contact Baxter. Robert snorted as he noticed that they were web-based email addresses. No wonder, then, that he hadn't found any suspicious messages on Erin's computer. She'd been one step ahead there. And not all of the letters were dated, so it was difficult to fit them into any kind of order or to determine which was the most recent. But judging by what was being discussed, how this man was sympathising with Erin about Ruby's troubles at school, and because some letters had been sent to Erin's shop, Fresh As A Daisy, he was able to conclude without doubt that this relationship had continued since their marriage. Four or five minutes to go, he reminded himself.

Robert made a mental note of the address in Brighton and consigned the matter to a professional compartment in his mind, as he might for a client at work. He gathered all the cards and letters in the correct order and replaced them in the tin. He hesitated before locking it, staring hard at the collection of keepsakes Erin couldn't bear to part with. He randomly pulled one of them from the bundle, the lawyer in him unwilling to pass over conclusive evidence. He snapped the lid shut, turned the key and replaced the box behind the drawer just as Erin called out that she was home.

Swiftly, he returned to his own study, stashed the stolen letter inside a file and opened up a couple of documents on his laptop.

'I thought you might like this.' Erin was suddenly behind Robert, passing him a glass of wine, sinking her fingers into his shoulders. He groaned, completely unable to sip his drink as his emotions battled over Erin. He hated her for being so deceitful yet his body adored the deep massage. 'Why don't you quit work now and come downstairs. I've got salmon for dinner.'

Against his better judgement, Robert allowed his body to loosen under her touch. With every stroke of her strong fingers delving into his overwrought muscles and tendons, he began to relax. Already he was starting to doubt his judgement. It was his Erin, for heaven's sake. He loved her. He *adored* her. She wouldn't betray him, would she? That he had doubted her integrity made him unable to take her touch without each stroke stirring his guilt. Erin was a good woman, who had struggled to survive as a single mother. Now she was working hard to build up her new business and raise Ruby as best she could. He sighed. He had surely read this all wrong.

Finally, as he greedily drank in Erin's touch, Robert recalled the promise he had made to himself after Jenna died. He couldn't let it happen again.

He turned to face Erin and pulled her face down to his. 'Can the salmon wait for a while?'

Their kiss was long and slow, unlike any they had shared recently. Erin tasted of wine with a hint of toothpaste; smelled of herbs laced with shampoo. As she collapsed onto him, Robert couldn't help it that Erin's close-up face blurred and then briefly refocused into that of Jenna.

'You're all sweaty.' She grinned, unbuttoning his shirt. 'How about I scrub you clean in the shower?'

Robert allowed a brief smile to whip across his mouth, pushed as hard as he could to shift the notion that his wife was having an affair. He stared deep into Erin's eyes – pale blue discs with a dreamy coating urging him to give in. He felt his body respond but checked it by standing up, easing Erin off his legs. Like a recovering alcoholic reaching for the bottle, Robert couldn't fend off the doubt. He had seen the evidence.

'I've got work to do. There's a complicated case.' He turned away, knowing that if he stared any longer into Erin's eyes he would succumb. 'I'm sorry.' Robert shifted files around on his desk, pretending to search for something until she left the room. She banged the door so hard that Robert felt the anger shake through his feet and up into his heart.

He dropped down into his chair and retrieved the random

letter that he had stolen from Erin's tin. He skimmed through the scrawl as best he could but the impossible writing – it was Erin pouring out her feelings again as if her hand could barely cope with such a task – and the years of subsequent crumpling had ensured that reading the incomplete letter as a whole was virtually impossible. And it wasn't addressed to anyone either.

'. . . If you knew . . . safe at least . . . that tragic . . . my baby back . . .'

'Erin, Erin . . .' he sighed, allowing his head to drop back, his eyes to close. His wife had transformed into a puzzle. Too much of his life had been wasted on obsessing about Jenna and her every movement, not to mention the tragic result. He didn't think he would survive if it happened again.

TWELVE

At the hospital they X-rayed my skull because I'd fallen, checked me for concussion and bandaged my head. I was heavily sedated for twenty-four hours and talked gibberish to the police officers as they interviewed me.

In those early hours – the most vital stage of the entire investigation, they said – I made no sense whatsoever. The kidnapper, I was told, was putting more distance between me and my baby with every second. I thought about this, in my chaotic mind, and it didn't seem to mean anything. Then they informed me that Andy, my husband, was at his parents' house, Sheila and Don's. I remember wondering why he didn't come to see me in hospital, remember wanting him to hold me, remember the vomit each time I was given a sip of water. Really, that first day was a blur.

The next evening, Natasha minus thirty hours, I was driven home by two police officers, PC Miranda Hobbs and Detective Inspector George Lumley. She was nice but he made eyes at me as if I was the worst mother in the world. PC Hobbs made tea for me and Lumley wired my telephone while I sat and watched, glancing at his broad, experienced back and then at the empty baby bouncer.

PC Hobbs stayed with me until her shift ended because Andy now couldn't be located and they didn't want to leave me alone. The policewoman regularly telephoned Sheila's house but was simply told that Andy had disappeared.

Disappeared, I remember saying over and over until PC Miranda had to put a tea towel over my mouth to make me quiet. How can so many people disappear? But Andy was home by the next morning, dirty, drunk and sobbing in the doorway before falling to the floor. We cried together on the carpet while a fresh pair of police officers hovered over us, lunging for the telephone every time it rang. Over Andy's shoulder, as we hung on to each other, I spotted Natasha's hairbrush. She had a lot of hair from the day she was born, and would gurgle as I swept the soft baby brush across her scalp. I crawled across the floor and picked it up.

'Don't, love,' Andy said.

I pushed the bristles to my nostrils and sucked in a faint whiff of Natasha. I plucked out a few wispy brown hairs. I still have them in an envelope. There's nothing else left of my baby.

Sheila and Don arrived next, a couple of hours before the journalists that camped in the street. Sheila brought a casserole covered with tin foil. Don crushed me in his arms while Sheila stared at me, shaking her head, rubbing her boy Andy's shoulders. I thought: you're lucky. You still have your baby.

Sheila had never liked me, rather tolerated me for Andy's sake. Not that he was anything special or much to be proud of, just a car mechanic. But Sheila cherished him and nothing was ever good enough for him, especially me, and now I had proved her right because I had lost her only grandchild.

Sheila took control. She sent the lady police officer, who was supposed to be looking after me, down to the corner shop to fetch one hundred tea bags, two pounds of sugar and six pints of milk. 'There'll be a lot of brewing these next few days. Best be prepared.'

Within minutes, Sheila had removed all trace of Natasha from the living room of our tiny terraced house. I watched her stuffing furry animals, bright plastic toys and a rag book into a bin liner. Most of the toys had never been touched. Natasha was only two months old and could barely hold anything yet. Sheila dismantled the baby bouncer that Andy had bought from Mothercare. I'd hung a couple of mobiles above where Natasha used to lie when I changed her nappy but Sheila made quick work of plucking them off the ceiling.

Our lounge was soon transformed back into a grown-up domain. Not a trace of anything to do with babies remained. Natasha's toy box was stashed in the loft, and Sheila rearranged the chairs in our tiny front room. Then she took down our fake Christmas tree and boughs of tinsel that I'd hung when Natasha suddenly ceased her bawling and slept greedily. Sheila left our decorations in the street for the dustmen to collect. 'No more Christmas,' she proclaimed, brushing her hands together.

At 2 a.m. Andy and I were woken from our fitful sleep by a phone call. Natasha minus thirty-eight hours. There had been a sighting. A van driver had been spotted with a crying baby at a motorway service station. An elderly couple, travelling south from their New Year break in Scotland, had noticed a man and screaming baby going into the gents' toilets. They thought it odd but did nothing until they approached the Midlands and heard about the abduction on a local radio station. They called the police and that was it. Nothing more happened. The man was never located.

I hated knowing that Natasha had been seen screaming. She was screaming for me. Screaming, screaming all of the time for me as she stiffened and arced her body in uncontrollable wails.

They gave me some tablets at the hospital to dry up my milk. It didn't work. My breasts were hard lumpy packages fighting against each other in my bra and it hurt to put my arms by my sides. In the bathroom, with PC Miranda back on duty and waiting outside the door, I leaned over the sink and let them drip. I thought, what a waste, all that milk going down the drain. The smell of it made me cry so then there were tears and milk in the basin, like a massive weeping of my body.

PC Miranda had to get help to shove the door open because I'd flopped down behind it. Together Miranda, Don and Andy pushed against the door and shifted my slack body across the bathroom carpet. Andy helped me to my feet and I began to laugh hysterically. I didn't have my top on.

A few hours later there was another sighting. Hertfordshire Police had received two calls from motorists reporting a hitchhiker on the M1 southbound. A small figure, so bundled and hooded against the winter cold it was impossible to tell if it was male or female, was seen carrying a swaddled baby down the motorway slip road while thumbing a lift. PC Miranda held my hand as she told me that by the time Hertfordshire Police cruised up and down the motorway, the suspect had disappeared. But she smiled and warmed my frozen heart a little when she said that the surrounding fields and villages were being scoured and tracker dogs had been brought in. The police in neighbouring counties had been alerted too, and everything was being done and it wouldn't be long now, PC Miranda said, swallowing, averting her eyes, wouldn't be long now before there was more news.

'Do you have children?' I asked. Perhaps she'd got two, could spare one. She nodded.

'He's four. His grandma looks after him when I'm working.'

I'm glad PC Miranda didn't lie about having a child. I needed doses of normality in my surreal existence, like sticky sweet medicine. I don't know how I'd have got through those first few days without PC Miranda. Nowadays, I never see her.

Detective Inspector George Lumley returned to our house on Tuesday morning, Natasha minus three days, and said that he wanted us on the telly. His face was brown and wrinkled and he smelled of cigarette smoke. Even though I later learned he was only forty, he looked a lot older. He told us that from the evidence gathered so far, they had concluded that the snatching of Natasha was most likely a spur of the moment incident rather than a premeditated act and the perpetrator was, in all probability, becoming rather tired and fed up of a crying baby.

A number of cases, he reported to Andy and me as we sat miserably on our settee while he towered big and experienced in front of us, a number of cases conclude satisfactorily after a plea from the parents. Only a year previously, a toddler had been abducted from a nursery and subsequent to a tearful plea by the mother was found two days later in a McDonald's restaurant, playing happily in the ball pit. I thought of Natasha dumped in a place no one would ever find her. Smothered, strangled.

'Will you do it then? A press conference?'

Andy said we would.

I've got a new client today. She told me her name was Sarah when she telephoned but wouldn't give me her last name or number. She sounded very young and very shy. I'm half expecting her not to show up but as I'm preparing the tea tray – I always offer my clients tea and a biscuit – there is a knock on my front door. I pull the elastic band out of my long hair, run my forefingers under each of my eyes and tuck in my blouse. When I open the door I see a young Asian girl of probably no more than fifteen.

'Sarah?'

She nods and looks up and down the street before stepping into my small living room. She keeps swallowing, as if she is fighting against being sick. I don't take my eyes off her but smile and tell her to sit. I always do it in the living room, the client in the armchair, me on the sofa, the tea tray a bridge of comfort between us.

They are always nervous the first time, until they realise that it doesn't hurt and I am usually right. But I'm careful with what I tell them. I have a responsibility, a kind of cosmic accountability that if too much gets said, the balance sheet doesn't add up.

'So what's your real name?' I ask. 'Tea?' I pour her a cup anyway because it seems that two questions have overloaded the girl and she remains silent. Only after I have taken a few sips and half a digestive does she speak.

'If you were that good, you'd know.'

Her eyes are black globes but there's no lustre in them. She's a troubled girl. I know that much from her phone call and, anyway, most people who come to see me have problems. 'You'll waste most of your session if you make me guess.'

'Just call me Sarah.' Sarah bows her head and locks her fingers together. The backs of her hands have the residue of beautiful henna tattoos. Her nails are painted cerise.

'What would you like to know then, Sarah?' I haven't decided what to use yet. Tarot? The crystal ball? What does she suit? Maybe the runes, or should I take a look at her palms?

She sits perfectly still, staring at her fingers, her long dark hair falling across her face. She's like this for about four or five minutes then she pulls her head up, as if a great weight is attached to her forehead, and she stares at me with huge cinnamon eyes.

'I'm pregnant and I want to know if it's a boy or a girl because if it's a boy then Father won't kill me so much.' She sucks in a lungful of air because saying those words has winded her. 'He'll hate me but he won't kill me.'

I don't miss a beat. I'm used to it now, hearing about babies. It's been thirteen years, after all. Life goes on. Other people get pregnant. Other babies have died since mine. I'm not news any more.

'Then it's a boy,' I say, having to suck in air too because now I'm being a counsellor not a psychic and that's something I never do. Damn this Sarah girl. 'Does your mother know?'

Sarah's head drops again. 'She's dead.'

'Let's ask her what she thinks about all this then.'

'No, no!' Sarah falls off her chair onto her knees and covers her face with her hands. 'The shame,' she wails over and over.

'But if she's dead . . .' I was going to say, then does it matter, but for Sarah of course it matters. Her mother's dead and she's pregnant.

'How old are you?'

'Fifteen.'

Two years older than Natasha then.

'When did your mother die?'

'When she gave birth to me.' Sarah wipes her face on her sleeve and sits down again. 'Why are you asking me all these questions? Are you a fraud? You should know.'

'I only know what comes to me, Sarah.' Now it's my turn to get on my knees. I take her left hand and turn it over. She has six child lines, three of them jagged and broken. I take a risk and place my hand on her belly. Just by the feel of her I can tell she's probably nearly six months gone. Easy to hide under loose summer clothes and her trim young body carries the bump well. But I can feel the baby inside; know instantly it's a girl.

'It's definitely a boy.' I have to turn away as Sarah's face loses some of the pain she walked in with.

'Really?' She holds her belly and smiles. 'If I tell Father that I will name the baby after him, then in time he may forgive me. But I will not be able to marry Farhad, as he had planned. No boy will want me now.'

I take my tarot pack, shuffle and hand Sarah the cards. 'Cut them.' Anything to break up this psychiatric consultation. When she's done, I lay five cards out in a cross beside the tea tray. Death, the Fool, the Prince of Cups, the three of Swords and Strength. It comes to me in a flash, without the cards.

'You love him, don't you?'

Sarah nods, her cinnamon eyes syrup-coated.

'But he's white and your father won't allow you to see anyone but the boy he has arranged for you to marry?'

She nods again. I'm angry at myself because this is too easy. I'm not telling her fortune, I'm being her mother. I offer her a biscuit.

'What do the cards mean? I'm scared that death is there.' Sarah points to the array, showering biscuit crumbs over the Fool.

'Death? He's nothing to be scared of. He means new beginnings too, you know. Or perhaps the death of everything you've known in your life so far.'

*

The press conference was arranged for the next day at a hotel in the centre of Northampton. The speed of everything amazed me. Within hours of the announcement, reporters and TV cameramen converged from all over the country on my home town. It took me the next twenty-four hours just to wash and dress. My limbs were filled with wet sand and my will to even move around the house was weighted with lead. I couldn't believe that all these people had come just to see me.

Andy and I were taken in a police car to the Marriott Hotel and ushered into a private room. I could hear the commotion of the press nearby, checking their equipment, vying for the best spot to catch a shot of me pleading, crying.

I'd put on a pale blue suit, the one I'd worn to Natasha's christening, but I wished I hadn't. On my right shoulder was a small stain where Natasha had dribbled milk. I pressed my cheek onto the mark. DI Lumley handed me a piece of paper.

'Your statement to the press, Mrs Varney. When you read it, make sure you're loud and clear. I want the bastard to hear everything you say.' He gave me that look again, as if I was in conspiracy with the person who had done this. I looked at Andy for support. He was peering over my shoulder, reading and nodding in approval.

'I didn't write this,' I said.

'No, this one's been drawn up for you to read out. We have to be very careful what you say. We don't want them to know how much we know but, likewise, we don't want them to know that we don't really know anything at all.'

I was confused. One single point of fire ignited in my heart. Looking back, it was the beginning of my anger. I wanted Andy to react, to say that we weren't reading it, but by the expression on his face I could tell that he approved of my pre-written speech. I skimmed a few lines of it but knew it wasn't what I wanted to say. It didn't sound convincing enough and that, I knew, was paramount. It could all be thrown back at me in the future. I had to touch the hearts of the nation. I needed them on my side.

'Best if Mum does it, Mr Varney.' DI Lumley beat his fist against his heart and pursed his lips. Perhaps he truly felt sorry for us and just didn't know how to show it.

A waitress from the hotel came into the room with a trolley and served us tea. I didn't want it but was told to drink up to calm my nerves. I wanted PC Miranda to be with me but they said it was her day off. My cup and saucer rattled as we waited for two o'clock.

Every clock in the world got in my way. It was now Natasha minus four days and three and a half hours. What would I do when it was exactly a week later, a month, the anniversary? How would I feel on her birthday, at Christmas or the year she was supposed to start school?

'I want my baby back . . . *please* . . .' I cried, dropping my head to my knees. DI Lumley felt it was a good time to lead me out to the press, while I was animated enough to show some emotion. I stood, quivering, hyperventilating and sweating on a podium with about fifty journalists and TV crew waiting silently for my plea to the kidnapper.

Then, as I sat down at the table, as I leaned forward to the microphone and opened my mouth to speak, the flashing began. I scrunched up the piece of paper that DI Lumley had given me and dropped it on the floor. In my own words, I addressed the nation.

'Death really is nothing to be scared of. But let's look at this. The Fool is where you are now in your life. And see, he's reversed.' I watch for Sarah's reaction, tune in to her involuntary twitches, expressions, a flick of the hair or nail picking or anything else that might give me clues. Her eyes widen as she edges forward in the armchair.

'It means you're stuck,' I add. This, as I thought, elicits instant reaction from Sarah. I'm on to something.

'You're telling me.' Her face sheds a layer of mistrust, like a guest removing their coat. She takes a first sip of tea, an indication that she's warming to me.

'Tied up in knots is what I see, Sarah. Backed into a corner and you're only fifteen.' How I hate myself. I turn to the cards again because it's better than drowning in her eager spice eyes.

'When will the baby be born?' Now she asks something that takes only a bit of mental maths. I continue to stare at the cards, wishing she'd gone to see her family GP.

'I can see there's been much turmoil in your life.' She's said as much anyway. 'So much sorrow and pain. You've had a life of heartbreak, Sarah.' I'm sticking my neck out here, with little else to go on really. But she takes my lead flawlessly.

'Since I was born. Tell me, when will it end? Will I ever be happy?'

'Of course,' I say, wondering if she will. 'Your baby will bring you great joy and your father's initial anger will diminish once he sees what a beautiful child you have given to the family.' I've never told a child's fortune before; never had to wonder about so much blank life ahead. 'And you've got strength on your side. The cards are clear about that.'

'Really?' She takes more tea.

I spend the next forty minutes telling Sarah about all her good qualities and how to handle her father and young lover, how to breathe during childbirth and not once do I return to the cards for help. I feel like even more of a fraud than I already am. This is simply woman to young girl. Mother to daughter. It is all I can do not to beg her to give me her baby when it's born.

When I had finished, when I had begged with the population of Great Britain to open their eyes and help find my baby, when I had told them about my stupidity and negligence and implored mothers everywhere never to leave their babies unattended even for a second, when I had described Natasha in every detail down to the length of her tiny fingernails and the pale shade of her milk-speckled tongue, when I had said all that, I made a point of speaking directly to the person who took my baby – one to one, just me and him, full-on eye contact through the cameras. It had to be done.

DI Lumley opened his mouth, raised an arm, gripped my elbow but then thought better of it. He stepped back and remained perfectly still by my side, letting me have my say, in spite of the pre-written statement crumpled on the floor. That afternoon, he proved to me that he had a heart. I stared deep into the BBC television camera and took a long breath.

'When you first met my baby – she's called Natasha Jane Varney, by the way – she would have smelled a little of me, perhaps a tang of the washing powder on her sleep suit, maybe a trace of my perfume or shampoo had rubbed off on her clothing. What worries me now is that she'll smell of you. When I get my baby back, you're going to be on her. What worries me, too, is that I found a bootee after you'd fled so one of my baby's feet is going to be freezing. And I'm concerned that you won't wind her after a feed.' I can't believe that I found it in me to laugh here. 'If you actually bother to feed her, that is. Just so you know, she has six feeds in twenty-four hours but because she's always been breastfed, you'll probably have trouble coaxing her to take a bottle. You also ought to know that she likes to be held over your shoulder and patted gently on the back. She loves it when you lay her on your legs and sing nursery rhymes to her, pulling funny faces at the same time. "Rock-a-Bye-Baby" is her favourite. And she adores walks in her pram – I'm assuming you'll be investing in one of those – but if it's a really cold day, do wrap her up well, won't you?

'Natasha usually wakes about nine or ten times during the night. She's never been a good sleeper. Except in the day, that is, but you'll have far too much to do then to be able to catch up with sleep . . .' I felt a hand slide up my arm. 'You could always phone the health visitor but she might be too busy to come . . .' The hand grips my elbow and tries to lower me back into the chair but I'm not stopping; not now everyone's finally listening. 'If you get really worn out, you can always leave her in the car and go into a shop.' I pause and stare at the ceiling to make the tears stay in my eyes. 'Then maybe someone will steal her.'

There's something large and sticky in my throat, choking my words, making me swallow too much and now the hot tears are overflowing. The photographers go into a flashing clicking frenzy and Andy puts his arms around my waist. I hear someone call out, 'That's it, get close to your wife, Mr Varney,' and then loads more flashing so that my eyes hurt and all I can see are thousands of electric blue dots, as if I'm spinning through the universe.

The room, the noise of everyone in it, gradually falls silent. I let my eyes close and allow my body to relax into Andy's grip. Vaguely, I can hear questions being fired at me but I can't be bothered to answer. My world is filled with beautiful sparkles – perhaps what Natasha saw when she gazed up at the crystal mobile I'd hung above her cot.

Silence now as I head towards the centre of the starlit vortex. In the middle, there is nothing; complete blackness and emptiness and escape from all my pain. Then, at the very centre, I see Natasha, all wrapped up in her pretty baby clothes, gurgling and smiling and waiting for me. She isn't crying at all. I hold out my arms to my baby and beg her to forgive me.

Even though it's time for Sarah to go, I can tell she doesn't want to. My usual signals of glancing at my watch and stacking the empty cups on the tea tray haven't worked. I should probably just tell her that our session is over and she owes me twenty-five quid but I haven't got the heart. And she's got a baby inside her. One that might not be wanted.

'I don't have any other clients today. You can stay and keep me company, if you like.' It could be shame for not really knowing what her future holds or a desire for company. Either way, the thick guilt that I'm wearing must be visible and flashing green neon to Sarah although she doesn't hesitate in accepting my offer.

'Sure. But only for an hour or so because my father and brothers have their meal at six and I haven't even begun preparations yet.'

Something about her voice tells me that she is dolefully resigned to her lot in life. She, too, is wearing a suit of guilt, for killing her mother as she slid into the world, for shaming the family by carrying a child when she is only a child herself.

'What about your school work?' I pick up the tray and beckon her to follow me into the kitchen. Kitchens are good places for talking. I should see all my clients in the kitchen. I dump the crockery into the sink and put on my rubber gloves. Sarah sits at my wooden table. She is far more relaxed now.

'I've never bothered to study hard. Since I was little, my father has always talked of the man I will marry and how happy and well-set-up in life I will be.' Sarah pulls a face, one that tells me she wishes she could tell the future. 'But now that I'm going to be a single mum, exams suddenly seem important because I'll need a job.'

She rests her constantly mobile fingers on her belly for a moment, pulling her cardigan taught over the bump. Suddenly, I long to touch it again, to feel the hardness of her skin, perhaps the jut of an elbow or heel. 'I doubt if anyone will give me a job now though. Or marry me. What *am* I going to do?' Then she drops her head to the table and, within the privacy of the long dark hair that curtains her face, Sarah sobs for nearly two hours.

When she's finished, I wash her face with a flannel soaked in warm water and lavender, make her another cup of tea and send her on her way feeling a whole lot better. She even manages a laugh when, at the front door, I bend down and plant a little kiss on her belly.

THIRTEEN

The M23 was a solid ribbon of cars. Multicoloured metal stitched permanently to the hot tarmac. Robert turned off the engine and stood up in his seat to see if he could spot the problem up ahead. He considered putting the roof up again, to shield himself from the sun that at only ten thirty was baking everyone's anger and frustration rock solid. The radio, which had only been on in the background, suddenly interrupted Robert's thoughts with a local traffic alert announcing that the M23 was closed southbound at junction 10A due to a jack-knifed lorry having dumped its load across all three lanes.

The car in front moved forward six feet. Only when the car behind hooted did Robert bother to start his engine and also move forward six feet. He couldn't be bothered with road rage, not today. He studied an alternative route on the satnav. There was a junction coming up ahead although it would most likely be gridlocked with desperate motorists trying to find an alternative way around the mess.

As the car to the left of him moved forward, Robert pulled on the wheel and swerved his car into the nearside lane. He ignored the flashing headlights from behind and instead put his own headlights on main beam and set his hazard lights flashing. He drove his vehicle at the hard shoulder and accelerated towards the junction up ahead. He had to get to Brighton, which meant getting off the motorway. His nerves simply wouldn't accommodate any further delay. The hard shoulder was for emergencies, he knew, but to Robert this was an emergency. He was going to save his marriage.

Robert's instincts, fired up and on red alert, told him that Crawley was going to be congested from the still-stranded rush-hour traffic so as he approached the roundabout at dangerously high speed with his lights flashing and his horn blasting, he headed east and then south where, directed by the GPS, he eventually found open roads followed by deserted country lanes.

After twenty minutes, Robert pulled over into a field gateway and turned off the engine. Completely off course, he sighed and pushed his sunglasses to the top of his head. He wiped the sweat off his forehead with the back of his hand and let his head drop back onto the seat. The heat had frazzled his nerves and shrivelled the determined spirit with which he had left home that morning.

He'd kissed Erin briefly, more of an accidental swipe of lips, as she'd left for work, without mentioning his planned trip to the south coast. Then he saw Ruby safely on the school minibus. Nothing out of the ordinary so far; he just prayed that neither of them would need him today. Explaining that he wasn't around because he was in Brighton would ruffle Erin's curiosity and suspicion enough to require him to lie about a business meeting and then they'd be as bad as each other. Both liars.

He pulled the cap off a bottle of water and sucked until it was nearly gone. He got out of the car to stretch his legs and gather his thoughts. Knowing what to wear to meet his wife's lover had proved difficult. He'd dressed in his usual dark business suit with a short-sleeved summer shirt underneath but as soon as Ruby and Erin had left the house, he changed. He decided on jeans and loafers with a loose shirt and dark sunglasses. He wanted to leave behind as many years as possible because he had a foreboding that Baxter would be about ten years younger and far better looking.

He brought down his fist on the car bonnet and instantly regretted it. A dent in the silver metal reflected the glaring sun. At that moment he could have hated Erin for her lies, for her easy concealment of the truth but most of all for doing this to Ruby who would, after all, suffer the most. But it didn't stick, the hate, so instead he hated himself for sneaking off to Brighton.

An hour later, Robert slipped the Mercedes into a space along the Promenade. The beach was spotted with pink and stripped bodies basking on the smooth pebbles. He locked the car and snorted, thinking that if he couldn't locate Baxter then he would buy some shorts and take a dip in the sea to cool off.

He took a piece of paper from his back pocket and studied it. He had searched for King's Flowers on the internet and printed off a street map. It was only a couple of blocks away from the seafront and within a few minutes of entering the darker lanes of historical Brighton, Robert had located the quaint shop on Market Street. The cream and green painted façade sported fashionable gold lettering advertising 'King's Flowers, Blooms for all Occasions. Proprietor: Baxter King'.

A quick scan of the window display told Robert that the flowers and other decorative goods for sale were very expensive, even compared to Erin's London shop. But it was the minimalist sprays of twisted bamboo and fiery orchids, the roughly painted wooden palettes used to display bold arrangements of anthurium and bear grass, oriental lilies strewn horizontally over sand and beach stones – all of it sprayed with sugar water to make the whole scene appear as if it had woken up to a spring dew – that caused him to take a sharp breath. Erin's shop window in London was virtually identical.

Robert leaned against a lamp post, hardly able to look at the frontage of King's Flowers. Had Baxter King copied his wife's ideas or was Erin so besotted with the creative Mr King that she had reproduced the Brighton display in London? Either way, Robert felt nauseous when he realised just how close they must be. Opposite the flower shop was a café bar. Robert took a table in the window and ordered a strong coffee while he mulled over what to do next.

King's Flowers was obviously very popular. In fifteen minutes, Robert counted a similar number of customers leaving the shop, all with beautifully wrapped arrangements. Inside, he could see two young women wearing jeans and short tops with dark green canvas aprons slung low on their hips. They chatted and busied themselves with the customers and the blonde one took off her shoes and climbed into the window display with a pump spray to douse the arrangements. Robert had seen Erin do the same thing many times. He supposed she had picked up the tip from Baxter King. He wondered where the man was. Too important to be bothered with the everyday running of the shop, he supposed. He might not even catch sight of him at all, in which case his journey would have been wasted. Robert was keen to study him from this perfect vantage point before making himself known. Knowledge is power, he told himself, swirling the last of his coffee around the cup.

He stood up and was about to leave the café but froze. A

man, short and stocky, wearing a purple and yellow seventies-style shirt, strode into King's Flowers and immediately embraced both of the shop assistants. He then ducked behind the counter and leafed through some papers before laughing with the women and pacing around the shop, making minute adjustments to the stock.

'Baxter King,' Robert said, slowly sitting down again, relieved that the man was about five feet six tall and possibly as wide. From where Robert was, and through two layers of glass that bounced the sun jaggedly across the narrow street, he could see that King had a red face with a patchy beard in yellow and brown and a smattering of grey-streaked hair that clung to a sunburnt scalp. Robert laughed and ordered another coffee.

The man was so unattractive he was unique. Robert wondered what it was that Erin saw in him. He had assumed, because Erin had chosen to marry him, that she went for more conventional-looking men – although Robert winced as he thought of himself that way. He knew his dress sense was conservative although he shopped in upmarket stores, and he had worn his hair the same way forever but he'd rather hoped that Erin viewed him as attractive and distinctive.

It suddenly struck him that maybe that wasn't enough. Maybe the type of man Erin craved was like Baxter King – wild and outlandish without a care what others thought of him. The flower shop owner was drinking from a mug and holding the telephone to his ear with his shoulder. Maybe it wasn't even Baxter King at all. Maybe he was really six feet tall, muscular and tanned and owned a yacht in—

'Just go and find out,' Robert snapped at himself, interrupting his ludicrous thoughts. Several customers in the café glanced his way. Robert paid and stepped out into the hot street. He pulled his sunglasses down off his head, pushed his fingers through his hair, breathed in and went through the door of King's Flowers.

The sudden rush of chilled air prickled his tacky skin but didn't unsteady him. He was in the other man's domain now but felt strangely calm and composed. Perhaps it was the tranquil music that dripped from speakers in each corner of the shop or the cool polished marble underfoot that made him feel he'd come to see a friend. It could have been the blend of twenty different flower scents, all carefully chosen to relax the customer, that caused his shoulders to drop and his stomach to unravel.

Robert viewed the different displays – everything from beach flora through zesty tropical arrangements to perfumed English country wildflowers at their summer best. Robert knew that Erin would love every one of them, take sheer delight in studying the colours and textures of the different plants and props. He grinned, felt a pang of love, as he almost heard her exclaiming and clapping her hands together.

'Can I help you, sir?'

Robert immediately tensed as he realised the blonde shop assistant was beside him. Up close, she was even more attractive than when he had seen her in the window. King obviously adored beautiful women.

'I want to send some flowers to my wife.' Robert could see, without looking directly at him, that King was still on the telephone behind the counter.

'Do you have anything in mind?' The assistant smiled, semi-flirting, probably on commission, and steered him to an array of what looked like herbs to Robert. 'This kind of thing is very popular at present and really unusual. We can do a lavender-based arrangement or even rosemary and add other herbs to suit. Lots of ladies love these in the kitchen. Or you could go for something sparse, like the bamboo with oriental lilies, or something with lots of grasses?' She waited for Robert to make a comment but he was busy watching Baxter King.

'Freesias,' he said, without looking at the assistant. 'Two bunches.' Robert approached the counter. He was only three feet away from his wife's ridiculous lover and could smell his cologne. He tried to repel it from his nose, wondering if it had been a gift from Erin. At this distance, he could see that the skin on King's face and neck was pockmarked and, down one side, it was white and blistered as if he had been badly burnt. He tried not to stare as King suddenly guffawed with laughter, exposing a rack of yellowed teeth. The shop assistant came to the counter and gently nudged King out of the way. She opened an order book and picked up a pen.

'When would you like the flowers delivered?' She smiled, the antithesis of the wild creature looming behind her.

'Tomorrow?'

'What's your wife's name, please?'

'Erin Lucas,' Robert replied loudly, deliberately using Erin's previous name and directing his reply at King. Robert felt like a bit-part actor on a vast stage, who has stolen the crucial line of the leading man. The assistant began to write but before she had a chance to ask anything more, Baxter King ended his call and leaned forward on the counter.

'I'll deal with this order, thanks, Sally. Take Alison outside and freshen up the street displays.' He urged her away from the counter and turned to Robert. 'Erin Lucas? You're sending flowers to an Erin Lucas?'

In those few words, the size of Baxter King diminished further. The crazy flora on his tasteless shirt wilted and the bulging skin on his cheeks and hands sank as if it had been seared on a grill. The greyness in his eyes occluded like miserable rain clouds and his pitted cheeks flushed to highlight hundreds of purple thread veins.

'Yes. I'm sending flowers to my wife.' Robert stood tall and removed his sunglasses.

'Is she OK? Is she sick?' King's fingers twitched around his mouth and he began to tug on a tuft of scant beard. 'Did I miss her birthday?'

Robert snorted and stared hard at the man. He rested both hands on the shop counter and leaned forward. 'No, she's not ill and it's not quite her birthday. I'm sending her flowers because I want to. Because I love her.'

'That's a relief.' Baxter King stood back a little and managed a small smile. 'But you can't send her freesias. No, no, no . . .' He came out from behind the counter, his small smile now a chunky yellow grin. He offered his stubby hand to Robert. 'Baxter King, by the way. You must be Robert. I've heard all about you.'

Robert found himself shaking hands with King and, completely unable to respond – partly from shock at the casual admission that he knew Erin and partly because he kept on talking – Robert followed him around the shop and listened to what exactly his wife preferred in the way of cut flowers.

'Personally, I'd send heliconia, probably the Mexican Gold. Simply stunning in a tall vase with glass beads. But you could go for some stems of red ginger. Horrendously expensive because I get them flown in from Puerto Rico.' King wiped his nose with the back of his hand. 'But she's worth it.'

'I'll stick with the freesias, thanks.' Robert deepened his voice.

'Not the heliconia?' Baxter King stepped back, a theatrical

stance, and raised his eyebrows. His chapped lips formed a horizontal question mark, his watery eyes begging Robert to change his mind, and for a moment Robert was tempted to take the heliconia.

'I gave her freesias when we met.' It was becoming a battle of the blooms and Robert refused to give way. 'Knowing Erin as well as I do, I can safely say that she'll love them.'

'*Safely*, you see. That's the problem I face each and every day. So many men come into my shop with the intention of buying chrysanthemums for their wives, girlfriends and lovers.' Baxter King held out his hands to Robert and waited a beat. 'I don't even *sell* chrysanthemums in here! Bloody waste of petals. It's my job to make sure that men buy what women really want. The *exotics*. I ask my customers, if the woman in your life was a flower, what would she be? I encourage them to tell me about her, about her shape, her smell, her height, her colouring. Then I ask what she's like in bed, as a mother or . . .'

Robert could see King, like a large dish of melting jelly, and he could feel him, because he had now taken hold of both his hands, but he couldn't do anything to stop King. The man was like rampant ivy, planting his enthusiasm all over Robert. He had to admit, the man was good at his job. Had he not come into the shop to confront King about the relationship he was having with his wife, Robert would have been persuaded to order the Puerto Rican red ginger and hang the price.

Robert glanced uncomfortably at his hands, still held by Baxter King although the man's fingers were sweaty and losing their grip.

'So you see, you really can't send my beloved Erin freesias. They're not *special* enough and she's a very special lady.' King finally released Robert and stepped back to lean against the counter. He mopped his forehead with a handkerchief and waited for a response.

Robert didn't know what to say. He paced around the small shop again, pretending to ponder the various blooms but really wondering if he had got the right man. He thought back to the letters he had found in Erin's study. There was no doubt in his mind that the two of them had a special relationship and no mistake either that it had been going on since their marriage.

'When did you first meet my wife?' Robert's tone was accusing. He stood with his arms folded.

Baxter glanced at the ceiling and thought. 'Oh, years ago. It was when her daughter was only about three, possibly four.' Baxter King tipped back his head, revealing more scarred flesh on his thick neck. His breathing became rasping. 'I caught her stealing my bloody stock.' Robert opened his mouth to speak but Baxter continued. 'When she fell to the floor sobbing and begging and telling me her sorry story, well, that's when I took pity on her. So desperate, she was. Poor lamb and with a child to feed.'

Robert's open mouth transformed into a choke and everything he'd planned to say slid back down his throat like a foul bolus of food. There was obviously some mistake. After a moment, when it seemed as if Baxter King was lost in memories and gazing into an arrangement of purple rhododendrons, Robert began to laugh.

'You realise we're on crossed wires here?' Feeling relieved, he relaxed and blew out hard. 'We must be talking about two completely different women.' But Robert's relief was short-lived. King had mentioned a daughter and he could hardly ignore the letters that King, *this* King, had sent to Erin. 'Erin

Knight – I mean Lucas? About five foot six, fair skin, blonde hair this sort of length?' Robert's hand dithered around his neck trying to recreate his wife's hairstyle while the bolus worked its way back up his gullet. *Stealing flowers?* His thoughts kicked up several gears as he tried to imagine Erin doing such a thing.

'Yes, Erin Lucas and I know she's called Knight now. She told me all about you. It was such a relief when I heard that she'd married someone decent. Things are finally going right for her.'

Robert felt his forehead prickle as dots of sweat forced through his skin and turned to a salty crust in the air conditioning. Here he was, faced with the man he thought was having an affair with his wife and instead of trying to conceal his knowledge of Erin, King was brazenly open about their relationship. Robert needed to sit down. He felt dizzy and ludicrously confused.

'Could I have a glass of water? I've had a long drive and—'

'Of course. Come out the back and we can talk in private.' Baxter called the shop assistants back into the store and led Robert to a kitchen area which faced out onto a shady cobbled courtyard. Buckets of flowers and ornamental trees in terracotta pots were stacked everywhere but there was a small space outside with a table and two chairs.

Robert, feeling not at all as he had expected, sat down and gratefully took the cold drink. He leaned forward, elbows on his knees, and wiped his hand across his mouth. He knew he had to play this carefully.

'Yeah, you're right. Marrying me was good for her. And she's got Fresh As A Daisy to keep her on the straight and narrow now.' Robert tried for a frivolous tone and, although a little bitter-sounding around the edges, King didn't seem to notice.

'My man, you're so right. From the minute she began working for me I knew she had talent. A real eye for colour and beauty. Her floral designs earned her quite a name around here. And Patrick just adored her when she first came to stay with us, which was just as well because she ended up living with us for nearly eight years!' Baxter King let out a laugh the likes of which Robert had never heard before. Fleetingly, he was reminded of a donkey.

'Poor Patrick.' Baxter sighed, glancing at Robert who was staring hard at the cobbles, trying to decode what Baxter had told him. 'A terrible way to go.'

Robert realised that, if he was to play the game correctly, humouring the peculiar King was imperative. He needed to know everything. 'Patrick?' Robert said it as if he should know but couldn't quite remember.

'My partner. He died in the terrible fire.' As if centre stage, Baxter hung his head and paused.

'Your business partner?'

'My lover, dear man. My *lover*.'

Robert arced his head long and slow in an overstated nod, time enough for him to assimilate this huge new piece of information. Baxter King's lover had been a *man*?

Robert's first thought was that Baxter must now prefer women but a moment's reflection made him see that this was highly unlikely. The man was very definitely and openly gay. Robert had been so concerned about Erin having an affair that he'd missed the signs completely.

Once again, a brief swell of relief but then more agitation as a thousand questions beckoned. It was clear now that they were both talking about the same Erin. What Robert didn't understand was the part about Erin stealing from King's shop. It didn't sound in the least bit like his wife, although, as his belief in her honesty dwindled, all sorts of unusual scenarios became possible.

'I'm so sorry.' Robert hung his head out of respect.

'Thank you. It's fine. I can talk about it now. I have to, you understand. At least Erin and Ruby escaped unharmed.' Baxter King made a show of massaging the scars on the left side of his face and neck. Robert couldn't help staring, as if the chewing-gum stretch of his skin would reveal the entire story.

'I think Erin finds it hard to talk about.' Robert was leading, he knew, but the man seemed eager to divulge information. 'I was in Brighton and had heard so much about you from Erin that I couldn't resist a meeting.' Robert slowed himself. He was relying on the scant information he had to sound credible. It would be easy to slip up.

Baxter King looked at his watch and grinned. 'Have you time for an early lunch, my man? I'd love to know how she's getting on. And I want to hear all about Ruby.'

Robert stood up and took his cue. 'My shout,' he said, allowing a reciprocal smile to widen his face.

The two men ordered a light lunch of warm chicken salad drizzled with a pesto dressing. Baxter studied his meal as if it were a striking bouquet of summer blooms before disposing of it greedily.

Idle chit-chat concerning running a flower shop, life in Brighton compared to London, and Patrick's acting career which was finally coming to fruition before he died, occupied them while the waiter served chilled beers and presented their food. They both knew there was much to discuss and instinctively waited until their privacy was assured. During these twenty minutes, Robert found himself growing to like King. There was something about him that he found appealing, an honesty that he hadn't expected to encounter in the man he suspected of having an affair with his wife. Still, Robert had to know.

'Forgive me for asking but I've always wondered, because Erin talks of you so highly, have you ever been in a relationship with my wife? Are you, or were you, her lover?' Robert knew instantly he sounded ridiculous and he drove his knife into a piece of chicken.

That same guffaw again, from deep within Baxter's cavernous belly – an explosion of disbelief surfacing like a small volcanic eruption. 'Erin and I, lovers? She's far too lovely for an old faggot like me. I wouldn't let myself anywhere near her. Never fear, my man, your wife's perfectly safe with Uncle Bax. Cheers!' Baxter King lifted his dew-covered glass high and then chinked it against Robert's untouched drink, downing most of the contents in one draught.

Robert picked up his beer and did the same.

'Tell me about Ruby. She must be quite a young lady now.' Baxter wiped salad dressing off his mouth.

'She is. More and more like her mother every day.' Robert didn't know why he said that. It was completely untrue. 'She's growing up fast.' He didn't want to have to go into detail about Ruby's troubles at school. He felt inadequate enough as a stepfather.

'But?' King had latched onto Robert's evasive tone.

'No buts, really. We moved her to a different school recently. She's doing really well, although Erin took a fair bit of convincing that it was the right thing.'

'Were those bullies still beating up on her?'

Robert was relieved that King already knew, obviously a result of his correspondence with Erin. He nodded. 'She goes to a private college now. They're heavily into music. In fact, there's a trip to Vienna coming up—'

'But Erin won't hear of Ruby going, right?'

Robert was stunned. 'You're right. She didn't even want her to go to Greywood College. She said Ruby shouldn't run away from her problems.'

'That doesn't surprise me. Erin's done enough running away in her life. And she's incredibly protective of Ruby. When the child was younger, Erin literally wouldn't let her out of her sight. Even when she went to the bathroom.'

Robert froze, chicken halfway to his mouth. Another fragment offered.

'Where do you think that's come from?' His most leading question yet, Robert knew, but it had to be done. He'd never get another chance.

'Well, we both know the answer to that,' Baxter said, assuming that Robert's knowledge was equal to his. He placed his cutlery carefully on the edge of his plate and leaned forward, his elbows resting on the table, his sieve-like face tipped towards the ceiling.

Robert nodded slowly in agreement. 'Yes, of course,' he said, trying to sound convincing. His expression urged King to continue.

Baxter spoke in a low voice that was hushed by his loaded words, but after the first few seconds, Robert couldn't hear anything except the banging in his ears. The noise of his blood pulsing through his head gave him a sudden migraine, which, he decided, was infinitely preferable to what Baxter was telling him.

His vision slewed and the entire restaurant distorted as if it was underwater, every inch of skin on his body rupturing with a cold sweat. A demolition ball had smashed through his life and he wasn't sure if there would be a way to rebuild. He stared at the wall opposite, his breathing tight and painful.

Robert desperately wanted to call Louisa.

FOURTEEN

Louisa cancelled her meeting in Birmingham, but only because it was Robert. Anyone else would have taken their place in her diary.

He was waiting at Euston Station, holding a half-drunk cup of coffee and looking as if he hadn't washed or slept for two days. If it wasn't for the designer sunglasses and Mercedes keys he was clutching, he would have looked like just another homeless person.

Louisa's long stride scissored her between impatient passengers and she was soon standing beside Robert.

Their conversation the previous afternoon, when Robert had called her from the blustery Promenade in Brighton, had been short but intense enough for Louisa to know that this was more than Robert speculating about his wife's honesty. This was history repeating itself.

Without begging or divulging any need other than business, he had coldly requested that they meet. He'd said that he wanted to hire her professionally.

'So,' she said in her usual crisp, uncomplicated voice. 'Here we are.'

There was a pause, a shutting out of the station's midmorning noise, each of them noticing their hearts kick into the same rhythm before a brief embrace. Robert could hardly bear the brush of her thick hair on his cheek. She was wearing it loose today, the russet waves spilling on her shoulders. She smelled of raspberries.

'Here we are.' Robert laughed and looked away, turning on his heel and wiping his palm over his stubble. He knew he was a sight, even more so in Louisa's fresh light. 'My car's downstairs. Shall we go?'

They both knew it was pointless talking about it until they were somewhere quiet, a place where their voices could cut cleanly through the summer humidity without either of them having to say pardon or frown or cup their ear. Robert only wanted to go through this once. Even the hooded interior of the Mercedes provided a less than suitable environment. Louisa moved a chiffon scarf from the passenger seat as she got in.

'Erin's?'

Robert nodded, half expecting her to smell it as if it was a leading clue in the investigation he was hoping she would agree to take on. How to present it to her so that she didn't jump to conclusions, assume things were heading the same way as with Jenna, he didn't know.

'I wasn't sure if you'd even answer my call.' They both slipped on their sunglasses as Robert accelerated onto the street.

'I nearly didn't.' She briefly touched his hand as it rested on the gearstick.

The wine bar was cool and dark, barely open, all the tables and chairs perfectly positioned. They didn't want to eat, for which the waitress seemed thankful, and they sat on a leather settee at the rear of the premises. An air-conditioning unit buzzed overhead. They drank chilled house white.

'I know what you're thinking but you're wrong.' Robert put his glass on the marble-topped table and leaned his forearms on his knees. Louisa sat next to him, her pencil-slim legs crossed. Her cropped linen trousers rose up to expose her smooth knees.

'You have to admit, Rob, that you're an unusually suspicious person.'

'And wasn't I right about Jenna?'

'That message on her phone proved nothing.' Louisa sighed but it was lost in the hum of the air conditioning. Sucked up and recycled.

'It proved she was meeting a man without my knowledge or—'

'Does Erin know that you're here with me?'

'Of course not.'

Louisa shrugged, her palms wide and upturned. She reached for her wine. 'Then she has as much reason to accuse you of having an affair with me as you had with Jenna.'

'The difference is that we're *not* having an affair, are we?' He paused as their hearts realigned. Another early customer passed by on the way to the toilets. 'Anyway, I don't see what that's got to do with me hiring you for a job. Are you willing to work for me or not?' Robert took a long sip of his wine, chilling his lips, his thoughts.

'Just like old times, eh?' Louisa laughed. 'Except I have a niggling feeling that it's not documents that need serving or a missing person you want tracing.'

Robert hadn't yet told her what Baxter King had said. Just that it was urgent, that he needed her. That they had to meet.

'In a way, I do want you to locate a missing person. Someone I once knew. Thought I knew,' he added. 'I'm having trouble getting Ruby's birth certificate—'

149

'Yes, I know that, Rob. You already told me. I regularly use an agency that can run a nationwide search for Ruby's details on pretty limited information. I expect you've just been in touch with the wrong register office or something silly. Next problem?'

'It's Erin.' He sighed heavily. 'She's not being honest with me. The thing is, Ruby's new school have called several times and sent notes home about returning Ruby's enrolment papers. Erin's done absolutely nothing about it.'

'You said yourself that she was never keen for Ruby to go to the new school.'

'Oh, but she was.' Robert laughed incredulously. 'It was Erin who sent off for the prospectus and made the appointment with the headmistress in the first place. It was only when the final, more official side of things needed wrapping up that she cooled right off. And even mentioning the school trip to Vienna is—'

'Like banging your head against a brick wall.'

Robert noticed Louisa's wedding ring, a plain gold band, glinting in the yellow lamplight. He nodded. 'Exactly.'

'The poor woman's probably so wrapped up in running her business, not to mention her daughter's troubles, that she's simply overlooked what you call "the official side of things".'

'That's why I got Tanya to sort out the passport for the trip. She fell at the first hurdle. No birth certificate.'

'Rob, if I get this certificate for you, will it help? Will you let go?' Louisa put a hand on his shoulder.

'This time yesterday, I would have said yes, that getting the certificate would make me believe that over the years, Erin had lost her copy, been too busy to get another – even that she was an overprotective parent and that's why she won't let Ruby go to Vienna. I could have handled that.' Robert reached for his wine glass. Louisa's hand fell from his shoulder and he felt a cool patch where her warmth had been. 'But now, in light of what I found out yesterday, I'm not sure about anything.'

Louisa flagged the waitress and they soon had a whole bottle of chilled wine sitting on the table. 'You'd better tell me everything then,' she sighed, trying not to sound as though she had heard it all before. She opened her leather folder, slid a silver pen from its holder and positioned her hand to write.

'No judgement? No interruptions?'

Louisa nodded, her mass of hair falling forward. She tucked it behind her ears and unconsciously slipped the pen between her lips.

'As I told you, I drove to Brighton yesterday. I'd gone to find a man named Baxter King because over the last few years he's been communicating with Erin by letter and email. I found this out when I was looking in Erin's office for Ruby's birth certificate, in case she had an old copy that she'd forgotten about. In fact, it was Ruby herself who showed me where her mother kept such papers although I didn't find much except an expired passport of Erin's and these letters from Baxter King.

'They showed him to be the proprietor of a flower shop in Brighton, King's Flowers, and so I went to see him. The letters were quite suggestive in places. King expressed his deep love for Erin and how he missed her and that she should prepare the bed for when he comes to stay.'

'Oh, Rob,' Louisa whispered but he didn't hear.

'Anyway, it turns out that King's clearly not involved with Erin romantically.' Robert's tone lifted and small laughter lines formed beside his tired eyes. 'He's gay.'

'You see, there's always an explanation for—'

'You've not heard the good bit yet. Erin actually lived with King and his partner – who apparently died in a fire – for a number of years and before that she lived in London. King caught her stealing his flowers, learned her sorry story, took pity on her and tucked her and Ruby under his arm. They were one, albeit unusual, happy family.'

'And?' Louisa said, having only jotted down a couple of notes so far. Robert finished his second glass of wine and poured another.

'And,' he continued, 'it turns out that before her career in flower-stealing, Erin earned a living by opening her legs.'

He swiftly downed the third glass of wine and leaned back in the deep leather settee, draping his arms wide over the cushions. He levered an ankle onto his knee and stared sideways at Louisa, waiting for her reaction, waiting for her to tell him he was mistaken or paranoid or making something out of nothing.

Her words didn't come. She sat stiffly, silver pen hovering over the paper, the tune of the air-conditioning unit and the chatter of more customers taking away the need for words. Finally, Robert added, 'My wife was a prostitute, Louisa. A hooker. A whore. A call girl.'

Robert watched as her expression toggled through various forms of shock, although none of them seemed appropriate. Already, having unloaded the heavy information, Robert's breathing became easier and his thoughts stirred in the sump of his mind. Sharing this news with Louisa, he hoped, was a safeguard against it all happening again.

'Whoa,' she finally said. 'That's a pretty serious allegation to make about your wife. Do you think it's true?' Louisa reached for her wine.

Robert shrugged. 'If I say yes, you'll tell me I'm being

paranoid. If I say no, which is probably what any sane person would do if they wanted to preserve their marriage, then I'm going to wonder forever what else she's hiding.'

'She mightn't be hiding anything.'

'See? I knew you'd say that.' Robert pushed his fingers through his already messed hair. Dark and unruly, without styling, it made him appear like a rock star ten years past his prime.

'OK, let's say Erin was a prostitute, that she did earn her living that way. As a single mother struggling to bring up a young child, she probably didn't have a choice.'

Suddenly, Robert wished he had met Erin a decade before, even before Ruby had been born. Then he would have had a chance of saving her and being Ruby's real father. 'So you're saying that all young mothers should turn to prostitution to support their kids?'

'Of course not, Rob, but in this case, maybe that's what happened. She was obviously desperate. And by the sound of it, she was desperate enough to eventually break away from such a life when she went to live in Brighton and took up stealing instead.'

Robert pulled a face that implied he considered that scenario possible but it quickly transformed into one that looked as if he had slammed his finger in the car door. 'What about Ruby?' he asked, as if Louisa had all the answers. 'Do you think she knows what her mother did for a living?'

Louisa shook her head impatiently and fished her ringing phone from her bag. She glanced at the caller ID, sighed and then switched off the phone without answering. Robert liked it that she considered him more important than whoever was calling. 'Who knows? It depends on how old the kid was at the time.'

'King said Ruby was young, only three, I think, when Erin came to Brighton. She wouldn't have understood exactly but she would have picked up feelings, vibes. God, she was probably in the house while it went on.' Then Robert went pale as the realisation struck him, pretty much at the same time as Louisa thought of it too. It was she who voiced their shared suspicion.

'Don't think like that, Rob. It's hardly Ruby's fault, is it? She's your daughter now, and her father, whoever he was, probably doesn't even know he has a daughter.'

'Yup, he paid his fifty quid, got what he wanted and delivered Ruby deep inside Erin.' Robert let out a pained moan that caused several customers to look over. He leaned forward, head between his knees, feeling sick. How could he ever look at his stepdaughter again without seeing her as the by-product of some long-forgotten, easy transaction? How could he ever touch his wife again without wondering how many men had gone there before? He stood and started towards the gents. 'I need your help, Louisa, to get to the bottom of this without trashing another marriage. I want to hire you full-time, professionally, until this mess is sorted out.'

As he strode to the toilet, leaving Louisa pondering his demand, he wondered how committed she would actually be to helping him save his marriage. He also considered: was hiring Louisa, knowing her do-whatever-it-takes work ethic as he did, any more moral than Erin selling her body? He believed it was.

When he returned, Louisa said, 'I'll need a place to stay, a car, access to the internet, five hundred pounds up front plus another thousand to cover the job I'll have to cancel.' She removed her dark-rimmed glasses, uncovering her unnaturally green eyes so that Robert had no option but to agree.

*

An hour later, Robert checked Louisa into a hotel, watching her runner's legs stride the patterned carpet of the foyer as she telephoned her previous hotel and arranged to have her luggage sent to London. He didn't think he should accompany her to her room but, as she was talking on her mobile and he didn't want to leave without saying goodbye, he continued to walk by her side. He glanced at his watch. He wouldn't be missed yet.

FIFTEEN

It's cold; so cold that my baby and I have become one, wrapped up together in my dirty parka. I press her face into my neck and feel her tiny breaths on my skin. She smells milky and sweet, her eyes wide with wonder as we run. We're running away, charging dangerously across the ice-glazed supermarket car park, escaping down the high street, pinballing through the Saturday shopping crowds and down Holt's Alley to a warren of terraced houses beyond. That should do it; keep them off my scent. I kiss my baby's head through her little woollen hat.

'Don't worry, chickie. Mummy won't let them catch us.'

I haven't a clue where we're going. But it's been such a cold morning of effort, a winter-blue, throat-burning escape, that I'm now exhausted and need somewhere warm to settle and feed my baby. We head for the train station because I know there's a café on platform two and a train would be a good thing to get on, to take us away.

I stop running and catch my breath in a brisk walk. I'm simply not capable of charging through town with the weight of my baby pressed to my front. I only gave birth a week ago and my insides still feel loose, my breasts way too heavy with milk to keep running, even though I know we have to if we are to survive this.

In the baby magazines, it said that new mums should take it easy and get friends and relatives to do the running around. Here I am, running, running and probably drawing more attention to myself by doing that anyway. I'm not going to let them catch me. She's my baby. All mine now.

I have named her for her deep red lips. Ruby. Apparently, you forget quickly, about the birth – nature's trick to ensure a repeat performance – but I can still remember every detail. What I'm finding hard to recall and put into order are the days that followed.

Mother and Father didn't return from their New Year celebrations at Uncle Gustaw and Aunt Anna's house until the sun had burst well above the horizon. I woke, perhaps from the rays touching my eyelids or perhaps from the merriment that haemorrhaged through the front door (New Year is the only time my mother is ever merry), and for a moment I forgot all about the night's happenings.

It was only when I felt something wriggling in the crook of my body that I realised my baby wasn't inside me any more. She had wormed her way down under the covers in an attempt to be back in my womb again or perhaps she was burrowing for my nipple. Instinctively, I drew her up to my breast where she knew exactly what to do and after a dozen agonizing sucks, my baby slept peacefully.

We have reached the train station. I have only been on a train twice before. Once when I was ten and we went to London to visit Father's cousin, who had recently arrived from a village just south of Warsaw, and the second time, well, that was when we went to Broadstairs for a holiday but came home after two days because Mother saw Father touching a maid's tits on the landing of our guest house.

I go into the railway station café and sit down at a table,

adjusting Ruby so that she lies on my knee no more obtrusively than a small cloth bag half hidden under my coat. I feel in my pocket for the money. Two twenty-pound notes and some silver. It was all Mother had in her purse; the remains of the housekeeping.

I carry Ruby to the counter and buy a hot chocolate and a bar of Dairy Milk. Ruby is being such a good baby, tucked under my arm and still fast asleep, that the café woman doesn't even notice I have a baby. Surely, if she'd seen, she would lean forward and coo and talk in a high-pitched voice. All she does is slam my change onto the counter and turn to the person waiting behind me. I am not special to her.

Back at my table, I sip my hot chocolate and study the timetable that someone has left lying in a pool of spilled tea. Trains to London go every half hour. The next one is in twelve minutes and I shall be on it.

Mother didn't knock on my door until well after midday, when she left my usual lunch tray on the landing. I could barely get up out of my wet nest on the floor, but hunger drove me on all fours to get the food. No one knew I had pushed out my baby. I ate like a wolf and slipped the tray back outside my bedroom door, as I would normally do. Then I slept again. I don't remember for how long. Ruby was thankfully silent, barely aware she was alive and quite content to suckle or sleep.

I'm standing on the platform now, close to the edge. A train rushes through the station, three feet from Ruby and me, drenching us in debris and excitement. We will soon be on our way. A garbled announcement tells me that the train to London is next. I don't know what we will do when we get there, except be safe, anonymous.

No one will know that I am running away from my parents

– parents who ordered my baby to be given up for adoption. No one will care about us in London and that, I know, is why we will be safe.

I am breathing each breath carefully, tiptoeing through each minute with my precious new baby, living it as if it's my last. I expect my father's strong hand on my shoulder at any time, my mother sobbing by his side, whimpering accusations at me. The police will suddenly blanket me, take my baby and hand her to some other woman, my parents nodding approvingly. I will be sent to prison and the only person allowed to visit will be Uncle Gustaw . . .

The train lumbers up to the platform and I climb aboard with the baby pressed against my body, her eyes peeking over the top of her blanket. What she makes of the world through those new, watery eyes, I don't know. I read that newborn babies can't focus on anything further away than their mother's faces.

Ruby is suddenly alert, writhing in her cocoon and watching the scene around us as if she can make sense of everything she sees. I smile and kiss the top of her head. She is precocious and I am a proud mother. Ruby is already an intelligent baby. I walk sideways down the narrow aisle.

The train is crowded but I find a vacant seat next to a young man wearing headphones and reading a magazine. He doesn't look up as I sit down but puts his elbow on the chair rest so I can't have it. I unfurl Ruby, who is becoming restless. I notice that she has lost one of her little knitted bootees and her foot is cold. I rub her toes. My arms are aching from carrying her through the town and I don't feel very strong today, a bit like I'm getting 'flu.

I fidget and get myself comfortable and the young man peeks at me sideways, then glances at Ruby. She is leaning against my body, trying to pull her arms from beneath her blanket wrapping. She lets out a frustrated yelp. Surprisingly, the young man smiles and then looks away again. I can hear the *tss-tss* of his music. Someone's mobile phone rings and another baby squawks further down the carriage.

If I wasn't on the run, if I didn't want to keep it a secret that I'd got this baby and was fleeing to London, then I'd go and sit near the other baby so Ruby could make eyes at it. I could talk about babies with its mother, about which nappies she prefers and if she breast or bottle feeds. I'm a mother now, although I don't feel I have any right to be at fifteen. I don't feel proper. I bet that other mother would look down her nose at me and shift her baby out of reach. The train begins to move and I realise I'm travelling backwards.

Twenty minutes into the journey and Ruby is screaming. The young man next to me turns up his music and the lady across the aisle is staring. I am sweating in my parka. The sliding door at the end of the carriage opens and the ticket inspector leans against the first set of seats while the passengers open their bags or search their pockets for their tickets. Another six rows of seats and he'll want to clip my ticket. I don't have one. I stand up, gripping my screaming baby, and walk towards the conductor as if I'm drunk, one hand on the back of each seat as I go.

'Excuse me.' I turn sideways and slide past him as he is questioning someone about their ticket. I go through the sliding door and duck into the toilet. It stinks and the floor is wet. I kick the toilet lid down with my foot and slump onto it. There's a tiny window. I could jump out. I did that when I ran away from home. I sat on the window sill and dropped into the bush below. I probably won't see my family ever again.

'What?' I say to Ruby. She's squirming and crying and

twisting. Her arms have popped out of her shawl and her legs are beating. I hold her up, so her face is level with mine. For a second we lock eyes, an unfathomable connection, then her face reddens and crumples and she howls like she's in terrible pain. I thought I would be a good mother.

'Are you hungry?' I fumble with my coat zip and layers of sweaters and T-shirts and finally dig out my aching breast. Ruby stops howling and begins to grumble. She makes a throaty snuffling sound, as if she can smell the milk that's leaked all over my clothes. Within a second, her mouth is around my bursting nipple but she's chewing and fussing and not latching on properly. She wants to drink but doesn't seem able, as if something is wrong. Her little fists are clenched and beat about as she tries to feed from me. Milk has dribbled all over her face so I dab it with her blanket but that angers her even more. It's as if she doesn't like my milk.

'Don't have any, then,' I say and pull down my clothes. We sit in the loo for about twenty minutes, waiting for the ticket inspector to move on, and the steady rhythm of the train gradually forces Ruby into reluctant sleep. Careful not to disturb her, I leave the toilet and stand in the space between the carriages. I think I'll just stay here until we arrive in London.

I ran away because Mother and Father tricked me. All those months locked in my bedroom and they were plotting to steal my baby.

'Hand over your baby, Ruth,' Mother said tersely as if it was something to be disposed of before the dustmen came.

'Come on now, Ruthie, be reasonable. What about your school work, the rest of your life?' Father loomed over me, arms folded, looking so much like his brother.

Locked in my room pregnant, I went along with it,

pretending that it was for the best, but all the while I was thinking of a plan. Too long I've played their game. I'm a woman now, I've got a child of my own. I'll need a job, a place to stay. I'm going to get a new life. If they thought I was going to go back to school – I blow out in disgust and, just at that moment, I see the ticket inspector enter the carriage ahead through the far door.

The train seems to be wheezing and slowing so I push down the window and stick out my head, gripping Ruby so she doesn't get sucked out. Half a mile up the track, I can see a station. I look back down the long carriage. He's midway through now, not checking tickets any more because he thinks he's done everyone. Signs for Milton Keynes flash past and the scrub grass gradually turns into concrete as we enter the station. I have my hand ready on the door lever and just as the train reaches a standstill, just as the carriage door slides open and the inspector walks into the void, I hit the button to open the door and leap off the train. Ruby's head lurches forward and then back onto my breastbone. She wakes with a high-pitched scream and we're running again, running away from the train and into the warmth of the dismal waiting room.

We sit and wait, me shaking, the baby whimpering.

Finally, Ruby is sucking on me. It's taken nearly half an hour to coax her into drinking my milk and now she is guzzling on me. While she's feeding, I remember my Dairy Milk and unwrap it with one hand. Ruby's little head is nestled on my left arm and her knees are drawn up to her chest. She's a ball of baby and blanket. I drop chocolate flakes onto her so I pick them off and pop them in my mouth, thinking that one day she'll be able to eat chocolate too. I realise that I don't know when that will be. I haven't a clue when she should eat normal food or walk or talk or go to school or learn an instrument or do exams or leave home or get pregnant.

Ruby's sucks are becoming less vigorous and less urgent, which is a good thing because my nipple is on fire. I was alone in the waiting room but a man comes in and, out of all the vacant chairs, he chooses the one right opposite me. I don't want a stranger to see my tit.

'How old?' The man, probably in his forties, puts loads of shopping bags down and leans forward to get a better look. He's out of breath and smells of the cold, earthy air. I'm not sure if he's asking *my* age, disapprovingly, or Ruby's so I ignore him. 'My daughter's fourteen now.' He leans back again and sighs.

I lower my arm, so that Ruby's head drops an inch or two in the hope she might let go of my nipple so that we can leave. But she's stuck on hard and I want to scream out because it hurts. I pull the blanket up over Ruby's head and my chest.

'Make sure you cherish these early days,' the man continues. 'You never get them back.' He cracks open a can of Coke. 'So convenient too, that you've got, you know,' he jerks his head at my chest and takes a swig of Coke, 'milk on tap.' He thinks he's funny and laughs. He's making me scared. There's no one else in sight and even though it's only half past two, the light is already turning purple-grey, like we're in for some snow. I'm freezing and my nose is running.

'Going anywhere nice?' He's staring at me.

'I'm waiting for my husband, actually. He's coming in on the next train. Then we're going home.' I say it like it's real and for a second that's almost as delicious as my chocolate bar, I believe it myself and imagine a handsome young man with slightly tousled but styled hair and wearing an expensive suit stepping off the train from his highly paid job in the City. He marches up to me, embraces his wife and daughter and then announces that he's taking us both out for dinner before we go home to our warm, comfortable house . . .

'That'll be the train I'm catching then. It should only be a couple of minutes now.' He stands up to leave. 'Well, good luck with baby.' He walks away and I'm about to call after him because he's left one of his shopping bags under the chair, but I don't. I let him get on the train when it arrives and, after he's gone and Ruby's fallen asleep again, I hook the bag across the floor with my foot. It is stuffed full of groceries and it makes me think: did he know?

Carrying the shopping and Ruby is hard work. It's forcing more of my insides out. I don't know if I should still be bleeding like this but I'm not going to the hospital. They'll just send me home again or, worse, call the police.

I get a bus into the centre of Milton Keynes. I came Christmas shopping here once with my mother and Aunt Anna but they didn't like it and complained about how expensive everything was. I thought it was magical.

Today it's not magical. Every shop window has 'sale' posters and I feel like I'm walking through melted toffee because there are so many people. I go into John Lewis and find the baby section. It's warm and filled with the joys of owning a new baby – matching lampshades and quilts and towels and packs of soft sleep suits. Sagging festive decorations hang from the ceiling and there's a Christmas tree leaning at an angle as if it's had enough and wants to be packed away.

'If you need any help, love, just let me know.' Even though she sounds nice, I bet she thinks I'm going to steal something.

I hoist Ruby onto my shoulder, so everyone can see I have a baby and it's OK for me to be browsing.

'Just looking.'

'There's a mother's room over there, if you need to change baby.' She smiles and crinkles her nose. She's right. Ruby stinks. I don't have any nappies.

'Oh, Ruby, you *do* need changing but, silly me, I left your nappy bag at home.' I don't normally sound like that.

'Everything you'll need is in the mother's room. With our compliments.'

The room is empty and smells of talc and tepid milk. I lay Ruby on the changing mat and shake out my aching arms. When I pull away her blanket, I see that her baby suit is damp right through. No wonder she's been restless. I peel away the layers of clothing, right down to the vest that has poppers between her legs. I pause and study the garments, getting a whiff of fresh washing powder through the stench of soiled nappy.

'Mummy'll get you cleaned up in no time, chickie.' I tickle her tummy but she gives me that look again, our souls connecting angrily before a single tear drips out of her left eye. I change her nappy, badly, but have to dress her in dirty clothes again as I didn't have time to pack a bag. It was a now or never escape. I was lying on my bed then I was lying in the bush beneath my window. No chance of picking out a winter wardrobe.

I sit and feed Ruby and it suddenly hits me that we have nowhere to spend the night. My friend Rachel ran away once. Only for three days. She went to a hostel for battered women. She wasn't battered and she was only thirteen at the time but they took her in. Then the hostel reported her to the police because they suspected that she was a runaway. She was returned to her family.

Rachel was protesting because she wasn't allowed a puppy. I'm protesting because I wasn't allowed my baby.

Another mother comes into the room and says a brief, 'Hi,' glancing at me then Ruby. I think she was going to start chatting but changed her mind. She undresses her baby. She has a really nice pushchair. It's huge and comfortable and has a nappy bag to match. She talks to her baby as if he can understand everything she's saying. I'd like a pushchair like that for Ruby. It would save my arms breaking.

After Ruby's change and feed, I wrap her up in her shawl again, get her fixed firmly in the crook of my left arm and stuff half a dozen nappies and a packet of wipes into my grocery bag when the other mother isn't looking.

'Bye,' I say and spend the next hour wandering around the store looking at all the lovely things. I didn't mean to, but I steal a lipstick. I've never had one before. No one stops me when I leave the store and I end up in McDonald's for a cup of tea, laughing.

It's dark outside. Ruby and I have a giggle together because she's happy now that she's dry and fed and I put on some bright red lipstick, which makes her gurgle even more. I think she really likes me.

I never thought that I'd run away. I never thought it would be so easy. Maybe that's where I've always gone wrong – I never think. I didn't think I'd get pregnant or that anyone would ever like mousy me enough to make me pregnant but I don't want to remember that so I screw up my eyes until it goes away.

I'm sitting next to a large window. With the night a black background outside, I can see my reflection. Big holes for eyes, grey skin stretched across bones that are too, well, bony. My hair hasn't ever been styled and my fringe is ragged.

Mother doesn't believe in vanity. Since I could listen, she drummed into me the terrible hardship the Polish people suffered during the war, the Nazi invasions, the Warsaw Ghetto, the uprisings. She said that alone cancelled out all the vanity in this family. My forebears suffered for me to live but I would never possess an ounce of the courage that my grandparents had when they fled Poland.

I never understood what she meant. I learned about the war in history and it didn't sound very nice but it was hardly my fault. I make a promise to myself to get vain, because Mother isn't around, because the war's over now.

I'm doing all right. Ruby and I are in the Holiday Inn. Finding a place for the night was important, with a baby to look after, and I didn't want to crouch in a shop doorway in this freezing weather. I walked away from the shopping centre and, like a welcoming beacon, I soon saw the neon sign of the hotel. I've always wanted to stay in a proper hotel but Mother and Father insisted on bed and breakfasts with fusty sheets and orange swirly carpet whenever we went away. This is much nicer.

I'm looking a bit conspicuous in my old parka and trainers but I think the lipstick helps, makes me going on twenty. There's a nice bar with settees and lamps, and music flutters around like summer butterflies even though it's mid-winter. Ruby certainly likes it here. She was howling but as soon as she heard the tune, she stopped crying.

Uncle Gustaw once told me that the trick to getting what you want is confidence. He should know. So I hold my head up high and smile at the receptionist as I walk past, shifting Ruby up onto my shoulder for everyone to see. Babies make you credible, I've discovered.

The sign above me says: 'This way to the pool'. A swim

would be nice. I find the ladies' changing room and two middle-aged women are forcing their bodies into swimsuits. I can smell warm lady-flesh and chlorine. I sit on a bench and fiddle about with Ruby until they pack their belongings into a locker and curse because the lock won't take their pound coin. It makes me think. They're talking about their grandchildren as they go through to the pool.

Ruby and I take a shower instead of a swim. Ruby's naked body is pressed against mine as we get squeaky clean. There's even a soap dispenser. The towels are soft. I hope the two women won't mind too much me helping myself but it's hardly my fault that the locker was jammed. They should have used another one.

Inside their sports bags I find an assortment of huge under-wear, a towelling tracksuit, a couple of T-shirts, a size 18 skirt from BHS and a toiletries bag stuffed with really nice things. I put my own clothes back on for now but wrap Ruby up in the tracksuit because her stuff stinks. I rinse out her dirty clothes in the basin, pack the groceries that the man at the station left behind into my new sports bag and head off into the warren of corridors.

Carrying a load of luggage through a hotel looks credible. There are doors every few feet, mostly bedrooms but some of them have names on them like Balmoral Suite and Windsor Room. I rattle the knobs but they're locked. We go up in the lift to the next floor and twist a few more knobs. Two cleaners are chatting halfway down the corridor. They're leaning on a trolley loaded with sheets and sachets of coffee and little packets of biscuits outside what looks like a storeroom. By the sound of it, they're packing up for the day.

'I'll sort it in the morning, Sandra,' one of them says. I'm walking slowly past, to find out what's going on. I'm being confident, like Uncle Gustaw said, and they don't notice that I stare right into that cosy little storeroom, nor do they notice that I hang around about ten feet away pretending to look for something in my bag. And they certainly don't notice when, after they've parked their trolley in the storeroom and walked off, letting the door swing shut by itself, I scamper up and jam my trainer just in time to stop it locking.

'What d'you think, Ruby?' My voice is dulled by the piles of linen and towels.

How proud I am for securing us a room for the night! I don't reckon they'll be back until morning, which gives us ages to indulge in the stack of pillows and duvets and sheets and little bottles of whisky and sugar sachets to dip my finger in like a sherbet dab.

I dump Ruby on a pillow and spin around with my arms wide. There's only just enough room to do that, what with the trolley and the shelves taking up most of the space. I kick off my trainers and pull a pile of folded duvets onto the floor. I make a nest, padding up the walls with pillows, just like a mother bird. Then I unzip the sports bag and dig out the food that the station man gave us. I open a packet of Nice biscuits and eat three at once. There's a tin of peas, which are useless since I don't have an opener, an Iceburg lettuce, a bag of carrots, a can of Spam, which I love, and a packet of cream crackers.

'We'll have a feast tonight then.' I squeal with delight and Ruby spits up all her milk on the duvet nest so I get another one down from the rack.

I make an early supper of crackers with Spam and lettuce followed by a nice crunchy carrot. Then I start on the sugar cubes and whisky and then I sleep for hours with Ruby curled up beside me. Really, she is a very good baby.

★

I had to leave in the end. I folded up the sicky duvets and put the pillows back in their place and fiddled about with the trolley so it looked untouched but after two nights in the cleaners' store, I reckoned it was only a matter of time before I got caught.

On the first morning, after my Spam-fest, I woke feeling quite ill. I tidied up the room and lingered the day away in the shopping mall. I spent a few quid on maternity pads and a cup of hot chocolate and agonised over a vacant pushchair left outside the ladies' loo. I would have had it, too, if she hadn't come back so quickly.

Then, in the evening, I did exactly the same as I had the night before. We even had another shower. Curled up in the storeroom, I dreamed of finding us a nice house and a job where I earned hundreds of pounds a week. Then we left without a trace because no one's luck lasts that long.

So now we're trekking along the icy verge, thumbing a lift to London. I know we're near the motorway because I can hear the rumble of traffic. A couple of cars slow down and the drivers stare at me but they don't stop. A van goes by and a hundred yards up ahead I see its brake lights flash on and off, like he's not sure whether to stop. But he does and once again I'm running with Ruby wedged in my left arm and the sports bag bumping against my back. My throat is burning from the cold.

'Where you going, love?' He's blond and messy, probably a builder.

'London,' I pant, leaning on the passenger door.

'I can take you up the road to the motorway junction but that's all. It'll get you a couple of miles closer.' Builder-man grins, exposing horrible teeth that are the same colour as the flashes of yellow in his hair. But he seems nice so we climb in beside him. His van is warm and smells of oil and coffee.

'What's a young girl like you doing hitching a ride so early on a Monday morning?' He drives on, glancing at me a couple of times, his sly grin telling me that he doesn't really care but wouldn't mind knowing anyway.

I stare straight ahead, keeping quiet until I think of what I can tell him. Ruby squeals and squirms on my knee.

'Cute baby,' he continues. 'How old?'

'Not very,' I reply, thankful for the diversion although I can tell he doesn't really care. Builder-man is humming along to the song on the radio and tapping his fingers on the wheel but he's obviously been thinking.

'And you're hitching a lift with a not very old baby?' The song has ended.

'Yeah,' I reply, picking my nails. I can see the motorway junction up ahead now so I get Ruby locked into position, even though she's screaming, and gather up my bag. I just want to get out. Builder-man drops me in a lay-by without any more questions. He toots and drives off.

In the cold, with my toes like fossils and my cheeks stinging from the bitter wind, Ruby and I stand at the head of the motorway slip road. It's nearly an hour before anyone stops and this time it's a juggernaut with about a hundred wheels that smoke and wheeze as the great truck comes to a stop.

'London?' I shout up to the driver and he beckons me in. I virtually need a ladder to get into the cab but the man pulls us up and straps me in. There is a bed up behind the seats. I ask him if he's going all the way to London although my lips barely work from the cold. The truck driver holds up his hands like he's stopping traffic.

'Eh, no Engleesh.' Then he howls with laughter and gets us on our way.

Two and a half hours later and we're in North London. We say goodbye to the truck driver at an industrial estate and a man who works in a warehouse gives me directions to the nearest tube station. I've always wanted to ride on the Underground and I'm chuffed to bits that I worked it out by myself. We ride the bumpy train to the very heart of the city that's going to save us.

We get off at Tottenham Court Road for no particular reason. The weight of Ruby is dragging me down as we walk along the platform and I have cramps in my belly like I've burst open. Under all these clothes, I'm sweating and on fire and out of breath and a little dizzy and my heart is banging behind my swollen breast but I keep trudging on, thankful for the escalator that takes us as high as a house back up to ground level. I stand and rest while everyone else rushes past.

At the top, I slide my ticket through the machine and then feel a bit better as the cold air outside slaps my face. I keep walking although I don't know where and I can hardly keep hold of my baby because she's getting so heavy. I have to get away from the crowds and the noise in my head so I go down a side street but it feels like the buildings are crashing down on me and the noise gets worse, as if one of those trains is whooshing between my ears. At the end of the street there are several skips that stink of sour drains and old food. A man in a chef's uniform comes out of a back door and tosses two black plastic sacks into the waste. He stares at me for a moment as I stagger down the alley, no doubt assuming I'm drunk in charge of a baby. He bangs the door shut.

Next thing I know, I'm on my back feeling the thud of the

ground hit my skull and there's complete darkness and silence for I don't know how long.

Then someone's prising my eyes open but I can't see who because there's a bright light behind them hanging from the ceiling.

'Wake up, wake up now.'

I sit bolt upright and a pain slices through my head. I search frantically for Ruby.

'Where's my baby?' I scream hysterically. I can taste blood. I can taste my own fear.

SIXTEEN

Robert sat in his office and leaned back in the swivel chair, propping his feet up on the leather-topped desk. He'd come directly from Louisa's hotel. In her room he'd drunk coffee, called the office, left a message for Erin on her voicemail and breathed deeply as Louisa emerged from the shower wearing a hotel robe and smelling like oranges. He didn't want to leave but knew he must. She promised to call in the morning.

He hadn't been home since he'd left for Brighton the previous morning, having spent the night in the office. Home and family seemed out of kilter in his mind, as if Baxter King's revelation had eroded their existence.

As he sat, unable to work and still in the same clothes he'd worn to Brighton, still wearing the same expression of grim disbelief – *his wife had once worked as a cheap hooker* – Robert assimilated the information as coldly as if it was a new case placed in front of him. But however he pieced together the facts, he couldn't escape one grim discovery: Erin had deceived him. Knowing the truth was one thing but he didn't think he could truly accept it until he had heard it directly from her.

Wrecked by lack of sleep and too much caffeine, Robert buzzed through to Tanya and told her to put more coffee on to brew. He also requested that she bring the Bowman file through immediately. Distraction was what he needed. He would submerge himself in Jed's dirty case.

'You look done in, Mr Knight,' Tanya said when she brought the files. She wore her hair loose today instead of the usual tight ponytail.

'Pulled an all-nighter, Tan.' Robert's voice was weary and he knew his stubbly face, messed-up hair and creased clothes were unsettling for her. He smelled too but didn't care. 'No calls, no visitors, no disturbances. Understand?'

Tanya nodded and left.

'And bring me coffee!'

Robert opened the Bowman file, stared at the first page for ten minutes without reading a word of it and then walked to the window. He rested his forehead against the glass and stared at the street below. He wondered how many of the people he saw going about their everyday lives had problems. None of them looked very cheerful, he thought.

Then he remembered Mary Bowman, the way she had sat in his office and sobbed, declaring that she hadn't enough fight left in her to plead for her children; that she was prepared to let Jed win in court just to end it all, to finally be done with the beatings that she had taken every day of their eleven-year marriage. She confessed to Robert that she had slept with Jed's brother. It was a one-off, a moment of desperation in an attempt to win comfort and kindness from someone, anyone. A Jed-replacement to provide the love that she'd never had.

Of course, when Jed had found out he'd beaten his wife to within an inch of her life. He forgave his brother, who in fact gained Jed's sympathy for being led astray by the sinful Mary Bowman. But one act of kindness from her husband shouldn't be overlooked. Mary had told Robert, as she ran both hands up her swollen face and massaged her temples, that she had received one loving gift to help her through the blackest period of her life. Jed had given her some medicine, bought from one of his mate's mates, and told her that if she took it when he said, he would lay off her face. Mary was now completely addicted to Valium. And Jed still didn't lay off her face.

Robert spent the next hour trying to figure out how best to represent his foul-mouthed client. However he planned to spin it, to himself or the court, the case left a loathsome taste in his mouth. If he hadn't actually met Mary Bowman and seen first-hand what Jed got up to behind closed doors, he would have happily persuaded Den to take over the case, flattering the senior partner into handling the file. But Robert felt a strange responsibility towards the woman, similar to how he felt towards Ruby now that he knew the truth about her mother, his wife. He wondered how desperate Erin must have been to turn to prostitution. Worse than Mary Bowman? He shuddered as he thought of his wife in Mary's shoes and wondered what lead he could offer the defence lawyer to ensure that Jed never got his children.

Unable to concentrate on anything other than his own problems, Robert left the office and drove to Fresh As A Daisy. As he was inserting coins into a meter across the street from Erin's shop, he recalled the day when he presented her with her new business.

It had been a complete surprise to Erin. They'd parked in a similar position and Robert led his new wife across the road with his hands over her eyes. Once outside the small, run-down premises, he handed her a gift-wrapped box, which he insisted she open right there. She hadn't a clue that the recently closed-down flower business in front of her was now hers. When Erin saw the set of keys, she stared at Robert with a half-smile, the beat of her heart almost audible from the excitement. She looked all around, to check if she was missing something obvious, but then Robert flung his arms wide at the boarded-up premises and shouted, 'Ta-da!' Erin was speechless as the knowledge sank in that she finally had her own business – a lifelong dream at the end of an exhausting journey.

Looking back, Robert realised that there had been a moment of sadness before Erin unlocked the door and stepped inside; a barely detectable thread of hesitation that perhaps, Robert now considered, was because she thought she didn't deserve such an extravagant wedding gift.

Robert darted across the busy street and into the heavily scented domain of his wife's shop. Instantly, he was reminded of Baxter King's shop in Brighton. It seemed an age since he was there although it was only yesterday. His mind, which struggled to contain the powerful urge to confront his wife in a fit of rage, had morphed time. He felt as if he had flu, his world thick and groggy and filled with dark light, despite the bright day.

'Darling, what a surprise!' Erin jumped backwards off a small stepladder with a spray canister in her hand. 'You said you'd be away all day.' She wrapped her arms around Robert's neck. 'Den's just terrible, making you go to that conference at such short notice. I missed you last night.' Erin was about to press her mouth to her husband's but she held back. 'You need a shower, Mr Knight.' She grinned, misting Robert's face with water. 'Remind me to give you a good scrubbing later.'

Robert, his body in turmoil, part of it responding to his wife's attention and part of it replaying Baxter King's words over and over, strode across the shop, knocking over a bucket of yellow flowers. He was about to slam his hands on the counter but stopped. His body stiff and hunched, he simply stood with his back to Erin. His breaths were quick shots of anger and love. Seeing his wife, having her wrap her arms around him, looking at all that she'd achieved in the shop prevented him, for the moment, from speaking his mind.

He turned and, as if wearing a mask – the one that perhaps he had always been wearing – he managed a small smile. 'A shower is just what I need. I feel wrecked.'

Erin grinned coyly. 'Just let me bring the buckets in from the pavement then and I'll shut up shop early.' She winked at Robert as she dragged the heavy containers indoors. Robert should have helped but he didn't. Instead, he stared at her lithe body. Underneath the skinny-fit T-shirt, the low-cut jeans and jewelled flip-flops, he saw the lean lines of a beautiful, intelligent, confident woman. It was the body of a prostitute.

Robert hadn't wanted to confront Erin at the shop. They would have been interrupted by a string of customers, and honesty, which was what Robert needed, would have been easy for Erin to avoid. His incertitude, as they drove home in separate cars, beat down on him like the desert sun. His head throbbed and his throat was tar-like from too much coffee. He tailgated Erin's Mazda, blowing out through his teeth in despair as he recalled giving her the personal registration plate as an out-of-the-blue gift.

'It's your birthday in a couple of weeks,' he said out loud with both hands locked rigidly on the wheel. 'What shall I get you, eh?' He was yelling at the Mazda now, his temples pounding as his blood pressure rose. 'A bloody red light to stick in the front window?' He shoved his elbow into the door panel and ground his teeth as the stop-start traffic reluctantly allowed him nearer the truth.

The house was thankfully cool, which helped to slow his racing pulse. Robert went into the living room, assuming Erin would follow although he realised she had other reasons for closing the shop early. Within seconds he heard the shower running upstairs. Erin called out to him a couple of times but Robert pretended not to hear. He waited for her to finish, then it would happen. He would confront her. Robert wondered how he would ever make love to his wife again.

'Robert, help! Come quickly!' Erin's voice was urgent and he wasted no time in taking the stairs in twos and dashing into their en-suite shower room. He didn't like the way he'd responded without delay and as he stood in the steam-filled bathroom, his brain beat against his skull.

'What is it?' Robert couldn't see Erin properly through the steamed-up glass of the shower cubicle although he was aware of a slim figure moving behind the droplets and mist.

'In here,' she said. 'Open the door.'

Robert did as he was told and slid the door aside. Hot water rained out on him and he was faced with his naked wife soaping herself, leaning against the tiles with her head thrown back and her hands between her legs.

'Take your clothes off and get in.' She giggled as she ran her fingers over her breasts. 'You're disgusting. I have to wash you.' Erin blew him a silent kiss, her blonde hair darkened by the water and slicked to her head.

Robert squinted through the steam, which only served to make Erin look more beautiful, more mysterious. He realised it was the mystery that had attracted him to her in the first place – her secrecy, her perfect unknown status making her anything he wanted her to be. Erin had always been vague about her past, only ever revealing details when absolutely necessary. Until now, it had never been a problem. Rather it served as bait, teasing and tempting him to spend more and more time with her until he finally felt ready to commit. When they married, Robert felt as if he had set sail on a beautiful yacht and was cutting through the waves to uncharted territory. Each day he spent with Erin tantalised him and he was always left wanting more.

Standing in the bathroom, he had similar feelings but now he felt he was on a sinking ship in a turbulent ocean. As he watched her playing in the shower, Robert wondered if any amount of soap could make her clean in his eyes.

Suddenly, Erin reached out of the shower and yanked him by the arm. He lost his balance and stumbled into the cubicle fully clothed. Erin leaned back on the tiles and laughed, water streaming down her face and neck.

'Told you I'd get you clean.' She giggled, pressing her soapy body against his clothes. 'Take your shirt off and let me wash your back.' Erin began to fiddle with the buttons but Robert pushed her hand away and did it himself. He was left with no alternative but to take off his sodden shirt anyway, although being semi-naked in the shower with Erin was not how he had envisaged confronting her.

'Now, now,' Erin continued. 'Don't get stroppy. If you're going to be a dirty boy then you have to face the consequences.' Again that laugh, that sinewy stretch of neck. Robert worked hard to keep his eyes from wandering across the geography of his wife's body. But his peripheral vision told him that she was as beautiful as ever – gentle curves in all the right places with toned muscles across her shoulders and belly. With the soap coursing down her body and legs, Robert couldn't help but feel aroused, despite the trouble he held in his head.

His body was reacting to Erin one way, while his mind was pulling him quite another.

'There's something we need to talk about.' Robert pressed his palms to the tiles, trapping Erin between his arms. 'It's serious.'

Erin giggled again. 'Talk dirty,' she ordered, rubbing shower gel over his exposed chest. 'And don't even *think* of being boring right now. Anything serious will have to wait.' She tilted the shower head so that it doused Robert's chest and when he was rinsed, she trailed her mouth over his clean skin.

Robert retreated as far as the shower enclosure would allow. He banged his elbow on the glass, which Erin instantly made a point of kissing better. Before he knew what was happening, she unbuckled his trousers and dropped the saturated material to his ankles.

'While I'm down here . . .' She grinned, staring up at Robert and massaging his buttocks with gel.

Robert felt himself respond. If he didn't stop her now, he knew he would succumb and while part of him was screaming out to allow her to continue, the sensible side, the lawyer side of him, forbade it. With a massive surge of self-control, he stuck both hands under her armpits and hauled her upright. Their faces were close, the magnetic space between them filled with thick steam and the zing of lime shower gel. Robert tried, but failed, to gain an insight by staring deep into Erin's eyes, in case he saw something that would make him change his mind.

'How many times do you think we've made love?' Robert heard himself asking. He had no idea how this was going to come out, only that he knew it had to.

'Let me see.' Erin thought it must be a game and began

counting on her fingers and then borrowed Robert's and then dropped to her knees again to use his toes. She stared up at him and said, 'Two or three hundred?' before continuing with her mouth on his wet skin.

Robert dragged her upright again, roughly this time. Erin rubbed at her sore shoulders and frowned.

'Hey . . .'

'So what do you reckon I owe you then, considering it's all been on account?' Robert levered Erin aside and turned off the water. He pulled up his wet trousers, which wouldn't come up easily, and wiped his hands over his face. He studied his wife, searching for any reaction, however minute, that would convince him that Baxter King had made a terrible mistake. There was nothing. Erin stood completely still, staring at the droplets on the glass.

'Time to settle my bill, I think.' Robert took a step forward, knocked Erin back against the tiles. He truly didn't know what he was doing when he took each of her wrists in his hands and raised them above her head, pinning her to the wall. He pressed his face close to hers but she turned her head to the side and closed her eyes. 'How much do I owe you for all the sex? Tell me what you charge.' Robert's voice ricocheted off the glass. 'Tell me!' he yelled.

'I don't know what you mean, Rob. Stop this. You're scaring me.' Erin dared to open her eyes. Robert's face was veined and red and mapped with worry lines that she'd never noticed before. 'Let me get a towel. I'm freezing.'

Whether it was the sound of his wife's voice or the sight of her small body trembling beneath his grip, Robert wasn't sure, but something in him gave a little, and he allowed her out of the shower. He knew that she couldn't possibly be cold. The room was stifling. She was shaking with fear.

Robert followed her out and stood, dripping, in their en-suite bathroom while Erin put on her robe. She wrapped the white towelling around her, pulling it closed up to her neck. She eyed the doorway to their bedroom but Robert was standing in it, both arms stretched across the opening.

'How much?' he spat.

'Robert, what happened last night? You're acting so strange.' Erin's voice was several tones above its usual pitch and faltered over each word. Robert noticed immediately.

'I didn't go to a conference,' he admitted. He fixed himself in the doorway, determined to keep Erin trapped until she confessed. 'I went to Brighton.'

They both felt it, as if the humid air was suddenly freeze-dried and the gap between them had become an impenetrable pack of ice. Robert watched Erin for a reaction but she was silhouetted by the midday sun streaming in through the opaque window behind her. It had no effect on the chilled atmosphere.

'Brighton?'

'I went to see Baxter King.' All Robert's senses were on red alert to gather Erin's response. But she simply stood, hugging her robe around her body, shivering, her soaking hair dropping rivulets of water down her face. She made no attempt to wipe them away. The seconds before she spoke seemed like hours.

'Is he a lawyer? A client?' Erin pulled herself flawlessly into a role Robert didn't recognise. Her voice transformed into that of a confident woman and she appeared to gain an extra six inches in height. She strode up to Robert with an inner calm and deftly ducked under his arm into the freedom of the bedroom.

'I've not heard you mention him before,' she called back as

she swiped clothes from the wardrobe and tossed them onto the bed.

Robert turned in the doorway. He couldn't believe what he was hearing. With her back to him, Erin slipped into denim shorts and a halter-neck top and wrapped her dripping hair in a towel. She was acting as if she'd never heard of Baxter King. At her dressing table, she wiped on face cream and applied a stroke of mascara. She seemed positively upbeat, as if Robert had mentioned a completely inconsequential name that would never occur in conversation again.

Robert desperately wanted to accept the wash of relief that his body was begging for and his heart was in need of a break from the steady stream of adrenaline which had fuelled it for over twenty-four hours. It would have been easy to accept Erin's assertion that she had never heard of Baxter King; easier still to fall into bed and carry on what she had started in the shower. His wrecked body needed it. Robert pressed on, fighting away the memories of Jenna hanging on every word.

'So you're telling me that you've never heard of anyone called Baxter King?' Robert paced around the bedroom as if he was briefing a jury in court.

'Correct.' Erin spoke without moving her lips as she applied lipgloss.

'And am I right in thinking then that you've never lived in Brighton?'

'Absolutely. I've never even been there.' Erin put on her watch.

'So if I said to you that I've heard otherwise, that you do know Baxter King and you did live in Brighton for a number of years, what would you say?' Robert stood directly behind his wife, staring at her in the mirror.

'I'd say you'd heard wrong.' Erin didn't blink, barely breathed and returned Robert's look with perfect composure and an honesty that was hard to question. Her hands were locked together on her legs, the only discernible movement being the minute flicker under her left eye.

Robert saw it and noticed also how she was unable to help a tiny swallow followed by a minuscule jaw twitch – all the things his years of experience trained him not to miss. He'd sat in enough police interview rooms to know the symptoms. Erin was *too* controlled, just too artificial.

'And if I asked you another question, one that could change everything between us forever, do you swear that you'll answer me truthfully?'

'Of course but—'

'Did you once earn a living by having sex for money?' Unable to use the word 'prostitute', Robert spat out the words like machine-gun fire, aimed at the back of Erin's neck.

She swung round to face Robert and stood up. Their faces were inches apart. She held a perfect defence, her frosted blue eyes melting with tears in order to win Robert's sympathy, in order to buy precious seconds to think. Her lips parted a little, not to speak but to display ultra-feminine shock. Robert wondered if she would wipe the back of her hand across her brow and fall gracefully to the carpet.

Instead, they were both knocked off balance by a loud bang downstairs and frivolous teenage banter in the hallway. Within moments, piano music filled the house as Ruby played her latest composition loud and strong.

Robert didn't know what to do. The moment of strike had been missed. Like an army general standing in the war zone with his troops gathered around him, weapons poised, Robert quickly assessed the situation. A third party had inadvertently entered the battlefield, stumbling across territory that was about to become an area of destruction, smoke and bleeding bodies. To spare the innocent, Robert allowed Erin to flee the bedroom. As she went down the stairs, she called out to her daughter, asking why she had come home from school so early.

Robert sat on the dressing-table stool and stared at his reflection. A worn-out face grimaced back, not directly at himself but over his shoulder, following the path by which his wife had just exited. He could still smell her and he felt the warmth of her on the stool. The signs had been there, no doubt. Robert debriefed himself by playing over the scene again in his head.

'So I put it to you,' he said quietly to his reflection, 'that your beloved wife is a skilled liar and a common hooker. I also put it to you, for careful consideration, that you are an idiot for not realising it sooner. Case closed.' He banged his fist on the dressing table. There was nothing more he could do. Erin had answered his question by not answering. He would go back to the office to think, to figure out a suitable sentence. Since his mind was bereft of sense or any vision of the future, he didn't expect he would do much more than sit and stare at the paintings on his wall.

Robert changed into dry clothes. He went downstairs and was about to leave the house but froze in the hallway when he heard a deep voice crooning and laughing around Ruby's words and her now intermittent music. In the dining room, he found Ruby sitting at the piano and a teenage boy leaning awkwardly over the body of the baby grand. The two kids were engrossed in coy conversation and affected giggles and didn't notice Robert listening in the doorway.

'It's *not*!' Ruby insisted, covering her chocolate eyes but leaving her beautiful smile exposed.

'Sounds like it to me,' the boy teased, poking at a few random notes on the piano.

'Well, maybe just a little bit,' Ruby confessed. 'But not a love song in the traditional sense, 'cos I don't know you well enough yet. It's more a song of admiration.' Then they both giggled again and Ruby flicked her long hair back over her shoulders, a nervous habit Robert had seen her do many times before. The two teenagers obviously fancied each other like crazy. Robert wasn't sure if he had any rage left in him to fend off the attentions of the scruffy-looking boy.

'Dad!' Ruby squealed. The boy turned round and stood up straight, losing the inane grin on his greasy-skinned face. 'This is Art. Remember I told you about him?'

Robert nodded grimly at the boy, allowing his eyes to briefly study his lanky body. He wore shredded jeans that barely held on to his hips and a faded T-shirt with 'Nuke' splashed across the front. His hair, a muddy, unwashed brown, was long and unruly with glints of yellow smeared at the ends. The boy surprised Robert by holding out his hand.

'Pleased to meet you, Mr Knight,' he said in a voice too deep for someone so skinny. 'Rube was just playing me her new song. It's cool.'

Robert managed to offer his hand in return but didn't bother replying to Art. 'Why aren't you at school, Ruby?' His voice was raw and jagged.

'Study afternoon, Mr Knight,' Art replied when he realised that no credible words were going to come out of Ruby's open mouth.

'Well then, shouldn't you be studying?' Robert hated himself for being cruel to Ruby, especially when she appeared genuinely happy.

'We were going to study up in my room together.' Ruby finally found her voice and blushed at the sound of it.

'I think your mother and I would prefer it if you stayed downstairs to do your work.'

'Nonsense, Robert.' Erin came into the dining room from the kitchen carrying a tray of pizza and cans. 'They'll have peace and quiet upstairs. Here you go, love. Can you manage?' Erin handed the tray to Ruby and shot a look at Robert. The teenagers disappeared and so did Erin, back into the kitchen where she began to make a show of banging plates and pots and slamming cupboard doors.

'And I'll get more peace at the office,' Robert yelled towards the kitchen. He left the house with a floor-shaking bang of the front door and drove back to Mason & Knight.

Den was obviously talking to a woman on the telephone. He'd got his feet spread wide apart, his chair pushed back from his desk and he'd loosened his scarlet tie. His face shone with tanned approval as he pushed his fingers through already tousled hair and flirted with the woman on the other end of the line.

'I bet you say that to all your gentleman callers, you tease.' Den grinned into the phone. 'Oh, oh, I don't think that's fair! I'm a perfect gentleman. I hope to show you sometime.' Den raised his arm when he saw Robert standing in his open doorway, beckoning him to sit opposite. 'Yes, I'd like that. Well, maybe I will. I'll call you later and we'll arrange a time. Gotta run now. Bye.'

Den sank back into his chair and broke the knot of his tie completely, leaving it dangling around his open collar. 'Phew, red-hot babe,' he said, expecting a pat-on-the-back kind of response from Robert. Then, sizing up the stiff figure in front of him, Den silenced himself and frowned. 'Robert?'

Robert breathed in deeply, the first decent breath he'd had in hours, and blew out a desolate, choked sigh. He put both hands on his neck and dug his fingers into the tight muscles stretched over his aching bones. As much as he wanted to say, 'There goes another marriage,' he didn't. Instead, he gathered his thoughts and dragged his mind back to business.

'It's the Bowman case. I need you to take over.' He gave no reason; that could wait until he heard Den's reaction to his plea.

'Now tell me what's *really* on your mind, sunny Jim.' Den closed his office door, opened his mahogany drinks cabinet and poured two shots of Jack Daniels. 'Take, drink, and tell me everything.' Den perched on the arm of the leather Chesterfield and waited for Robert to speak.

When Robert did finally manage to produce words that were connected with what was really on his mind, they were broken and incomplete and skirted hesitantly around the issue that he had reason to believe his wife was once a prostitute.

'Basically, we're not getting on too well. Bit of a mess, truth be told. Stuff in the past, that kind of thing.' Robert knocked back his drink.

Den shifted uneasily and waited. Dealing regularly with difficult clients, he knew that squeezing facts, the extra gem that could secure victory in court, depended on giving them time, room to think. Leave a big gap for the truth after all the lies and confusion are done with.

But when, after several minutes had passed and Robert continued to drop further from reality with the weight of his problems, Den realised that his usual tactic wasn't going to work. He said, ordering rather than asking, 'Dinner at my house tonight. I'll call Tula and let her know. If you need, you can stay overnight.'

Robert nodded and held up his glass for a refill. As he downed the next shot, his head and chest began to unravel and Erin and Baxter King and Jed Bowman and Ruby's new boyfriend all went a little muzzy at the edges.

Den instructed Robert to go for a head-clearing walk while he wrapped up some work on a case due in court first thing in the morning. He said they would leave the office at six because Tula always served dinner at seven and that would give them time for a pre-dinner drink and private chat in the library before they ate.

Robert was comforted by the routine of it and did as he was told by taking a walk through Greenwich Park. He ended up beside the Roman ruins, a spot where he and Erin had taken picnics on several occasions soon after they'd met. Their stroll along Lovers' Walk had sent pinwheels of excitement through him as he anticipated what it would be like to make love to the exquisite and mysterious woman he had recently met. Just the suggestion of anything to do with lovers while he was in Erin's company – be it a film or book or the words of a song – aroused him insanely. But the best part, and he wanted to savour it for as long as possible, was the waiting, the not having her completely. He treated her like one of the rare flowers in the shop where he had first noticed her, arranging displays and dealing with paperwork while he watched and pretended to choose flowers. He cared for her like he wanted the exotic beauty to last forever. Even then, he knew he would love her. Even then, he knew flowers wilted.

Robert walked back towards the boating lake and took a bus, something he never did, and returned to the office. Den had been right. The still summer air and hazy sunshine had eased the pressure in his head and for half an hour at least he had been able to think of the good times he and Erin had shared. It made everything seem not so hopeless. That even if Baxter King was right, that if his wife did have a messed-up past, there was a flicker of optimism he might be able to deal with it.

Now he was standing in the Masons' kitchen, a thirty-foot-square room with stainless-steel appliances and a black and white checked floor, while Den popped the cork on a bottle of Faustino.

Tula was like a tiny mammal, Robert thought, as she scurried about the vast room in which everything was enormous. Even the refrigerator was the size of a double wardrobe. Tula wore tight black trousers with a lacy top stretched over her new, improved breasts, and a mass of gold jewellery accented her neck which was ridiculously smooth for a woman of her age. She also had on a navy and white striped butcher's apron which, because she was so petite, came down past her knees.

'My poor darling,' she'd crooned when Den and Robert had arrived. Robert thought she was talking to her husband but was quickly embraced by the spindly woman, who had to stand on her toes to kiss him. 'Den's told me you have woman troubles again. And so soon into your marriage.' Tula returned to the car-sized professional cooking range and stirred a sauce. 'You want to do what Denny does to me, sweetie, when we have a tiff. Send her off to a health farm. It'll do her no end of good. She's obviously stressed and probably needs a good detox.' Tula dipped her finger in the sauce and tasted it. 'I can give you a number.'

Robert smiled, warmed by the familiarity and inane

comments that he could always rely upon from Tula. Everything about her had been reshaped or uplifted or enhanced or implanted or removed. When she wasn't in a Harley Street clinic begging her beloved surgeon to take away just a little more of her nose or to stretch her skin a little tighter, she was either at Madeley's, the private club where he and Den played squash, being massaged or cleansed or shrunk in some kind of wrap, or she was lunching with friends, planning their next tropical vacation. And children weren't a possibility for the couple, even if Den had wanted a family. Her body, she'd said, would be ruined.

Robert loved Tula deeply. She was everything he didn't want in a woman and they got along flawlessly.

'Come here,' he said, placing his wine glass on the marble worktop. 'I'm being rude.' He walked up to Tula and grabbed her round the shoulders, lifting her off the floor. He pressed his face into her stiff, dazzling blonde hair and kissed her head. 'I'm a grumpy old sod at the moment so forgive me. It's good of you to have me over and dinner smells . . .' he took the wooden spoon from Tula and tasted the redcurrant and rosemary sauce, 'it smells and tastes divine. Just what I need.'

'Summer lamb.' She grinned up at him. 'You can't beat it.'

Den guided Robert into his library. Their footsteps echoed as they walked through the Travertine-lined reception hall and into the oak-panelled room that was Den's private retreat. 'Welcome to my botox-free zone,' Den had said when he'd first shown Robert around their newly acquired pseudo-Georgian house. 'Tula and her cronies aren't allowed in here. Strictly off limits.'

The room had everything he needed – a plasma screen television concealed behind an oil painting of a hunting scene, a well-stocked bar with built-in refrigerator, a mahogany desk which masked the latest computer technology, a half-sized snooker table, a dark green leather suite positioned around the fireplace, and a wall of well-stocked bookshelves. Robert could see no reason why his partner needed the rest of the house, except when he had to eat or bathe.

But Robert wasn't envious of Den's fortune. His father, the late William Edmond Frederick Mason, had set up Mason & Mason nearly fifty years ago with his own father. When Den's grandfather passed away, Den naturally filled the gap, having newly graduated from law school.

Robert had qualified at the same time but instead of having an easy passage into a family firm in the City, he fought his way through provincial firms further north. The experience he gained was invaluable and when Den's father died of a heart attack, Robert was the man Den called upon to become his new partner and Mason & Mason became Mason & Knight.

But the old firm, in the last years of William Mason's life, had lost the prestige it once had. Too ill to keep the important corporate clients he had nurtured for decades, Mason senior entrusted the business mostly to his son, Dennis, who spent the next few years enjoying the good life. Mason & Mason suffered as a consequence. Most of the cases they dealt with now were matrimonial, with the occasional litigation client coming their way. But it was a living, and these days a good one; Mason & Knight had earned a reputation as a specialist international family law firm.

Den had finally succumbed to routine. Perhaps more a result of age and lack of time than anything else, although once or twice a year he treated himself to an extra-marital fling. But Den was a loyal friend and an invaluable ally so Robert kept quiet.

'Is she getting it elsewhere?' Den eased himself into a chair.

'Not that simple.' Robert didn't think he was capable of divulging everything he'd discovered about Erin's history and he certainly didn't want Den to know that he'd been digging through Erin's private letters. It smacked too much of last time. 'Suffice it to say that she's lied to me and even when I confront her with what I know, she still won't admit it.'

'Where is she now?'

'At home, with Ruby. Keeping a close eye on her, I hope. Ruby's got a new boyfriend. A bloody gypsy, would you believe.' Robert leaned forward, the leather squeaking beneath him, and asked his partner earnestly, 'How do I do it, Den? My wife's not who I thought she was and my daughter's in love with a dope-head hippy despite sending her to one of the most expensive private schools in London.' He managed an incredulous laugh when he heard the words out loud instead of banging about in his head.

'Not who you thought she was?' Den latched on to the snippet of information.

'She hasn't been honest about her past and I'm not sure whether to believe her denials or the source of my information.'

'Denials? So she's declaring her . . .' Den paused, searched for the right word, '. . . her innocence?'

Den had hammered the truth home. While Erin had flatly denied knowing Baxter King or ever living in Brighton, she hadn't actually rebuffed his accusation. She'd had the chance, a tiny window of opportunity before she had run downstairs to greet Ruby, but instead she had avoided answering.

Robert sighed. 'No. She's not declared anything.'

'I see,' Den said thoughtfully. He was stabbing in the dark to figure out what Robert was implying. He wouldn't press his partner too hard. 'Have you thought of getting Critchley's bloke involved? What's-his-name, the chap who does all his digging?'

Robert wasn't sure if he should say, but he did anyway. 'I looked up Louisa when you told me she was back in England. We met at a country hotel and I saw her in London earlier today, got her a place to stay—'

'Hang on, Rob mate.' Den wasn't sure he was keeping up. 'You had a dirty weekend with Louisa, saw her again in a hotel today, and you're angry at Erin?' Den was laughing, approving almost.

'It's not like that.' Whatever he said, he knew Den would read it as he pleased. 'I've hired her. She's going to investigate this mess for me. It's best that I don't go steaming in any more than I have to. After last time,' he added. 'But keep it quiet. If Erin finds out I've hired Louisa, that'll be it between us.'

It made Robert realise that he didn't want it to be over. It also made him realise that because he'd been wrestling with guilt and dealing with grief after Jenna's death, he'd completely overlooked the signs, glaring and obvious to most, that Erin wasn't all she claimed to be. He'd not even been on the rebound; he was *ricocheting* through the post-Jenna days. Erin had been the light, him the moth.

Tula called them for dinner. The conversation reverted to the ghastly garden design team who had made a botch with the Japanese maples – they were in quite the wrong place, Tula moaned – and the Bowman case, which Robert again asked Den to take over. Den refused.

'Got too much on, I'm afraid. You're on your own on that one.'

'Oh well, I'll just have to represent him then. With any luck, we can wrap it up in one hearing. It's those kids I feel sorry for, living with the man they've seen beat up their mother countless times.' Robert instantly realised what he'd said.

'Your client's admitted that?' Den said through a mouthful of lamb.

Robert sighed and laid down his knife and fork. 'His wife, Mary Bowman, came to see me the other day. She said she was going to let her husband have the children. She looked like she'd been in a car accident.'

While Den remained silent, chewing and pondering, Robert thought about what he had just said. Mary Bowman was going to let her husband *have* the children. What right did she have to give them away? And what right did Jed Bowman have to claim possession in the first place? It seemed clear to Robert now: the children should be allowed to speak for themselves. At their age, one was eleven and the other thirteen, they were capable of deciding where they wanted to live. He considered the same situation with Ruby in mind and knew without doubt that he was right. Both he and Erin, if they should split, would respect their daughter's wishes about where she would reside, although in this particular instance Robert had no claim over his stepdaughter. But it proved to him that no one had the right to ownership, least of all parents like Jed and Mary Bowman.

'I'm not sure that colluding with the opposition is entirely—'

'Leave it, Den. I'll handle it.' Robert raised his hands to halt the conversation.

Robert paid the cab driver and walked carefully up the steps to his front door. He was well fed and after the wine and cognacs his thoughts were pleasantly numbed and ready to deal with Erin in a mellow way.

Following the lamb, Tula had served baked fruit with crème fraîche and then Den had led Robert back into his library where they sat and talked and drank brandy for another couple of hours. With Den's help, although Den still wasn't aware of the entire truth, Robert decided that he needed to adopt the 'innocent until proven guilty' tack and lay off Erin. He was a lawyer, after all, and slamming his wife on the say-so of Baxter King, a complete stranger, was a pretty low act. Den convinced Robert to go home and apologise, whatever their problem was, and talk things over calmly in the morning.

The house, as Robert expected, was dark and quiet. The neon-green digital display on the oven clock blinked eleven thirty. Robert drank some water and collected his thoughts before going up to his bedroom. He knew he would feel rough tomorrow, having consumed more alcohol in one day than he usually did in a week.

Erin had forgotten to close the bedroom curtains and an orange glow from the street light flooded the room in a dangerous shade of amber. Robert stopped when he saw that their bed was empty. Stupidly, he pulled back the undisturbed quilt to make sure Erin hadn't slipped out of sight. She must be sleeping in the guest room or tucked up beside Ruby. He crept across the landing, only to find that the spare bed was also unoccupied, and as he pushed Ruby's bedroom door open a few inches, his breathing halted completely when, again illuminated by amber light, he saw her bed was empty, too.

Cursing, Robert marched back to his bedroom, snapped on the light and flung open the wardrobe doors. Most of Erin's clothes were missing while some lay heaped on the floor of the cupboard. On the dressing table, her jewellery box was gone and in the bathroom all female toiletries and Erin's toothbrush were absent. He checked Ruby's room, and while more belongings remained, it was obvious that clothes and personal items had been packed and removed.

Robert fell onto Ruby's bed and pushed his face into the pillow. He felt as bereft as the day when he'd finally managed to dispose of Jenna's possessions from their home. Piece by piece he had packed her away and shipped her off to charity shops, grieving relatives, the dustbin; her life nothing more than a couple of visits to the council tip.

Robert, she said.

He jerked his head up, hopeful it was Erin. When Robert realised it was Jenna's voice, urging him not to repeat his mistakes, he finally acknowledged that Erin and Ruby had left him.

SEVENTEEN

Sarah comes to see me every week. It's a comfort for both of us. I never take any money from her but I always lay out the tarot, always scam a shot of hope in an otherwise bleak life. She hasn't told her father that she's carrying a baby. It tells me how much attention he pays to his beautiful daughter because her belly is proving like bread dough.

She's visiting on Saturday at six o'clock this week. Her father and brothers are going to a family celebration, and like all good Cinderellas, she's not invited.

'It's men only,' she tells me when Saturday finally comes. The week has dragged by and clients have been scarce. I get ready for her visit two hours before she's due. 'I'm glad not to be going,' she says. 'I'm not feeling very well.'

I guide her to the chair and switch on one bar of heat on the electric fire. The sun seems to have dropped too soon and, despite being June, there is an unusual chill in the air. Andy and I were going to open up the tiny fireplace and have real log blazes but we never got round to it before he left.

I reach my arms around Sarah's belly, as if to welcome the baby into my home. Sarah smiles.

'I can feel his shape,' I tell her. 'That's his foot there and that lump could be an elbow.' I place Sarah's hand on her baby's protuberances and her grin broadens. I make her

199

happy and I'm happy because there is a baby in the house again. 'You will still visit me, won't you, when he's born?' It suddenly occurs to me that perhaps she won't need my friendship when the new love comes into her life.

'I want you to be his godmother,' she says. The roof lifts on my miserable existence and sunshine pours in, making everything look like it's been painted bright yellow.

After the press conference Andy and I didn't take our eyes off the telephone or the television. Sheila moved in with us although she sent Don back home, mainly because he was offering me sympathy and that, as far as Sheila was concerned, wasn't something I deserved.

The next day our story was on the front page of most newspapers, local and national. When it was obvious there wouldn't be any immediate developments, like a body, the reporter's vans gradually diminished as other news became more exciting.

That was it really, apart from a couple of mentions on the evening news and radio bulletins. Our story slipped further down the list until we fell off the bottom. Several of the nationals ran a follow-up story and more pictures of Natasha a week later, reminding the country that our baby was still lost. But before long the people of Britain had forgotten us; we were old news and our plight was in the hands of the police.

Of course, had Natasha been found alive and well, that would have caused a spatter of stories for a day or so but what the press really wanted was a body. Natasha's dead body would have set the presses rolling triple time, but for now, more important things were happening in the world like Russia announcing stuff about their nuclear stash.

Sheila, despite her pursed lips and severe hairstyle and

choppy way of speaking, kept us alive in the weeks that followed Natasha's disappearance. By attending to the basics of life, such as cooking, cleaning, washing, deflecting phone calls, shopping and sending away unwelcome visitors, she allowed Andy and me to grieve as the faint thread of spider-spun hope stretched and thinned and eventually snapped. As February drew to a close, Natasha minus seven weeks, we knew that we would never see our baby again.

Andy lost his job during the same week that they suspected me of murdering Natasha. I can't remember clearly whether Detective Inspector Lumley and PC Miranda hauled me in for questioning before or after Andy came home early, angry as sin, saying he'd been fired for spending too much time in the toilets. I could tell by the clear lines cut through his grimy face that he'd been sobbing a while in the loos. We both sobbed every day but not in front of one another and not for the same reasons.

Sheila finally moved back to her own house but visited regularly, mainly to see Andy, to bring round bags of frozen stew and soup. The day I was taken in for questioning she'd called by unexpectedly and handed me a box of food for the freezer, knowing I was still incapable of shopping, but she wouldn't come in when I said that Andy was out.

A few minutes after she'd left, there was another knock at the door and I recall thinking that she'd changed her mind, that perhaps I wasn't such a careless daughter-in-law after all and maybe it wasn't entirely my fault that her granddaughter was gone. I skipped back to the door, desperate to be loved by Sheila, feeling the first pang of hope in ages that something good could come of this, but it was the police standing there. Detective Inspector George Lumley and PC Miranda, all serious, requested that I accompany them to the station for questioning. Once again my world crashed into an unfathom-able vortex of noise.

I was allowed to put on my shoes and a coat and lock up the house. I sat in the back of the police car with PC Miranda next to me. I wanted to grab her by the shoulders, pull her hair, scratch her face, poke out her eyes – anything to make her consider the time we had spent together in the days immediately after Natasha was taken. She was my ally in the endless and lonely search for my baby. She was the person who had reeled me through the early days, consoled me and talked endlessly to me about the future, that there would be one, and once she had even bathed me when I'd vomited and my hair was matted. PC Miranda had gone above and beyond the call of her duty. Now she was just doing her duty.

'You're not being arrested, Cheryl. The detective inspector just wants to get a few things clear about what happened that day.' PC Miranda patted my leg and gave me a forced half-smile, which told me I was as good as arrested.

At the police station I was taken to an interview room and told to wait. PC Miranda sat with me but didn't talk. The room was cold and everything in it was grey. When she saw me shivering, she went and fetched me a coarse blanket. That was grey, too. She offered me a cup of tea but I couldn't drink it. While I waited, I was thinking, am *I* the criminal now?

DI Lumley came into the room with another policeman who I didn't recognise. Lumley was tall with broad shoulders and an impatient face with small features. His eyes looked like boiled sweets that had been sucked away and his nose was a crooked line, too narrow for such a wide man. Now that he wasn't on my side any more, he didn't look very nice.

PC Miranda moved me over to a melamine table and I sat on one side while the police sat opposite. They each had clipboards and there was a tape recorder between us. They switched it on and began to log dates and case numbers and state who was present in the room. I'd seen all this before, on the television, when criminals were arrested. I tried to remember what it was I was meant to have done but all I could focus on was that I'd lost my baby.

Lost my baby, I repeated over and over. Lost my baby.

Perhaps they were questioning me because I'd been so careless. That could be a crime, leaving your car unlocked or indeed leaving your baby in the car in the first place. Maybe I was unfit to be a mother and I deserved to be locked up.

'This won't take long, Mrs Varney. There are just a couple of things we want to clarify about . . .' DI Lumley paused, glanced at his partner and then continued. 'About the day that your baby was abducted. I know this isn't easy and I want to assure you that I have a number of my top men working on this case. But we have very little to go on and just need your clarification on a couple of points.'

'Of course,' I said. My shoulders were hunched and hurt whichever way I sat. Since Natasha had gone, my body had begun to shrivel and desiccate. I was managing to eat a little these days and had sips of water and tea but even so, my bones dug into whatever I sat on and ached as if they were going to snap. My hair was falling out too. 'I'll try to help.'

'I'd like to start with the bootee.' Lumley looked at his associate and nodded. The other man produced a sealed plastic bag from behind his clipboard. It contained Natasha's knitted boot, the one that I'd found in the street. It was squashed flat and looked greyer than I remembered. 'Do you recognise this item, Mrs Varney?'

I wanted to kick their legs under the table, reach out and punch their chins, gouge out their eyes to show them a fraction of the pain I was suffering, would always be suffering. But that would only bring them closer to their goal, to find a suspect. I would fit the bill nicely, because they hadn't made any progress. Unsolved cases cluttering his desk obviously didn't please DI Lumley. He'd never really been sympathetic to my trauma. Now he was reduced to searching under his nose for a solution. Futile follow-ups on the leads they'd so far investigated had driven them to me. I took the plastic bag from the policeman. Inside was Natasha's bootee, a little muddy, but definitely the one I found that awful day.

'Of course I recognise it. I've already told you all this.'

'Take another look, Mrs Varney. Study it very closely. Is there any possibility that it isn't your baby's?'

'No. It's hers, I tell you.' I gave the bootee another quick glance. 'Sheila, my mother-in-law, knitted a pair of bootees and a matching hat. I found this on the high street when I realised Natasha was gone and I saw someone running away through the car park. They were carrying a baby. It must have fallen off Natasha's foot when the . . .' it's hard but they're making me angry, 'when the kidnapper took her. They always used to fall off.'

'I see.' DI Lumley made some notes on his clipboard and then requested something else from his associate. He was handed a piece of paper. 'Mrs Varney, what if I told you that this isn't your baby's bootee and that you are mistaken. Naturally, we have interviewed your mother-in-law, Sheila Varney, and requested that she provide us with a sample of wool from the bootee and hat set that she knitted. Fortunately, she had some wool left over and when the sample was analysed, it was found to be a completely different brand and mix of wool to the one this bootee is made from.' DI Lumley took the bag from my fingers and held it up, shaking it so that the bootee danced. 'The lab report is conclusive. This bootee is not the one made by Sheila Varney.'

DI Lumley slid the piece of paper across the table to me. I stared at it but didn't understand it. It was scientific jargon from the police forensic department.

'But it is Natasha's, I swear.' My voice began to crumble and my eyes filled with tears. How could they do this to me? It was the only glimmer of hope I had, a finger pointing them to Natasha, and now they were disputing the trail. 'How many little bootees like this can there be? Perhaps Sheila gave you the wrong sample of wool. She's got a whole basket stuffed full of wool.' I was desperate for them to believe me.

'Of course we considered that possibility so we also ran a DNA test on the skin cells harvested from the bootee.' Lumley stopped there, his lips chewing together as if he could hardly contain the words he wanted to hurl at me. His partner slid another piece of paper across the table to me. I glanced at it but again it didn't make sense. 'We hoped to match it to Natasha's DNA sample that we took from her hairbrush.'

'And? ' I gathered my thoughts and compacted my voice into a terse missile. I didn't want DI Lumley to think that I was getting agitated.

'The test was negative, Mrs Varney. No match. This bootee is definitely not your baby's.'

How can they know all this? I wondered. Be so sure about the opposite of what I'm telling them?

I came out of the shop and my baby was gone. The car was empty. I saw someone running . . . I found the bootee . . .

'Moving on, Mrs Varney, we also need to clarify about the cake.'

'Are you going to show me that too, all sealed up in a bag? It'll be a bit mouldy after all these weeks.' My head dropped forward onto the edge of the table and I exhaled. PC Miranda was suddenly beside me, stroking my back, probably warning me to watch what I said. I'd heard of innocent people being arrested for crimes they didn't commit. If I offered enough little signs of desperation, they would eventually add up to one big piece of evidence and I would be arrested. But what crime was I supposed to have committed? How could I steal my own baby? What were they implying?

'In your statement from the afternoon of Saturday, the fourth of January, you told us that you parked your car in the supermarket car park, see attached plan for exact location of vehicle, and went into the shop carrying your purse in order to purchase a cake to take to your mother-in-law's house. You left your baby Natasha asleep in the car. You paid cash for your cake at the express checkout and when you returned to your vehicle Natasha was not there.' He stared at me, his trained eyes boring into me.

'That's right,' I said.

'Perhaps you could explain then, Mrs Varney, why the supermarket's accounting records show that you paid for your cake on your Visa debit card a full twenty minutes *after* you claim that you purchased the cake for cash?'

How could I explain to Detective Inspector Lumley and his mute assistant that I had paid for the cake twice? Would it not alert their police instincts that something was amiss if I told them that the pathetic woman sitting before them had actually purchased the cake for a second time when she should have been alerting the police and searching for her stolen baby?

'I didn't mean for her to scan the cake again. I was going to tell her.'

'Who?' Lumley snapped.

'The girl at the checkout.'

'Tell her what?'

'That I'd lost my baby.'

'So why didn't you?'

'Because . . .' This is hard. I'll be in a pickle, I know, but he's asking me for the truth. 'Because I thought I was mistaken. When the checkout girl scanned my cake, it all seemed so *real*. Like I'd just gone into the supermarket for the cake as I'd planned and anything bad that had happened was all in my mind. For a few minutes I convinced myself that Natasha was still in the car and I was buying my cake.'

'For the first time?' Lumley added.

'Yes. I thought I was buying it for the first time and Natasha was still in my car.'

'But really Natasha was missing at this point and you were buying the cake for the second time.'

'Yes.' I hated myself. I was going to tell the checkout girl, who could have called the police. But I didn't. I didn't tell her. It was my first mistake.

'Why do you think you got muddled, Mrs Varney? After having already seen that your baby wasn't in your car, what was it exactly that made you think she *was* in your car when you were waiting to buy the cake for the second time?'

I swallowed and coughed. PC Miranda slid the cup of tea towards me and I sipped but it had gone cold.

'I don't know,' I whispered. 'I was tired. I'd been up all night. I got confused.'

'Why had you been up all night?' Lumley pushed back in his chair. It creaked under his weight. He was the kind of man who would have to buy his clothes at the big and tall shop.

'Natasha wouldn't sleep. I couldn't settle her.' It struck me that perhaps she sensed what was going to happen to her and that had caused her screaming fits.

'Did you often have nights like that? Was she a good sleeper or a bad sleeper generally?'

'Was?' I said.

'I mean "was" to describe the period before your baby was abducted, Mrs Varney. Not "was" in the terminal sense of the word. Well, was she a good sleeper?'

I nodded at Lumley and suddenly they both began scribbling notes frantically. Lumley glanced across at his associate.

'We have the health visitor's report, Mrs Varney, and it would suggest that Natasha wasn't a good sleeper at all. Since her birth in November, it appears that you visited or telephoned the health visitor thirty-seven times reporting problems with Natasha, mostly to do with sleeping or crying. Did Natasha cry a lot, Mrs Varney?'

I shrugged my shoulders. 'She was a baby. Babies cry.' *Is* a baby, I screamed in my head.

'Did you ever harm Natasha because she cried continuously or wouldn't sleep?'

I stared at Lumley. I fixed him with cold eyes. I wouldn't let him do this to me. Someone had stolen my baby.

'Perhaps you shook her to shut her up? Maybe held the pillow over her face for a few seconds too long, just to get some peace?' Lumley leaned forward across the table. I could smell coffee on his breath. 'Is that what happened, Mrs Varney?'

Gathering all the strength I had left, I leaned forward also, bringing our faces close. 'I didn't kill my daughter, if that's what you're implying, Detective Inspector. I'm only speaking calmly like this now, instead of screaming at you, because I scarcely have the will to live any more. If you knew how I had to force myself to even take the next breath, you would withdraw what you just asked me. If you have just one nerve of compassion running through your body you will let me go home and grieve with my husband.'

But Lumley was relentless. 'Grieve, Mrs Varney? Surely grieving is a little premature? We mustn't give up hope of finding Natasha alive and well. You've said so yourself. You've let hope keep you going this far.'

'OK, I meant—'

'Interview with Mrs Cheryl Varney concluded at fourteen seventeen p.m.' Lumley stood, looming over me like a cold front from the north. 'You're free to go. We very much appreciate you helping us and rest assured we'll be in touch if there's any news of your baby.'

The two policemen left the interview room and PC Miranda guided me to the reception area where I was told a car would take me home. I waited for an hour and a half and when nothing happened, I called a taxi. I went home and slept.

Two days later, Lumley arrived on my doorstep at 6 a.m. with three other officers and a warrant to search my house. For twelve hours I watched as they sifted through drawers and cupboards and took apart furniture and discovered things that I'd long forgotten. They crawled in the loft and picked through old photos and books, helped themselves to my underwear and clothing and spent a curiously long time bagging items from Natasha's room.

Then they went into the garden. I made myself a cup of tea and sat at the kitchen table, watching them crawl through my untidy patch like giant beetles. There was a flurry of activity when they exhumed the skeleton of our long-dead cat. They didn't find anything else.

*

I ask Sarah how she thinks her father will react to her having a christening for the baby. She says that her father will have used up all his rage and cut her off from the family by then anyway so he will never know about the christening. She wants to do it for the baby's English father, Jonathan. He is in the year above Sarah at school and she tells me that Jonathan isn't his real name, like Sarah isn't hers, but she still wants to keep coming to see me because I provide her with comfort and a safe place to be.

'Will you tell me your baby's real name?'

'Of course,' she replies, biting into one of my home-baked scones. Crumbs settle on her bump. I am a bit upset that, after the six or seven weeks she has been coming to visit me, Sarah has not been able to tell me her real name. I know that she worries I will tell her father and give away her secret but surely he will find out anyway soon, when his daughter arrives home with a baby.

'Why don't you bring Jonathan round to see me one day? I'd like to meet him.' Sarah looks shy and just eats her scone. She doesn't reply.

We talk for a couple of hours and watch television and I fetch some photographs down from the spare bedroom to show Sarah. I sit close to her and put my arm around her. Her shoulders feel bony so I make her eat another scone. I don't want her baby to be underweight. You'd barely notice she's pregnant and she's nearly due. I've left one box of photographs upstairs. That box contains pictures of Natasha.

'There's Andy and me on holiday. What a state I looked!'

'Was he your husband?' Sarah asks.

'Yes. We divorced a long time ago.'

'You had a husband and you let him go?' Sarah is wide-eyed and has crumbs on her bottom lip. She is beautiful and I know her baby will be too.

'We had many problems,' I tell her. 'Problems that could never be worked out.'

I miss out the bit about Andy transforming into a festering, nervous sack of hate who spat at me and beat me and destroyed my clothes and cut my hair when I was asleep.

I don't tell Sarah that Andy rigged my car so that I crashed into a hedge and how he tried to poison my food with turpentine. She perhaps wouldn't understand that Andy's anger towards me grew so colossal that I could feel it rubbing red-hot against me even when he was out of the house. He dragged it around like a stretched and infected tumour, refusing to let go of it or get help or let anyone lance it. Andy blamed me entirely for Natasha's disappearance.

'Jonathan and I won't have any problems. We love each other.' Sarah lifts her toes and warms them in front of the electric fire. She is wearing a sari today to help conceal her bump and she has luminous pink and green toe socks on her feet. The material of her sari flows over the baby in generous folds of emerald and purple, which are stitched and edged with gold. She isn't wearing any make-up and now that she is in her final trimester, her skin looks like finely brushed suede and her hair is long and glossy. I am so excited about the baby.

'Read my palm again.' She laughs, snuggling up against me. 'Show me the baby lines.' Sarah smells of cardamom and cumin and cinnamon. She is like a big tandoori cooking pot. I take her hand and study the crazed brown grooves in her beige palm.

'Look, that's your baby.' I don't mention the broken lines or all the other children she will bear.

She grins and takes my left hand, tracing her long nail

around my palm. 'So that must be *your* child line there. Cheryl, look, you're going to have a baby!'

I smile too and slowly look up at her, our faces so close, our thoughts so far apart.

'Yes, I am,' I say and bring her hand to my mouth for a little kiss.

EIGHTEEN

Robert spent the night on Ruby's bed. He was fully clothed and when he woke, his neck was creased with pain and his legs were cramped and tingling. He didn't remember immediately but as his eyes adjusted to the early morning sunlight, Erin and Ruby's sudden departure cut through his drowsy consciousness.

He sat up and the remains of Den's cognac and Tula's rich food coupled with the nauseous truth curdled his stomach. Calmly, without overreaction, Robert showered, dressed in fresh clothes and drank a gallon of black coffee while he decided what to do. He called Den at home but was greeted by the answer machine. At seven thirty, Den would most likely still be asleep and wouldn't even be thinking of going into the office for another two hours. Robert left a brief message telling his partner he would be taking the day off. He left another message on Tanya's voicemail asking her to cancel all his appointments.

Then he called Louisa. On the second ring, she answered with a cheery although breathless greeting.

'You just caught me. I've been in the hotel gym,' she said. 'I didn't fancy running in the rain.'

Robert glanced out of the window. Large droplets of a weighty summer shower had begun to pelt the glass. His

213

stomach rolled at the thought of Erin and Ruby out in bad weather.

'You're a driven woman, Louisa.' He paused, hoping she would make another idle comment but she didn't. She perhaps sensed the underlying layer of stress in his words, like one of those voice lie detecting devices. 'Look, something's happened,' he confessed.

'Oh?'

Robert thought he heard her sipping on something. 'Erin and Ruby have left me.'

'Oh,' she said, swallowing. 'That's not good.'

'Will you come over?' Robert didn't like the sound of what he'd just asked. It made him sound needy, and while in one way he was, he knew that a needy man would likely turn Louisa off helping him. He scoured his hand across his stubbly chin, making a mental note to shave, and wondered why he was bothered what she thought.

He was married. His wife had just left him.

He continued resignedly. 'I'd like you to get started on this case as soon as possible. I want to know where Erin and Ruby have gone and I have to know the truth about Erin's past. If I get involved, I'll get swept sideways and mess things up. I need you to take control, Louisa.'

'Give me half an hour. I'll bring my laptop and by then I should have received the birth certificate results.' She was eating something now.

'That was quick work.' Robert poured more coffee, wishing he could be as disciplined as Louisa.

'They don't mess about. We may not need to take this any further, you realise, Rob. When Ruby's birth certificate is located and Erin comes back with her tail between her legs, you can kiss and make—'

'It's not that simple any more, is it?'

'Look, I can't possibly know where they've gone but what I can do is prove a few basic facts to you to illustrate that actually nothing is wrong in your life.' Robert started to speak but Louisa wouldn't have it. 'Rob, half an hour and I'll be there.' The line went dead. He sighed. She was still acting as his friend, not a private investigator.

Despite Louisa's promise, Robert felt something unfurling and stretching within him, a phoenix-like creature that had lain dormant for over a year since Jenna had died and suppressed by the magic of his marriage to Erin. But now that she had gone and the lid on suspicion had lifted, the phoenix was rising, woken by the heat from Robert's welling anger and paranoia. A fire deep inside him was sparking and spitting with familiar obsession. It felt as if Jenna had returned and was making him live through it again, perhaps this time to get it right.

Robert took the stairs two at a time and went into Erin's study to retrieve the box containing the letters from Baxter King. He needed to take a closer look at their correspondence. But the box was gone. Erin had taken it with her.

While waiting for Louisa, Robert trawled through his wife's computer files again but found nothing relevant. He rummaged through papers lying on the desk, work that Erin had brought home from the shop, but again it revealed nothing. He wondered about the shop – would Erin be opening up as usual? Would she take Ruby to school? He hoped that she would keep routine as normal as possible for Ruby's sake and he decided to visit the shop after Louisa had begun work.

Forty minutes later, when Louisa still hadn't arrived and he had exhausted the possibilities in Erin's study, Robert stopped on the landing outside Ruby's slightly open bedroom door. Saddened by its emptiness, he went in and flopped down on her bed.

'Erin, Erin,' he sighed, pummelling his tired eyes. He breathed in the soft scent of Ruby's sweet body spray and smiled at the tatty layers of rock star, actor and cute animal posters covering her walls, showing that she was indeed on the cusp of little girl and young woman.

Robert stared up at the ceiling. From this angle, he had never noticed what a jewelled universe of sparkles and trinkets and treasure Ruby had created in her room. From every point on Ruby's ceiling there hung a glittering mobile, each one twirling in its own fantastic current. He recalled fighting one or two of the things off his head when he came in to say goodnight but, lying on the bed staring up into the cosmos they formed, Robert could see why Ruby collected them. They were magical. An escape – perhaps to that other place Ruby always seemed to be.

One mobile in particular caught Robert's attention. It was made up predominantly from quartz crystal, maybe twenty or thirty chunks arranged like a decadent chandelier hanging heavily above the bed. But dropping from the centre and virtually concealed by the crystal when viewed sideways, was something gold and oval, something fat and tarnished like an overripe fruit begging to be picked.

Robert stood up to take a closer look. He was desperate for any snippet of information, anything to offer Louisa so she could begin the hunt. Protected by the surrounding crystal, Robert could see that the gold nugget shape was in fact a large locket. It was hanging by its chain from the centre of the mobile and was nothing more than cheap carroty gold and clearly not part of the original decoration at all.

Carefully, he unhooked the chain and locket. He turned it over in his palms, realising that it hadn't been touched in a long while because it was coated with dust and fine, stringy cobwebs. It was hinged on one side and Robert dug his fingernail between the two halves to prise it open. The ornately engraved front of the locket was slightly dented, making it difficult to release but when it finally gave, a faded black and white portrait photograph of a young woman with her hair neatly curling from beneath a fur hat was revealed. Her neck disappeared inside a large fur collar and the background of the picture was nothing more than blurred fuzz. Robert guessed the picture to be from the nineteen forties but he couldn't be sure. He also couldn't be sure of the woman's age although he reckoned she was no more than twenty-five.

Robert slid the photograph out of the locket. It had no doubt been there for many decades and was brittle at the edges. He turned the picture over and saw old-fashioned handwriting. He squinted at the dull ink and virtually illegible words.

'Babka Wystrach,' he read slowly, not knowing if he had pronounced the unusual name correctly. The tiny script was in blue-black ink and very faded. He looked back at the young woman. She was smiling but appeared nervous, a little crease between her eyebrows making her seem unsure about something.

Robert replaced the photograph and snapped the locket shut. He slipped it in his back pocket and went downstairs, glancing out into the street to check for Louisa before telephoning Greywood College. The secretary advised him that Ruby's class register had been returned to the office with his daughter marked as absent. Robert apologised and excused his stepdaughter from school with a stomach bug.

He sighed, dropping down onto a kitchen chair. As he dialled the number of Fresh As A Daisy, he saw a couple of dirty plates and a saucepan left by the kitchen sink – remnants of Erin and Ruby's last supper. If it hadn't been for their missing possessions, he would have worried that they'd been in an accident. If it hadn't been for his paranoia, Ruby would be at school and Erin at the shop.

The number rang out. Erin hadn't opened up. Knowing the result before he tried, Robert called her mobile number, followed by Ruby's. Both times he was diverted to their voicemail services. He didn't bother leaving messages.

'Oh dear,' Louisa said as she strode into the kitchen and booted up her laptop on the table. She scanned the dirty plates and overflowing rubbish bin. 'You might want to think about hiring a cleaner.'

Robert ignored her remark and poured her a black coffee, remembering she didn't take milk. 'I found this in Ruby's room this morning. It may be of some use.' He slid the locket across the table, along with her coffee.

'Don't you have anything herbal? Peppermint or chamomile?'

Robert shook his head. He wasn't paying her to be fussy. 'Open the locket. There's a name inside.'

'One thing at a time, Rob.' Louisa leaned forward, the effect emphasising her slow deliberate words. 'Right . . .' She bit her gloss-slicked bottom lip as she pulled up a newly received email. 'It's from the agency.' Robert leaned over her shoulder, resting his hands on the table as she tapped the mouse pad. He held his breath, reading the message as fast as he could.

' "Search status failed. No documents attached." What

does that mean?' He knew exactly what it meant but wanted Louisa to confirm it.

'That's not what I expected,' Louisa whispered as if Robert wasn't there. 'Surely they've messed this one up.' A quick phone call to the agency confirmed that indeed they hadn't been able to procure a birth certificate for Ruby using very broad search criteria, which should have turned up at least one person named Ruby Lucas. Louisa pulled a face. 'And Erin convinced you that Ruby was definitely registered under the name Lucas?'

'Without doubt,' he replied, remembering how he'd finally pulled the information from her. He dragged out the adjacent chair, careful not to allow his thigh to touch Louisa's as they both stared at the laptop monitor as if it might suddenly explode with answers.

'Well, I don't understand then, Rob—'

'It's obvious. Erin didn't think it necessary to register her daughter's birth, the product of quick, paid-for sex,' Robert interrupted. 'Perhaps she was even going to give her up for adoption but couldn't be bothered with the nuisance paperwork.'

Louisa sipped her coffee. 'Let's think about this, Rob.' But her mobile phone rang and, after a glance at the caller display, she hesitantly took the call. 'Hey,' she said and then listened. 'I can't. I'm working.' She listened again. 'Another few days at least.' A breath verging on a sigh. 'I know. I'm sorry. Bye.' She snapped the phone shut and continued the conversation with Robert as if the call had never happened. 'Let's think about this carefully, Rob—'

'Was that Willem?'

'Yes.' The single word dragged into a thousand.

'You didn't sound very pleased to hear from him.'

'He wants me to come home.'

'That's reasonable.' Robert thought how much he wanted Erin and Ruby home.

'The main issue isn't the birth certificate any more, is it? It's about Erin's shady past, right?' Louisa refused to speak of Willem further.

Robert allowed his leg to relax and it accidentally nudged Louisa's. She was wearing loose black trousers that clung to her runner's thighs and rode up just enough for Robert to catch sight of her ankle and the silver chain round it.

'Yes,' he replied, not really thinking about his reply. As much as he needed to discuss Erin, Louisa's avoidance of her husband had intrigued him. 'But don't you want to go home?'

Louisa sighed. 'I'm working. For you. When this job is wrapped up, I will go home to Willem.' Her voice snagged on something in her throat as she said her husband's name. Robert noticed. 'Although I'm not sure what it is exactly that you want me to do.' She smiled but perhaps didn't mean it.

'You can find out who this woman is, for a start.' He tapped the locket on the table. Louisa turned it over and then popped it open. Like Robert had done, she removed the photograph. 'Then you can get one of your clever agency folk to dismantle Erin's computer and dredge the depths of the hard drive for deleted information. Apparently, it's all recoverable.'

'Rob, don't you think that's going a bit far? Isn't that a bit too much like last time?' She flipped the photograph over. 'Unusual name,' she commented. 'No doubt I can find something out about her. Give me a day to do some research.'

Robert nodded. He wasn't convinced about the computer though. 'Feel free to use my house as a base for internet and, well, whatever. I can give you a key.'

'Thanks. Do you mind if I take a look in Erin's office?'

'Help yourself. She's taken the juicy stuff with her but I can give you Baxter King's details, the man who told me . . . you know.'

'Chances are she'll be home before it's dark. And then where will you be, Robert Knight, having to explain away another woman in your house?' Louisa's face split into a grin worthy of a beauty pageant. 'Now go to work or something and let me get on. I will not allow you to drown in all of this.'

But Robert realised he was drowning and stood staring at nothing in particular as Louisa tapped at the computer as if he wasn't there.

NINETEEN

It occurred to Robert that he should notify the police about Erin and Ruby's disappearance. But police were for crimes and whichever way he looked at it, Erin hadn't actually done anything wrong – not provable in the eyes of the law, anyway, and leaving your husband for being paranoid was not a police matter. Erin had gone freely, taking her belongings with her. The police would laugh and pack him on his way.

Robert took a taxi to Den's house to pick up his car then drove to Fresh As A Daisy. He carried a spare key and let himself in, hoping that Erin hadn't changed the alarm code. She hadn't. The shop was surprisingly dark without its carefully chosen lighting switched on and the air smelled of sugary pollen and stale flower water.

The rain had worsened and the drive to the shop had been slow and expectant, like the clouds that shifted heavily over London. He gained some comfort that capable Louisa was moving things forward but a further layer of guilt clouded his world as he thought of her dry and safe in his home, while Erin and Ruby could be anywhere in the world.

Robert peered up at the fully laden sky through the large front window of the flower shop. He wondered if Erin could see the storm too. Had she noticed the horizontal streaks of lightning that blazed across the horizon? Was she running through the streets, Ruby tagging behind her, both of them soaking and homeless? Robert thumped the plate-glass window and the low resonating sound coincided with a bright flash in the sky.

'Damn you, Erin Knight!' A knot of pain tightened his heart. It was only because he loved her.

Not knowing what else to do, or trusting himself enough to tackle the cases at the office, Robert set about freshening up the flowers. He had a rough idea of what the stock cost and to allow the twenty or so buckets of blooms to perish would be a pricey mistake. He hoped Erin might somehow sense that he was tending to her flowers in her absence, or pick up on the thread of love that really, even with what he knew about her past, had not been totally severed.

Being in love with Erin, as he had been from the minute he first saw her, was as critical as tending to a rare flower, Robert realised as he carefully removed a dozen saffron and cerise orchids from a bucket. He felt as if he was holding a selection of beautiful women, all dressed in exotic silk saris, bowing their heads as he laid them down. He went into the back room and tipped away the stale water, filled up with fresh water and rearranged the stems. This he did for every bucket of flowers and then he methodically sprayed all the arrangements and picked out the wilted heads from the window display. As he worked, several customers rattled the door of the shop but Robert had left it locked with the 'Closed' sign showing.

When he was finished, he sat down behind the counter, pushed back in Erin's chair, and wished he had a cigarette, feeling as empty as he ever had.

Robert kicked the tyre and left the car where it was when he saw the ticket tucked under the wiper blade. He walked without knowing where he was going and ended up in a pub drinking bourbon and, after he pushed a few coins into the machine, he was chain-smoking Marlboro. He hadn't bought a pack since he'd quit when he met Erin and greedily and self-destructively he enjoyed the heady rush of a novice smoker. For another couple of hours he sat alone, silently protesting against everything he had thought was stable in his life but was, in actual fact the complete opposite.

When he left the pub, Robert didn't notice the continuing rain. It was only when he wiped his hand over his drink-numbed face and it came away soaking that he realised he was drenched. The streets around him felt like those on a map – removed, unfamiliar, as if he wasn't really there. He wandered around with nowhere particular to go. His shirt clung uncomfortably to his skin and he was fleetingly reminded of confronting Erin in the shower, fully clothed, fully aware he was driving her away.

He lit another cigarette, the first drag releasing another dose of the bitterness that he'd kept locked up since he'd visited Brighton and learned the truth about Erin. But it was a blurred view of how he felt, an anaesthetised and swirling picture devoid of sensible thoughts that caused him, in his drunken state, to decide to call Baxter King and demand that he tell him everything that he knew about Erin's past.

With half a dozen shots of whisky searing his mind, he huddled in an empty shop doorway and fished in his pocket for his mobile phone. It wasn't there. After cursing and kicking the wall, it slowly dawned on him that he must have left it in the pub but when he tried to find the pub again, he couldn't. He'd walked for ages in an unfamiliar area and hadn't a clue how to retrace his meandering steps. But he still had his wallet and searched for a public telephone box.

Inside the silent, urine-marinated cubicle, Robert was relieved that at least he was out of the rain. His wet clothes and irregular breathing soon fogged up the glass. He picked up the sticky receiver in order to call directory inquiries but stopped suddenly when he saw half a dozen pink, red and black business cards pinned above the telephone.

Red Hot Massage . . . Steamy Sauna with Kinky Nurse . . . Dominatrix . . . Foreign Girls . . . Blonde Girls . . . Busty Girls . . . Young Girls . . .

Robert's sight blurred as he read the grubby advertisements. Some of the cards had pictures of girls who didn't look much older than Ruby. He randomly plucked one off the booth and his eyes filled with grit as he saw the over-made-up face of a woman, older than the others, advertising her body for sale. Her image morphed into Erin's smiling fresh face on their wedding day.

'Helena,' he whispered, 'will massage your troubles away in a private room.' Despite the provocative pose and thick lines of theatrical make-up, Helena was an attractive woman with a shapely body and nipples that pointed at her telephone number.

Without knowing what he was doing, without any sense of reality remaining because it had all been washed away by the drink, Robert dialled Helena's number. All he knew was that he needed someone, *anyone*, to provide answers and expunge him of his misery. Helena, he thought, could be the woman.

Robert found a cab and gave the driver Helena's address. She'd sounded pleasant enough on the telephone and keen to have his business. Robert couldn't wait to meet her although his reasons for their union were very different to Helena's. She was out to make money; he was looking for explanations.

On the journey there, he pictured the woman stripping and slipping between satin sheets in her boudoir, spraying herself with vanilla and musk to tantalise his senses, preparing herself to satisfy her client's needs – as Erin would have done hundreds of times. The only thing Robert had in common with Helena's punters was desperation.

'Thirteen quid, mate.' The driver pulled up next to a row of terraced houses and opened the glass screen. Robert paid and stepped out into the rain. He tentatively walked up to Helena's house and rang the bell. Already he felt dirty.

The front curtains of the house were closed even though it was the afternoon and the doorstep was strewn with litter and dog-ends. He'd sobered up a little during the cab ride but not enough to make him back out. He was prepared to find out about Erin any way he could.

Robert mussed his fingers through his damp hair and remembered his stubble. He knew he looked a mess but it hardly mattered. He wasn't trying to impress anyone. The door opened and he was greeted by a woman wearing a man's navy towelling robe.

'Robert Knight?' she asked. Her voice was rough and deep. She held a cigarette down by her thigh. Robert nodded. 'Better come in then.' She wasn't the woman in the photograph. She couldn't be Helena.

He followed her upstairs, unable to see much of the surroundings because of the poor light but he could smell beer and heard a football match on the television downstairs. 'In here,' the woman said, allowing Robert to enter the bedroom first.

'Nice to meet you, Mr Knight,' she continued, grinning. 'My name, as you know, is Helena.' She closed the door and leaned against it, as if to indicate there was no escape.

But Robert didn't want to escape from Helena, whatever she looked like. He wanted, no, *needed* her – perhaps even more than her usual clients — and was desperate to find out about and understand his wife's secret life. But the thought of touching her body repulsed him. He had to find a way into her mind, to see what drove her. Simply to find out *why*.

'Take a seat and make yourself comfortable.' Helena indicated to the bed and slid a bolt home on the door.

Robert could see more clearly now even though the purple nylon curtains were closed. The room was small and lit by a single lamp. There was little else in there, apart from a chair holding a pile of clothes and a wooden coat stand behind the door. Robert shuddered when he saw that it was draped with whips and leather garments and several pairs of handcuffs. Helena noticed him looking.

'Fancy a bit of that?' She winked.

'Not really my scene,' he croaked. Helena approached the bed and sat down next to him.

'What is your scene then, Mr Knight? What can Helena do for you this afternoon?'

He studied her before answering, trying to see behind her worn-out eyes and catch a shred of reason, to find out why she had turned to prostitution. Her skin was like waxed crêpe paper clinging to her cheekbones and her long hair was over-washed, over-bleached and badly needed styling. Even without seeing her naked, Robert could tell that Helena was very thin. The way her bony fingers pushed the cigarette into an ashtray, the way the collar of her robe swamped her scrawny neck, the way her forehead jutted above her face as if the rest of it had been eroded told Robert that she didn't eat much.

'Just, you know, perhaps we could talk.' Robert swallowed,

wondering why he felt so powerfully protective towards Helena's over-used body. At that moment, he wanted to get to know her more than any other woman in the world and yet he found her as attractive as a dead rat. Was it that she represented Erin? Was she the next best thing?

Robert found himself being pushed gently back onto the pillow. Helena unbuttoned his shirt and attempted to remove his trousers but Robert stopped her with a hand firmly on hers.

Suddenly, the noise from the television downstairs grew louder and Helena scuttled to the door.

'Turn it bloody well down, Josh!' She returned to the bed and removed her robe, grinning at Robert as he lay perfectly still. He couldn't have moved if he'd wanted to. She started to rub his chest, pulling his skin around in rough swirls. 'Don't look so scared, Mr Knight. I won't hurt you.' Helena coughed violently, layer upon layer of tar and phlegm working loose through her cigarette-deepened voice.

'No!' He sat up and stared at her body, unable to speak as an image of Erin's perfect body transposed itself over Helena's. He wanted to reach out and touch her, to see if she really was Erin. He longed to brush his hand along the concave stomach which was made from fabric that had long since lost its stretch, just in case he met with the firmness of Erin's skin.

But Erin disappeared and Robert stared at Helena's breasts. Her huge nipples, hugging the lower portion of the flaccid sacks, looked as if they'd been dipped in melted chocolate.

Not taking no for an answer, Helena's bamboo-like arms and hands pressed firmly into Robert's upper body, lowering him back onto the bed, in what was undeniably a deep, relaxing massage. As she moved around him, he could feel her body warmth and he caught a whiff of her natural scent, the smell of soil after heavy rain mingled with old sweat.

'That's my son downstairs with the bloody telly too loud.' Helena cackled as she worked on Robert. 'Ready for a bit more now, love? You don't seem quite so tense.'

'Your son?' Robert sat up again. It didn't seem right.

'Don't worry. He's used to it. How else am I going to afford the amount of food he puts away or get him through university? I'm a student myself, you know. I've gone back to school to learn something useful.' Helena pushed Robert back onto the bed and dragged her fingers around the rim of his trousers.

'What are you studying?' Robert was incredulous.

'I'm doing psychology and English A levels. Then I want to train as a counsellor. A women's counsellor to help all them screwed-up bags out there.' She laughed and coughed again. 'Like me,' she added when her throat was clear.

Then, in one nimble action, Helena brought her body down upon Robert's. She lay on him like a thin leather hide and began to move provocatively.

Robert lay perfectly still, frozen by what he had learned about her. How desperate, how determined must she be to sell her body to strangers while her son watched television beneath her? As she reached for the button on his trousers again, apparently admiring what she had to work with, Robert swiftly drew up his legs and rolled to the side.

'I'm sorry, I can't. Not with your son and . . . everything.'

That was when Robert realised that everything was Erin; that everything was his life. That everything was what he wanted back and he would stop at nothing to get it.

'And everything?' Helena wasn't angry; she seemed more amused by his withdrawal.

'Stuff in my head.' Robert reached for his shirt. 'I didn't come here wanting to have sex with you.'

'I can cater for all tastes. Just the massage if you prefer.' Helena's low voice betrayed a tinge of desperation. 'Or the whips. You can do it to me if you like.'

'I'll still pay you. It's just that . . .' Robert fingered his hair, '. . . I wanted to know more about how you work. About prostitutes.' He didn't like calling her that, labelling her with such a loaded title. He didn't want to class this woman with his wife.

'What is there to know?' Helena put on her robe and sat on the end of the bed. 'I do it because it makes me a living. Perhaps it's desperation, I dunno. I don't feel desperate though.' She said that as an afterthought and reached into her robe pocket and fished out her cigarettes. She offered one to Robert, who accepted, and they both sat in a sphere of blue-grey smoke discussing how Helena first got into the game.

'I don't see nothing wrong with it. It pays my bills, keeps my son in education and a roof over my head. I provide a service to all you deprived men who might otherwise go preying on young girls.' Robert cleared his throat in protest. 'Present company excluded, of course.' Helena winked. 'I had to do it when my husband left. It started off casual down the pub. If someone came onto me, I'd make it quite clear from the start that they'd have to pay for it. If I met a builder in a pub and wanted an extension building, I wouldn't expect him to do it for free.'

Robert decided not to mention the small issues of love and marriage, trust and respect. Instead, his mind filled with Erin striking a deal, stripping, having sex and hoarding her cash. Did she do it for Ruby? Did Ruby even know that her mother was a hooker? Silently, Robert buttoned his shirt and prepared to leave.

'Why d'you want to know so much, anyhow?'

Robert stared directly at Helena, shuddering partly from his still damp shirt and partly because the image of Erin working like Helena was now firmly burned in his mind. 'Someone I love once earned a living this way. I wanted to find out why.' He breathed out heavily.

'And have you?'

A gap of time, only seconds, but as Robert looked at Helena – her eyes open and honest, her body spent and used – he knew that, yes, he had gained a glimpse of Erin's life before they met. He had coloured in a tiny corner of his paint-by-numbers wife. He didn't like it one bit.

'I think I have,' he admitted. 'She's like you. Determined and a survivor.' Robert leaned forward and kissed Helena hesitantly on the cheek before opening his wallet and removing fifty pounds. 'Most expensive kiss I've ever had,' he said flatly and gave her the money. She took it and stuffed it in her dressing-gown pocket.

'Count yourself lucky, Mr Knight. I don't normally do kissing.'

'Thanks,' Robert added, although thanking the woman for illuminating how his wife once lived seemed a contradiction. He felt worse than ever now about Erin's past. A push-pull game of love and loss. 'And good luck with your studies.'

'Good luck yourself,' Helena growled as she showed him out.

After Robert left Helena's house, he was overwhelmed with need for his wife – to hold her and touch her and love her in all the ways that she would have done for hundreds of others.

He fought hard to keep down the repulsion and begged himself to remember, when he was finally sober again, that his wife must have done it for a reason.

But when he arrived home, when he saw the remnants of life with Erin, when he saw her haphazard possessions, the drooping flowers, the jumbled laundry, the jacket hanging crookedly over the back of a chair, the notes stuck on the fridge to buy tamarind paste and flaked almonds, when he saw all these things with the memory of Helena ghosting his thoughts, he knew that before he'd met with Helena, forgiveness would have been as hard as having sex with a prostitute. Now it was merely a mountain he had to climb and with determination, he reckoned he could do it. If only she'd come home.

The house was empty – Louisa had left no trace of her earlier presence – and so Robert slept off the remains of the bourbon.

The telephone woke him the next morning although, when he answered it with a thin hope that it would be Erin, he believed he had only slept for a couple of hours. It was Louisa. She was calm and soothing and, after a gentle laugh at his sleepy state, she said that she had some interesting news.

TWENTY

I'm so silly. It's not until I'm wrapped in a blanket sipping sweet tea beside a coal fire that I realise he has Ruby safe and he's not going to kill me or nick what's left of my money. I manage a smile as he perches on the arm of an old ripped chair, watching me, licking his lips.

'Gonna get you looked at, sweetheart,' he says and I wonder why because he doesn't know me and didn't have to pick me up off the ground. 'I don't think you're very well and that's a shame because you're a pretty girl.'

'Where's my baby? What's wrong with me?' It hadn't occurred to me that I was ill.

'I ain't no doctor, sweetheart, but Freda used to be a nurse. When she gets back, she'll give you the once-over and get you some medicine.'

'Freda?' She must be his wife, I think, although he doesn't look the marrying sort. I can see his shadow on the wall opposite, flickering in time with the flames. His nose sticks out like a shelf and his mouth joins straight down onto his neck. 'I want to see my baby? Where is she?'

'Freda looks after things around here.' The skinny man pauses, staring as if he's trying to recognise me. 'And your baby's quite safe.'

'Oh,' I say, thinking that he's nice and how lucky I am not

to have been picked up by the police. They'd have marched me straight home.

'Freda and me, we run a sort of hostel. A place for pretty young women to stay.' His mouth forms a point as he speaks, chiselling the other features on his face as if too much bone has been carved away. He's very thin and tawny.

'Do you mean homeless women?' I sit up now, hardly believing my luck but cautioning myself as I remember how my friend Rachel was sent home by the hostel when she ran away. I will pretend I am older, which will also make having a baby more plausible. God knows what's been on the news about me.

As he thinks, as I wait for his reply, I can smell hope on my hot breath but suddenly I am gripped with pain. My belly feels like it's burst open and the mess is soaking into my clothes while my left tit is as tight as a brick in my bra.

'Yeah, for homeless women.' He grins and comes over to me, crouching down by the chair. He puckers his already distorted lips. 'You wouldn't be looking for a roof, would you?'

I nod, not wanting to appear too keen. I've really fallen on my feet but shouldn't let on that I'm desperate or he'll hike the price sky high. I'm not stupid. I really wish he'd bring me my baby.

'I dunno about vacancies though, sweetheart. You'll have to speak nicely to Freda when she gets back. We're bursting at the seams. All these homeless girls to look after.'

My burning belly chills and sinks. 'Is it because I've got a baby? She's very good and hardly cries.'

'It's not to do with your baby, sweetheart. Several of our girls have ended up with babies and they all help each other out. I can't promise nothing though. Drink your tea.'

'But can you get my baby? When I fainted and you found

me, I had a baby. She's called Ruby. My baby. Will you get her?'

He stands and walks away. His words echo in a vapour trail behind him as he looks back over his bony shoulder. 'What baby, sweetheart? There's no baby, lover.' And he locks the door behind him.

In my head I make a cold, precise scream that, although I don't know it yet, will cut me in two for the rest of my life. I don't run for the door and beat my fists against the locked panels, not at first. I don't fall to the floor and thrash and sob and break a window and escape, searching, searching for my baby. I haven't even asked him what his name is or where exactly I am and suddenly the quest for my baby drops to the same level of importance because who am I, a teenage runaway with a newborn baby, to question anything?

I passed out in the street and he rescued me and brought me to wherever I am now. It seems nice, although shabbier than the semi that my mother kept tidy and sterile. The man seems nice and I bet Freda will be, too. I will do as he says and finish my tea and wait for Freda. I'll hope that she'll take me into their hostel and I'll think a thousand times a minute about my baby, and then maybe I will get her back.

I am so hot. My forehead is tacky and seeping sweat as I stand up, as I stagger to the locked door, but I still manage to rattle the handle and smack my fists against the wood and press my lips to the crazed paint and squeal out for my baby. I do this until my voice dries up and I slide to the floor not knowing if it's tears or blood or fear dripping down my cheeks. Then, for the second time that day, the world goes black.

I don't know how long it's been but there's a hand on my shoulder gently tapping and nudging me. I open my eyes.

There's a woman beside me and I can't think where I am and for a moment I think it's my mother but then I remember the skinny man who rescued me off the street although I can't see him, just this woman leaning over me. She's wearing sweet perfume. I remember they've got my baby.

'Hello,' she says. 'I'm Freda.' She bends down lower, giving me a glimpse down her low-cut top. 'Who are you?'

'Where's my baby?' I whisper, quite tired of hearing the words and wondering if Ruby ever existed.

'What baby, love?' And her words echo like the beat of butterfly wings in the sun. 'You don't look too well.' She reaches for a cushion and plumps it behind my head. 'Go on, tell me your name.'

I'm tired and hot and shivering and hungry although I couldn't eat. I'm aching and sore and scared but not so stupid that I'd give my real name. I'd thought about this on the train, about how telling everyone who I really am would be a bit silly seeing as I bet my folks have reported to the police that I've run away; a fifteen-year-old on the loose, in the papers, on the TV. They'll be after me for sure.

'I'm Milly,' I say as confidently as I can although it sounds strange. I saw the name Milly on the badge of a girl working in McDonald's. She was pretty and wore rings and had a cross on a chain around her neck. She smiled and was nice to me even though most people usually aren't.

'That's a pretty name.' Freda pulls up a footstool and sits beside me. 'Becco tells me he found you passed out in the street. What's a lass like you doing wandering around in this weather?' Freda's voice is like chocolate milk. She takes off her jacket, exposing more of her deep, wrinkled cleavage. She lights a cigarette, the glow from her lighter showing me that she has furrows ploughed around her mouth and eyes. Her hair is short and grey but sleek, not brittle like grey hair can be, and her skin is the colour of smoked fish. Freda's eyes are dark and hardly have any whites. She could be my fairy godmother.

'Not sure,' I say, picking my nails. At least that's the truth. 'I think that man's got my baby somewhere. Can you ask him?' My heart crashes against the back of my sore tit.

'Where do you live?' She sucks on the cigarette and when she blows out, the smoke is drawn towards the chimney.

'Further north.' Careful, I think. 'My baby?'

'Are you new to London?'

I nod. She's intuitive. I like that. My mother didn't know things about me; didn't notice I was pregnant until I was six months gone. 'Is she OK, though, my baby?'

'Do you have anywhere to stay? A job to go to?'

Loads of people run away to London and survive, don't they? Hundreds come to seek their fortune. I'll manage just as soon as she gives me my baby back. 'No, but I'll find something. I just wasn't feeling very well and fainted. I've got this pain in my stomach.' Even as I speak, it's like I'm turning on a spit over a fire with a rusty bar stuck through my insides. 'I'll be OK in a while. Will you fetch my baby now?'

'Baby?' She draws a lungful of smoke. Then, finally, 'Your baby's being looked after, love. It's best that way for a while, until you're both better.'

'Is she sick? Can I see her?'

'She'll be fine but it's best you let her rest. You need rest too, love.' Her voice smoothes my pain and when my vision goes foggy, as if I've washed my eyes in milk, I reckon that she's right. Ruby and I both need to rest. I trust this woman. She is nice.

We chat for a bit longer but then I need the toilet and when

I stand up, the room dips and spins. Eventually, I make it to the hall and down a dark corridor to the loo. It's a big old house, with tiled floors and not decorated very nicely but at least it's a roof. I don't notice much else because I'm in agony and when I pull down my pants, something bloody and sloppy falls out of me like the liver Mother used to buy from the butcher's. The smell makes me retch and I yell out for Freda.

She takes me upstairs and gets me into a bed. She cleans me up and wipes my face with cold water. She presses her fingers all over my belly, sinking them deep into the empty pocket where a baby lived only a week ago. Each time I yelp she purses her lips and says, 'Hmm.' Then she asks if it's hurting anywhere else and I tell her that my left tit is on fire. When she has a look at it, she gasps because it's prickly red like a giant strawberry.

'You're a right mess, young lady,' she says and makes me scared because I didn't think I was. 'Did the midwife check that the placenta came out properly?'

I stare up at her, my lips slightly apart. I feel like I did at school when I was asked a question and I hadn't been listening. The teacher's eyes would bore into me and the others would giggle. I shrug and take a quick glance around the bedroom. There are three other beds, each with white sheets and a yellow counterpane. A single light bulb hangs from the ceiling, too bright in my eyes, and the orange curtains are half closed. It's cold, too. I remember the hostel that Rachel described when she ran away. Part of me wants to go home.

'I don't know,' I whisper.

'Did you have your baby in a hospital?'

'At home,' I say and then wish I hadn't.

'Where's home?'

'Further north.' Not telling her any more.

'Who helped you have your baby?' Freda's sitting on the bed now, her weight pulling me towards her.

'No one. I gave birth alone.' I screw up my eyes for a moment because I remember that Uncle Gustaw was there but I don't want to tell her about him and his creepy hands slithering over my skin while I heaved and split like a wild animal.

'You've got a uterine infection. It's a bad one judging by the state you're in. And to top it all, you've got mastitis. I'll have to get you some antibiotics.'

'The man said you were a nurse and would make me better.' I'm glad she knows what I've got.

'Becco said that? Nursemaid, more like.' She grins. 'To all our girls. I'll get you some tablets to dry up your milk, too. You won't need any while your baby's being taken care of. It's bed for you for a couple of days. Lucky I had a spare one, eh?' Freda's face opens up like a spring flower.

'Oh yes,' I say, thankful that she is going to make me well again so I can look after my baby properly. Thankful, too, that I have a bed and there are other girls in the house that I can make friends with. 'I can really stay for a bit?'

'I can't turn you out onto the street, can I? Plus, if you're a good girl, there's a job waiting for you as well. You'll have to earn your keep somehow.' Freda strokes my forehead and tucks a strand of loose hair behind my ear. 'Get a bit of sleep. I'll get your medicine and then introduce you to the other girls later.' She bends down and kisses my cheek. I don't remember my mother ever doing that. I sleep for what seems like hours and I dream of trains and strawberries and hotels and jumping out of windows and the stench of smoky old London.

*

It's the noise that wakes me. Clattering and swearing and banging and squealing like there's a cat fight. The house rattles. A strange scent filters up from downstairs where all the fuss is taking place. It's sugar candy and pink lipstick and high heels and sweat and tobacco and old shirts and Uncle Gustaw and something else that makes the spit in my mouth curdle sour. Could he be here?

My eyes won't open properly but even so I sit up like a mole emerging from the earth, and feel around the bed for Ruby until I remember that they're looking after her. Just looking after her, I tell myself over and over, and then Freda creeps into the room carrying a packet of pills. I open my eyes wide in case she's bringing me my baby.

'Did you get some sleep?' She sits on the bed and hands me a glass of water and a tiny white pill. No baby. 'You'll need to take one of these four times a day for a week. I know a doctor. He said you'll be right as rain in no time. In fact, you might meet him one day if you're a good girl.' Freda pops one between my lips and guides the water to my mouth. 'The girls are going to eat. I'd like you to meet them before they go back to work again.'

'Have you seen Ruby? Is she OK?'

Freda nods and smiles and I feel a little better although I'm still fuzzy from sleep. I get out of bed and the floor falls away from me and I have to lean on Freda as she takes me downstairs to meet her girls. I am back in the room with the fire.

I hadn't noticed before but there is a table in the bay window with two wooden benches either side. On it, there is a loaf of sliced white bread spilling out of its wrapper and a huge tub of margarine with a knife stuck in the middle. There are no girls yet although I can hear a procession of noise in the corridor. I must look a state in my dirty clothes, my hair all sweaty from sleep and my body folded from pain.

The door opens and they shuffle into the room, each one bumping into the one in front when they stop dead at the sight of me. Everything goes silent and pairs of narrowing eyes focus on me. They flick up and down my broken body, assessing the threat of me, wondering if I am like them or better than them or worse than them. It's just like at school. Just like the kids outside my window when I was pregnant. I am a car crash and they have all slowed for a look.

Becco is leaning against the mantelpiece, smoking, his slim hips silhouetted by the bank of red-hot coals, his jutting nose a crag in his sunken face. He sneers at me, or it could be a smile – I hope it's a smile – and I see his dusty grey eyes flash to the line of girls. He jerks his head to the table and they slowly reanimate and drag themselves towards the table.

'Milly,' says Freda loud and slow to everyone, breaking the syllables in two while jamming a finger into my shoulder. She marches me to the forest of young girls and stands me amongst them. 'This is Milly.' And then she says to me, 'Just say hello. They understand that. They're all foreign.'

'I'm not,' says one, stepping forward. 'Hello, Milly. I'm Maggie.' Then she giggles. 'Milly, Maggie. We're already a team.' Maggie looks a bit older than me. She's wearing torn jeans and a red T-shirt that says 'I fuck on the first date' across the front. Her hair is pulled back and what I can see of it is curly and springing around her ears. She has dark circles under her eyes and smudged mascara. She might be pretty.

'Hi,' I say. It feels weird to be called Milly when I'm really Ruth. If I hadn't jumped out of my bedroom window I wouldn't be here now. If I'd stayed at home I could have gone back to school and taken my exams and got a job or gone to university or got married. It's hard to keep your head above water. I want my baby. I don't think I can go back.

'Milly's got a baby and we're taking care of it until it's better.' Freda's face morphs into my mother's, her grooves and lines stretching until they resemble the powdery surface of my mother's pale complexion.

We're taking care of your baby . . .

Why does everyone want to take my baby from me?

'Milly needs a place to stay,' Freda continues. 'She's going to work here so show her what's what, Maggie.' Freda takes hold of my shoulders as if she's going to hold me up for everyone to see. She sits me at the head of the table and the other girls whisper amongst themselves and, like Freda said, they are talking a foreign language.

Maggie sits herself down at the other end of the table and then all the other girls, about six of them, slide reluctantly onto the benches. Another two leave the room but soon return with a metal pot of food. Freda and Becco leave and the girls resume talking with each other, ignoring me completely, rattling in their foreign tongue that even through the layers of thick accent I can tell are angry words about me. I burst into tears and once again find myself in a heap on the floor.

Freda was right. A couple of days taking the tablets and my hot tit is normal again, although still bursting with milk for Ruby every few hours despite the tablets that were meant to dry it up. Thankfully, my belly has stopped hurting and today Freda says she will take me shopping for some new clothes because she says I can't do my work properly in the stuff I have. I've been wearing the same things since I arrived and washing my underwear in the sink. When Becco found me passed out in the alley, he didn't bring my bag of outsized gear. I'm hoping that Freda will buy some stuff for when Ruby's better too. Apparently she's in hospital and I can't visit because of my infection. I miss her but know they are looking after her even though they don't really understand how much I want my baby. It hurts my heart.

Becco has been lurking around the house like the shadow of a twisted branch. He seems to hide behind every door and wait around every corner and I'm sure he watches me through a peephole when I piss. I asked Maggie about him but she just laughed and reminded me that without Becco I wouldn't be safe and dry and fed while many other homeless people are coping with the January freeze. She's right of course and so now, when Becco melts into a shadowy corner of a room or his eyes glint from behind a door, I allow his stare to burn two holes in my back and pray in my bed that they will heal before morning.

Freda and I step out into the sharp edge of a winter afternoon and head for the shops. I feel strangely free even though I've been told not to leave the house alone. When I woke early on my first morning, I tried the front door but it was padlocked in three places and fixed firm with an iron grille. London is more dangerous than I realised. Freda and Becco are very protective of their girls and my heart warms a little from their care.

Twice a year my mother took me shopping for clothes, once in the spring and then again in the autumn. Aunt Anna always accompanied us with a watchful eye. I saw many things that I would have liked to own but knew that speaking up was pointless. I would be bought the same sensible pork-pie shoes and tartan wool skirt teamed with a plain white blouse for best. I was allowed corduroy trousers and an itchy sweater and underwear that turned grey and saggy after it had been through the wash.

Then of course there was the school uniform, with which the other girls in my year were creative and daring by turning up their collars and raising the hems of their skirts. They wore make-up and back-combed their hair and smudged kohl under their eyes. One day I left the top button of my blouse undone and Mother nearly fainted at the sight of me.

Freda grabs my hand and pulls me onto a bus. 'We'll go to Oxford Street for some bargains,' she calls above the traffic noise and stench of diesel. When we get there, it's so crowded I can hardly see any shops but Freda seems to know where she's going and I follow her closely. We go into a shop with loud music and mannequins with pink hair and wearing clothes that my mother would curl her lips at and turn away from.

'Speak up if something takes your fancy, pet. What about this?' Freda winds her way through a group of teenage girls and points at a dummy wearing the shortest ever denim skirt with a low-slung leather belt and knee-high boots. She has on a bright pink top that doesn't cover her middle at all and the sleeves are slashed to pieces. I love it.

'How can I work in this though?' I ask excitedly, wondering if anything will look good around my puffy baby waist.

'This is ideal for work, pet. What size are you, an eight, ten?' Freda harvests the outfit in several sizes, along with four or five other items that are similarly alien to my usual style. But having given birth to a baby and run away and whipped up this whole adventure, I don't mind that Freda squeezes my lumpy shape into cropped clothes. It seems perfectly normal now not to be normal.

We leave the shop with three bags stuffed full of luminous treats and don't stop there. She takes me to shoe shops and

gets me stilettos and boots and then to a lingerie store with
knickers I've never even seen the likes of before. Freda buys
me seven pairs of black and red and purple stringy things and
a couple of bras that hardly hold my heavy breasts. I don't tell
the assistant that I oozed milk onto one of her tissue-wrapped
undergarments when I was trying it on.

After we leave the underwear shop, we pass by Mothercare. I stop and stare at the burgundy pram in the window. It's
two hundred and ninety-nine pounds. I look at Freda, just in
case, and she smiles knowingly.

'Wait until your baby's better and you get your first pay
packet before you start spoiling her. Becco will pay you each
week if you do well.'

When I asked Maggie what work I would be doing, she
pointed at her rude T-shirt. I tried to ask the other girls and I
spoke really slowly and made signs with my hands. They
stared at me with vacant eyes and their tongues lolled on their
lips while I repeated what I'd said.

'Rina give good head,' one said as if her voice was coming
from somewhere else. There was a ripple of sullen laughter.

'What you like, mister?' said another.

'Lili stroke you.'

'Oh fuck me, mister.'

One by one the girls droned their pre-programmed
English at me and simmered with resigned chuckles like a big
pot boiling dry. I swallowed my food down my sandpaper
throat and kicked apart the pieces of the jigsaw in my head.

'What will I have to do for my job?' I ask Freda as she leads
me zigzagging down the crowded street. We seem to be
walking in the opposite direction to everyone else. 'What will
happen to Ruby when she comes out of hospital and I'm at
work?'

'Questions, questions.' Freda grins. 'Let's get a coffee and we can talk.'

We queue up in a café bar down a side street and have to sit outside because it's full. There's something exciting about breath you can see and wrapping cold fingers around a steaming mug of coffee. Freda has bought us biscotti and I swirl mine through the froth of my drink. The rusty metal bar through my belly has been replaced with warmth and security and I hardly dare believe that I have been so lucky.

If Ruby and I had been forced to sleep in a shop doorway, we would surely have died in the cold. Being so inexperienced, I wouldn't have noticed that Ruby was ill or taken her to hospital. I shudder at the thought of what might have happened. Freda has taken care of us and not asked for a penny for food or rent and now she's bought me a whole new wardrobe of clothes. She's the mother I always wanted.

'So what do I have to do?' I ask.

Freda's face relaxes like a sponge cake fresh from the oven. She smiles and takes my hand across the table. 'It's important work. You give a good service to men and if you're hot they'll leave you a big tip and come back. Most of them are regulars. Doctors and lawyers, teachers and bankers. Maggie has a politician.'

The jigsaw is re-forming and I smash it away. If the last piece fits, I will see my new life. I am scared that Uncle Gustaw will be in it.

'But what about Ruby?' My voice quivers and a tear shimmies along my lower lashes.

Freda takes my hand. 'I didn't want to have to tell you but your baby is very sick, pet. She's in intensive care getting the best treatment but . . .' Her eyes dip as she lights a cigarette. She blows smoke at me. 'But it's very expensive to care for a young baby. That's why I'm offering you this job. There are hundreds of other girls I could give it to but you need to pay for your baby's treatment. Then you can have her back.' She pushes the packet of cigarettes my way. 'Besides, I like you and so will your clients.' Freda's left eye narrows to a slow wink and I can't help the smile that stops the tear in its tracks.

'But she'll be OK, won't she?' I am trusting Freda like I wouldn't trust my own mother.

'If you work hard and do as I say, then she'll be OK.' Freda's tone suddenly hardens. She drains her mug and stands up to leave, even though I haven't finished. I was going to try a cigarette.

'I will work hard, you'll see. I want Ruby to be better more than anything in the world. I want my baby back. I want to get her a pram.' My voice trails away as I follow Freda through the crowds.

The next night Freda announces that I will begin work with Maggie. It seems that Maggie is different from the other girls because she is allowed out of the house. Perhaps it's because I'm English like Maggie, I don't know, but being allowed out seems like a privilege and causes a stir among the other girls. One of them trails her finger down my spine and whispers a string of foreign words in my ear. It sounds like what Uncle Gustaw used to say to me.

When I ask questions, Freda says it's safer to work in pairs and reminds me of Ruby lying ill in hospital. I see this little baby, all skin and tubes, looking at me through the glass of her crib. I see me earning her health.

'But why can't they ever go out?' I ask about the foreign girls and when Freda doesn't reply, I catch sight of Becco in the corner shaking his head and drawing a line across his neck. He pouts a kiss at me.

Maggie says we only have four appointments tonight although she's sketchy about exactly what it is I will have to do. We got ready together, Maggie lending me her make-up and telling me to put on loads. She helps me into the complicated knickers and suspender belt and when I put on the bra, we laugh because one tit doesn't fill my new bra and the other bulges out like a Yorkshire pudding. Finally, I dress and feel a bit silly in my new clothes despite Maggie's encouraging remarks.

At eight o'clock the foreign girls go to the other side of the house through a series of locked doors. I've only ever taken a peek into the corridor beyond and feel relieved that I am allowed out. As Maggie and I watch Becco herding them through to work, I squint my eyes and wonder why they are here. Perhaps they have sick babies too. As we leave, I wave to Freda and catch sight of Becco blending into the wall behind her, a glint in his eye and a leer on his face.

'Take care of her, Maggie,' Freda sings. 'Remember *your* first time.'

'Like it was my last,' Maggie chants back, clicking the front door shut behind her. I feel like one of the seven dwarves, whistling my way to work.

'We're off to a posh hotel first. I've had Norris for three years. A real sweetie and he's going to love you.' Maggie hails a cab and tells him to take us to some place I've never heard of. I like Maggie. She's so confident and knows just what she wants. She says that when she's twenty she'll have enough money saved to go to California and become an actress. Maybe Ruby and I will go with her.

In fifteen minutes we are at the hotel and Maggie pays the

driver and asks for a receipt. 'First rule,' she says. 'Always get a receipt because if Becco thinks you've diddled him, he'll get right mad and dock your pay.' She musses up her hair and lifts her chin high before striding up to the porter and whispering something in his ear. Then the porter has us in the lift and Maggie slips him a ten-pound note and I wonder whether I would need a receipt from him too.

'Room four eight seven tonight, Mags,' he says and the doors slide shut, sealing us in anticipation. Then we are walking down the thickly carpeted corridor. Maggie stops and turns to me with a serious expression on her flawless face.

'He's quite old and can be fussy but follow me and you won't go far wrong. Compared to some, he's a pussycat to please.' She winks and has me puzzled.

Are we cleaning his hotel room? Are we serving him dinner or taking dictation? Or, worse, perhaps he wants sex. Suddenly, I see Uncle Gustaw hauling his saggy body down the corridor but he turns the corner before I can be sure. Maggie stops outside the room and knocks sharply on the door.

'He's a bit deaf.' She knocks again before we are let in. Norris is about seventy and has dappled skin on his cheeks and head, like the skin on the belly of an old dog.

'Maggie, Maggie,' he says, standing aside to let us in. 'The sight of you is going to kill me one of these days.' Norris has an Irish accent. His old man smell reminds me of Uncle Gustaw, of pipe tar and oily scalp. 'Who's your friend? Introduce me.' Norris wipes his brittle hand across Maggie's shoulders. She slips off her coat and sits down on the bed, her long legs aimed at Norris. I stand nervously by the wardrobe, waiting to be introduced and wondering what I will have to do.

'Norris, this is the lovely young Milly. She's just started

working with us and Freda thought you'd like a special pre-view.' Maggie grins at me. My stomach knots and I think of Ruby.

'A premiere event,' Norris says, shuffling up to me. He touches my hair. 'How old are you?' His voice isn't quite as gentle as it was with Maggie. I'm about to say fifteen but think better of it.

'Nineteen, sir.' The outfit makes me look older. Norris's eager expression slouches.

'But she could be a lot younger, don't you think?' Maggie approaches me and takes my hand, guiding me to the bed. 'Easily fifteen.' Then, 'Sit,' she whispers to me. I remember that Norris is hard of hearing. 'And smile. He's paying good money for us.' She slides my already short skirt higher up my thighs.

'She looks divine,' Norris growls. He sits on the bed between Maggie and me and holds each of our hands. 'Which one of you first?' he ponders, his frail head clicking back and forth between us. When he stops and stares at me, I get the feeling that Uncle Gustaw used to give me when we were alone together.

Norris moves my hand and puts it at the top of his wool trousers. There doesn't seem to be much in there, not like Uncle Gustaw. But I know what to do. I remember that sometimes in life you have to do this and again Ruby's frailty and need flashes through my mind. Determined that my baby will get well again, I do what comes naturally while Maggie offers occasional instructions and Norris buckles under the lightness of my touch.

'You were superb, honey.' Maggie treats me to a thick milk-shake before our next appointment. 'He adored you. You'll soon be earning more than Freda had imagined.' Maggie rustles through the wad of notes that Norris gave her and pays for our shakes. 'Don't tell Becco.' She laughs. I suck hard on my straw but hardly any of the shake comes up. It's very thick. I just need something to get the taste out of my mouth.

We are able to walk to our next appointment, again in a hotel. He's a businessman and polite and clean and good-looking and afterwards he lets us help ourselves to the minibar. I choose a slab of Bournville and a miniature bottle of Beefeater Gin. He wanted to go inside me but Maggie gently told him no and presented herself instead. He offered an extra two hundred for me which meant that Maggie had to tell him firmly that I'd not long had a baby and wouldn't be fully available for another couple of weeks. When he discovered I was dribbling milk, he made do with that instead and told me that he loved me. I wiped his chin with a tissue.

Next we had to visit Maggie's politician. I didn't recognise his name but she swore me to secrecy anyway. We went to his London flat, which he stays in during the week. He goes home to his wife at weekends. He wanted it with me too and Maggie had to say no again. She laughed afterwards, saying I would put her out of a job. The stash of money Maggie has tucked inside her coat makes me think this is a better job than cleaning or waiting tables, which is all I could have done without Freda and Becco's help. And I've had practice at this before, for many years, so it means that Ruby will be cared for and I'll be able to buy that pram in no time. I wonder what would happen if we held back a few notes for ourselves.

Our last appointment involves sitting in a hotel bar and talking to a foreign man. Actually, he's dressed like a woman but I can tell he's a man. He's about fifty and wears a purple skirt and white shoes and has an accent that makes me raise my eyebrows and lean nearer to him. He buys Maggie and me tall blue cocktails and we sit, one each side of him, on a squeaky leather sofa while a beautiful lady sings and a man plays the piano.

The dressed-up man wants us to talk dirty. Maggie hasn't met him before and she pulls funny faces at me when he isn't looking. He makes us describe our bodies and gets us to tell him about going to the toilet.

Inside, I know Maggie is laughing, like me, but she's told me several times tonight that we always treat our clients' needs with respect because they are paying a lot of money. We both still think he's funny. Then he tells me to go for a pee, which I do, and when I come out of the ladies' loos, he's just coming in.

He barges me back inside and I wonder where Maggie is. He grabs my skirt and shreds my new stockings and knickers and folds me over the basin. I can tell that he's got his purple skirt around his waist and his pants around his knees because I can smell warm chicken and salt. I see the floor shunting beneath me and I hear his foreign grunts and I know the wall should be hurting my head as it bangs against it over and over but I've automatically slipped into the safest place I know, where nothing, where no one can ever reach me.

When he's gone, I pick up my torn knickers and go back to Maggie who is still sipping her blue cocktail. The foreign man isn't there and Maggie is furtively counting some notes. I stand in front of her, dripping with what he's done to me, and when she realises she holds her arms open. I sit with my head cradled against her shoulder and think of Ruby as I gradually crawl out of my safe place.

'At least he paid us,' she finally says.

★

252

Over the coming days, I impress Freda with my dedication and reliability. If she knew that's how I've been my entire life, she'd understand how easy it is for me to knuckle down and do what I have to.

At the end of my first working week, Becco hands me an envelope. He stares at me a beat longer than he should and I swallow, feeling the envelope's fatness between my fingers. Then I run up to my shared bedroom and rip it open. I have earned fifty pounds. I've never seen that much money before. My parents never had a great deal; Father earned little from his job as a clerk and Mother said her job was in the home even though Father used to sit up late and fret about the bills.

I persuade Maggie to take me to Woolworth's to buy a cash box with a lock. It's black and shiny and invincible and where I keep the money I'm saving for Ruby's treatment. Maggie says that she has a bank account but I don't tell her that I can't have one because the police would track me down.

By the end of my second week, Becco hands me another envelope. 'Settling in then?' he says. A long stem of ash hangs off his cigarette. I nod, ever thankful that he found me passed out in the street although I'm too scared to tell him how grateful I am.

Up in my room, I count another fifty pounds. Then I mentally add up what Maggie and I have brought home to Becco every night that week. Eight hundred, perhaps a thousand pounds each night. From then on, I decide to take a lick of the cream from my clients. For Ruby.

Some days, when I'm not thinking about Ruby – Freda tells me she's still terribly sick and allowed no visitors – I think about my parents and Aunt Anna and Uncle Gustaw all flying about in a panic looking for me. It's been six weeks since I ran away and they still haven't found a hair off my head.

I think about our house and my bedroom and how they kept me locked in there for such a long time when I was pregnant. I think about how safe Ruby was when she was curled in my belly and that since she was born, everyone's been trying to take her. I think about my friends at school and what will be said about me in the playground, stories that will probably mutate for terms to come as if I'm a disgusting disease. I think of Gustaw and his hairy body and how I fought the heave in my throat whenever he came near. I think about when I dropped from my bedroom window and ran away when I found out about my baby's adoption. I think of giving birth on my own. I think of going back. I think I won't.

TWENTY-ONE

Louisa standing on the front doorstep was like having fresh flowers delivered. Robert stepped aside to let her in. Her nose curled and a tiny frown nipped her otherwise creaseless brow.

'Open some windows, Rob. It stinks in here.' Louisa left a trail of sweet scent as she marched to the kitchen, not stopping but still noticing the blankets piled on the sofa and the dirty plates left on the floor. 'You've had worse than this before. Don't lose it.' She unzipped her laptop bag, took out the slim machine and plugged into the internet. 'There's something I want to show you.'

A current of ozone and cut grass wound around the kitchen as they waited for the computer to boot up. Their faces were close as they peered at the monitor.

'The name on the photograph you gave me from the locket, it's pretty unusual. It's Polish and *babka* means grandmother. Babka Wystrach was someone's granny.' Louisa smiled, stroked her finger on the mouse pad and pulled up a bookmarked link.

Someone's grandmother? Robert thought. Ruby's perhaps, or Erin's? Or perhaps no one's and Erin had simply bought the locket at a flea market as a present for Ruby. He felt a pang of loss as he momentarily pictured Erin hunched over a stall crammed with trinkets and jewellery and collectables – one of her favourite pastimes.

'*The Chronicle and Echo*?' Robert asked, reading from the address bar on the internet browser.

'Wait,' Louisa said as the page resolved then, 'Listen. A sixty-one year old Northampton resident has been arrested on suspicion of child abuse and lewd acts with a fourteen-year-old girl. Police arrested Gustaw Wystrach at his home in the early hours of the morning following a report from the girl's mother about the abuse. Wystrach, whose family is originally from Poland and has run the Knowle Hill Youth Club for the last seventeen years, will be released on police bail tomorrow pending further inquiries.'

Robert straightened and sighed. 'It's dated June two thousand and one. How did you find that?'

'Easy. I just Googled the name Wystrach.' Louisa posed briefly with her hands on her hips and pulled a silly face. A runway of sunlight cut across her back and shoulders, skimming the tip of her ponytail. It looked as if it was on fire. 'There were hundreds of results but this was the best lead by far. The story was top of the list. Most of the other stuff was to do with genealogy. Of course, the information we need to do with the locket may well pre-date the internet or never even have made it into any online resources.'

'And I'm paying you how much to surf the internet?' Robert paced the kitchen. 'Anyway, aren't we interested in genealogy, Erin's family history? I can't see what this man has to do with her. Do you think it's worth following up?' Robert opened the back door and stared down the garden. The grass stood about six inches tall and rippled like a meadow in the light breeze.

'Of course it is. I'm an investigator.' She came up behind

him. 'I'll do a full newspaper search on this particular story, follow up on what happened to that dirty sod. I'll get his address and we can pay him a visit if you like. The woman in the locket photo could well be a relative. It's such an unusual surname.' She stepped closer. Robert could feel her body heat between his shoulders. Her breath hadn't quite cooled when it reached his neck. 'On the other hand, it could be nothing at all and by eleven o'clock tonight, when Erin has come home, she'll be curled up against your back whispering apologies.'

Robert turned. 'You think so?' he asked dismally, wishing that it was Erin standing behind him now. He hardly dared think how much he missed her and Ruby. He reached out and slipped Louisa's hands into his. 'Thanks,' he said, meaning it. 'I couldn't do this without you.'

Louisa smiled and pulled her fingers away. 'In the meantime, you go and wash, eat, have a game of squash – anything to get you unhooked from this mess while I find out more about this man. It won't be long.' She started back to the computer. 'And Rob, don't be disappointed if it turns out to be nothing, huh?'

'I'm rather hoping it will,' he confessed and went to shower.

After Louisa had driven Robert to recover his car and pick up his mobile phone – she didn't ask questions – it took them less than two hours to travel to Northampton.

They arrived in the flat, unremarkable town around noon and Robert bought coffee, two sausage rolls and a packet of cigarettes for lunch. Louisa didn't eat anything and only sipped at her coffee and when Robert offered her a smoke, she refused it with a disgusted puff as if she was smoking anyway.

Robert's head banged from the previous day's drinking binge but he didn't care. It didn't hurt as much as the layers peeling off his heart. Louisa had brought along a local map and precise directions, which Robert could have printed off the internet himself, but it helped justify her fee – helped keep him sane before he wrecked another marriage.

'What if he's in prison?' Robert sat on the bonnet of his car while Louisa occupied the only bench in the lay-by, as far away from Robert's cigarette as she could be while still being able to talk. Robert ate the last piece of his sausage roll, brushed the crumbs off his shirt and took the final draw of his cigarette. He dropped the butt on the tarmac and slowly ground it with his heel. 'Did you consider that?'

'He's not in prison.' Louisa shook her head. 'Do you have to do that?' She glanced at the dog-end. Robert ignored her.

'But you said he got fourteen years.'

'He did.'

'If I promise not to smoke any more, will you tell me what happened?' Robert put on his sunglasses. The glare behind Louisa made him squint.

'Gustaw Wystrach is dead.' Louisa stood and hitched up her jeans. Her white T-shirt didn't quite meet the ornate buckle of her leather belt. 'He hanged himself in prison.'

'And you didn't think to tell me this before we left London?' Robert slid another cigarette from the packet and perched it between his lips.

'You said—'

'I haven't lit it yet. So who the hell are we visiting now then?'

'Search me. His mother, aunt, wife, daughter? I know not.' Louisa plucked the cigarette from Robert's lips, javelined it into a litter bin and opened the car door, briefly leaning on the soft roof of the Mercedes. 'Mind if we go topless?' She grinned before ducking inside.

As they drove through the town, the gentle summer breeze transformed into a warm wind and if it hadn't been another day without Erin and Ruby, Robert would have enjoyed the sun wrapping hot fingers around his neck and tanning the ridge of his nose a shade deeper than the rest of his face. They entered an unremarkable suburb on the north side of town where Robert slowed to allow Louisa to study the map.

'It's two streets away,' she said, squinting down the rack of dismal sixties concrete-fronted council houses. They couldn't have been more conspicuous, thought Robert as he moved the car forward through the grim neighbourhood. 'Turn left here.'

Number 72 Bell Grove Gardens was the least attractive of all the houses in the street. The concrete and pebble-dashed exterior suggested it was council property and unlike the neighbouring houses, it was most likely still owned by the local authority. Compared to the effort made by the other residents, such as hanging baskets of lurid orange and blue annuals and front gardens decorated with flaking gnomes and stone ornaments, number 72 was shabby and unkempt, perhaps even unoccupied.

'Nice,' Louisa commented, peering at the litter-filled front garden. 'Shall I wait here?'

'What, don't want to dirty your shoes?' Robert pressed a button and the car roof settled back into place. 'Come on,' he ordered. 'You're my investigator. You'll know what to say to whoever might be alive in there.'

'I will?' Louisa followed Robert, both of them fixing their eyes on the decaying house as they crossed the street.

Robert marched up the front path as if the building were the keeper of all Erin's secrets. When he knocked on the door and no one came, they ventured through the side gate and into a weed-choked rear garden. Some kids were fighting over a ball in the neighbouring property. They went around the side of a tatty extension to the back door. It was open and music crackled from a radio that sounded as if it was a tweak away from being tuned in. Robert rapped on the open door.

'Anyone home?'

An old woman was suddenly there, materialising from nowhere and holding a laundry basket. They stared at each other, perfectly still, each sizing up the other. Robert saw someone's wife, perhaps married for decades, her weary body resigned to pegging out the washing and dishing up pie and chips for the rest of her life before she died unnoticed in an old people's home. Her skin carried a light sheen of grease as if she was sweating and her eyes, probably once blue, looked as if they had cried too many times and the colour had been washed out.

The old woman would have seen a stranger on her doorstep, a threat. Robert slid his sunglasses up onto his head.

'Mrs Wystrach?' Robert said finally, not sure if he had pronounced the name correctly. The woman barely nodded. 'Would you have a few minutes? I'd like to speak to you about something important.' The woman frowned, glanced at Louisa who stood behind Robert, and became agitated, the expression on her lined face showing fear. 'Something interesting, actually,' Robert added, like a stranger would offer sweets to a child.

'Wait,' she snapped and pushed the back door to, slipping into the darkness of the house. A moment later she returned with a big man, also old and also frowning. He filled the entire space in the doorway, looming over Robert in height because of the six-inch doorstep.

'Good morning.' Robert held out his hand and heard Louisa clear her throat. 'I'm Robert Knight. I'd like to ask you some questions if you have time.' The big man finally took his hand. It was a suspicious handshake, too frail for a man of that size, Robert thought, and his skin didn't seem to have a temperature. 'May I come in?' The two faces continued to stare at them, their eyes flicking between Robert and the silent Louisa, the woman still pressing the basket of laundry against her hip.

Finally, the man moved aside, nodded and beckoned Robert into the gloom of their kitchen, which had the decor and furniture of the 1960s. The four of them stood around a pale blue Formica table. Mrs Wystrach placed the basket on the floor and adjusted her floral skirt. Robert focused his attention as if he were in court and preparing to cross-examine a witness. He saw the pilling on her grey short-sleeved sweater, the slight stain on her apron, her yellow-grey hair tucked back at her nape and an array of age spots on her cheeks as if someone had spilled tea on her face. He desperately searched for something that would link her to Erin, to Ruby, to the missing past of his wife that he longed to know.

The woman reminded him of nothing, of no one.

'Are you the police?' The man's voice was weighed down with accent.

'No, not at all. I wanted to show you this.' Robert unfurled his left hand to expose the locket. It shone in his palm, casting an aura of wonder and shock over the old couple. The woman gasped and steadied herself on the back of a chair. The big man said nothing but Robert noticed his succession of swallows, didn't miss it when his neck stiffened and his hands balled. Sweat beads erupted on his floury scalp.

'Do you recognise it?' Despite his recent assessment of the

old woman, Robert already knew the answer. A pulse of hope quickened his heart and then slowed again as he checked himself. Even if the pair recognised the locket, it still didn't prove it was anything to do with Erin.

'Edyta,' the woman whispered. The name seemed to summon spirits from another time, such was the atmosphere in the kitchen.

Robert prised the locket open and the woman slapped one hand over her mouth and crossed herself with the other when she saw the faded photograph. The man turned away and grunted but Robert knew he had seen. He could tell by the sudden prominence of the veins on the old man's neck.

'Mr Wystrach?' He was guessing that was his name. 'Do you know the woman in this picture?'

He didn't reply but turned off the radio instead.

'Of course he does.' The old woman approached Robert for a closer look. She wiped a finger under her eye. 'It's his mother. Edyta Wystrach. She's dead now.'

'I'm sorry.'

'She was old and—'

'Where did you get this?' The old man's accent thickened with anger and volume powering it. He banged his already tight fists onto the table.

'I didn't mean to upset you.' Robert took a step back. 'I didn't realise your mother was dead.'

'It's not the photo of his mother that's bothering him.' Mrs Wystrach shrugged and reached for the kettle. She filled it and lit the stove. She seemed resigned, as if something they had been waiting for all their lives had arrived as casually as a letter on the doormat. 'It's the locket that my husband's curious about.'

'Go on.' Robert held it out to the rigid man. 'Take it. Have a look.'

'Or should I say, he's bothered by where it's come from. *Who* it's come from.' Mrs Wystrach wiped her hands down her apron. 'It was Ruth's, you see.'

TWENTY-TWO

When Andy left, I knew I'd got what I deserved. Loneliness, misery, desolation and a vat of thick, stinking guilt in which to bathe – when I could be bothered. The sun never shone in my new world and days would pass when I wouldn't speak to a single soul. Except Natasha's soul, that is. I found myself offering her occasional words, like sorry or I love you, but she never replied. She just left me a tingle in the core of my spine and a whisper of cold air on my neck. For a time, that was enough.

After a while, I began writing letters to her. They're all in the Natasha box up in the loft. But it still didn't feel as if I was connecting with my baby and so strong was the desire to make contact that I went to see a psychic woman. She'd been advertising in our area for a few weeks. *Make contact with lost loved ones*. It seemed appropriate.

When I telephoned Madame Luna, she invited me for an appointment at her little semi-detached house across the other side of town. I took a bus and twenty-five pounds and a notebook and pencil to write down what she said. She led me upstairs and into a bedroom that was decorated like the inside of a gypsy's tent. It was all red and purple and gold silk and candles burned everywhere. There was a small table with a crystal ball on it and a chair positioned each side. She told me to sit down. Madame Luna was fat and looked like a man but she changed my life.

'Someone precious is trying to contact you,' she said with a husky voice and I fell into her black eyes, desperate to be reunited with Natasha. Her hands hovered around the glass ball and I swear I saw shards of light crackling between her palms and the afterlife. I began to cry. 'She says don't be sad or she'll cry too.'

'She?' I asked.

'There's a little girl wanting to make contact. A little girl who loves you very much.'

As soon as my body stiffened, the instant my pupils dilated, the very second that sweat erupted on my top lip, Madame Luna sank her tendrils into my fragile body like the quick-growing roots of a pernicious weed. Later I would learn she was just doing her job.

'How old is she?' I asked.

'Two, perhaps three.'

My body relaxed with disappointment.

'Although, wait . . .' Madame Luna stared at me, agonised over the crystal ball, studied the minute muscle tremors that danced beneath my clothing like a biography. She understood the whiff of hope on each of my exhaled breaths. 'I think maybe younger, older . . .' I must have signalled unconsciously because she suddenly exclaimed, 'This is a very young child. A baby, I think.'

I didn't care that she was asking me, not telling me. I nodded frantically, releasing Madame Luna into revealing a frenzy of facts, some close to the truth, some so far removed I ignored them. I learned that Natasha was in heaven and that she loved me and forgave me and would talk to me every time I came to see Madame Luna and paid her for the privilege.

Before I left, my eyes hot from crying, Madame Luna made the mistake of telling me that I was a very intuitive person, possibly even psychic myself. Perhaps it was her way of ensuring I came back for another appointment, to make me feel special, to flatter her way into my trust.

Instead, she set me on the path to clairvoyance and, before long, I had placed an advertisement in the local shop window promoting my services. Within a week I had three clients of my own and I finally felt I was doing something useful while at the same time remaining close to Natasha.

I'm not really psychic. I simply have an ability to see the thread of sadness stitched into so many lives. With a gentle tug, everyone will unravel.

Sarah is visiting me today. She's two hours late. I'm fretting now and don't like the vein on my temple bulging and pulsing in time with every second she's not with me.

Perhaps she's had her baby and not bothered to tell me. I couldn't bear it if I didn't get to see the little thing, couldn't stand to miss out on pressing my nose against its neck and nibbling its fingernails short when they get too long. 'Don't let me down, Sarah,' I call out, one minute checking on the cakes I have baking for our tea and the next sticking my head out of the front door and peering up and down the street.

I am briefly halted by the line of sunlight that dares to enter my house through the open door. It's like a bridge from my gloom to the place where Natasha and all babies live. I stare up at the sky and wonder what would happen if I crossed the bridge. I know I will get my baby back.

As the months turned into years, my contact with PC Miranda Hobbs and Detective Inspector George Lumley transformed into an annual update. An update of nothing. Natasha minus three years and they officially put the file into the hopeless pile.

In a way, it was a relief; a signal to move on and forget my baby. They didn't bother me again with accusing questions about wool and cakes, realising that they'd taken a wrong turn. I tried hard to get on with my life. I dragged my memories around like a dead weight attached to my ankle, hindering me wherever I went, whatever I did.

Each time I passed the local playgroup on the way to the shops, I pretended that I was going to fetch Natasha, that she would come running up to me with a wet painting or a monster made out of loo roll tubes and empty cereal packets. I saw all the other mothers standing there, waiting for their darlings, and wondered what would happen if I just stepped inside the gates to see if there was a spare child. But I never did. I always walked on by.

My divorce from Andy was swift and cracked my life like scored glass. Finally, everything had gone. I immersed myself in my new career, building up a regular bank of desperate clients all wanting to fondle their sadness, unable to let go. That was why I was so good at what I claimed to be: I couldn't let go either. Easily I wrapped my finger round their threads of misery, each time tugging a little harder, each time taking their twenty-five pounds, paying my mortgage, feeding on their grief.

I made quite a name for myself. I even got asked to have a stall at the school fête, now an annual booking, and I did an interview on the local radio station and regularly wrote columns for magazines. I began to work the pub circuit, and still do, hosting psychic evenings with other local mystics and healers. The punters queue up for their drinks and then queue up to see me. I tell them what they want to hear, pressing on the truth by clever deduction rather than super powers. I know I'm a fake, I know I'm a fraud but sometimes I get that feeling that something big is about to happen, something so life-changing that all I can do is gawp. Like I am now.

When Sarah doesn't come, when the bridge of sunlight has shrivelled behind the row of houses opposite, when the cakes have sunk and dried, I get changed ready for my evening at the Stag's Head.

The first Saturday of every month they buy a ticket and line up to have their fortunes told. I try not to let my anger influence what I say but I might not be able to resist predicting a little tragedy or disappointment for one or two of them. I snap the curtains closed against the street, even though it stays light until nearly ten o'clock, even though I like passers-by to get a glimpse of my solitude. I don't want Sarah peeking in if she decides to come knocking later. I wouldn't want her to see the baby basket I bought for her all tied up with ribbon and filled with tiny velvet sleep suits laid out as a surprise. I'd feel silly if she knew that I'd redecorated the back bedroom, Natasha's old nursery, in modern pastel colours and bought a lamp with rabbits on the shade and shifted the box of toys down from the loft that Sheila so speedily packed away when my baby was lost. Before I go out, I drop to the floor and hold all the new baby things to my face, crying and laughing at the same time.

The Stag's Head is already full. It hums with loud conversation, punctuated by an occasional peel of laughter, and reeks of smoke and beer and hope. I greet the landlord through the layers of punters at the bar and he rushes me through to the usual room out the back where three other clairvoyants are already doing their trade. It's as if he can't hold back the hordes any longer, all desperate to touch the other side of life.

But apart from the usual mêlée of clients, who get to see me for only ten pounds if they buy two adult meals at the bar, I sense that there's something else waiting for my attention. A rather more pressing matter than making contact with long-dead aunts or delving into the minutiae of someone's hopeless future. I'm getting that feeling, and I don't like it one bit, that something is about to happen. I think of Sarah and her baby. I look at my watch and then at the face of my first client as she sits down at my stall. I wonder what to tell her as I am heaped with a fear that has absolutely nothing to do with this woman.

'Hi,' she says but I don't answer. I stare at my upturned palms stretched out on the purple cloth covering the table. The lines are strawberry-coloured against the paleness of my skin, each one a map of truth or lies. I remember Sarah laughing, studying them and pretending to tell my fortune, predicting I was going to have a baby. And it is then, just as I look up, that I catch the eye of a stranger staring at me from beside the bar, slowly sipping his pint.

TWENTY-THREE

Robert and Louisa watched the old woman clattering about making tea. The Wystrach kitchen smelled of disinfectant and a faint tang of gas. When the tea was made and she had completed what seemed to be a sacred tray-laying ritual, Mrs Wystrach guided the pair through to the living room, while her husband carried the tray. Robert and Louisa sat beside each other on the edge of a floral sofa. They were offered a bitter orange brew in a rattling cup and saucer.

'Have you lived here long?' Robert didn't really care. He simply wanted to know about the photograph in the locket, weigh up the possibility of a link to his wife and then get the hell out of the depressing house. Neither of the old couple answered his question.

'Tell me where you got this.' The old man creaked to his full height, which was impressive, and dangled the locket in front of Robert as if trying to hypnotise the unwelcome visitors into telling the truth.

'It belongs to my stepdaughter,' Robert said honestly and with a tone that he would use for particularly mistrusting clients. He offered a reassuring smile and reached up for the item but the old man jerked it out of the way. The locket spun on its chain, glinting in the morning sun filtering through the grubby net curtains. Robert took a sip of his tea, winced and noticed a tear beading in the corner Mrs Wystrach's eye. A car cruised along the street. 'Who is Ruth?' he asked. 'You said the locket belonged to Ruth.' A faint trail of exhaust filtered through the open window.

Again, silence, but Mr Wystrach lowered himself back into the chair next to his wife. It creaked under his weight. The couple bowed towards each other, their shoulders touching, their united frailty showing.

'Ruth was our daughter,' Mrs Wystrach said, looking at her husband, perhaps for permission, when she spoke.

'*Is* our daughter,' the old man growled. A tiny muscle twitched beneath his eye.

'I'm not sure I understand.' Louisa's crystal voice cut a line through the heavy air. 'Is, was?'

Mrs Wystrach touched her husband's knee with her bony hand and when she replied, her accent made her sound as if she needed to clear her throat. There was great sadness in her voice, the pain transcending language. 'After all these years, I believe Ruth must be dead.'

'No!' Her husband exploded into full height again. 'Ruth is alive.' It seemed as if there was more the man wanted to say but the words choked his throat, clogging it up with fear, sadness and desperation.

'If she's alive, perhaps Ruth would like the locket back.' Robert spoke gently, familiar with the art of eking out information, although he wasn't convinced it would lead them anywhere useful or that it had anything to do with Erin. 'I'm sure my wife and daughter would like to see it returned to its rightful owner.'

Another long period of silence. Robert heard kids playing in the street and wondered why they weren't at school. The steady thud-thud of a ball repeatedly bounced on hot tarmac and the piercing wail of a toddler followed by a raised adult voice alarmed him so that he strained to see into the street. The warm summer air transformed mundane noises into tantalising sound bites. There was a whiff of burnt toast and then fumes as another car with a throaty exhaust chugged past the open window. Mrs Wystrach's greying nets billowed in the summer breeze and Robert thought that the old couple had died in their seats, such was their inertness.

'Is it possible to locate Ruth, to return the locket to her?' As if a switch had been flicked, Mrs Wystrach leaned forward, her gaze dancing cautiously around the room. Her eyes narrowed to slits and her thin lips disappeared as they stretched over her teeth.

'You won't find Ruth. Everyone's tried.' A glance at her husband brought him back to life also and he nodded in agreement. 'Ruth's gone, you see. Vanished.' The old woman gestured a mini-explosion with her hands and puffed air out of her cheeks.

Fleetingly, Robert had an image of Ruth, a faceless girl, dissolving into thin air before his eyes. Then he thought of Erin and Ruby's vanishing act.

'I'm sorry,' he found himself saying but really he meant it about his own situation. 'Have the police done all they can?'

'Of course. The investigation was over and done with many years ago.' Mrs Wystrach took the knitted tea cosy off the pot and stirred the contents. 'More?' Robert held out his cup; he needed to prolong the meeting to prise out information. 'She's been gone thirteen years. There's nothing else to be done.' She tapped the spoon on the side of the teapot. 'They say she's probably dead.'

Robert sipped his tea, anything to distract his body from mirroring the involuntary twitches that consumed Mr

Wystrach as he fought internal conflict, refusing to believe his wife's resignation. Common sense told Robert to get up and leave, that to be wrapped up in the old couple's story was both misleading and dangerous, that he might learn something that would steer him away from the truth about his wife, that he might learn something that would make him more obsessed.

'Mr and Mrs Wystrach, do you know anyone called Erin Lucas? Does the name have any connection with this locket?' Louisa asked, placing her teacup on the coffee table, glancing at Robert briefly.

'I have a photograph of her,' Robert said. He took his wallet from his back pocket and flipped it open, offering it to Mrs Wystrach. She took a look, leaned against her husband and clapped a hand to her forehead. Her head bobbed vigorously and her lips suddenly pursed as if a drawstring was tightening around the words that wanted to come out.

'He says do we know this woman,' Mrs Wystrach said to her husband, trying to control herself. She was acting as if he had suddenly become deaf or dumb.

'We don't know her,' he replied too swiftly. His face tightened at the sight of Erin and colour leaked into his broad cheeks, revealing doubt, distrust and certainly regret. A faint grimace curled at one side of his mouth like a leaf preparing for autumn. Robert glimpsed the pale blonde wisps of Erin's hair as Mrs Wystrach held the picture in trembling hands. He recalled taking the photo in a high wind on Anglesey. Erin had one hand at her neck and the other brushing back her flyaway hair.

Mr Wystrach pushed his fat fingers through what remained of his greasy hair and sighed. 'Have you lost someone too?' he asked, the tight accent receding a little, the signs of recognition ebbing, as if he had taken control of his feelings.

Mr Wystrach, for some reason, was striving to give little away.

'Possibly. I'm not sure yet.' Robert realised he sounded stupid – either someone is lost or they aren't – but the man's evasion, despite his obvious recognition of Erin, had thrown him. 'It's my wife,' he added, although they weren't listening. Mrs Wystrach was whispering excitedly in a foreign language to her husband and they both smiled and frowned, as if a small valve had been released but with a great pressure behind. Whatever they were hiding, Robert was reluctant to reveal anything about Erin. She was still his wife.

Mrs Wystrach crossed herself and stood up. 'You wait a moment.' She shuffled from the room, her rubber-soled slippers making no noise, and soon returned clutching a box file to her chest. 'We'd like to show you some things about Ruth.'

The old woman placed the box on the coffee table and carefully opened it, a light spray of dust scattering off its top in the sunlight. As she fingered through the many papers it contained, Robert could see that most were newspaper clippings. Louisa leaned forward, a shaft of sun filtered by the nets dappling her hair. Their bodies were close, their thoughts closer still.

'This is Ruth. And this one and this one.' Suddenly Robert and Louisa were wrapped in newspaper clippings and photographs as Mrs Wystrach handed them all over in an excited flurry. Her breath and anticipation were hot on his skin as Robert shared the pictures with Louisa.

Staring up out of the yellowed newspaper was an insipid girl with vacant eyes against a pale blue swirly background in what was obviously a school photograph. Above it, the simple headline stated: *Schoolgirl Missing*.

Robert's heart knotted in his chest as he stared at a much

younger Erin. In his mind, there was no mistaking that the girl in the newspaper had matured into his wife. He wasn't sure whether to leap up and hug the old couple – in case they really were his parents-in-law – or keep the discovery to himself in case they clammed up. From body language alone, Robert was certain they knew more than they were letting on and he didn't want to put up a road block. He would tread carefully; contact them again if necessary.

Either way, Robert couldn't help imagining that it was Erin and Ruby who never came back, that it was their pictures he had supplied to the police and the newspapers, urging the nation to search for his missing family. A line of sweat prickled underneath his shirt, dampening the length of his spine.

'I'm so sorry,' he found himself saying, hardly able to look at the young girl. She had already sent a jolt through him. 'It must have been very hard.'

Robert heard Louisa mouthing the words of the accompanying report of the missing girl, noticing only key words as they left her lips – *runaway, abducted, plea, police* . . .

'She was only fifteen. A child.' The old woman's voice contained a thread of hope, ridiculously, as if Robert, a complete stranger, had been delivered to relieve them of their loss. 'She was everyone's favourite little girl.' She placed a worn-out hand on her husband's back. 'We were a close family.'

At this comment her husband stood and moved to the window, angling his oversized and ageing body into the column of sunshine that struck across the room. 'One day she was here. Then she ran away.' Mrs Wystrach joined her husband in the light and they stood staring out of the window, leaving their visitors to riffle through the clippings.

There were several copies of the same newspaper, containing articles about the missing girl. One clipping had come from a national daily. All dated from the same month – January 1992.

'What do you think?' Robert lowered his voice, as if that would make his words unintelligible to the old couple.

'I was about to ask you the same question.'

'Look at the mole. Look at the cheekbones. I know the hair's different, but the foundations are there.'

'I have a mole,' Louisa whispered and pointed to her temple. 'It doesn't make me the girl in the picture.'

'This girl could never be you.' Robert held up the black and white photo again. 'But it certainly could be Erin.' If he'd been alone, Robert would have whispered to the girl directly. She looked as if she had a secret, the way her eyes were stilled with fear and her lips sat slightly apart with the story they wanted to tell. Did she know that she had been in all the newspapers?

'Uh-uh. Sorry,' Louisa chided. 'This girl was fifteen years old in nineteen ninety-two. That would make her twenty-seven, twenty-eight, depending on her exact birthday. How old is Erin?'

'Thirty-two. OK, Sherlock. I'm just telling you what I see. There is a very strong likeness between this young girl and my wife.'

'You're being suggestible, just like the old couple when you showed them the locket.' Louisa sighed and sat back. 'Rob, I can't see it. Don't hang out on this.'

Robert didn't respond to her scepticism. While he had the chance, while the Wystrachs' backs were turned, he removed several pages from one of the newspapers, folded them tightly and tucked the wad inside his shirt.

'She may yet be found,' he offered the old couple. 'Never give up hope.'

They both turned in unison. 'But the locket,' Mrs Wystrach

pleaded. Her eyes were dots, shrunken from the sunlight. 'You must tell us where you got it from. Ruth's grandmother gave it to her for her tenth birthday. She always wore it. The picture in the locket is Edyta Wystrach, the mother of my husband, Vasil, and his brother Gustaw.'

'Perhaps you could tell us more about your daughter's disapearance,' Louisa's direct approach flicked a switch in the woman.

'Ruth wasn't just a runaway.'

'Irena, don't.' Vasil Wystrach placed a warning hand on his wife's arm and shook his head.

'What harm can it do? The press told the world back then anyway.' Irena shrugged off her husband's touch. 'The police believe that Ruth kidnapped a baby when she ran away from home.'

'Why would she do that?' Louisa edged forward and withdrew a pad and pen from her shoulder bag. 'Why would a fifteen-year-old want to do such a thing?'

The woman hesitated before answering, swallowed away what she really wanted to say. 'This is what we said to the police but it seems that they have their evidence and it all points at our Ruthie.' The skin on Irena Wystrach's face paled, ageing her further. She swallowed several times. 'We don't believe our daughter did such a thing, do we, Vasil?'

'The evidence they had suited the police and the grieving mother of the stolen baby. What they didn't realise was that we were grieving too.' Vasil's voice was thin, cautious.

'What evidence did the police have that your daughter took this baby?' Louisa jotted a few notes. 'Don't worry. I'm not a journalist but we think that your missing daughter may have something to do with someone we are trying to locate.' She smiled in just the right place.

Irena riffled in the box of papers again and retrieved some later clippings. 'Read this and see if you think it is evidence. If they thought our Ruthie was a kidnapper, then they should have tried harder to find her.'

Robert pressed close to Louisa, who removed her glasses to read the new thread in an otherwise routine missing teenager story.

ABDUCTED BABY LINKED WITH TEEN RUNAWAY

Police suspect a link between the teenage runaway, Ruth Wystrach, last seen by her parents Vasil and Irena at her home on 4 January, and the abducted baby Natasha Jane Varney.

The infant was kidnapped from her mother's Renault 5 while parked in a Northampton supermarket car park also on 4 January.

Several witnesses have made statements to the police claiming that they saw a young girl matching the description of the missing teenager. Two witnesses were able to give an exact time and good description, stating that they saw a female youth running through the car park carrying a baby. The suspect was said to be in a distressed state. Another witness reported sighting a teenager with a baby hitching a lift on the M1.

Detective Inspector George Lumley, the officer in charge of the case, said, 'We are following up all leads but would particularly like to speak with the runaway teen so that we can eliminate her from our inquiries. The mother of the abducted baby is naturally very distressed and will be making a statement to the press shortly. Anyone with any information should contact the Northamptonshire Police on . . .'

'Whoa,' Robert said when he had finished reading. 'Somewhat circumstantial, don't you think?'

Then the knife dug deep in his heart.

'What they print isn't necessarily everything they know.' Louisa handed back the clipping. She replaced her glasses.

'Just tell us where you got the locket. It could only have come from our Ruth. She would never have given it away.' Vasil Wystrach coloured with his demand.

Robert stepped in. 'Most likely my wife bought it at a flea market. I'm guessing she gave it to my stepdaughter as a present.' Robert pulled on the knife that was lodged in his heart but it wouldn't come out. 'Have you considered that your runaway daughter might have sold the locket? She would have needed the money.' The pain in his chest didn't ease. 'Was she into drugs, Mrs Wystrach? Was your Ruth an addict?'

'Rob,' Louisa interjected.

'Did your Ruthie have some terrible secret that forced her to commit this crime? Perhaps your daughter wasn't the girl you thought she was. Have you considered that?' Robert shifted uncomfortably.

Vasil balled his fists and made to move but his wife halted him. The first flicker of their daughter in thirteen years and she wasn't going to have it end in a fight.

'Take another look, will you? Have a good look at Ruth.' Mrs Wystrach fluttered a different faded picture of Ruth in front of Robert.

He steadied the picture and stared into the vacant teenage eyes. He glanced at the date at the top of the page – Saturday,

11 January 1992. He controlled his rapid breathing and tried to recall what he might have been doing on such a day. Of course he couldn't, and wouldn't expect anyone to.

All Robert knew for sure was that he would have been twenty-four years old and fresh out of law school, and Erin would have been only nineteen. Ruby would have been barely born; an unwanted gift for such a young, troubled mother. He shook his head as the knife dug deeper. Robert removed his stare from the pleading eyes of the teenager. Erin's eyes.

'I'm sorry. I don't recognise your daughter,' he lied, trailing his finger over Ruth's mousy fringe and long hair. Robert refused to reveal anything about Erin. Not until Louisa had researched the story further. There was something, he sensed, that the couple was hiding. 'She's pretty,' he offered as consolation. 'She'd be a grown woman now.' He didn't care if he upset them. He needed a cigarette and a chance to think. He stiffened his legs, as if to stand, and handed the clipping back to Mrs Wystrach. 'We should go.' He addressed Louisa and gave her a look that told her not to protest.

Robert realised she hadn't finished with the old couple but he wasn't sure how much more he could hear; wasn't sure how much of the story Louisa had pieced together herself yet. Until he was somewhere safe, until he could let it come out, Robert would not allow himself to think of Ruby or her uncertain future. For now, the knife remained lodged in his heart.

He turned to Mr Wystrach. 'I'm sorry about your daughter.' Robert removed a business card from his wallet and left it on the tea tray. 'If you think of anything, if you want to talk, then call me.' Robert nodded at Irena Wystrach and showed himself out through the rear door, praying that Louisa was following.

He walked around the side of the house and bleeped the Mercedes unlocked, waiting without looking back until Louisa was beside him. He didn't want to hang about any longer than necessary in the drab, concrete-lined street.

'You look like you've seen a ghost.' Louisa buckled up. She swapped to her sunglasses, allowing Robert to glimpse his reflection in stereo.

'I have,' he snapped and belted the Mercedes to the limits of each gear.

Robert called Louisa on his mobile even though she was in room 224, the one right next to his. He hadn't planned on staying the night in Northampton and he hadn't planned on bothering Louisa again. They'd both agreed an early night was needed and parted in the corridor after a hasty and tasteless hotel meal.

He let his head sink into the dough of the fresh pillow while the phone rang. It hadn't been easy booking them into separate rooms when the receptionist assumed they were partners. Partners in crime, he'd said. God.

'You're still awake then.'

'No,' she said. 'What's up?' It was still early but Robert knew she was sleepy and fuzzy from the wine they had shared.

'Natasha Jane Varney is what's up.'

'We've been over this, Rob. Goodnight.'

'Wait.'

'What? I'm tired. I'm only staying the night so that we can visit the local register office in the morning. Then you can get whatever's in your system out of it.'

'I want you to find the abducted baby's mother.'

'Her name was in the newspaper report. Why don't you look in the phone book?' Louisa yawned. 'Let me sleep, Rob.

You won't like me tomorrow otherwise.' She hung up.

Robert smoothed out the newspaper pages he had taken from the Wystrachs' house on the bed. He felt like a historian piecing together someone's missing past, only in this case he'd been handed the entire puzzle on a plate, each piece of the jigsaw numbered clearly and fitting perfectly. Strangely, miraculously, tragically, he was the only person in the whole world who could see the picture it made, the consequences it bore.

BABY SNATCHED FROM CAR PARK

Northamptonshire Police have launched a massive hunt for a baby abducted from a supermarket car park on Saturday, 4 January.

Natasha Jane Varney, aged 8 weeks, was left in a vehicle while her mother went into the shop. On returning, Mrs Cheryl Varney, 23, discovered her baby had been taken and raised the alarm.

Detective Inspector George Lumley is treating the case as an abduction and asks the public to be vigilant and report anything they think may be of use. 'The infant was wearing a pale pink Babygro and a white woollen hat and wrapped in a matching blanket. We are concerned that the baby be reunited with her nursing mother as quickly as possible. Needless to say, parents Andrew and Cheryl Varney are extremely distressed and call upon the public for help.'

Such a small square of copy for a life-changing event. Heading the story was a picture of the infant and Robert stared long and hard at her shiny jet hair and depthless eyes. Her long fingers curled round the edge of the blanket and her newborn gaze was distant, a coincidence caught in the split second the shutter opened and closed, but so similar to Ruby's distant stare, when her mind seemed to wander off to that other place. The baby's mother, Cheryl Varney, was barely discernible in the picture.

Fighting the paranoia in which Louisa would claim he was drowning, Robert reached for the telephone directory that sat squarely next to the phone and flipped to the Vs. There were only a handful of Varneys and only one with the initial C. Robert entered the address and number into his phone and snapped it shut.

He didn't think telephoning was appropriate to let someone know that his stepdaughter was their kidnapped baby.

Oh yes, he thought, making a lunge for the minibar. He could see exactly what had happened back in January 1992 and suddenly possession being nine-tenths of the law had never seemed so wrong.

The setting sun was virtually hidden by clouds rumbling from the west. Robert sensed rain; he sensed a storm and snorted as he wiped his mouth after cleaning his teeth with a courtesy pack he had purchased at reception.

He didn't particularly care what the weather did and wondered if Erin's phone needed charging because it consistently diverted to voicemail without even ringing. He wasn't sure he'd know what to say to her anyway. He splashed water on his face and slicked his damp hair back with his fingers. He gathered his car keys and room key and, after requesting a local map from the reception desk, left the hotel. Louisa, he assumed, would be asleep by now or at the very least immersed in the bath or a movie.

Twenty minutes later, Robert turned into Windsor Terrace, a narrow street of tiny red-brick properties, as if each one was a building block rather than a whole house. The single front windows gazed into the ones directly opposite and Robert noticed that most had net curtains hanging in them all except one. Instead of nets, the curtains were completely closed. A finale of orange sunlight tracked a runway down the deserted road.

All the parking spaces were occupied and Robert was forced to park at the far end of the street. He walked back towards the Varney household with a light patina of sweat glossing his face. The evening was muggy and he reckoned the temperature between the two rows of houses was a couple of degrees higher than in open space. Robert wondered just how much the residents knew about each other's lives, living this close. He wondered if Cheryl's neighbours knew about her years of misery.

Number 18 was small and neat but strangely devoid of character. Many of the other houses had baskets of summer flowers dangling over the pavement or window boxes crammed with geraniums. Music or the low chatter of television slipped from open front windows and, like in the Wystrachs' street, Robert heard a baby wail, a toddler scream in anger. This time, the infant noise crashed into Robert's heart. One house wouldn't have any baby noise. One house would be filled with sadness.

Without knowing or thinking about repercussions or what he would say, or wouldn't say, Robert went through the front gate of number 18, tucked between two identical houses, and knocked on the door. This was the house that had the front curtains closed so when there was no answer, he wasn't able to peek inside to see if anyone was home. There wasn't any visible way to the rear either, being mid-terrace. He knocked again, louder and more urgently. A middle-aged woman came out of next door, a dog yapping at her heels, and stared at Robert as if he had just knocked on her door.

'She'll be out late,' she said briskly. 'Give her a call and make an appointment.'

Robert turned and leaned on the low wall that separated the two tiny front gardens. When his feet sank, he realised he was standing on soil. 'Do you know when she'll be home?'

'Late, like I said.' The woman wiped soapy hands on a tea towel. 'If it's urgent, she's at the Stag's Head up on the road into town. You might get to see her if she's not too busy.' The woman grinned as if she knew something Robert didn't and clicked the door shut.

The Stag's Head was crowded and filled with the smoke of seared steak and cigarettes. One by one Robert studied each of the bar and waiting staff to see if any of them matched the image of the woman he held in his mind. Of course, he might not recognise her now. The photograph in the newspaper was thirteen years old and focused mostly on the baby. She would have suffered over a decade of misery and grief, which would have taken its toll on her looks. He didn't think any of the staff at the Stag's Head even vaguely resembled the woman in the picture. Robert edged towards the bar and ordered a pint.

'Can you tell me where I can find Cheryl Varney?' he asked, slipping a ten-pound note across the wet counter. The young girl, agitated by the number of waiting customers, gestured to the rear of the pub.

'She's in there. Do you want a ticket? There's a long wait. Or you could see someone else.' The barmaid hovered between the pumps and the till while Robert figured out what she was talking about. He noticed the coloured chalk writing on a blackboard above the bar. *Psychic Night. Tarot, Runes, Clairvoyant* . . .

'I'll take a ticket for her and wait,' Robert replied as it dawned on him that Cheryl Varney was a psychic, although not psychic enough to find her own baby.

When he was handed ticket number thirty-two, a female voice, barely audible, sang out from the rear of the pub, 'Number twenty-five, please.' A young woman held up her ticket as if she'd won a raffle and made her way to a room leading off the bar.

Robert shouldered his way between clusters of patrons of all ages and finally stood at the far end of the bar, near the doorway to the room hosting the psychic readings, and watched as the client seated herself at a table spread with a purple cloth. A crystal ball sat in the middle of the table and, behind it, with her dark hair hanging in swathes around her alabaster neck, was Cheryl Varney. Unmistakably.

Robert drank his pint without tasting it. With his eyes fixed on Cheryl, he drew out a packet of cigarettes from his top pocket and took out the last one. He remembered he didn't smoke. Someone bumped against him, sloshed an inch of his pint down his shirt, apologised and then offered Robert a light when he asked.

Robert drew in a lengthy breath and blew out, squinting through the smoke at Cheryl – the woman who had lost her baby thirteen years ago. The woman whose baby he had found. The woman he just wanted to meet, to perhaps pass on a secret message that her daughter was safe and well and beautiful. The woman who believed her baby was gone forever.

Robert waited his turn and drank his beer and smoked his cigarette. He would wait all night if he had to. He wondered if

Cheryl really was psychic. He didn't believe in stuff like that although he could understand why she did. He watched her working.

Curiously, she had her own hands spread out on the table, palms upturned, studying them intently. Then she suddenly glanced up at Robert as if she sensed he was staring. For a moment, he couldn't hear anything, as if the pub had emptied and they were completely alone, just him and Ruby's mother.

TWENTY-FOUR

It took me three years to save up eleven thousand pounds. I tried to resist spending most of my regular earnings on clothes and toys for Ruby but the promise of her returning to me soon sent me to the shops for gifts.

After six months working at what I soon realised was nothing more than a brothel, Freda put me in a room with Maggie. A reward for being her best girls. We decorated it with curtains and cushions and pictures from the market and bought a rug for the floor so Ruby had somewhere soft to crawl when she was better and came back to me.

It wasn't that I was stupid or gullible or didn't know what they were doing to me. I understood that I was selling my body and giving most of the money to Becco and as time went by and the weeks turned into months and eventually years, I also realised that it wasn't being spent on Ruby's medical bills. There were no medical bills although I didn't look that one in the eye until much later. I continued on my course, set firmly in the belief that as soon as Ruby was better she would one day be snuggled next to me when I finished work.

I can't remember the date, the hour, the minute when it hit me that I would never see my baby again. I can't remember what I was wearing or who my clients were that night. In my situation, it was a little like losing a milk tooth: you wobble it and it falls out. Thing is, with a baby tooth, you know another one's right behind it.

Like I said, my weekly pay packet was often spent as soon as I earned it so I saved up a little stash by creaming a few quid off the top of my clients' fees or offering extra services for more cash – stuff the other girls wouldn't do. I wouldn't have had to steal from Becco and Freda if I'd been more careful with my money but I needed something to whitewash the pain, a little luxury here and there to help me forget that ten different men would be heaving their hairy bodies over me in any one night. Besides, Maggie was getting fired up about going to California and I desperately wanted to go with her. I had to get money for that and for Ruby's future when she got better.

Then Becco started stalking me more than usual. I kept thinking, it's only because he wants a bit of me for himself that he's so interested. In fact, I once offered but he slapped my face – the only time he ever hit me – and since then his beady eyes didn't so much watch me as become a part of me. He was even in my dreams.

He watched the other girls, the foreign ones, but not in the same way. He kept them on a visual cord that if snapped, if stretched beyond the walls of this house, would most likely have resulted in Becco disposing of them some place only he knew.

Again, I'm not stupid or anything, but it took me a while to figure out that the girls who couldn't speak much English, the ones from Albania and Serbia and anywhere Becco could score a decent-looking harvest, were kept against their will. Or maybe it was that they just didn't have a will to do anything else. Then, after that, I realised that Maggie and I were the decoys, the maids, the tolerated link to the outside world.

Norris died. He'd become one of my regular clients as well as my first client that night in the hotel with Maggie. Both Becco and Freda knew that he was a meagre payer but they let him get away with it because he was regular and nice to us girls. But when I found out he'd died, I didn't tell them. I let them think I was still visiting him and collecting his measly hundred and fifty when really I was visiting a lawyer in his swanky apartment who paid me twice as much. If I hadn't got the 'flu, if Maggie hadn't had to step in at the last minute to visit the long-dead Norris, I would have got away with it.

So then there was a row. The night hung heavy with the scent of hurried or desperate or violent or silent sex, like the stinking pile of laundry that built up in the foreign girls' bathroom. Everywhere reeked of dirty men layered upon dirty men layered upon skinny girls.

'You done a stupid thing, silly Milly.' Maggie slapped my face and showed me her bruised and bloody thighs. 'Turns out Norris is dead so I took a punt on the street and ended up with seven kinds of fury jammed between my legs.'

We fought and she slapped me and spat in my face and I bit her and then cried as she dragged me across the floor. Panting and hair everywhere, we'd smashed the only telly in the house before Becco separated us and pulled Maggie out of the room, making me believe I'd won. Making me believe that Becco liked me better. Making me believe I was special. Making me believe, later, when I was pacing around the house in the early hours, that Maggie wasn't really dead when I found her folded into the stone-floored pantry. Making me believe that the gash across her temple was residue from between her legs, that she hadn't been knocked out cold and thrown into the small room. Maggie wasn't breathing and wouldn't talk to me and I tried and tried to locate the tick-tick of a pulse on her lifeless body.

It went like this. As soon as Becco had hauled Maggie out of my hair, I went to bed. I was ill. I knew she'd simmer down. I woke at five, the first tendrils of light were weaving into my room, and I saw that Maggie hadn't come to bed. I needed some water and a pill to stop the aches. Freda kept paracetamol somewhere in the kitchen, which is how I came to find Maggie in the pantry. In a state of shock, I was walking back through the hall on my way to alert Freda – she would know what to do – when a ferocious yelling and pounding began at the front door like all hell had broken loose.

In a second, in pure fear, I ducked through a door that led to the cellar. In another second, whoever was smashing the door in was inside the house.

It was the police. A raid. I heard them spreading through the three floors with a trail of warnings followed by terrified screams as the foreign girls were woken. When they finally got to searching the basement, I was already hidden. I had discovered by accident, by falling into it, a water-filled pit at the back of the unlit cellar. As two policemen flashed torches around the vaulted cave, I held my breath, curled into a ball and disappeared underwater.

I saw the beam of light zigzag over the surface like a fish might see the moon. I said a silent prayer that they wouldn't notice bubbles as my lungs squeezed for life. Using all the self-control I had learnt during the last three years – when a punter's picking his way over every second of my skin, when he's close up examining every hole in my body and deciding what to shove where – I stuck my nose up so that my nostrils gently broke the surface of whatever kind of water I was in. Another prayer that it wasn't from the toilet. Even with liquid in my ears, I heard the murmurings of the police voices, their urgent raid-speak as they co-ordinated their blitz on our house.

When their lights were gone, when after hours and hours the house creaked only from its own weight, I slithered out of the pit and dragged my waterlogged body back up the steps into the hall. There wasn't a sound. It was the strangest thing. No foreign babble of sparring girls, no crack of the whip from Becco, no buzzer sounding from the other end of the house where the other girls worked and their customers called. Maggie and I were used to the orchestra of sounds, just your everyday brothel, but we were never allowed into that part of the house. Aside from mealtimes, we were kept completely separate.

I stretched out but couldn't straighten properly because my spine had fused in the cold water. I left the lights off and stalked the house. I went into Becco's office first and, by the orange spray of street lighting, I could see that most of it was missing. It was like everyone had moved out and forgotten to tell me.

Where papers had been piled, there was empty desk. Where boxes had been stacked, there was now blank carpet that looked cleaner and plusher than the rest. I went behind the desk and sat down in Becco's chair, the place where he'd counted out my money. I opened a drawer. Nothing apart from an elastic band and a biro cap. I stretched my legs, which caught on a carrier bag that had been left under the desk. When I stood up, the bag came with me and when I unhooked it from my ankle, something fell out. A little maroon book. Someone's passport. Something the police had overlooked.

I kept hold of it and went back into the hall, leaving a trail of water as my sodden dressing gown dripped. I was freezing.

Then I heard a whimper. A brittle mouse-like cry with a sniff behind it. I followed my ears and ended up in the attic room on the foreign girls' side of the house, although I wasn't sure whose side it was any more. In fact, I wasn't sure about anything except that unless I wanted to be hauled away by the police, I'd better get my stuff and bugger off quick.

I found her in the wardrobe and laughed and cried at the same time, my emotions as curdled as sour milk and as separate as oil and water. She was as folded up as Maggie had been in the pantry but this little thing was alive, snivelling pathetically and calling for her mummy, for me.

'Naughty Freda's been hiding you here all along,' I said to her, crouching and grinning and tickling her knee. She had a red crescent around her mouth as if she'd drunk fizzy pop and there was food matted in her hair. She wore a nappy although she seemed too old for such a thing, and the tops of her naked thighs were bubbled with blisters. 'And naughty Freda said that you weren't very well and I couldn't have you back yet.'

I scooped the little girl up and wedged her on my hip. She smelled of wee and stale milk. I loved her instantly and I knew she loved me back, even though she didn't understand a word I said.

'*Nënë, nënë, nënë*,' she wailed a thousand times, which I later discovered meant mummy in Albanian.

For the second time in my life I escaped by jumping out of a window. I had forty-eight pounds in my jeans pocket, the passport that I'd found in Becco's office and little Ruby attached to my front as we legged it, just like I'd done several years before.

When I'd gone to fetch my saved-up money from the cash box hidden under my mattress, it was jimmied open and empty. The police had got to it and I doubt very much they bagged it up as evidence. I stuffed the empty tin into a small bag and grappled my daughter into some clothes that I discovered at the back of the wardrobe she was hiding in. We left through the kitchen window as the police entered again through the boarded-up front door. We headed for the station, took a train to anywhere and ended up in Brighton. On the journey, I leafed through the passport to discover who I was.

We flashed into a tunnel and as we emerged into the daylight, I became Erin Lucas, born 29 June 1972. I was four years older.

It was easy at first, with the tourists eager to spend, and many of the locals soon came to know me. They made a point of finding me on the corner by the antique shop to buy their flowers. I was the cheapest in town.

It was summer and sleeping behind a beach hut or dodging through the hostels got me by. I never nicked from the same shop twice in one day. In fact, I don't think many of the shops even realised that some of their street displays had mysteriously vanished. The trail of water from the stems on the hot pavement soon evaporated.

I rearranged the blooms into splendid fragrant bouquets and sold them easily. I earned twenty pounds in one day, my best ever although a far cry from my London earnings. But I was glad to be out of all that and gradually Ruby's troubled behaviour began to change.

She learned English and soon forgave me for leaving her in the hospital for so long. Spending all that time with Mummy was good for her and when I wasn't stealing from shops or posh, flower-filled gardens or selling my wares on the street, we would pick through the pebbles on the beach as if they were washed-up sweets or hunt for shells and tide-smoothed glass from across the world. The sun shone and we were happy.

By the end of September, when the hotels emptied of their bustling summer trade and the wind kicked up and chucked weed and froth onto the beach, when the litter formed swirling flurries down the narrow lanes, a hand reached out and saved me. As I removed three cellophane-wrapped bunches of some exotic flowers I didn't even know the name of, a plump hand wrapped around my wrist and stopped me in my tracks.

'I hear you're the competition,' the man said, stooping down beside me. Ruby tugged at my other hand, whining, sensing danger, and I felt I was being torn in two. 'I can recommend a reliable wholesaler for your stock,' he continued and I couldn't understand why he gently guided Ruby and me into his perfumed flower shop. When I fell to the floor sobbing and pleading with him not to call the police, he sat me down and gave us orange juice and Belgian chocolates. It was all we could do not to scoff the lot.

'I'm sorry,' I said. 'I won't steal from you again. It's just that your flowers sell the best and we get starving.' The man liked my honesty.

'I've been watching you for a week now, when I realised that my anthurium hadn't grown legs and walked away. I even bought one of the arrangements you had made on the sea-front, although you won't remember.' I didn't.

He told me his name was Baxter King and that he was looking for an assistant. He offered me the job right there and then because I had an eye for colour. He called for his partner, Patrick, to come and see what he had found. The pair stood staring at me in a loose embrace while I sipped my juice and Ruby sucked on a coffee cream. Within a week I had learnt the ropes and been invited to move into the couple's comfortable flat to help them keep house.

'Baxter,' I say, breathless, as he comes in smelling of salt and the wind. 'Someone telephoned again. I know it's him.' Without taking his eyes off me, Baxter lets his jacket slide onto the chair, wraps his hands around Patrick's shoulders for a second and then comes up to me to give me a hug.

'It was all too long ago,' he says. 'There are things in life you have to let go of. There's no way he could trace you. It's a wrong number, you'll see. If it bothers you, I'll get the number changed.'

I nod and try to believe him although I don't. Not even Baxter knows my full story.

I saw the body. I nicked his money, a passport and a little girl. I've got secrets even though I know how to keep my mouth shut. I have a new life now, far away from anything I left behind in London, and the thought of Becco seeking me out and forcing me back to work . . .

I shiver and tell Baxter about my day at the shop, how popular the new stock is proving to be and how well Ruby is doing at school.

'She didn't get the part in the musical, by the way. She's not Annie, not even one of the other orphan girls. But she's pleased as pie.'

Baxter raises an eyebrow, one of his tricks, and seems relieved that I don't appear worried any more, even though I am. 'How come?'

'She's in the orchestra. The pianist.' I watch as his pale face turns pink with the pride of a father, even though he's not.

Baxter had Ruby sitting at his piano from the very first day we came to live with him. She learnt quickly and eagerly although she wasn't even school age. Playing the piano, simple nursery rhymes and jingles at first, became Ruby's passion. It was a vent for all the agony she had absorbed in the first few years of her life, a way to let it all out. I will love Baxter forever for giving her that.

'I'm so happy for her,' he says, staring out of the bay window of the first-floor flat, down the street to the sea. 'Looks like a storm's blowing up,' he comments and I know he's right.

Someone sends me flowers. Someone has sent flowers to a flower shop. The delivery man looks as bemused as me when he confirms my name and says, yes, they are for you.

I call Baxter to come from the storeroom but remember that he has gone out to run errands. I am all alone. I peel open the envelope and read the card. A chill works its way from my feet to my heart as I read his name in black handwriting. He has found me. He hasn't given up looking, after all this time. He wants me back, to keep me quiet.

I shut up the shop early and sprint to Ruby's school, waiting outside for her to finish, stepping from one foot to the other as if her class will never finish. She looks bewildered when she sees me. Normally, she will walk alone to the shop and take delight in rearranging the displays or beg for coins to buy an ice cream and sit on the seafront shooing away the gulls until it's time to go home.

Today I drag her by the hand and we take the bus straight home and bolt the door. Just in case and without Ruby knowing, I pack a bag. I cram in all the things I couldn't bear to lose and all the things we're going to need. Twice I have fled and left my life behind. The telephone rings. I don't answer it.

When I listen to the message, I know it's him. I would never forget that voice, those weasel eyes searching me out.

He wants me back even though I'm not me any more.

The stench of smoke wakes me. They say that fire spreads quickly but panic and noise fill the flat as much as the swathes of dense blackness that invade our bedroom.

'Ruby, wake up!' I scream. We sleep in the same room and she is so still that I wonder if the smoke has already got to her and I will be carrying a body as, once again, I flee for my life. But she stirs, her nose twitching and her eyes watering as soon as she opens them.

'What's happening, Mum?'

'Get up now. There's a fire!' I hear Baxter screaming, banging, glass shattering. I yank Ruby off the bed and undo the sash window catch. My fingers aren't mine and I can't make them work. 'Shut the door,' I cry. It'll give us precious extra seconds.

Finally, the window catch gives, years of paint crumbling as it opens. I slide up the heavy pane and push Ruby onto the window sill. The metal fire escape at the rear of the building clatters and creaks like the hulk of an old ship sinking as she climbs onto it. I drag the pre-packed bag from under the bed and sling it onto my shoulder. Without looking back, we clamber down the fire escape and run as fast as we can down the street. I know he won't be far away.

Even when we are panting on the beach I can smell burning in the night air, see the flicker of orange above the rooftops as sirens scream through town. We sit, shaking, Ruby in her ballerina pyjamas resting her head on my shoulder, me in sweatpants and a T-shirt, and once again I'm thinking of catching a train.

The tide creeps up the pebbles, the noise of the wash getting closer, and when we can feel the spray on our ankles, we move further up the beach and huddle under the storm wall. I think about the consequences of running away again as well as the outcome if we stay.

We could stand up now and walk back to the smouldering ruin that is Baxter and Patrick's flat. I can't bear the thought that I have brought this upon them. But they'll be OK; they'll survive. They can rebuild and they have each other and the shop. I know that they're better off without me. It's a fact that my parents are better off without me – the teenager who shamed them by getting pregnant at fifteen. Now it's a fact that Baxter and Patrick are better off without my sordid past darkening their lives.

When it comes down to it, Ruby would be better off without me too. But I am her mother now. She falls asleep against my shoulder.

In the morning we take a bus to the station and ride a train to the place Becco will never think of searching; the last place he'd expect me to hide. London.

At Victoria Station, I push fifty pence into the telephone and dial Baxter's shop to tell him we're OK. In a voice warped by grief, he tells me that Patrick is dead.

TWENTY-FIVE

She called ticket number thirty-two, oblivious of the consequences. At first, Robert didn't hear her over the noise in the pub. He had gone to sit down on a leather banquette but wished he hadn't because he was positioned beside a fruit machine that spewed out coins and jangled his thoughts. Then he glimpsed Cheryl's face through the crowd, watched her mouth his number. As if he was walking underwater, he pushed his way to the woman whose life he could to bring to a halt.

Something in Cheryl's eyes flickered as he approached. Without a word and only a heavy drag of her eyes up and down his body – a sure-fire way for a psychic to gain a starting point – she beckoned him into the sanctuary of the clairvoyant's room. It was peaceful and smelled of sandalwood and there was a hint of tranquil music trickling from a couple of speakers. Three other tables were set out with a generous gap between each of them so that the consultations could take place in privacy.

'Please, sit down.' Her voice was quiet and structured. Built on grief.

Robert did as he was instructed, not taking his eyes off her. She wasn't routinely attractive but there was something beautiful about the warp and weft of her skin, the way the fabric of her soul bared through as honest as her blushed cheeks or as devious as her dilated pupils. The saucer eyes made her look crazy. Robert would understand if she was.

'I'm Cheryl,' she said. Her gaze flicked over him, perhaps to read his past, his future.

Robert knew that was how they worked, these so-called psychics. One snippet of information, one fact too many and they were on to something, had you all wrapped up hey presto and pocketed your money. Except that in this case, he was about to predict her future, change it forever.

'Robert Knight,' he said and held out his hand which seemed to surprise her. She didn't take it.

'Did you want the tarot, crystal ball, runes? I can do most things.' She didn't look at him as she spoke.

'I'm not sure,' Robert replied honestly. He didn't care about his past and he didn't think he had much of a future any more. He would rather talk about her, the woman he believed was Ruby's real mother, the woman who had suffered incalculable loss because of his wife. The woman who, if he turned the whole matter over to the police, would have another chance to be Ruby's mother. Then he thought of Erin – he loved her, didn't he? – broken, in prison, unable to forgive him if he turned her in. His heart beat so hard he could feel it in his throat.

Was it coincidence that Cheryl's hair, although deep brown, almost black, shone silver-blue in the light of the many candles positioned around the room, like Ruby's sometimes did? Was it not hereditary that she had the same full lips as his stepdaughter, the long limbs, the bony fingers and extra-slim neck that disappeared elegantly inside a purple chiffon top?

'What do you recommend?' He was gentle with her, hardly able to imagine what her life had held.

'Give me your hand,' she instructed, still not making eye contact. Does she know why I'm here? he wondered. She's meant to be psychic, after all.

She wiped her fingers over his palm. 'Ah.' She laughed, her smile a temporary tributary of her innate sadness. 'A businessman.' It wasn't as if he was wearing a suit or carrying a briefcase. He wondered why she found the fact amusing. 'And the usual stress to accompany that?' It was a question not a statement.

Finally, she made eye contact with Robert. He knew she'd seen the stars of sweat seeping from his palm. He nodded, not wanting to give too much away. 'Everyone has problems, don't they?'

The low voices from the consultations around them dissolved and the background noise from the bar passed to another dimension.

Cheryl closed her eyes and sighed before opening them. Her hand quivered and she let go of Robert's before he could notice.

'Well, you're going to live a long life, if that's any use.' Cheryl leaned back in her chair, the smile daring to spread.

'A long life full of stress? Hmm.' Robert mirrored her grin.

'It's not all bad.' She took a swift look at his palm again. 'But now is the hardest time. Once you get through that—'

'Couldn't that apply to anyone? Don't most of the people who come to see you have problems?' Robert instantly regretted challenging her. It wasn't what he had come to do.

'We all have our problems, Mr Knight. It's how we deal with them that makes each of us unique.' She slid Robert's hand off the velvet cloth, a sign that she was rejecting what he'd said, and positioned her own hands round the crystal ball. Robert could see her reflection in it, her glassy face morphed by refraction, twisted and wrecked by events outside her control.

'Tell me about my family and what their future holds.' He had now revealed that he had a family but he wasn't testing how credible she was. He was trying to find a way to talk about Ruby. Ideally, he wanted Cheryl to see her future through his and save him the ordeal of breaking the news; save him betraying Erin completely.

As she lost herself in the crystal ball, Robert considered the consequences if he had got it wrong. But the police had drawn the same conclusion thirteen years ago; the detective who had handled the case of Cheryl's kidnapped baby, Robert had noticed, had also handled Ruth's disappearance.

He, too, stared into the crystal ball and contemplated the impossible scenario of Ruth, his Erin, stealing another woman's baby. But all he saw in the glass was the face of Mary Bowman as she was denied her children.

'I can see a woman. Her life is as fragile as the wing of a moth.' Cheryl's voice was barely there. She continued to stare into the glass. 'She's always scared. Always running away.' Cheryl suddenly pulled her hands away from the ball. Her face went blank and her eyes hardened. She turned round and pulled a mohair wrap off the back of the chair and slung it around her shoulders. Robert noticed the hairs on her arms standing upright.

'Go on,' he urged, knowing she'd seen something, even though he didn't believe in this kind of thing.

She gazed at the ball again. 'Do you want me to be honest?'

'Of course.' He wished he could be honest but the truth, although it would change this woman's life, would destroy Erin's.

'You lost someone dear, not so long ago. You blame

yourself and live in circles, dizzying yourself with old habits, tired ways.' Cheryl hugged the shawl tighter. 'So scared,' she whispered with a look that said the same about her.

'And?' Robert's hunger for more information nearly outweighed the reason he had come. Cheryl had clearly seen Jenna.

'I don't see any more.'

'Can't or won't?' Robert said too loudly, wounded by her words even though he knew they were true. He wanted to shout at her and shake her cold body then cup her face in his hands and whisper that she could stop hurting now, that the pain could be over, that he had found her lost baby; that his wife, Erin, had stolen her and brought her up as her own, for whatever reasons, when she ran away from home, and that if she liked, she could have her back, to keep.

Except that to say those words would also be to shatter the life of a young girl who had just discovered confidence and happiness. How could he strip Ruby of the only mother she had ever known? How could he betray the woman he loved? Without doubt Erin would be tried and sentenced and the whole nation would know her story.

How could he?

Robert slouched in his chair. He groaned loudly, causing several other clients to stare. 'I'm sorry.' He straightened again when a look of surprise swept over Cheryl's weary face. 'It's been a tough week.'

To ease the awkward moment, Cheryl dealt a spread of tarot cards. Robert focused on the elaborate pictures, not caring what they meant. She could tell him that he was going to be run over by a bus tomorrow and he wouldn't mind. He just wanted her to mention her baby.

'As I thought,' she said, businesslike again, as if the moment between them, that thread of near connection, had never happened. 'A long life with lots of changes afoot. But for the better,' she added. Then, 'You must have specific questions. Everybody does.'

Oh, I do.

'Does anyone ever tell *your* fortune?' he asked.

Cheryl relaxed, amused. 'I can read my own future. Why would I need anyone else to?'

Robert let it pass. She continued to translate the cards, while he tried to lay the map of what she said over real life. There was something about a dilemma, crossroads perhaps, nothing that wouldn't fit the next punter as easily. Cheryl mentioned his work but told him he was in the wrong job. He knew he wasn't. Robert looked at his watch, wondering how long he had left.

'Can I buy you a drink when you've finished working?'

'I'm running late. I have five more clients to see yet.' No eye contact. Her cheeks reddened.

'Lunch tomorrow?'

'Mr Knight, did you come here to ask me on a date or do you want a reading?' She folded her arms, abandoning the tarot.

'I'm sorry. You're probably married with a family and think that I'm a sleaze—'

'You already told me that *you* have a family!'

'It wasn't meant to be a date. Just a drink.' Robert swallowed, felt his jaw twitch. He knew she was experienced in noticing the signs, just as he was. 'So *are* you married?' He remembered there was a husband – Andrew Varney? – mentioned in the newspaper reports following the abduction. Robert instantly regretted probing. Cheryl dipped her head and clasped her hands on her legs. She was barely breathing.

'I'm divorced.' It was as if she was lifting a boulder. 'A long time ago now.' Signalling a degree of bravery, she shuffled the tarot cards around.

'I'm a widower but married again now.' Robert waited for her to absorb their connection, that they had each, somehow, lost loved ones. He waited for her to cross the bridge. 'Do you have children?'

The gap of time was intolerable. The moment stretched to infinity but the immediate blankness on her face was what he had expected. Robert knew that underneath the layers of chocolate hair, beneath her flawless skin, behind the unfathomable eyes that had seen so much pain, was the core of her feelings.

'No, I don't.' Her reply was the javelin of an Olympic athlete. The words were driven with finality: *don't ask me any more.*

'I have a daughter.' There. It was said. He had shown her Ruby. 'She's thirteen.'

Cheryl smiled. 'Difficult times then.' She seemed grateful for the reprieve.

Robert heard the clairvoyant at the next table delivering a glimpse of the future to his client. He stole a look. A young woman sat riveted by the older man's revelations. He was reading her palm.

'Does anyone ever come back and tell you that you got it wrong?' Robert didn't know where he was taking it now.

'Complain?' Cheryl laughed. 'It's a bit hard to moan about fate. Not like you can take it back and ask for a refund, demand another life.'

'But what if you were so wide of the mark, you know, with your information that they asked for their money back?'

'If they were that unhappy then, no, I suppose I wouldn't charge my fee.'

'What if something should have been glaringly obvious but you overlooked it? Would you charge then?'

'I can only tell my clients what I see. I access this information in a number of ways.' Cheryl gestured to the crystal ball, touched the cards. 'If you're that much of a sceptic, Mr Knight, I suggest you don't make appointments with clairvoyants.' Apparently recovered from the sudden glimpse of her past, Cheryl defended her occupation.

'How did you first get into it? The psychic stuff.'

'I went to see one myself. She told me I had a gift.'

'Why did you go and see a clairvoyant?' Robert didn't realise he had incised and touched a nerve.

In an instant it was all over. Cheryl stood up. 'Mr Knight, I will not charge you for this consultation because you obviously have no desire to learn anything about yourself. If you wouldn't mind,' she levered her arm at the door, 'I have other genuine clients to see. Goodnight.'

Unperturbed by the outburst, in fact relieved that it had reached this point, otherwise how else would he know how to say the words, Robert also stood and leaned his hands on the small table. It wobbled.

'I *know*,' he began in a controlled tone, not too loud. Years of experience in court, impossible clients, even his recent struggle with Erin levelled his words. 'I *know* what happened.'

Cheryl cocked her head. The space between her eyebrows tightened.

'I know about your baby.'

Cheryl staggered and leaned on the chair, gripping it for support. Her knuckle bones turned yellow, nearly erupting through the skin.

'I've found your baby, Cheryl. It's all over.'

TWENTY-SIX

I soon learnt how hostels worked. Don't ask for much and neither will they. Two nights here, another couple there. If I stayed too long in one place, they began to ask questions that I was no good at answering. I managed to track down several old clients and earned a few hundred so that one night I was able to treat Ruby to a night in a posh hotel. We ate ice cream out of the tub and watched weepy movies until we fell asleep in the king-sized bed.

Then I saw the advertisement. I might have missed it if Ruby hadn't stopped to tie her trainer lace. *Assistant wanted*. I left Ruby standing in the street and impressed the flower shop owner with my extensive floral knowledge. I began work the next day and by the end of the week we'd rented a room in a house full of students. They didn't care who we were because I paid two weeks up front with an advance on my wages. In some ways it was good to be back in London.

I enrolled Ruby at the local comprehensive school two weeks after the start of term. It should have been a new beginning; her first year at secondary school. She was eleven. It was a whole month before I realised she'd been truanting. Her bed was soaked from tears and I found her sobbing with the sheet stuffed in her mouth to silence her misery. When I pulled it out, she screamed. When I walked in on her in the bathroom, I saw the bruises on her back.

I made an appointment with the headmaster but he had little time for my complaints.

'We have other itinerant children in the school. Why doesn't she play with them?' He thought we were gypsies.

I allowed Ruby to come to the flower shop where I worked. It was situated on a respectable high street and mid-morning she would run to the bakery and fetch doughnuts and hot chocolate. But she soon got bored and tried school again. I had to re-enrol her because the school secretary thought we had moved on.

With several months' salary behind me, I rented a small bedsit that was all our own. No more sharing bathrooms or labelling food in the fridge. When the school asked for a copy of Ruby's birth certificate, I kept promising I'd send it in. I never did and in the end they gave up asking. To them, we were trouble.

The florist was next to a music store. At three forty-five Ruby would step off the school bus right outside the shop. I'd see her trying not to smile as she spied me through the foliage of the window display and instead of coming to greet me, she'd go next door and run her fingers across the keys of the Bluthners and Steinways.

At first the owner was cautious of a pre-teen girl trailing sticky fingers over his expensive instruments but one day, when Ruby plucked up the courage to allow the fingers of her right hand to strike a complicated tune, he pulled out the stool for her and adjusted the height.

'Do you play?' he asked and Ruby nodded, too terrified to speak. Through the partition wall of the shop units, I heard my daughter lose herself in Debussy, Chopin and Mozart, everything Baxter had taught her over the years. From then on, whenever she wanted, she was allowed to go into the music shop and play the piano. The owner said it helped his business.

Months later, I was able to afford a second-hand piano for Ruby and I'll never know how the removals men squeezed it into the living space of our tiny bedsit.

I'm rearranging Fresh As A Daisy. I've learned over the years that customers expect a completely new look every couple of weeks. It lures them back. Baxter taught me the importance of window arrangement. 'Your invitation to the world,' he said.

I'm aiming for the bleached driftwood New England kind of look today – lots of twisted, weathered branches, beach pebbles with whitewashed pallets to support galvanised pots of stunning grasses. I managed to get hold of a fishing net and I'm trying to hang it up at the back of the display but it keeps dropping down. The number of people who walk by and stop to stare, you'd think one of them would lend a hand. I pause to make a coffee, leaning against the counter to study my work while the kettle boils.

Eventually, the window is looking pretty much how I want it. It seems to be attracting attention and I get a nice comment from one of my regulars. She comes twice a week to buy an arrangement for the firm of accountants where she works. Some of my other displays are looking a little limp. I fetch my spray canister and a stepladder and barely before I have misted anything, Robert strides into the shop. My heart skips and I smile. I like it when he drops by unexpected.

'Darling, what a surprise!' I jump backwards off the ladder, still holding the sprayer. 'You said you'd be away all day.' He'd left me a brief message yesterday saying Den had sent him to a legal conference. 'Den's just terrible, making you go away at such short notice. I missed you last night.' I think of kissing him but stop short. 'You need a shower, Mr Knight.' I squirt him playfully and grin. He doesn't respond. He looks flat. 'Remind me to give you a good scrubbing later.'

Robert still doesn't say anything. He strides across my shop as if he's looking for something and skittles a bucket of gerberas. He leans against the counter, his fists balled and white. He's breathing as if he's been running. Finally he turns to me and says, quite calmly, 'A shower is just what I need. I feel wrecked.'

I've got him. I grin again. 'Just let me bring the buckets in from the pavement then and I'll shut up shop early.' I wink at him and begin to drag the buckets in from the street. If he'd help, we'd be home quicker. But he doesn't. For some reason he just stares at me like I'm a stranger. We drive home in separate cars and as I look in my rear-view mirror, the sun glints off Robert's Mercedes as if it's on fire.

Nine months after the squashed-in bedsit, I moved us to a two-bedroom flat. I was earning just enough to pay for it and, tempting though it was, I didn't go back to selling my body. I wanted none of it. And, remarkably, Becco appeared to have lost my trail.

When we first moved in, the flat was grotty and smelled of cats but we soon had it our way and filled with the scent of lavender and home-cooked food. For the first time in my life I had my own kitchen.

Ruby seemed to be getting on well at school, despite being taunted by several kids. I prayed it wouldn't turn into anything worse. She enjoyed French and music lessons and made a friend called Alice who came back for tea. I worked hard for the owner of the flower business, using the skills I had learned in Brighton to transform his rather dull shop into one of the most popular florists in the area.

I wrote and told Baxter about our life in London and at first he didn't reply. I was worried that he had cut me off, holding me responsible for Patrick's death, which in a way I was. But I persevered and eventually his letters filtered back, short at first but then he revealed more about his life and how he had hired two assistants to help him in the shop. Baxter was strong. He'd saved my life even though I'd shattered his.

We arrive home and my skin prickles with evaporating sweat. The house is so much cooler than the inside of my car. Robert's obviously in a bad mood about something and I'm going to snap him out of it. I blow him a kiss but he doesn't see so I run upstairs, leaving a trail of my clothes across the bedroom floor. I step into the shower and let the water flow between my breasts. I feel wicked.

When Robert doesn't take the bait I know I'm going to have to be devious. It must be a very bad mood. 'Robert, help! Come quickly!' I scream as if there's a burglar in the house and before I know it, Robert's outside the shower cubicle panting like a beast.

'What is it?'

'In here. Open the door.' He does and instantly he's doused with water. I'm all lathered up and I can see he can't believe his eyes. 'Take your clothes off and get in. You're disgusting. I have to wash you.' I blow him another kiss. I know he wants me.

When he just stands there gawping, I reach out and pull him in. He wasn't ready for that and staggers into the cubicle fully clothed. I'm laughing my head off, not sure if the water on my face is from the shower or tears. Robert looks hilarious. 'Told you I'd get you clean.' I giggle. I push my soapy body against him. I don't care if his clothes are a mess. 'Take your shirt off and let me wash your back.' He does as he's told but reluctantly. 'Now, now. Don't get stroppy. If you're going to be a dirty boy then you have to face the consequences.' His eyes, creased to slits, dance all over me. I know he wants it.

'There's something we need to talk about,' he says, leaning on the tiles. I'm pinned between his arms. 'It's serious.'

For the first time ever, I wonder if he knows.

Ruby was in the shop next door playing the piano. She banged out an angry melody, something she'd composed herself, and from that I knew she'd had a bad day at school. The shop had been quiet all day, the rain not having let up since first thing. I hadn't bothered with the outside displays that morning because the petals would have been washed away.

Apart from the 'Open' sign on the door, I might as well have been closed. The owner of the shop rarely stopped by these days. He trusted me completely to manage the stock and the accounts, somehow knowing I wasn't going to rip him off, knowing I needed to keep my job.

The autonomy gave me confidence and I began to dress differently and had my hair highlighted and cropped into a flattering, jaw-length cut. I even hoped that one day I might meet a man. I didn't know what it was like to have someone to love me, not pay me. The thought of allowing a touch of my body without first agreeing a price confused my understanding of intimacy.

I was adding up the week's takings. The bell jangled and I looked up, pushing my reading glasses onto the top of my head. I didn't really need glasses and had bought a weak pair from the chemist. I liked the tortoiseshell frames. They made me look purposeful, as if I had a life. The man stopped in the doorway, politely wiping his feet over and over again. It didn't matter. I mopped the floor every night. He folded up his umbrella and stood it against the wall. I thought: you'll forget that.

'Hello,' he said and smiled. He walked around the shop and I went back to my calculator. Once or twice I looked up, a habit I have when customers are in the shop. He didn't notice.

'Can I help?' My question seemed to fluster him and, after staring blankly at me for a couple of seconds, he plucked a bunch of roses from a container and put them on the counter.

'Thanks,' he said while I wrapped them. He leaned on the counter with his left hand and I noticed there was no ring. He had nice hands.

'Eight ninety-nine then, please.' When I studied his face, I could see he was tired. His dark hair was mussed from the wind and rain and his eyes looked as if the soul had been sucked from them. He smiled and handed me his credit card. I swiped it through the machine and after a quick look at the signature strip I handed it back.

'Thank you, Mr Knight. Check and sign, please.' He held the pen and paused.

'I can hear music.' He tilted his head towards the partition wall.

'My daughter. She plays the piano in the shop next door until it's time to go home.'

'She's very good,' he commented. 'You must be proud parents.'

'Parent,' I corrected. 'Just me.' I wanted him to know, in case.

'Well, thanks.' And he walked out of the shop into the rain.

*

What can I do but carry on? He has me pinned to the wall, hot water raining down on us and he wants to talk about something serious. I don't. 'Talk dirty,' I order and smother him with shower gel. 'And don't even *think* of being boring right now. Anything serious will have to wait.' I rinse him with the shower rose and run my tongue up his chest.

Strangely, Robert flinches and thwacks his elbow against the glass. I take the opportunity to kiss it better. I will kiss anything for him. I loosen the belt on his trousers and drop to my knees, sliding the wet cloth to his ankles. 'While I'm down here . . .' and finally Robert's body responds to me.

Suddenly, he has his hands under my armpits and roughly pulls me upright. Our faces are close. 'How many times do you think we've made love?' he asks. I have no idea why.

'Let me see . . .' I hold up my fingers one by one and then take hold of Robert's and do the same. I crouch in the small space again and continue counting on his toes. 'Two or three hundred?' I drag my mouth over his wet legs but before I know it, he has me standing again. 'Hey . . .' He's hurt my shoulder.

'So what do you reckon I owe you then, considering it's all been on account?' He turns off the shower and hoists up his wet trousers. Robert stares at me and I don't move. There's heaviness in the cubicle and it's more than the steam. 'Time to settle my bill, I think.' He shoves into me, jamming me against the tiles and the shower control pokes into my back. He grabs my wrists and pulls them above my head roughly.

I'm scared and want to get dry. I block it all out. All of it. Nothing happened. I'm OK. I'm all right.

'How much do I owe you for all the sex? Tell me what you charge.'

I screw up my eyes and turn my head away from him.

'Tell me!'

'I don't know what you mean, Rob. Stop this. You're scaring me.' I open my eyes to slits and see the veins on his neck. 'Let me get a towel. I'm freezing.'

Like a sigh held in for too long, Robert releases me and I slide past him into the bathroom. I grab my robe and wrap it around me. I'm not going to hear what he said. I'm not going to hear.

'How much?' He's blocking the doorway to the bedroom.

'Robert, what happened last night? You're acting so strange.' My voice quivers. It's too high. Don't panic. He doesn't know. He doesn't know.

'I didn't go to a conference. I went to Brighton.'

'Brighton?' I barely say the word. He doesn't know. He *can't* know. The sun is on my back, streaming through the frosted window. It doesn't feel warm.

'I went to see Baxter King.'

'Is he a lawyer? A client?' My voice drops back to its normal level. I walk up to Robert, trying my best to appear unfazed, and slip under his arm into the bedroom. 'I've not heard you mention him before.' Quick as a fox, I grab some clothes. I pull on shorts and a top and wrap my hair in a towel. I don't care if it's wet. I just need to get out. I smear cream over my face and a kiss of mascara. It will do. I haven't time to bother with foundation or put concealer on the annoying mole on my cheek. I smile at Robert's reflection. Best to appear casual.

'So you're telling me that you've never heard of anyone called Baxter King?'

'Correct.' I add a bit of lipgloss. He knows I always wear it.

'And am I right in thinking then that you've never lived in Brighton?'

'Absolutely. Never even been there.' I put on my watch and curse the awkward strap. I ignore my thumping heart.

'So if I said to you that I've heard otherwise, that you do know Baxter King and you did live in Brighton for eight years, what would you say?'

He's right behind me now, glowering at my image. 'I'd say you'd heard wrong.' I don't blink, breathe or move. I stare back at him, knowing I've faced worse.

'And if I asked you another question, one that could change everything between us forever, do you swear that you'll answer me truthfully?'

'Of course but—'

'Did you once earn a living by having sex for money?'

Even though my entire world has come crashing down, even though I can see Ruby and me fleeing and running away and starting all over again, I know I can't afford to hesitate. I stand up and face Robert. *He can't do this to us.* Why couldn't he have left everything alone? Tears collect in my eyes and I don't have to feign the shock that rushes through me. Suddenly there's a loud noise. Someone is in the house. There are voices. It's Ruby. She's playing the piano.

Taking a chance, I run out of the room, calling my daughter's name.

I knew he'd forget his umbrella. It took him two hours to realise. I'd had a few customers since him but not many. The doorbell jangled and there he was again although not so wet because the rain had finally let up.

'I forgot my umbrella.' He was wiping his feet again.

'I know.' I reached down behind the counter and retrieved it. I'd curled it up neatly with the strap.

'Actually,' he said. 'I want some more flowers.'

'Wow,' I said back and I passed his umbrella across the counter. 'OK.' We smiled at each other and I shuffled some bills around. He went to look in all the different buckets.

'What do you recommend?' He was half hidden behind my new display of lilies. I stepped out from behind the counter. He was taller than me.

'What's the occasion?' My hands were on my hips.

'What are your favourites?'

I didn't have to think. 'Just freesias. It's their scent.' I pointed at the bucket containing the out-of-season blooms. I didn't have many left but he scooped them all out. They dripped on the floor. I went and wrapped them and told him the price. This time he paid cash and held the bunch against his coat.

'For you,' he said and passed them back.

'Me?' I took them. My hands shook. This was it.

'Dinner?'

And it was.

Ruby has brought a boy home. Too bad she's never going to get the chance to see him again. He looks interesting. She's playing her new song to him and he stands, enraptured, leaning against the piano. I make them pizza and drinks, to get them out of my way, and Robert slams his way out of the house. I wonder if it's the last time I will ever see him. I swallow it all down, everything that's rising up my throat. That shell is beginning to coat my body again. It's thickening all around me just when, over the last few months, it had finally melted away.

When Ruby and her friend Art go to her room to study, I gather up a bunch of her sheet music and a handful of the CDs she recorded with Robert. I know she couldn't bear to leave those behind. Upstairs, I pull two large holdalls out of the cupboard on the landing, quietly so Ruby doesn't hear, and dump them on my bed. I stop still and think that it won't be my bed any more; the quilt set I chose, the matching lampshades and the fur rug for Robert to step onto in the morning. I fight it all back down.

I'm not seeing straight as I stuff clothes into one of the bags. Each time I run away, I manage to rescue more of my existence. Perhaps one day I'll hire a removals van.

In the bathroom, I scoop up my toiletries and I pick out some make-up from my dressing table along with my entire jewellery box. Some of it's valuable and could be sold. The wardrobe's a mess. Clothes have fallen to the floor but I don't care. I take the stairs to the top floor and get the key to my cash box. I remove the box from the secret compartment in my desk and, back in the bedroom, I jam both key and box into the holdall. The other bag I leave empty for Ruby's stuff.

I sit on the bed unable to cry and then tell Art it's time to leave. There's a fuss of course when I tell Ruby that we're going away.

'It's just a holiday, only a few days.' Although I know it will be forever. She stamps her feet and pulls her belongings out of her bag as quickly as I put them in. 'We have to,' I tell her. 'We'll go and see Baxter. It's been so long.' I don't know where the thought came from but Ruby's face relaxes and she finally allows me to pack her clothes. I instruct her to gather anything else important and when she is done, I click the front door shut and take one last look at my house as the taxi driver helps us haul our luggage into the boot.

'Victoria Station,' I tell him.

TWENTY-SEVEN

Robert and Louisa left Northampton after a fruitless search at the register office. The motorway was choked and for three hours they crawled south along the M1. It gave them time to talk and Robert too much time to think.

'If you could prove conclusively that Ruby was Erin's daughter, would you let this go?' Louisa craned her neck out of the window to see if she could spot an accident up ahead. 'Nothing. Just miles of cars.'

'Then I'd only have to be concerned about my wife's secret life as a prostitute.'

'But if you could get round that, by talking, by understanding, would you get off this ridiculous train if I could prove to you that Ruby belongs to Erin?'

'You're assuming that Erin's coming back and—'

'Rob, just answer the question!'

'Yes.'

'Right, then we need to run a DNA test.' Louisa picked her phone from her bag. Robert thought about the implications then listened as she spoke to someone she obviously knew quite well. 'No, not that kind of favour.' She giggled. It was the first time Robert had heard her stoop to such an immature display of need. 'I need a maternity test like lightning.' Another giggle and she trailed a finger along the leather trim of the Mercedes door. 'Ha ha. Very funny. No, not for me and no, I'm already taken. Just tell me how long it'll take if I get the samples to you this afternoon.' A pause and then, 'James, you're a doll. I owe you big.' Louisa snapped her phone shut and killed the silly laughter as soon as the call ended. 'Twenty-four hours if I get samples to him today.'

Robert, still dizzy from Louisa's obvious flirting, considered the implications. 'If the test shows negative, that Erin isn't Ruby's mother, then what? Are we any further forward?' He drummed his fingers on the wheel as the car in front began to move. 'At last.'

'I can only tell you the scientific answers, not the moral ones.'

Robert removed his seat belt and fumbled in his pocket for cigarettes but realised he'd run out. Up ahead, he saw a service station and pulled off.

'Promise me you'll give up when this is all over?'

Robert sat on a low brick wall in the car park and smoked four cigarettes in a row. The fumes from the slow-moving traffic, trapped in the air by the day's heat, fused with the smoke from his Marlboro.

Jenna hadn't liked him smoking either. Maybe that's why he was doing it again, to annoy her, to prevent her voice, her memory, her smell, her pervasive spirit from haunting his thoughts further. Robert hoped the stench of his smoke – his guilt – would repel her enough to allow him to do what he had to do.

Robert ignored Louisa's plea. 'So tell me, how do we get DNA from a wife and daughter who have run away?' He recalled several cases over the years that involved paternity testing but he hadn't had anything to do with the actual test or sample methods. All he'd ever been interested in, as now, were the results.

'You'd be surprised what we can find in your home. It'll take a bit of searching but all we need are, say, hairs from a brush or an envelope Erin's licked.'

A piece of Erin and a piece of Ruby, Robert thought, to patchwork back together his broken family. Spit and hair, that's all it would take.

'If Erin's not Ruby's mother, what do I do? Do I go to the police? Do I tell Cheryl that I've got her daughter?' Robert considered that Cheryl might already have notified the police of their strange encounter. But he doubted she'd be able to find him through his name alone.

'If you report Erin to the police, Robert, not only will you lose your wife, *another* wife, but Ruby will lose the only mother she has ever known.'

'I just wanted to tell Cheryl how beautiful Ruby is but I didn't get the chance. I wanted to let her know that she's thirteen and talented and a wonderful pianist and that she's just got her first boyfriend and hasn't long started her periods and . . .' He broke off, lit another cigarette and squinted up at Louisa, who was standing over him scowling like the nicotine police. 'Truth be known, I wanted to tell Cheryl that she *couldn't* have her daughter back.'

Robert recalled the look on Cheryl's face when he had delivered the news. It was somewhere between fear and relief and bore the trademark paleness and shaking of someone who had seen a ghost. Why, Robert wondered, hadn't she fallen to her knees and hugged him and begged him to take her to her long lost baby? When the shock waves had dissipated, why hadn't she sat and allowed the many questions Robert was sure she would have stored away to come flooding out?

In reality, when her muscles were able to function, Cheryl had simply run, as best she could in her long skirt, and disappeared through the crowd. Robert simply stood motionless, hoping she'd come back. Before he left he picked up a tarot card and slipped it into his pocket. It was the Justice card. The ruler of truth.

Louisa didn't waste any time. 'The university genetics department will be closed if we don't get a move on. Now, show me the bathroom that Erin used.'

If she hadn't grabbed him by the arm, Robert would have stood there forever in the hallway of his house staring blankly at the couple of letters that had arrived for Erin that morning. Return to sender, he thought before taking Louisa into his en-suite bathroom.

'She's taken most of her stuff from in here.' Robert watched as Louisa scoured the shower cubicle and the sink for traces of his wife. Rather than search for the whole woman, they were picking about for minuscule fragments of what made her whole. He wondered: does DNA show traces of dishonesty? Is a person with a certain genetic sequence liable to develop a propensity to lie, to be unreliable, to steal or murder even?

'Damn,' Louisa said, holding a fine blonde hair up to the light. 'No root. James said a hair must have a root for them to harvest a suitable sample. Where did Erin usually keep her hairbrush?'

Did, Robert noticed. As if she was dead. 'In here.' He showed Louisa to Erin's dressing table and discovered that she'd dropped a lipstick on the floor beneath the stool. When he bent to pick it up, he saw the small waste bin under the dressing table. It had tipped over and spilled its contents on the carpet. 'No hairbrush but look.' Robert carefully lifted a clump of woven blonde hairs, like a tiny fragile nest, and handed it over. 'Any good?'

'Possibly perfect.' She grinned, examining the hairs, which had obviously been pulled from Erin's hairbrush. She extracted a couple from the clump. 'There are certainly some roots in here. I'll give the whole lot to James to be on the safe side.' She eyed Robert cautiously. 'Are you sure these are definitely Erin's hairs?'

Robert laughed and ignored the pain it caused. 'Ruby's got long dark hair.' He frowned when he thought how dissimilar it was to Erin's. 'And it's certainly not mine. It couldn't be anyone else's.'

A search in Ruby's small bedroom didn't reveal a suitable sample. In the kitchen, Louisa was about to telephone her contact in the university's genetics department when Robert stopped her and pulled a face. 'I've told her a thousand times about this. But now I'm pleased about her disgusting habit.' He pointed to a piece of gnarled pink bubble gum stuck to the side of an unfinished glass of milk. It was sitting beside the unwashed plates from Erin and Ruby's last meal. 'Will gum do?'

'Fine, except you can't prove that it's Ruby's.'

Robert smiled. 'Erin wouldn't be seen dead with this in her mouth. Ruby always had a packet of the stuff in her pocket. It's hers all right.'

Louisa prised it off the glass with a knife and allowed it to drop into a freezer bag. She collected the other bag containing the hair, said, 'Keys, please,' and snatched them from Robert when he held them out.

'I'll be back soon. Meantime, sit tight and don't do anything rash.' She turned and walked a couple of paces but then stopped. Looking back at Robert, she saw the worry hanging on his features, dripping from his eyes and mouth and jaw. She approached him and kissed his cheek. 'I won't be long,' she whispered and gave his arm a squeeze.

Instead of waiting in the empty house, Robert found the keys to Erin's car – which had been left in the street since she'd gone – and, after a frenzied solo squash session at the club, he headed for the office.

There was peace and stillness, the hum of the computer network silenced by Tanya and all the harsh lights turned off except for the dim fire exit signs illuminating a path to his desk. It was only ten past six but all the clients were asleep already, tucked neatly inside the filing cabinet, their troubles and battles silenced for the night. At the end of each day, Tanya would put a finger to her lips and say, 'Sshh, quiet now.'

The leather creaked as Robert dropped into his chair. He saw that one file had been left out on his otherwise clear desk. He liked to keep things organised in his office. It gave him a sense that urgent cases weren't piling up around him, even though they were. He picked up the file and read the label. As he thought, it was the Bowman case.

He remembered Mary Bowman sitting opposite, her rotten-fruit face begging him to let go even though she confessed she had given up. Robert knew she hadn't. How could anyone relinquish their children without a fight? What right did he have to persuade the judge that her kids should be taken away? They were pawns in a dirty game. He wanted no part of it. It occurred to him that sometimes, in some cases, the mother had no choice.

Robert went into Den's office and poured himself a drink. He looked around the senior partner's office. The original paintings, the antique furniture, the shelves of leather-bound books all made a statement: I'm wealthy and I will win your case. Den took the important clients, not that they had many of those, and he was left with the trash. The Jed Bowmans of the world.

It would be easy, he thought as he took the glass of whisky back to his office, to pick up the file and leave it lying on Den's desk with a note saying, 'Over to you.' But to do that would be to guarantee a victory for Jed. Without doubt, Den would destroy Mary's case and Jed would receive custody of the children. Mary Bowman was an unfit mother. She was a drug addict and had been unfaithful. She was also without a job and without courage. Jed on the other hand had been the strong arm of the family and saw it as his duty to remove his offspring from danger. He had a job now, determination, and a will so strong he would stop at nothing to see his wife left in the gutter. Jed Bowman was fuelled by revenge.

Robert took a red marker pen and scrawled 'Case Closed' across the front of the file. Mason & Knight wouldn't be dealing with the man any more. As for Mary, he would see to it that she received the best legal representation in London.

Kicking back in his leather chair, feet up on his desk, Robert wondered what had driven Erin to steal baby Ruby from Cheryl's car. He'd read the newspaper article a thousand times. The baby's mother had been in the supermarket for such a short time. Then he wondered about Cheryl, how she must have felt when she discovered her baby was gone. He remembered her eyes, the way she scoured his palm.

If Erin met Cheryl, would she say sorry?

After an hour of thought, Robert picked up the phone. He didn't believe Erin would show regret; didn't really believe she should. How could anyone regret thirteen years bringing up a child? As he looked up the number on the internet and then dialled, he wondered if Detective Inspector George Lumley was still in the force. He could have retired, moved to another area, died.

It rang only twice before he put the receiver back on its base. He couldn't do it. He saw Erin being taken away. He pictured Ruby watching. He tried to imagine Ruby's new life with Cheryl but it simply wasn't there.

Cheryl didn't know that Ruby liked to eat Coco Pops in front of Saturday morning TV. She had no idea that she was prone to leaving her homework until the last minute and needed to be badgered to get it done. How would she know what to do if Ruby had a nightmare or wept for Erin?

Strangely, out of everyone, he felt the most qualified to offer Ruby the stability she needed but as far as the courts were concerned, he had little right to her future. Robert picked up the telephone three more times before finally leaving the office and returning home.

Robert couldn't sleep. Louisa had returned to her hotel. He had rather hoped, after the Chinese takeaway and bottle of wine she had returned with from the university, that she would feel like occupying the guest room for the night. He hadn't much wanted to be alone and he might have taken the chance, before the pressure that he felt morphing into a storm, to talk openly with her. To finally tell her how he had once felt about her. What he should have said years ago but never did. And he wanted to make it clear that it was Erin he loved now, even though she seemed as unreachable as anything in his life ever had. Even though he was losing his grip on her hand because of unfathomable forces pulling her from him.

But Louisa had left. She'd hovered, true, on the top step, perhaps hoping for more than the see-through kiss on her cheek as the taxi ticked, waiting to take her back to the hotel.

'I'll call you when I get the results. James said twenty-four hours is the best case. It could even be the day after tomorrow.' A pause, then a look – a safety rope being dropped down a cliff to a stranded climber – before she finally left.

Robert watched until the taxi was out of sight and then went back inside, dialled Erin's mobile number then Ruby's mobile number before going to bed and staring at the ceiling. He imagined that all the hairline cracks in the plaster were the mistakes he had made in his life. He knew, too, that despite its creaky boards and sticky sash windows the old house had been standing for well over a century. He predicted a couple more.

Robert rolled and shifted beneath a single sheet draped loosely around his waist. He was naked but still hot. The humidity of the day was trapped in the bedroom even with a window open and although his skin prickled as if cold, his mind seared with feverish thoughts. He turned again and placed a hand on Erin's pillow. He knew it was over. He had been prepared to forgive her for lying about the way she'd fought to survive, by selling her body – he could eventually come to terms with that – but what he couldn't obliterate, ever, was that she had stolen Ruby.

Slowly, gradually, like a laborious mathematical equation, everything began to add together then multiply and square to infinity. It explained the dissimilarity between mother and daughter in looks. It explained why Ruby was often so distant and far removed in thought. Deep down the girl knew she didn't belong. There was no genetic link to hold her steady in her place in the world. When the results came back from the lab, they would show Ruby's genetic heritage, and somewhere in the world was the mother it came from. That someone, Robert was convinced, was Cheryl.

Aside from gut instincts locking together, it was clear to Robert that Erin never had any intention of allowing Ruby to go on the school trip to Vienna. How could she get a passport without a birth certificate? How can a mother register the birth of a baby she has kidnapped? Robert guessed that the out-of-date passport he had discovered in Erin's study must either be a fake or stolen. Thinking about it, the small photo was a sketchy likeness and of course the little mole on her cheek that he assumed she had covered with make-up for the photograph wasn't even present. He wondered who the young woman in the photo was.

A car hummed down the street. A cone of light momentarily flickered through the voile drapes and then the clunk of doors, low voices, the jangle of keys in a lock. Robert sat up in bed, praying that his finally groggy mind hadn't conjured another symptom of guilt; another do-good visit from Jenna, laughing, breezing her way through, rectifying his life. He looked at the digital clock. 2:12 a.m.

He padded across to the window and saw a black cab drive off. He threw on some clothes and went to the landing and peered between the banisters down into the dim light of the hallway. A duffel bag was dumped on the tiles.

Ruby stood alone, staring up at him. Robert took a breath and held it, feeling he'd never be able to let go.

TWENTY-EIGHT

I run home. I forget my takings. I don't tell anyone I'm leaving.
I trip on the stupid long skirt that I wear to make me look more
gypsy-like, spiritual, and now I can't see because of the tears.
The air outside is as cloying as the pub but without the stench
of cigarette smoke and beer. I suck in the humid night but the
air doesn't want to come into my lungs. I can't breathe. I am
choking. I stop and lean against a brick wall, knowing I have to
keep running in case he catches up with me.

What does he know?

A man walking his dog stops and stares at me and asks if
I'm all right. He asks if I'm having an asthma attack. An
attack, yes, but not from asthma. He walks away. My chest
heaves in and out but I still can't get enough oxygen. I force
my body to carry on, taking me home so I can be alone and
never come out into the world again. Finally, I arrive at my
front door, having survived on micro breaths, and realise my
handbag is at the pub. It contains my keys.

I creep through the tunnel a little way down the street,
leading to my rear garden. I have a pain in my chest, or maybe
my heart. There's nothing to be heard except my frightened,
short breaths and the indignant howl of a cat as it skittles off
down my long garden.

What does he know about my baby?

I know the kitchen window catch will be undone – it never closes properly. I jam it open with a garden cane and slide through it. I end up standing in the sink. I climb out and stare at the cakes that are still on the table. The cakes I made for Sarah.

I take a bite from one but spit it onto the floor. There is no saliva in my mouth so it sticks to my tongue. In the living room, I trip over the baby basket filled with clothes. I switch on a lamp and kneel down beside my gift to Sarah. I wonder if she ever came knocking and I glance at the front door to see if a note has been slipped onto the mat. There's nothing.

I bury my face in the basket of clothes, as if I'm trying to climb in to be a baby myself, and eventually I fall asleep. I dream of that man from the pub finding Natasha and wake in a cold sweat and with a pain in my neck. The milkman is clinking bottles in the street. I've been on the floor all night.

It's best that I do something so I begin folding the little baby clothes. Because I fell asleep on them, they are creased and one side of the straw basinet is squashed. When they're all neat, I take them upstairs and pop them in the painted chest of drawers. I stencilled rabbits and flowers on it to match the ones on the wall.

I think of Sarah giving birth and it hurts me to picture her cinnamon face screwed up in pain and her belly heaving and the midwife yelling at her to push, no don't push, pant, pant.

When Sarah still doesn't come to show me her new baby and eat the cakes, I decide to go out and look for her. I put on my sandals and run my fingers through my tangled hair, not caring that my make-up from the night before is smudged like bruises underneath my eyes or that there are muddy streaks down my cheeks. After all, a baby doesn't care what its mother looks like. It just wants love and milk and warmth.

In the park, it seems like all the world has a child. There are mothers and fathers and grandparents everywhere pushing prams or holding the hand of a toddler or watching a little one's eyeballs spin as they cling to the roundabout. It's a nice day for the park.

I sit on a bench and watch all the grubby brothers and candy-pink sisters playing on the equipment. When a swing becomes free, I sit on it and go as high as the clouds. Perhaps from up here I will spot Sarah and her new baby out for a morning stroll. The wind swipes across my face and the sun makes me squint. I laugh out loud.

Then, in the distance, crossing the road, I think I see her. Her bump has gone and she's cradling a bundle in her arms. Then I swear I see the Knight man from the Stag's Head, laughing beside her and pointing up at me as I fly high, high on my swing.

I could tell your fortune, I yell at him in my head but he doesn't hear.

I could tell you my fortune, too. But I don't and the next time I swing up high, they are gone.

I jump off and go back to the bench. There is a woman sitting in my place but she smiles and shoves up. She smells of fried food and cigarettes and has a grubby little boy whining at her and tugging her sleeve while she wrestles a baby back into its pram. The pram is old, as if it has held many infants. It is made of grey cloth and has stains on the edges that could be old sick or food. It's not a very nice pram and the little boy has his laces undone and his knees have scabs that he's picked.

'Bloody hell, Nathan. Give it up.' The woman looks at me and pulls a weary face. She is thin and worn out. The human equivalent of the pram. Her baby is screaming now it's been put flat on its back. She's after some sympathy.

'Is he a handful?' I ask, having to clear my throat because I haven't spoken yet today and I'm clogged with regret.

'Terrible twos.' She says 'twos' like 'toes'. A bird squawks and flaps out of a branch above, making us curl up our shoulders for a second.

'Is it just the pair that you have?' A boy and a girl, I deduce. The baby is wearing pink.

'I got three more at school,' she reveals. She says 'three' like 'free'. The woman takes a packet of Embassy from the concertina hood of the pram and lights a cigarette. The smoke blows directly over the baby. 'You got kids?' she asks. Nathan kicks the wheel of the pram, sending the baby into another screaming fit.

'No,' I say as she belts Nathan's legs. I look at the baby's little legs kicking within the pink cotton sleep suit and think that one day those legs will get slapped too.

'Need a wee-wee.' Nathan is jiggling beside his mother, clutching his groin with one hand then the other. His face is flushed and already I can see a damp patch circling the front of his shorts.

'Oh bloody hell, Nathe. You've just been.' The woman squints across the play area to a concrete toilet block. 'Just go behind a tree,' she tells him. 'I've got Jo-Jo in her pram.'

Nathan shakes his head and points to his bottom. His cheeks are crimson now and he's fighting everything back. The woman grabs his arm. Her fingers sink easily into his flesh. It's as if they are sinking into the knot of my heart.

'Can I help?' I ask.

The woman stops, half standing, Nathan jiggling frantically beside her, and looks at the pram. 'You could watch her for a tick. I won't be a minute.' She drops her cigarette on the ground, leaving it burning. Smoke twists up underneath Jo-Jo's pram.

'Of course,' I say. I already have my hand on the pram's handle, rocking it gently. The baby's shrieks change to curious shouts, as if she's never been rocked before. The woman drags Nathan across the playground and they disappear into the graffiti-covered concrete building.

'There, there.' I lean forward and peer at Jo-Jo. For a second, she stops shouting and stares at me, gumming a half smile before stuffing her fist into her soft mouth. She stretches back her head and I see a necklace of dirt. I reach into the pram and slip my hands under her little armpits. Her head lolls slightly before she stiffens, eyeing me warily. I glance across at the toilet building.

She said she'd only be a minute.

I press Jo-Jo to my front. She smells of stale milk and her nappy is soggy and full.

'You need changing, little one,' I tell her.

Only a minute.

I stand up. My legs don't belong to me. I can hear Natasha crying. No one is paying me any attention. Jo-Jo dribbles on my collar and I can hear her fist squelching in her sore mouth.

Crying, crying, I can hear Natasha crying as again I stare over to the toilet block. The sun sprinkles down on us through the tree above, dappling the grass. I press my foot on the woman's smouldering dog-end and still Natasha screams at me.

To get away from her noise, I sprint across the playground with wide-eyed Jo-Jo.

TWENTY-NINE

Ruby sipped hot chocolate and if things hadn't been the way they were, Robert would have made a joke about her brown, milky moustache. As it was, he hardly dared breathe in case she shattered into pieces and floated away.

He asked her again. 'Your mum's in Brighton?' It figured, he thought.

Ruby nodded. Her fingers were laced round the mug.

'And your train got into Victoria at one o'clock?'

Another nod, her hair unwashed and clumped in heavy strands around her face.

'So what have you been doing for the last hour?'

Ruby carried her mug to the sink and splashed in some cold water. 'Sitting. Thinking. Stuff.' Her body folded into the kitchen chair again, barely containing the will to bring the drink to her lips. 'I called Art.'

'You were out in London after midnight doing . . . stuff ?' Robert couldn't stand to think of what might have happened. 'Does your mother realise how worried I've been about you both?' An understatement. 'And now she'll be worried about you.'

'I left a note at Baxter's house.' Ruby's voice was even.

Robert tried to coax her chin up with his finger. Her head hung, forehead parallel to the table. 'Why did you leave me?'

Ruby shrugged. 'It was Mum's idea. I didn't want to.' She was a kid again, avoiding blame for breaking something.

'Well, did Mum say why she wanted to?'

Ruby sighed. 'She said it was a holiday. When we got to Baxter's place, I heard them talking about finding us a flat, getting Mum a job. She mentioned running away for the last time.' She lifted her head. Her eyes were liquid. 'Some holiday. I didn't even get a walk on the beach or coins to take down to the pier.'

'So it's permanent? You and Mum are leaving for good?' Robert suddenly wished Ruby hadn't come home. Then there would still be some hope.

'As permanent as we ever do things.' And Ruby silently drained her mug.

It was 4 a.m. when Louisa arrived. On the telephone, she'd told Robert that there was little point in her coming over but his persuasion skills far outweighed her ability to say no at that time in the morning. Besides, he offered to pay an extra fee for the inconvenience.

'Ruby's in bed.' Robert had tucked her up, protecting his precious catch from predators. She was his only link to what he could barely remember as normal life.

'I doubt she's enjoying this any more than you are.' Louisa slipped her wedding ring on and off. 'By coming back, she's telling you where she wants to be.'

'Try telling her mother that.' Robert wasn't sure whether to offer alcohol or tea or bacon. He noticed a pale streak low in the eastern sky.

'What exactly did you want me to do,' Louisa glanced at her wrist before realising she hadn't put her watch on, 'at this hour?'

'Nothing.'

'You're paying me to do nothing in the early hours of the morning?'

'Yep. You can help me wait.' When she looked puzzled, Robert added, 'For the DNA test results.'

They drank coffee and Robert beat some eggs. Louisa sat with her back to where he was cooking. 'You realise that if the results show Erin is not Ruby's biological mother, things are only just getting started.' She swivelled round.

'That's why I'm cooking eggs,' he said flatly, signalling with the spatula. 'Mine are the best.'

Later, when the blackness outside had stretched into pink, blue and orange and the traffic had kicked up, they stood in the garden while Robert smoked.

'Must stop soon.' He held the cigarette between thumb and forefinger and sucked deeply. Then, remembering, he pulled the tarot card from his jeans pocket and turned it over and over between his fingers.

'What's that?'

The face of Justice flashed at him, grinned at him, teased him, but most of all the card of Justice, dealt by Cheryl herself, told him he was doing the right thing.

'The answer,' he replied, squinting somewhere beyond the rising sun and taking another long draw.

The fuss started mid-morning. Robert decided to let Ruby sleep in but when Louisa prised her bedroom door open to check she was OK, he wished he hadn't.

'Rob, Ruby's gone!'

'What do you mean gone?' He'd never heard Louisa squeal before. He took the stairs two at a time.

'She's not in her room. Not anywhere.' Louisa ran quickly from door to door on the landing, shoving each one open.

'OK, don't panic. Maybe she went to school.' Robert ran downstairs and called Greywood College. He hung up and shook his head. He tried Ruby's mobile number but it went straight to her voicemail. He left a message instructing her to call home as soon as possible.

'She'll be OK,' Louisa offered. 'Wherever she's gone, it'll just be to clear her head.'

An hour later and Robert couldn't take it any more. He paced back and forth, struggling to block out what was happening to his family.

At noon, Louisa telephoned James in the university's human genetics department. The results weren't ready although he confirmed viable specimens.

They spent the day waiting, talking, watching the phone, listening for the sound of footsteps in the front porch, a key in the lock. By five o'clock, Robert was desperate.

'Of course!' He landed the heel of his hand on his forehead. 'She'll be with *him*.' Already he was gathering his keys, jacket, phone. 'What's the date?'

'The twenty-first. Why?'

'She was invited to a summer solstice party at Art's house.' He sighed heavily, not knowing whether to be concerned for his daughter's day-long absence or the company she would be keeping.

'Do you know the address?' Louisa gathered her own belongings and slipped her arms into a thin knit cardigan. 'I'll leave my laptop switched on in case James emails the DNA results.' She placed a hesitant hand on Robert's arm. 'It won't be long.'

Robert stared at the holiday-brochure sky as they stood on the front step of his house. 'I haven't got a clue where Art lives.' He clapped his arms hopelessly against his sides but then strode off with the confidence of a man who knew where he was going. He bleeped the Mercedes unlocked. 'Hurry. We have to get to Ruby's school before they close for the night.'

On the way, Robert made a futile and anonymous call to the school secretary, who, as he thought, refused to give out pupils' personal information. He wove dangerously through commuter traffic to Greywood College. Only two cars remained in the staff car park and Robert didn't hesitate in barging straight into the empty corridors of the school and yelling out for someone, anyone.

A teacher that Robert didn't know casually emerged from a classroom, sliding a pair of glasses from his nose. 'Can I help you?'

'Yes you can. I need the telephone number of a pupil. *Now*. It's urgent and the police are involved.' Robert heard Louisa let out a little gasp at his lie. The police should be involved, he thought.

'Go to the office. You might find the secretary still there. Second corridor on the left, third door down.' The teacher limped away, leaving a faint smell of Scotch in his wake.

They headed for the office and when no one replied to their knock, they went in.

'Looks like she's still in the building.' Robert pointed to the white sweater draped over the typist's chair, a cup of tea still steaming, a handbag on the floor. The computer glowed in the small room.

'Allow me.' Louisa quickly navigated her way around the desktop. Within thirty seconds, she had pulled up a pupil database. Robert stood half in and half out of the office, keeping watch.

'What's his surname?'

Robert shrugged, still fixed on the corridor. 'God knows. Can't you just search for Art? He's here on a scholarship.'

'Why didn't you say?' Louisa grinned and opened a list of pupils who had been awarded assisted places. There were about thirty names on the list. 'Art Gallway, 23 Meakin Avenue.' Louisa wrote down the full address on a Post-It and returned the monitor to its previous display.

'Oh,' said the secretary. She was clutching an armful of files. Robert blocked the doorway.

'So sorry to invade your office,' Louisa chirped, easing Robert out of the way. She slipped the piece of paper into her leather shoulder bag. 'We were after a school prospectus. Do you have one?'

After a cautious beat, a quick glance to each of their hands to confirm they hadn't lifted anything from her office, the secretary managed a small smile. 'Of course,' she said and handed them a bundle of brochures and forms from a rack in the corner.

After Robert and Louisa had left, when the secretary sat down on her chair, she noticed that it was warm.

Louisa entered the postcode into the satnav and Robert pulled away from Greywood College, narrowly missing a large van.

'Same to you too,' he yelled and swung the Mercedes in a wide U-turn. 'Of course,' he said in his normal voice, 'we don't know that she'll be at Art's house. Next stop Brighton, otherwise.'

They drove through London for twenty minutes, heading south of the river to a part of town neither of them knew. About a hundred years ago, Meakin Avenue would have been a desirable place to live. Dilapidated and derelict Edwardian houses sat neglected in a wide street.

'You should look at buying here,' Louisa commented, scanning the once-impressive buildings. 'Really,' she added seriously although she knew that Robert couldn't think of investments at a time like this. 'There, number twenty-three.' She pointed to a house with hundreds of candles burning in the tall windows. Their light was virtually unnoticeable in the solstice sun.

It's the longest day, Robert thought. *The longest day of my life.*

They parked, walked up the short, weed-littered path and banged on the front door.

'Hardly surprising,' Robert commented when no one answered. Loud music made the windows rattle, the foundations shift. The landslide of voices indicating a party in full swing prompted Robert to try the handle of the weathered front door. It gave and opened.

Louisa followed close behind Robert as they entered the darkened domain. They waded through a sea of bodies, some upright, some sitting on the floor with their backs against the wall. Others were slumped on the stairs, drinking from cans, smoking reefers, oblivious, apart from a casual glance, of the strangers who had just entered the house.

Robert would have called out Ruby's name but knew it was futile amid the mess of sound. As they went deeper into the house, part of him wanted to pick up a drink, take hold of a second-hand joint, let his body fuse into the crowd and forget Erin forever. He reached behind him and took Louisa's hand.

Forgetting Erin, even for a second, was impossible.

'Do you know where Art is?' Robert yelled at a youth sprawled on a dirty sofa. The boy shrugged and grinned inanely. Someone turned up the volume of the music. Robert trawled on, studying each person they passed. There were all sorts at this party, young and old, most of them travellers or drop-outs, New Age types with congealed hair and flowing clothes.

With his heart quickening and still towing Louisa, Robert went into the kitchen. There was a spread of food on an old pine table, interspersed with tea lights. Two men were filling their plates with bean salads and flatbread.

'Rob, look.' Louisa tugged Robert's fingers. He turned to where she was pointing.

In the back garden, Robert saw a cluster of teenagers, some embracing, some dancing with their hands high above their heads, and some swigging from cans, sucking on cigarettes. Ruby tossed back her hair and laughed before wrapping her arms round Art's neck. Robert marched outside.

'Ruby!' He pulled the pair apart. 'What are you doing?'

'Hey, Pops,' Art said. 'Weren't you young once?' He buried a hand in his pocket. Robert tensed.

'It's OK,' Louisa interrupted. 'Just leave it, Rob. At least we've found her.'

'Time to go, young lady.' Simple words that Robert never had the chance to practise, making him feel even more of a fake father. What right did he have to order her to do anything? She didn't even belong to her mother, let alone him.

'Go where?' Ruby struggled like a fish being landed.

'To see your mother,' Robert replied.

It was only when they were all in the car that Robert wondered which one.

THIRTY

I was right. Jo-Jo's bottom is sodden. She is lying completely naked on the soft carpet in the bedroom I'd reserved for Sarah's baby. She's a little padded prawn, the colour of lightly boiled shellfish.

I really don't know what has happened to Sarah. She promised that she'd stop by and show me her new baby. But no matter now. Jo-Jo dribbles pale yellow pee on the carpet. I scoop her up and take her to the bathroom. One hand is pressed under her puckered bottom, the other spread across her weak back. Like I used to hold Natasha.

I turn on the bath taps, drizzle in a dose of bubble bath and prop her on my lap while we wait. I just want to get her clean.

When she's in the bath, Jo-Jo begins to scream. She's obviously not used to being washed. I'm kneeling down, my back aching over the side of the bath, swishing water over her protruding belly and supporting her head with my other hand. I take a face cloth and begin to scrub at the lines of dirt on her neck.

Her mother hasn't taken very good care of her and that's why I don't feel bad that I've taken Jo-Jo. The woman has four other children, probably all dirty as well, so I bet she's relieved that I've unburdened her. It's one less baby to smack.

Jo-Jo is shrieking and howling, her little milk-furred tongue quivering inside her red mouth. Her cry warbles through my head, bringing back memories. Nightmares.

After her bath, I wrap her in a warm towel and hug her to my chest. I dance about until she stops crying and then take her back into her bedroom. It's Jo-Jo's room now. I tape her into a nappy and wriggle her into one of the velvet sleep suits from the stash I made ready for Sarah's baby. The sleep suit's a bit of a tight squeeze because it's meant for a newborn. So her toes don't curl, I snip the seam of the foot open.

She screams again. I think she's hungry so I lay her in the straw basinet and go to the kitchen to see what I've got. The cake that I spat out is still on the floor. Something smells bad. I think it's the rubbish bin. I have some semi-skimmed milk in the fridge, showing use-by yesterday. It will have to do for now, until I can buy some proper baby milk. I haven't got a bottle so I pour some into a bowl, warm it in the microwave and then take the bowl and a teaspoon back up to Jo-Jo's room. She is still screaming.

I pick her up and balance her on my knee, supporting her back in the crook of my arm. I spoon up a tiny bit of milk and brush it against her lips. She's silent for a second and then bats the spoon away, spilling the milk down her clean suit.

'Oh, Natasha!'

The baby stares up at me silently, big wet eyes. She gums a grin and then squeals. I reach for a soft fluffy duck and press it against her palm. She grapples for it, holds the toy for a second but then drops it. She screams. I try another spoonful of milk but the same thing happens. This goes on for another ten minutes and the baby consumes none of the milk. I have to change her suit because she's in such a mess. The whole time, she is bawling.

'Shut up!' I shriek. I clap my hand over my mouth when I realise this was not a nice thing to say. 'I'm sorry. I'm so sorry.' I press her face against my shoulder so that her wails are smothered. 'Let's go into the garden. The fresh air and sunshine will do you good.'

That's what Sheila always used to say. Fresh air is good for babies. I mull over all the advice she gave me when I was pregnant and soon after Natasha was born. I wish I'd taken it. It's not just the guilt from losing my baby that torments me but the little things, the things I could have done better that haunt me. But none of it seems so bad any more, now that I have another baby. I scoop her up and carry her into the garden.

The grass needs cutting. It's knee high and I'm not one for flowers or shrubs. There's a craggy old apple tree down the end but I never eat the fruit. The apples are sour and full of maggots or mottled with scaly brown patches. My garden is only as wide as my house, about twelve feet, although nearly a hundred feet long and has a wire fence on either side separating it from my neighbours' neat strips.

'One day, Tash, I'll get it sorted. We'll have to nag Daddy into getting the mower out, won't we?' I tickle her cheeks and for the first time she laughs. Her eyes are slits from the sun.

I pick my way through the long grass, tracking a wide arc around the concrete slab covering the old well, and sit down in the shade of the apple tree.

The baby nestles in my crossed legs, on her back, staring up at me, gnawing on her hand. Thick, clear saliva coats her chin. I wipe it off with the hem of my long skirt.

The sun is warm on my back. My neck is stiff from having slept on the floor and no amount of fingering the knotted muscles makes the pain ease. I gaze down my long garden to the house and smile as I notice the pale yellow curtains in the open bedroom window snapping in the breeze.

But my peace is shattered by the baby's wails. She squirms on my legs and plops off into the grass. Her cries are even more frantic so I pick her up by the shoulders and march her back indoors.

'I think you need a sleep, Miss Natasha.' I deposit her upstairs in the basinet and bang the door shut.

She screams and screams and I slump down on the landing, my back against the wall, my legs and hands aquiver because I've finally got my baby back.

THIRTY-ONE

Robert bundled Ruby into the Mercedes. She spat and cussed at being dragged from the party.

'Quit the wild-cat routine, Rube.' He adjusted the rear-view mirror so he didn't have to witness her poisoned expression. He deflected the 'I hate you' and 'You've ruined my life' with an imaginary squash racquet. She was thirteen. It was normal.

'Just take me back to the party, yeah?' Ruby poked a knee into the back of Robert's seat. 'I'm allowed to go to a freaking party. Do you know how much you embarrassed me?' But the remark that hit Robert's jaw hardest was when she spat, 'You're not my real father. You can't tell me what to do.'

'Where are we going, Rob?' Louisa asked when she realised they were several miles off course to return to Robert's house.

'I'm taking Ruby to her mother. It's about time she met her.' Robert gripped the steering wheel and stared straight ahead. He wanted to voice his feelings about the Bowman case, about children being with the right parent but he knew it would come out wrong. Besides, while he was paying Louisa for her time, he didn't expect her to doubt his motives.

Robert swiftly negotiated the traffic and soon joined the beginning of the M1. For the second time in two days, he steered the Mercedes towards Northampton. Part of him didn't feel real, while part of him felt like he was playing God.

He stole a quick glance at Louisa. She was sitting calmly, looking elegant even in jeans and a T-shirt. On her feet she wore leather sandals. Her toes were long and straight, the nails painted deep burgundy. How he wished it was Erin sitting next to him, perhaps returning from their weekend in Somerset, life as normal, then climbing into bed to curl against her slender back, Ruby content and asleep in the next bedroom.

'Don't you think we should wait for the DNA results?' Louisa spoke quietly even though Robert had tossed his MP3 player into the back and Ruby's ears were plugged. The girl's head bobbed in time with the music. Robert's knuckles whitened as he gripped the wheel, snapping back to reality.

'No,' Robert replied. 'The results will confirm what I already know. And I can't wait any more. I want my life back. Besides, the police will have to conduct their own genetic investigations.'

'Police?' Louisa asked but did not receive a reply.

Robert drove in silence, thinking, trying to keep Jenna from attacking the inside of his mind, begging him not to do it all over again. He made a deal with her. If she stopped ghosting his thoughts, he would steer away from the paranoia that had eventually killed her. It was as he left the motorway at the exit for Northampton, Jenna's voice echoing inside his head like a bee, that Robert realised he could switch her on and off at will. For now, he clicked her gently into silence.

Ruby, having removed the headphones and slept for most of the journey, exhausted from no sleep the previous night, squirmed on the rear seat. 'Where are we going, Dad?' she asked, dragging the back of her hand across her cheeks. The slowing of the car had woken her.

'To see someone who's been dying to meet you for thirteen years.'

Ruby didn't ask any more.

They cruised through the town and turned into the street of terraced houses. The evening sun sent jagged daggers of light from the windscreens and bonnets of parked cars. Robert pulled down the sun visor and searched for a space.

He reversed into a tight gap, cut the engine and got out of the car. When Ruby didn't get out, he opened the rear door and, leaning inside, gently stroked her head. She was sweating and black hair was stuck to her forehead – the same black hair as her mother, Cheryl. Slowed by her sleepy state, Ruby searched the street with dark eyes and Robert could see that she was wondering where she was.

Home, he thought. I've brought you home.

He watched Ruby peel her sticky skin off the leather seat. She must never be without a mother, he thought. At no point did he want Ruby to feel she wasn't loved, owned or cherished by whichever woman she ended up with. Considering that it might be anyone other than Erin nearly killed him. Knowing the pain that Cheryl had suffered sent his guts into spasm.

Over the last couple of days, he'd become used to imagining the emotions that Cheryl would have spent thirteen years stage-managing. He'd guessed at her guilt, her sense of loss, her self-loathing and anger. Now he would have to imagine the feelings of his wife when she was arrested, prosecuted, tried. The two women would be swapping lives.

The jail sentence wouldn't be Erin's punishment. It would be losing Ruby, and Robert couldn't stand the thought.

As for Ruby, well, she would eventually understand. When the open wounds had knitted together in a cross-hatch of mistrust and new beginnings, she would tentatively ask when her real birthday was, what the weather was like as she'd burst into the world, what her father had said when he first held her. But the answers would stop at week eight. When she was taken. After that, only Erin knew.

'Hop out, love.' If they take her away, I can still see her, he thought. I can appeal for visiting rights. Fleetingly, it occurred to him to offer to represent Cheryl in court but it would be too similar to the Bowman case, only this time Erin would be Mary Bowman and he would be no better than Jed.

'Where are we?' Ruby climbed out of the car. She frowned at Louisa. 'I want Mum.'

Robert sighed, wondering if she realised how laden her words were. 'There's someone I want you to meet.' Robert took Ruby's hand and guided her to the door of number 18. Cheryl's house. The house where Ruby had once lived. He closed his eyes, breathed in and knocked.

An old Ford Escort screamed past, windows down, loud music rippling the air. Cheryl didn't answer. He knocked again and looked at his watch. It was nearly eight thirty, still light, the air warm and thick.

'The Stag's Head,' he whispered when no one answered after a few minutes.

It was a long shot but he didn't know where else to look. It hadn't occurred to him that Cheryl wouldn't be home.

He parked the car right outside the pub on double yellow lines. Leaving Louisa and Ruby to wait, he went into the bar.

'Is Cheryl Varney here tonight?' The barmaid was calmer, with only a few customers drinking. She ran a towel across the polished bar.

'Nope. She only comes in once a month.' The young woman reached down behind the bar and retrieved something. 'But she left this last night. Don't suppose you'll be

350

seeing her any time soon?' The barmaid held up a brown leather bag.

Robert stared at it as if it was a limb that Cheryl had left behind. 'I will. Yes, as a matter of fact I will be seeing her tonight.' The woman shrugged and handed it across the counter to Robert. 'Cheers, then,' he said casually and left the pub before she had a chance to change her mind.

Leaning against the rear of the Mercedes, Robert unzipped the bag. It was a glimpse into the life of the woman who had been destroyed by Erin. It was probably the closest he would ever come to her once Ruby had been taken away.

Robert removed a small purse. He unfastened it to reveal the photograph of a baby. It was the same picture that had appeared in the newspaper after Ruby's abduction. He tucked it back inside the bag as if he was saying goodnight to an infant. There was a chequebook, a driver's licence, a hairbrush entwined with long black hairs and two lipsticks. Underneath a packet of tissues, Robert pulled out a set of keys. The key fob was a small picture holder containing another baby photograph.

He slipped them into his top pocket and smiled. He had the keys to Cheryl Varney's house. They would go inside and wait.

THIRTY-TWO

We went Italian – that same night. I didn't want to sound too keen when he asked but in the end it was him who suggested it. I shut up the shop half an hour early so that I could take extra time to get ready. Truly, I'd never been on a proper date before. I was twenty-eight – although the whole world thought I was thirty-two because I'd got by with the stolen passport – and I'd never been with a man who might end up loving me. I would have to remember not to ask for my payment at the end of the evening.

I arranged for the lady in the flat below to sit with Ruby. She was kind and had been friendly since we moved in. She didn't ask questions.

'So, who was the first bunch of flowers for?' I tipped my head sideways, giving him a playful grin. I forked my food, not really hungry.

'My secretary. It's her birthday.'

'No one's ever given *me* flowers before. I feel like it's my birthday too.' I didn't count the ones Becco had sent me in Brighton and realised soon after I'd said it that I must have sounded strange. Everyone got flowers at some time.

We talked and he told me he was a lawyer. He said he'd been married before and his eyes dropped when he told me he was a widower. I didn't ask how she'd died. He said he played squash and liked the movies and had a house in Fulham. He was normal. He paid the bill. He kissed me in the street.

Even though he tries not to show it, you can see that half of Baxter is missing. No one will ever replace Patrick.

He welcomes us and our holdalls, as if he knew all along that we were coming back, and makes us hot pancakes and syrup and insists we have seconds. He has scars down his neck but we don't talk about the fire. Enough has been said in our letters.

'I'll never understand you, Erin.' He musses my hair like my father should have done. 'I'm going to send you back. You can't run away any more. Your husband is a good man.'

'He said things,' I say like a pouting teenager. 'About stuff he shouldn't know. He's been prying into my past.'

'You're married to him. You owe him.' Baxter drizzles extra syrup on my pancakes. 'Besides, he wasn't prying. It was my fault. We were talking about you and I thought he knew and—'

'He'll divorce me anyway. Now that he knows what I was.' Over the years, I'd told Baxter everything. He listened to my full story.

Nearly everything.

Ruby is beating away at the piano. She sings along to the tune she composed for Art.

'I want you to call home to let Robert know you're OK, stay here for a couple of days to calm down, and then go back to your life.' Baxter is filled with sadness, I can tell. He's thinking that either Robert or I could die in a fire, and he's probably right. The blaze is already out of control.

I don't call Robert to tell him we're OK. Ruby and I trudge

around the streets of Brighton, remembering. We sit on the shore like we did when we escaped the fire. Baxter's flat has been restored but Patrick can't be. I take Ruby to see his grave. We leave flowers from Baxter's shop. I miss Robert. I miss my home. It's the only place I've ever wanted to be. My past ensures it never will be.

It's Baxter who tells me Ruby has left. He can't sleep – he hears exploding glass and screams at night since the fire – and he has found Ruby's hastily scrawled note on the kitchen counter.

'All holidays come to an end. That's the point of them. I've gone home to Dad. Ruby x.'

'That's it then,' I say. 'And I didn't even write any postcards.'

Baxter fingers my shoulders as if my bones are the keys of his piano. He grinds at the knots of muscle that cling to my skeleton. 'I have a feeling that Robert will understand why you did what you did. Tell him everything. Be so honest it hurts.'

It takes me most of the day to pluck up the courage. It's like sweeping leaves on a windy day. My courage tumbles away on the first breathy gust of trouble.

By lunchtime, Ruby texts me to say she got home OK and that Robert wasn't cross. I try to call her but her mobile phone diverts straight to the message service.

'I'm coming home too, babe,' I confide and hang up.

The train pulls in to Victoria Station just after 5 p.m. Knowing Ruby was safe with Robert, I didn't leave Brighton until mid-afternoon. I took a walk on the beach with Baxter, slipped my arm round his fat girth while he played with my hair.

From the station, I take a taxi home.

The house smells of dirty laundry and stale food. Robert hasn't emptied the bins. I see a crumpled packet of Marlboro on the counter and wonder who's been smoking. I walk around the entire house, like a ghost searching for someone to haunt. The place is completely empty.

'Rob?' I call, in case he and Ruby are hiding. They'll jump out at any minute with kazoos and balloons and party poppers.

Welcome home, darling. You are forgiven.

The thing is, I've forgotten what I've done wrong.

The house telephone rings, making me freeze. I stalk back into the kitchen, like a lioness pacing around injured prey. I hang back from the machine as it takes a message.

'Rob? You there, Rob?' A pause and then, 'Pick up if you're there. Damn it, call me.'

The machine beeps and clicks. I'd recognise Den's voice anywhere. So Robert's not at the office. I comfort myself by imagining that he's taken Ruby to see a movie and then for ice cream. A coming-home treat.

There is a laptop computer on my kitchen table. It's not Robert's. It has recently been used because it's plugged into both the power point and the telephone point and a screen-saver, made up of rotating pictures of a man I don't recognise, swims across the screen. He's nice looking. Someone's husband.

I brush my finger across the touch pad and the man dissolves to Outlook Express. There is a rack of unfamiliar emails. For some reason – perhaps my unconscious eye glimpses it first – my heart quickens at the list of unread messages.

Without taking my eyes off the laptop screen, I slide a chair behind me and sit down. I don't understand whose computer this is and why it is in my kitchen. I can only guess, my heart a caged animal, why my name is mentioned in the subject line of a message from someone called James Hammond.

To: Louisa van Holten
Subject: Maternity Test Results: Erin Knight

I double click on the message. There is no saliva in my mouth.

Hey Lou,
The tests ran OK. The results indicate that from the genetic material harvested there is less than a 0.1% chance that Erin Knight is the biological mother of Ruby Knight.
It's pretty conclusive. She's not the kid's mother. Hope this helps rather than hinders your investigation and don't forget, you owe me a drink.
Best,
James

I have to get away from this computer. I run to the bay window in the lounge and scan the street for Robert and Ruby walking home, drunk on ice cream, fizzy pop and a feel-good movie. Perhaps they've been bowling or shopping or eaten a hamburger and chips. I study each car cruising by in case they've been for a drive but no cars pull up into the empty space outside our house.

I want to smash that computer and burn it so its black plastic warps and bubbles and no one will ever know. I go back to it as if it's a sleeping beast snuggled up with my past tucked in the crook of its arm. What it also holds is the key to my future.

Can I manage one last fight? I ask myself.

'So let's get this straight,' I say to the machine. 'You're telling me that I'm not Ruby's mother? That there's someone else in this world better qualified than me to fill that role? That I'm only *one-tenth* of a per cent capable of being her mother?' I slump down in the chair and sob. 'If only you knew,' I whisper to the computer, 'you would have ditched that message in cyberspace.'

I don't cry for long. It's not my style. Quickly, I figure out that if it's Louisa's computer then she's working for Robert. He's hired an investigator, *Louisa*, to unpick me as if I'm a dirty old quilt. Louisa has obviously been in this house, *my* house, with Robert, trying to second-guess my moves, my motives, my plans.

Did they sleep together in our bed?

Louisa will soon be back for her computer and her emails and then they will continue with their cat-and-mouse games until they have me arrested and I will be tried for kidnapping.

I tap my fingernail on the edge of the keyboard. Louisa will read the email. She will bask in the thrill of having undone me completely before ever so gently telling Robert the bad news.

I'm sorry, Rob. Erin is definitely not Ruby's mother. She has been lying to you.

She has been lying to herself, I think.

Then Louisa will comfort my husband, the only man who has ever truly loved me, and wrap him up so swiftly in the beautiful complications of her own life that he won't realise he's switched wives. For him, it will be seamless. For her, she gets what I know she's always wanted.

I stare at the list of emails. Three are from someone called Alexa Lane, another is from Amazon confirming an order, four look like spam messages, there is James Hammond's message about the rest of my life and then there is one from someone called Willem van Holten. I double click it and read the blue text.

I quickly deduce that Willem is Louisa's husband. I also deduce that she has recently told him she wants a divorce. This is his reply, begging her not to go, promising her the world, the children she wants, the return to England that she desires. Poor Willem, I think. Poor me. Louisa has freed herself just in time to claim Robert.

Recklessly, I delete the email and then erase it from the deleted items box. It's nothing more than a moment of control over her life, like she is playing with mine, but it gives me an idea.

Of course, deleting the message from James Hammond, the expert in genetics but not in love, it seems, would be a disaster. This is an email that Louisa has been waiting for. This is the email that will make or destroy my life. This is the only thread between Robert and me that hasn't been snapped. I cannot delete this email.

No. I need to change it.

Now I am no expert when it comes to computers but I know there's a simple way – not entirely foolproof but then who's saying Louisa's not a fool? – to mess with this email. I ring Baxter.

'Hey, Bax,' I say. He's just shutting up shop. It's a little after five thirty.

'Are you at home?' he asks, the quiver in his voice almost equal to that in mine.

'I am,' I reply, trying to sound bright. 'I need a favour.'

I remind him of the time we had to rescue Ruby. She was ten. She'd been seeing a boy – *seeing*, I laugh – and she was totally besotted with everything about him from the way he walked, slightly lopsided with his jeans showing six inches of his underpants, to the way his hair concealed his huge brown eyes. Just like hers. Micky carried his books in a retro Adidas bag and at the end of maths, he asked her out. They went to see *About A Boy* and shared a bucket of warm, buttery popcorn.

'You remember when that Micky kid dumped Ruby in an email?'

'The knife is still in my heart.' Baxter feels everything as if his skin is missing. 'How can young love be so cruel?' he asks no one.

'You know we changed it and re-sent it so it looked like it had still come from Micky?' Truth was, if we hadn't been able to fiddle with the contents, I would have deleted the message. For a couple who had only enjoyed the cinema, Burger King and a walk along the beach with me fifty yards behind pretending not to know them, Micky's method of dumping my daughter was a little harsh. His words would have ripped her in two.

'I recall,' Baxter said. 'We made it so that she didn't land with such a bump.'

'That's the one. Well, how did you do that?' I position my fingers over the keys of Louisa's laptop, keeping one ear on the front door and the other tuned in to Baxter's voice.

'Let me think. Well, first you need to click on the Tools menu and select the Accounts option. A separate window will open with all the email accounts listed.' He paused and sighed. 'Patrick showed me this when we wanted to play a practical joke on his previous lover.'

'There's only one account in the list,' I say. 'Does that matter?'

'Not at all. And Erin?'

'Yes?'

'I'm not going to ask why you're doing this so please don't tell me.'

'Thanks,' I said, meaning it.

'Next you need to click on Properties to get the details of that account.' He waits for me. 'Now you need to change the name in the User Information to the person you want the email to appear to have come *from*.'

'OK,' I say, holding the phone with my shoulder. I type James Hammond where Louisa van Holten had been. Fleetingly, I think of Willem. 'Now what?'

'Click Apply and OK and then close the window.'

Then Baxter talks me through the next stage. I pull up the original email from James Hammond, click Forward, fill in Louisa's own email address in the To field, remove the Fw: tag from the subject line, which would instantly spoil the result, and delete everything in the body of the email, which would again indicate that this wasn't a virgin message.

'Now you're free to write what you want in the email, hit send and you're done. But don't forget to delete the original email well and truly or it will all be pointless. And you must change the name back to what it was in the Account settings. OK?'

We chat for a moment longer and I promise to call soon. He senses that, as yet, there is no news about the rest of my life.

I alter the message from James Hammond.

Hey Lou,

The tests ran OK. The results indicate that from the genetic material harvested there is more than a 99.9% chance that Erin Knight is the biological mother of Ruby

Knight. It's pretty conclusive. She's definitely the kid's mother. Hope this helps rather than hinders your investigation.

    Best,

      James

I take out the bit about Louisa owing James a drink. The less these two have to do with each other, the better. I send the email and delete the original. Then I put Louisa's name back in her account settings.

Within minutes, a new email arrives from the ether from someone called James Hammond. It all relies upon Louisa and Robert not digging too deeply into the email's true source.

Then I remember something that Robert once told me about a client he was defending. The judge was having a hard time believing his client was homeless, favouring the appeal of the congruent prosecutor from the outset. The defendant had bought a suit from Oxfam to impress the judge. Next day, Robert told his client not to shave and to wear ripped jeans and an old T-shirt. He won the case.

'People believe what they see,' Robert said.

Praying he's right, I leave the computer and go upstairs to unpack.

THIRTY-THREE

Robert opened the door of Cheryl's house and ushered Louisa and Ruby inside. He glanced nervously up and down the street before going inside himself, ruffling his hair with his fingers. He felt he was about to drop off the edge of the world.

'Cheryl's house, I take it?' Louisa asked.

Robert silenced her with a finger over his mouth. They were breaking and entering but with a key; they were intruders who wanted to give, not steal. They had come to mend Cheryl's heart.

The three of them stood in the small square of living room, Louisa waiting for Robert to do something and Ruby frowning and sighing at the nuisance of it all.

'Cheryl?' Robert called out. 'Are you home? I've got your handbag.'

'So much for being quiet,' Louisa muttered.

'Don't touch anything,' Robert continued but Louisa was already holding a strip of photographs in a silver frame.

'Look,' she said. Robert peered over her shoulder. 'Who is she?'

Robert shrugged. He saw a pretty Asian girl and she was pregnant. The pictures were more of her bump than her. He glanced out of the window. Still sunny in the street but twilight in Cheryl's world.

'Wait here,' Robert instructed and silently thanked Louisa as he saw her take hold of Ruby's hand for comfort. He walked towards the back of the house and stopped, noticing that Louisa and Ruby were right behind him. 'Listen. Do you hear it?'

'Someone's crying,' Louisa whispered.

'No, they're singing,' Ruby said. Robert cocked his head and closed his eyes to listen.

'Upstairs?' Louisa suggested.

Robert nodded and began the procession up the steep staircase. Louisa held tightly onto Ruby's hand.

The haunting noise grew louder, like a tomcat staking his claim on an alley at night. There were no windows on the tiny landing and Robert had to wait for his pupils to adjust before he could see anything.

Suddenly, he was on his knees, crawling across the floor to a shadow in the corner. Someone was huddled there, humming a broken song and sucking back snot and tears. The air vibrated with the tune.

'Cheryl,' Robert said. 'What's happened?' His voice was thick and clogged and his heart pounded. He hadn't expected this.

Louisa turned on the light and everyone screwed up their eyes. For a second, no one could see anything at all.

Robert stifled the gasp lodged in his throat but Louisa couldn't hold hers back. The woman was rolled up into a ball on the carpet and the sight of her made their eyes widen and their mouths go dry. Her face was a scrunched map of slime and fear and her back curled like that of a foetus. She shifted rhythmically to a looping song, rocking back and forth as she sang. In a second, Robert was there, lifting the matted curtain of hair from her face. The woman was completely unaware of her visitors. All she knew was her own misery.

'Louisa, what's happening?' Ruby whispered. Robert looked up and saw Louisa mouth, 'It's OK,' even though he knew it wasn't.

'Cheryl, listen to me. It's Robert Knight. We met at the pub.' He tried to lift her but she was a sack of wet feathers. Louisa stepped in to help but Robert put up his hand to stop her. He didn't want to overwhelm Cheryl. 'Will you come downstairs? I'll make you a cup of tea.'

Cheryl slowly lifted her head, as if the weight of her grief would barely allow it, and dragged her eyes first to Robert, then to Louisa and finally to Ruby. She clearly wasn't focusing, her mind was fixed somewhere far from reality. Her lips still formed the outline of a fractured lullaby, an occasional clogged syllable. Every part of her shook.

Suddenly, Cheryl was on her feet – an alert fox sniffing the morning air. Her eyes were liquorice, glinting, searching but still not seeing properly.

'Where's my baby?' she snarled. 'What have you done with my baby?'

Robert recoiled as Cheryl leaned forward, baring her teeth, her arms dangling and dribble foaming around her lips. Her head twisted from side to side and her eyes were big wet beach pebbles.

'Your baby's fine,' he reassured her and then he turned to puzzled Ruby. 'Look. See? She's fine.' His voice was suited to a four-year-old. Cheryl's behaviour suggested she was exactly that age.

'Come on, you.' Louisa was beside Robert, encouraging Cheryl to calm down, taking control, cajoling and sweetening, all those things she was being paid to do. The role suited her.

Robert took hold of his stepdaughter's arm – if she could be called that now – and pushed her gently towards Cheryl.

Presenting Ruby to her real mother felt like peeling Erin's skin from her body. Treachery flowed like blood through his veins.

Ruby was having none of it. 'Get *off*,' she complained and used Louisa as an anchor. A brief tug of war ensued, Ruby in the middle, and then suddenly everyone froze as a baby's cry cut clean through the air. Small bleats at first but in a second it was shrieking at full volume.

Robert let go of Ruby and pushed through the door behind the crazed Cheryl. The howling grew louder. In a moment, he returned with a squirming packet wrapped in pink velour. The bald baby continued to cry for all it was worth, even when Robert attempted to rub its back. His inexperience showed in the way he held it – like a plastic doll.

'Is this your baby?' Robert asked Cheryl over the din. In a flash she snatched the infant from him, its head whipping forward as she sped down the steep stairs out of sight.

'Oh God,' Robert groaned.

They found Cheryl sitting in the living room cradling the baby, singing again, rocking again, back in the senseless state in which they had found her. The baby had quietened and was staring up at Cheryl.

'Robert, I really think we should leave—' Louisa's words were interrupted by an urgent knock at the door. Because Robert was preoccupied with extracting sense from Cheryl, Louisa answered it.

A young Asian girl stood on the doorstep. She was the pregnant girl in the photographs.

'Is Cheryl home?' she asked. Robert looked up and beckoned her in. The girl's eyes widened at the state of Cheryl. 'Oh,' she whispered and walked up to the distressed woman. 'What do you think made her like this?' Cheryl sat, inanimate, soulless, transparent but for the veil of grief draped over her and was completely oblivious of the gathering forming around her.

'We just found her in this state,' Robert said and he was about to ask the young girl about the baby but Louisa interrupted.

'Rob, can I have a word?'

Robert raised his hand to put her on hold. He was listening to Cheryl as her song shifted to something else, something unintelligible.

'I need to speak to you, Rob.' The front door was still open and Louisa hovered between the house and front garden. An easy escape. 'Rob, listen, I'm going to call James Hammond at the lab. The test results should be available now and we need to know.'

Louisa's look told him to wait until she had news but he didn't see it. He didn't notice, either, the way her mouth curled into a tiny bittersweet smile of sadness as she watched him handle Ruby and Cheryl. The Asian girl did her best to break through the brittle glass house that surrounded the scene but Louisa could already see the shards glinting on the carpet. 'Rob, just wait. I'll be back in a minute.'

Robert glanced up. He caught the tail end of Louisa's stare and acknowledged her intentions with a slow nod. This is it, he thought. This is confirmation of what I already know.

Cheryl sat rigid with her legs cooped under her. The baby continued to squirm on her lap but mostly it chewed its fist and gnawed in time with Cheryl's ranting. Robert felt a breeze swill round the stuffy living room from the open door and it revived him a little, making him realise that only a few minutes in Cheryl's company had affected his thoughts like lungfuls of carbon monoxide. The woman's grief was palpable. He wanted to ball it up and hurl it far away.

'Hi, James . . .'

Robert heard Louisa's voice carry but a passing car obliterated her next words. Then the baby let out a long squawk and Louisa's conversation with James Hammond was cut up into odd words and broken sentences. Robert tried to gather their meaning but all he could see was Erin stealing Cheryl's baby. Then she ran for her life.

My wife, a kidnapper, he thought, and in the same internal sigh he wrapped his arms tightly around her frail image because he wanted her back; he wanted her so badly he would have done anything to change the moment. But in an instant Erin was crushed and she floated away in a million pieces.

'Say that again. I can't hear you. Reception's poor.'

The front gate creaked and banged. Robert saw Louisa through the window. She was pacing about the street, struggling with poor signal. He tried to lip-read her words but couldn't.

What if he was wrong? He knew full well that any lawyer worth his salt would crumble the circumstantial movements of the young Erin, Ruth Wystrach, and sprinkle them under the jury's noses. Just because the police had a hunch thirteen years ago and his own paranoia was likely to rear up annually didn't actually mean that Erin was a kidnapper. Neither could anyone prove that she had actually ever worked as a prostitute or that Baxter King had been telling the truth. When it came down to it, Rob knew he was relying on gut instinct. What worried him most was that he was never usually wrong.

He glanced out at Louisa again, torn between trying to hear her conversation with the lab and Ruby quizzing him about what was going on. He knew the DNA test results would prove irrevocably what he already knew. He touched Cheryl's hand then did the same to Ruby.

Let them sense the bond, he pleaded in his mind. Let them feel the connection.

Louisa stepped back inside the house. She pulled the band from her ponytail. Her hair flopped around her shoulders.

Robert looked up. His face was a white wall. Ruby tugged impatiently at his hand.

'Dad, let's *go*.'

The baby cried and Cheryl sobbed through another tormented song.

Robert was truly torn. He was in the eye of the storm and whichever way he turned, he faced bad weather. Then he saw Louisa shake her head from across the room. Her expression was blank, her gesture loaded.

'Dad, I want to leave *now*!' Ruby tugged at Robert and tried to walk away.

Shocked into stillness, Robert slowly brought together the cold hand of Cheryl and the squirming fingers of Ruby.

Louisa did nothing to stop him.

THIRTY-FOUR

Robert took a wool throw and draped it around Cheryl's shoulders. His heart dug a deep hole in his chest. Like Cheryl, he was losing sight of what was real but he realised that for Ruby's sake, he must remain in control.

'Cheryl, is this your baby?' He knelt beside the shaking woman, touching the infant. He hadn't considered that Ruby might have a sister or brother.

'She's not well, is she?' the Asian girl said. Robert glanced at her as she squatted beside him. She had a waterfall of black, silky hair and shifted to adjust the bump at her middle.

He shook his head. 'And you don't have any idea what's happened?'

'I've been coming to see her for readings recently. Usually once a week and she's always been fine.' A Midlands accent licked at her words. 'But I've had some troubles at home and couldn't make it this weekend.' She smoothed a hand over her belly. 'But earlier today I came to visit and when no one answered I let myself in the back door. I found her in a terrible state with this baby screaming in the spare room. I didn't know what to do.'

'And?' Robert stroked Cheryl's sweating head. He tried to prise the baby from her grip but she tensed and chanted louder. 'Did you tell anyone?'

'I went home and told my older brother. He said he'd go to the police station and alert them before coming here. I've just come back but it took me a while.' Again, she cradled her belly. 'Will she be all right? She's been ever so good to me.'

Robert nodded. 'I think so. She's just had a bit of a shock.' There was no way out of the guilt. If he hadn't told Cheryl that he knew where her baby was, if he'd handled it with the full weight and consideration it deserved, she wouldn't have fled from the pub. They could have talked, arranged a time for her to meet Ruby, involved counsellors, social services, done whatever it took to ease the blow. Now he expected the staccato of a neon blue light and the chaos that accompanied such an invasion.

'This isn't your baby, is it, Cheryl?' The Asian girl stroked Cheryl's back. 'Come on, tell Sarah. If you think of all the things I told you, you can tell me.' Her words caught everyone's attention. She sounded wise beyond her years.

Cheryl gripped the baby harder. It stopped whimpering. 'Natasha,' Cheryl whispered, ducking her head and planting a kiss on its downy scalp.

'No, Cheryl,' Robert intervened. 'This baby is not Natasha.' Now was the moment to explain fully. '*This* is Natasha.' He caught Ruby, who tried to sidestep his reach but failed. He pulled her by the arm and once again set her before Cheryl.

'Robert, what is this all about? Get off!' Ruby struggled, her eyes two darts aimed at him.

Robert's heart snagged on the impatient tone in his stepdaughter's voice – that she had said Robert, not Dad, that she swiped at his shoulder with her free hand and glared at him as if she truly hated him. It was the first phase of letting her go.

'Ruby, this is your—'

'No!' Cheryl screamed, halting the breeze that wound

around them from the street. The knife cut cleanly through all of them as she sang in perfect tune, fondly caressing the baby in her arms.

> Rock-a-bye baby asleep in the well,
> I put her down there, now I'm in hell.
> When the rope snaps, the cradle will fall,
> And down will drop baby, cradle and all.

Everyone was motionless, no one knew what to do or say, all words or possible explanations had been surpassed. The temperature in the room dropped by several degrees and a darkness seemed to enter it.

Detective Superintendent George Lumley filled the doorway of the small house as if he'd been hovering outside, waiting for his prey to be still before he swooped. Three other police officers, one a woman, stood beside him.

It all happened so quickly, although by the end, time had become an immeasurable skid so that no one knew when they had last eaten or slept or been home or done anything that resembled normality.

Robert, Louisa, Ruby and Sarah were initially herded into the tiny kitchen to wait with the WPC. They were ordered not to leave the house. Voices shot like rapid fire from the living room, mostly the clipped questions of DS Lumley, who had briefly made his identity known to Robert. He was a solid man, a superintendent now.

'It's been a while, Cheryl,' he said, a whip of annoyance detectable when she showed no signs of intimidation. It took up-close, space-invading interrogation to get anything other than song from her. Finally, she admitted that the baby in her arms did not belong to her. Through another song,

Cheryl confessed to the infant's abduction.

Paramedics arrived and examined the baby before removing it to hospital. The distraught mother, having notified the police of the kidnapping from the park earlier in the day, was already on her way to meet the ambulance.

The small terraced house was filled with the static of police radios, the stares of neighbours as they lined the street for a quick snatch of the fuss and a steady stream of officers coming and going through the guarded front door. But mostly the house was filled with the stench of death.

When the room was cleared, George Lumley lowered his body into a chair opposite Cheryl and prepared himself for the confession he had hoped for thirteen years ago. He didn't want it in rhyme; he didn't want it in song or poetry. George Lumley wanted Cheryl Varney to spill her story in plain English.

'Mrs Varney,' he began. He filled his lungs with air. 'Did you murder your baby daughter Natasha on Saturday the fourth of January nineteen ninety-two?'

The WPC opened various kitchen cupboards and filled the kettle with water.

'Might as well have a brew,' she announced. No one else seemed to agree.

'Dad, what's *happening*?' Ruby shifted her chair at the table closer to her stepfather. It was Dad again, he noted. A good omen written over bad.

'Let's just say I made a mistake. A terrible, ghastly mistake.' He pulled Ruby's hand into his. He felt Louisa's cold stare on his face. 'You OK?' he asked. The ridges of her cheekbones were white and the flesh beneath visibly sunken. She looked as if she knew something he didn't.

'Yeah,' she said vaguely, her thoughts somewhere else. 'I'm OK.'

When DS Lumley ordered the garden to be searched, it was dark and floodlights were soon erected down the thin strip of land like brilliant sentries. Officers tramped through the small house, in the front door and out the back, carrying tarpaulin, shovels, camera equipment, and when the forensics team arrived, they carried metal cases containing precision instruments and technology. Everyone held their breath, waiting for a find.

Robert, Louisa, Ruby and Sarah were brought into the lounge one by one to make statements to DS Lumley. When it was Robert's turn, he saw that Cheryl had gone – except for the sickening song that still hung in the air like steam winding out of simmering manure. The policewoman sat opposite Robert while Lumley questioned him about his involvement with Cheryl Varney.

'And did she mention all this when she told your fortune?' Lumley's tone was unnecessarily mocking, his smirk too obvious. He wafted a hand, indicating he was referring to the situation generally.

'She said a few things that impressed me. But like I said, I didn't originally track her down because I wanted my fortune telling. I went to see Cheryl Varney because I believed I had found her abducted daughter.'

'Let me get this clear one last time.' The smirk fell away and was replaced by a grim expression, one that consisted of a tight jaw, narrowed eyes and the flushed, veined cheeks of a man who drank too much. 'Certain evidence led you to believe that your stepdaughter was in fact the kidnapped baby of Cheryl Varney?'

'Yes.'

'Having located your wife's parents, Mr and Mrs Wystrach, they then told you that their runaway daughter stole—'

'No,' Robert interrupted. 'They showed me newspaper clippings reporting that their runaway daughter was a suspect in the Varney kidnapping case. It happened the same day. You, the police, stated that you wanted to locate the runaway Ruth Wystrach, now my wife Erin, in connection with the abduction. And my wife has a daughter the same age as Cheryl's baby. You do the maths, Superintendent.'

'I will.' He paused, swallowed. 'There was certainly reason to believe that the missing teenager was linked to the abduction. A girl fitting her description was seen running through a car park carrying a baby. The same car park in which Cheryl Varney had left her baby unattended in the car.' Another pause. 'Of course, if you are unsure, you need to think about the identity of your stepdaughter.'

Robert stopped to think. The detective was correct. He had obviously misread Louisa's solemn head-shake after she had spoken to James Hammond. Ruby's paternal heritage was still uncertain and would possibly always remain a mystery. But what he did know was that he would love her as if she were his, as if her entire life, past and present, rested in his hands.

'Tell me one thing, Mr Knight. You're a lawyer, a sensible man, a fair man, a level-headed man, no doubt with the canny ability to see the truth when it knocks on your door.' DS Lumley removed the pen from the WPC and slid the statement pad from her grip. He placed them on the table. 'Off the record, what made you first suspect that your wife was a criminal?'

Robert folded his tired body forward, leaning his forearms on his knees. He stared at DS Lumley.

'Honestly?' Robert said, eyeballs rolling upward. 'It was the fear of losing her.'

Suddenly a young constable came running through the house and pushed through the front door into the street. His hand was cupped over his mouth and his face was ashen.

'I think I'm needed,' Lumley said, rising. He sighed. 'Hang on to your wife, Mr Knight. Running away isn't a crime. Being unduly paranoid should be.'

The major scramble occurred at 2.25 a.m., when Ruby had finally given up demanding answers that Robert couldn't supply, and she'd fallen asleep.

Young Sarah had been sent home, her older brother escorting her away. She offered Robert a brief smile as she left, lips the colour of hazelnuts, her eyes like coins.

'Rob,' Louisa said. They were still waiting in the small living room, hoping for DS Lumley's dismissal at any time. He was preoccupied in the rear garden, off limits to non-police.

'Yeah?' Robert yawned, wondering how he would stay awake on the drive back to London. Ruby was a puddle on his lap.

'There's something I should tell you.' Louisa's face had lost its usual glow over the course of the evening. Her eyes appeared skinned with cataracts and the natural sheen on her hair was missing. She was wrapped in Robert's jacket – fear and the night responsible for lowering her core temperature. She stared somewhere beyond Robert's shoulder, looking for the right words.

Then two police officers clad in white coveralls, masks and gloves guided an unmarked metal casket the size of a coffee table through the house and out into the street. The officers' eyes, the only portion of their faces visible to tell a tale, showed nothing.

The crate was labelled simply: Police Property. A clear plastic sheet protruded from the lid as the procession, flanked by DS Lumley, made its way out of the house. Moments later, blue lights flared silently down the street. DI Lumley returned to the house and spoke to Robert.

'You can leave now but we'll need further statements from you in the coming days.' The superintendent was weary, the lines on his face disappearing into his grey hair. It had been thirteen years.

Robert motioned to the door, his throat knotted around what he wanted to say. 'Was that . . .?'

'It was Natasha,' Lumley said solemnly as if the child had nameable form after all these years. 'She was deep in the well, suspended in a basket. Forensics suspect strangulation. Initial examination suggests at least three of her cervical vertebrae were crushed.'

Robert bowed his head. He joined hands with Louisa, an attempt not to think about the scene Lumley had just described. For now, he couldn't speak but Lumley answered what he was thinking anyway.

'When we searched the house thirteen years ago, after we initially suspected Cheryl, we found nothing except a dead cat buried in the garden. The slab covering the well was completely hidden beneath turf and weeds. As it was, we were there on gut instinct and a lucky warrant.' Lumley stiffened, arming himself against accusations. The baby would have been dead anyway, even if they had found it back then. 'Cheryl's already claiming insanity, that her post-natal depression was never flagged.'

'Let's go,' Robert said. He had to get out. He roused Ruby

and got her into the street before she remembered where she was. 'What did you want to tell me back in there?' Robert said to Louisa as he steered the Mercedes out of the narrow street.

Louisa glanced back at Ruby, who had balled herself up on the rear seat. She slept with the earphones on. 'It's nothing. Really.' She gripped Robert's outstretched arm with her fingers. 'Nothing important at all.'

Soon, the car was cruising south on the M1 and Robert was focused on the ribbon of tarmac ahead. Every so often, he stole a look at Louisa to see if she had succumbed to sleep. Each time he saw her watching the night, unblinking, with nothing to say.

THIRTY-FIVE

Robert knew she was back. There was a lightness to the air, a whisper of things to come as the indigo night sky gave way to a mottled, tangerine-coloured dawn.

He pulled the key from the lock, after ushering Ruby and Louisa inside, and closed the door quietly. He wanted to be sure first.

'Go through,' he told Louisa. 'Let's get some food.'

'I want to go to bed,' Ruby moaned, unable to keep her eyes open.

'OK, love. You go up. I'll be there in a minute.' Robert stroked her head, suddenly familiar again, as she sloped off.

'What a night,' Louisa exclaimed, roping her arms round Robert's neck just as Erin emerged from beneath a throw on the settee.

For a second, both women locked eyes and then Erin's sleepy state turned into alertness and disbelief.

'Robert!' she cried.

'*Erin*,' he replied loudly, unwrapping himself from Louisa. 'You've come home.'

Erin struggled to her feet. Her skin was equal to her mussed hair in colour, pale and fragile, and her eyes were ice drops assessing what they saw.

'Like a fool, I see,' she said, softly now. 'I should have

realised that you'd pass up on me as soon as I was gone.' Each word was cut and pasted perfectly onto her tongue from her overwrought mind.

'No, Erin, that's not true.' Robert spied the empty bottle of wine on the table, the last inch of red in the glass. Erin lost her balance as she untangled herself from the throw. He could see she'd not long stopped drinking.

'Don't worry. I'm gone.' Erin smiled sweetly and shoved her bare feet into her sandals. 'Where's my daughter? Where are my car keys?'

'*Our* daughter has gone to bed. She's exhausted. And you're not going anywhere.' Robert caught her by the wrist as she skittled past.

'I'll get her tomorrow then.' Erin squirmed and pulled a face although clearly not in any state to put up a fight.

Robert smelled the alcohol on her breath, her hair, her clothing. He pulled her close to make it a private moment. 'You're talking nonsense. I'm not letting you go anywhere in this state. I'm not letting you go anywhere ever again.'

He marched her into the kitchen, realising that was what he should have done with Jenna. Instead she had fled the house and driven off in her car after drinking; drinking and driving because he'd left her with no alternative. 'You're going to have a gallon of coffee and we're going to talk.'

Robert paused, drew breath and listened for Jenna. She wasn't there. He glanced around the room – a final check – but there was nothing. Just the room. He stared into the black depths of their garden and all he saw was Erin, reflected in the glass, and his own image staring back.

Silently, privately, he said goodbye.

'I'll put the kettle on,' Louisa offered, feeling like a spark at a petrol station.

Robert seated Erin at the kitchen table and then leaned over Louisa's laptop, tapping the mouse to bring it out of sleep mode. 'Louisa, check your email.'

'No, Rob. Let's have a coff—'

'Now, Louisa, or I'll do it for you.' Robert wanted to finally prove that his suspicions about Erin had been ridiculous, that now the police had unearthed the grim truth about Cheryl's baby, he had nothing to fear about Ruby's maternity. Of course she belonged to Erin.

'Rob, why don't—'

'There it is, look. An email from James Hammond.' He pushed Louisa's finger off the mouse pad and opened the email himself. Louisa slumped into a chair where she couldn't see the screen. 'She's all ours,' Robert said after a moment, realising that Erin wouldn't have any idea what they were talking about. She was thankfully unaware that he had even questioned where Ruby came from. 'Ninety-nine point nine per cent, anyway,' he finished under his breath before stamping a kiss on Erin's neck as if she'd just given birth. To Robert, she had.

Erin watched them, alert but silent, sitting straight in the chair.

Louisa reached for the laptop and rotated it so she could read for herself.

'Mum!' Ruby exclaimed. 'You're back!' The girl bowled into her mother's arms. 'Oh, don't leave Dad again. I never want you to split up.' She pulled Robert into the three-way embrace, her tiredness forgotten in the excitement of having her family reunited.

Louisa looked up from the computer. She said nothing. She watched as Ruby's promises and chatter strung her parents together like a broken necklace.

Erin and Robert's fingers slowly entwined either side of their daughter, their own promises to each other contained in the unspoken messages they swapped.

Then Louisa caught Erin's eye – just a brief connection between the two women but enough to convey a silent plea. Louisa held her breath, nodded slowly at Erin. She looked away.

'Right, coffee then,' Louisa said when the moment was firmly in the past. Swiftly and without fuss, she deleted James Hammond's email from her computer. The computer breathed a heavy sigh as she shut it down.

THIRTY-SIX

It's cold and raining and I wrestle the door as it tries to bang shut in the wind. Inside, I prop my umbrella against the wall and realise that I'll probably forget it when I go. It makes me smile, the way Robert and I met – a forgotten umbrella. I scan the café to see if she's here yet.

A hand rises over the heads of the many customers. It belongs to Louisa. She gives me a wide grin.

'Well done for getting a table.' I shrug off my coat and drape it on the back of my chair. I glance about. 'Is it waitress service?'

She nods and raises her hand again. A young girl is suddenly beside me, offering coffee, tea, whatever. 'How've you been?' Her eyes flash green beneath her grey shaded lids.

'Whoa,' I say. 'Where to begin?' I drink coffee, let her wait awhile.

She waits.

'Take a look.' I unbuckle my bag and fish out a pocket-sized album with a dozen or so photographs inside. Louisa takes her time, poring over each one, noticing every detail. I do it a hundred times a day.

'She has your eyes,' Louisa says. 'Well, and your nose and mouth and—'

'She's totally beautiful,' I say, realising I sound vain.

'Have you told her?'

I drink more coffee, unfurl my leg and cross it the other way. 'I haven't spoken to her.'

'Ah,' Louisa says. 'No rush.'

She's right. There isn't a rush any more.

It took several months for things to get back to normal. Thing is, if you've never been normal, you can never really be certain that things have got back to it.

But Robert took himself off to work and became a vigilante lawyer specialising in children's rights, appealing tirelessly on behalf of minors who would have otherwise remained unrepresented. It all started, he said, with two kids called Joe and Alice Bowman. He helped them untangle their lives from their warring parents and they are now, I believe, living with a foster family while they decide where they want to live. Rob says they are learning about how happiness is meshed with forgiveness. I think he is learning this himself.

Rob's new focus at work also came from my story, or so he said as we lay in bed about a week after Ruby and I returned home from Brighton. Things were still brittle; bone china on the edge of a shelf. Robert was coming to terms with Ruby's paternal heritage and my childhood abuse but better that way, I told him, because there was no other father for Ruby to adore. Aside from me, there was zero competition for her love. I didn't mention that our daughter was no more the product of Gustaw's interference than any other child.

'We can get through this.' He shimmied his hand over my belly, a craftsman sizing up his materials. 'I know that because of how I felt when you weren't here.'

'And I wasn't here because of how you felt.' I rolled onto my side so that his hand rested on the crest of my hip. He frowned at me. 'Your obsessive lawyer side. Driving the truth from me.' I had to look away. There is one thing he'll never know. 'My whole life I've excelled at keeping people the other side of my barrier. It was second nature until you found a way through.' I hoped he understood what I meant. 'Imagine a wound. Now rip the plaster off it. Don't just touch the raw skin and see the person flinch, stick your whole finger in and gouge about with your nail.'

Robert made a noise. 'That's what I did to you?'

I nodded. 'The wound's always been there. It's just that no one ever touched it before.' He was getting it now, I could see it in his eyes as they narrowed and darkened and tiptoed across my body.

'The thing is,' he said, 'how did you get the wound in the first place?'

To avoid answering, I rolled on top of my husband and distracted him the only way I knew. Later, he pushed inside me, searching for the truth, believing he found it before slipping into sleep.

Really, the only truth he found was the answer to his own question.

We order paninis with mozzarella, basil, rocket, and a pesto dressing that runs between my fingers as I bite. Louisa laughs.

'Here, wipe your chin.' She smiles as her panini does the same. We don't bother with cutlery. 'Did Ruby's birth certificate come?'

'Finally,' I tell her. 'This is good,' I lick my lips. 'It arrived a couple of weeks ago. Rob took care of all the paperwork at the courts.' I sigh, like I did when I finally held the certificate in my hand. I showed Ruby that she was officially born. She grinned and squeezed my waist, her head on my shoulder. She's going to be tall.

'And the adoption?'

'It's in hand. Technically, we need the agreement of Ruby's biological father before Robert can officially adopt Ruby.' I put down my panini and wonder what right either of us have to really keep Ruby. When I found her in the wardrobe, I truly believed that she was my sick baby. I'll go mad if I wonder about her real mother scouring the country for her although in my heart I know that Ruby had been abandoned, just like Becco dumped my first baby. 'Considering that my uncle abused me since I was four and he's dead now anyway, getting his permission isn't an issue,' I continue, coaxing a smile to run parallel to the charade.

I'm used to talking to Louisa about such things and she is the only person who knows the truth. I am getting used to talking to my counsellor, too, but if I tell her the truth, then I risk losing Ruby again. But without the talking, the therapy, these last few weeks, I wouldn't have survived. Robert and I wouldn't have survived. 'But what about you?' I ask. 'Are you sticking around for a while?'

'Ah,' she says. 'Me and Willem.' And she sinks her teeth into the bread.

Lots of things happened that week. Firstly, I won an award for Fresh As A Daisy. Silly really, because I never even entered any competition. It turns out that Baxter put me forward for some national florist's showdown and my shop won for its innovative window displays. I even got my picture in the paper. I kept a copy this time.

Then, as the last shreds of autumn gave way to the first fingers of winter, Ruby shuddering and waving goodbye one morning as the air frost nipped down her back, as the bell of sky above hardened with a veneer of ice, my medical notes tumbled through the letter box with the gas bill and a couple of bank statements.

Reading through the notes, I learned I had been a surprisingly healthy child. Of course, everything stopped when I reached the age of fifteen. My last recorded visit to the GP was when I told Mother I was getting fat and she took me to see Dr Brigson. Looking back, I think I knew. And as I read on, it seemed that Dr Brigson did, too.

Visible scars consistent with local trauma to the vaginal area . . . child clearly disturbed and unable/unwilling to discuss cause of pregnancy . . . possible rape/abuse? Notify Social Services . . .

It occurred to me, as I read the notes, that I wanted my parents; a childish desire to be owned, protected, cherished. While it's too late for protection – in fact, soon it will be my turn to protect them – I want them to know what I have become, that I survived. I want to ask them why they tried to have my baby adopted, why they thought I would be a bad mother, why they never noticed what Uncle Gustaw was doing to me.

I want them to see me. To take me back. And, after I admitted this to myself, I resolved that one day very soon I would drive to the dismal house where I gave birth. I promised myself I would go home.

No one ever did report my abuse to social services. But it was the medical proof, detailed accurately within those notes, that was precious now. They stated I was pregnant, estimated delivery date first week of January 1992, with a viable single foetus. What happened to me thereafter didn't particularly interest the Registrar General. To file the form for a late, a very late, birth certificate required certain details, all of which I was now able to provide. Thanks to Louisa.

I called her two days after I returned home from Brighton. Robert and I were making a go of things and since I'd changed the email from James Hammond on Louisa's computer, and since I knew that she knew, I wanted to talk to her – despite our brief moment of understanding. To explain. To make sure she was OK with knowing. I couldn't risk losing Robert again.

'Hey, I'm an investigator. I know when to stop digging.' She told me that it was seeing Ruby and me slotted around Robert like three pieces of a unique puzzle that made her understand. 'I don't care who Ruby is,' she said. 'But I do care about what she can become.'

She didn't mention her feelings for Robert. She didn't need to.

So, with my consent and Robert's backing, we paid for Louisa to pull up my medical records. Robert accepted what had happened, with Uncle Gustaw – God knows he's seen enough child abuse in his line of work – and an understanding stitched itself between us about my life thereafter. That's when I began seeing the counsellor. Once a week, on a Wednesday.

Then, without telling Robert, I asked Louisa to find out what had happened to Ruby. My first Ruby.

'Let me take another look,' she says. I slide the album across the table, careful not to get dressing on the cover.

'It felt a bit creepy, taking pictures of a young girl without her knowing.' I crane sideways so I can see the pictures too. 'That was when she was coming out of the cinema with her friends. We went to see *Oliver Twist*—'

'We?'

'I sat behind her, eavesdropped on her conversation, watched her eat popcorn.' Truth is, I tailed her so closely it's a wonder she didn't call the police.

From the minute I first laid eyes on my daughter, my

biological daughter, I fell in love with her. She is everything I had imagined and more. Think of a lioness surrounded by cats; think of a sleek yacht in a sea of rowing boats; think of an orchid in a field of daisies; think of a ruby in a pot of glass beads.

'Will you tell Rob?' she asks.

'What, that I lost my baby?'

'You didn't lose your baby, Erin. You lost your mind.' Louisa snaps the album shut. 'Someone took your baby. Someone threw your baby away.'

She called me at the shop, breathless with the news. The phone line was twanging between us. 'I've found her,' she said and I marvelled at how easy it had been. 'She lives in London.' I sat down, as if folding my body behind the counter would aid the absorption of shock. All this time and she'd only been a breath away.

The first time we met at the café, Louisa provided me with newspaper articles. They'd really made a thing out of it, a nationwide feel-good story of the baby who was thrown away. I never read the papers or watched the news. I was too busy earning money to pay for my baby's treatment.

'When you told me what happened, Erin, it didn't take a rocket scientist to figure out that if your baby had been found, a story of some kind would be in the papers.' Louisa tucked a strand of fiery hair behind her ear.

'They told me she was ill,' I said again, just so Louisa didn't think I had a hand in disposing of my baby. 'That I would get her back just as soon as she was better.' I was past bowing my head. I'd been a child myself. 'They told me she was in hospital and I believed them.'

BLOOD TIES

5 January 1992

NEW YEAR BABY THROWN OUT
WITH THE RUBBISH

A baby girl, just days old, was found dumped in a skip
yesterday afternoon. A passer-by, who wishes to remain
anonymous, heard the infant crying at around 3 p.m.
and alerted the authorities.

The baby, currently being cared for in St Thomas'
Hospital, has been named Felicity by the nurses
because, 'Despite her unusual start in life, she is a
happy little soul,' commented the sister in charge of the
infant's care.

A police spokesman said, 'We have secured and
examined the area around the skip in which the infant
was found and at this point in time, cannot make any
announcements. We are extremely concerned for the
mother and her well-being and urge her to come
forward for assistance.'

Felicity, I thought, as I positioned myself outside her house. It
was just after six in the morning and I'd told Robert that I was
going to a trade show. He promised to look after Ruby, while
I went off to spy on the baby that had been thrown away.

It was a nice house; very middle-class in a suburb with
trees and clipped hedges and no doubt a competition of fairy
lights at Christmas. Felicity's house was painted white and
had fake black beams criss-crossing the front. There was a
Volvo estate parked in the drive and at ten past eight exactly,
Felicity's mother came out of the house laden with school
bags, calling back inside the house and beckoning frantically.

She was more like someone's mother than me. Better all round, with her neat brown bob and sensible shoes.

Then Felicity came out of the house, looking like any other teenager with her school tie knotted short and her black trousers trailing in the wet – *except that she was my teenager.* She eased herself into the Volvo, not in any hurry, after which her mother sped out of the drive.

I started up my car and followed closely, inhaling the tang of exhaust that blew in through my heater vents in case I got a whiff of my baby. Fifteen minutes later, we pulled up outside a high school and Felicity got out of the car without kissing her mother goodbye.

I never got to kiss you goodbye either.

I saw her three times during the day. Once at ten thirty when the bell rang and she marched across the front of the school to the science block. She was at the head of a V-shaped formation of five girls. She was the prettiest, the tallest and obviously the most popular, the way the others all flowed behind her like a bridal train. She had nothing of Uncle Gustaw about her. Her blonde hair whipped about her shoulders in the cold wind.

Put your coat on, young lady.

At lunchtime, Felicity sloped off to the fish and chip shop a couple of blocks down from the school. I got out of my car and went for chips too. Nice big fat greasy ones and I leaned against the wall while Felicity sat on a bench with a friend and shared cod and chips. I couldn't hear everything but they mentioned a couple of boys, sprayed Coke through their noses and bent double with fun.

A warm river of blood flowed through my heart. Felicity was happy.

I saw her at three forty, when she loitered in the street for her mother. Many kids got onto the school bus but I was pleased to see that Felicity was picked up by a parent. She managed a quick brush of her lips across her mother's cheek after she'd hurled her school bag into the rear.

I let them drive off into the distance. Next time, I would bring my camera.

'The Yorks seemed happy to share their story. They even went on a daytime TV show for adoptive parents and discussed the morals of taking on someone else's baby without knowing its history. They said that was the least of it. Getting to know and learning to love your child was the bigger part of the journey.'

'They did?' That's good, I think, as I sew my baby's name together in my head. *Felicity York*. It sounds nice. She sounds nice. I think of her lying in a skip. I think of her lying in another woman's arms. 'Louisa,' I say. 'You're still sure you won't tell Rob, aren't you.' It wasn't a question. Her eyes go wide at the mention of my husband's name.

'I'm sure,' she says earnestly, pulling a crumb from her lip. 'Why would I want to hurt him? Why would I want to hurt you or Ruby?'

And I believe her as we finish our paninis with runny pesto dressing and talk over the noise of the cappuccino machine and watch silver bulbs of rain wiggle down the window. We do this until it is time for me to go home.

Robert is taking a thrashing from Ruby on the Playstation. He rolls on his back like a dying insect, groans and lays down his controller as a sign of defeat.

'Ha, you'll never beat the Mighty Red,' Ruby says and begins to tickle Robert's ribs with her foot. He grabs it and tickles her back and I have no chance of being noticed as they begin death by tickling. I go into the kitchen to unpack the groceries that I picked up on the way home from my meeting with Louisa.

I wonder if Robert will sense that I have been with her. Will he smell her scent on me, catch her words on my breath or the shadow of her kiss on my cheek as we parted? I wash my hands in case.

'Oh, you scared me,' I gasp. Robert is pressed behind me, his arms round my belly.

'Hey, fat woman, how you doing?'

'You wait,' I say. 'Cooking later or going out?' It takes him less than a second to decide that we are going out.

'Why don't you have a lie-down or a hot bath before we go?' He gently massages my stomach. It'll be classical music pressed to my skin soon.

'Why don't you come with me?' He knows what I mean and follows me upstairs while Ruby plays the piano. Briefly, I wonder if Felicity plays an instrument.

'Will you look at that?' Robert is pointing at the stuffed bag on the landing.

'She's so excited,' I say. 'She packed yesterday and the school trip's not for another week.' Robert takes my hand and leads me into our bedroom. He lays me down on the bed and a waft of fabric conditioner pillows around me. I smile as he closes the door.

'What?' he asks, pulling his shirt off over his head without unbuttoning it.

'Nothing,' I say, meaning everything.

Just that my three children are safe. Ruby, Felicity and the one tucked inside me, growing at a million miles an hour.

Julia Marshall never knew her father.
She's about to find out why.

**The first chapter of the breathtaking new novel
from Sam Hayes,
UNSPOKEN, follows here . . .**

PROLOGUE

As a child, there are things you learn not to talk about; that the very utterance of certain words sends some people into a flat spin.

I was four when I first spoke of my father, having just started nursery. 'Where's *my* daddy?' I asked my mother. It appeared that all the other little girls had a father and, until I discovered this fact, the absence of my own had meant nothing to me. It was simply never spoken of. As if he never existed.

That first day at nursery, we'd been asked to paint a picture of our family. I'd done one entirely of him; just my daddy standing tall and proud and gazing at me with handsome blue eyes, exactly the same shade as mine. He was smiling, his arms outstretched, as if he was beckoning to me to run into them, knock him back a few paces as I hurled myself against his body.

Really, it was just a soggy piece of sugar paper with brown and orange swirls for a body, and a pink blob head. But how I loved my new father.

'Look, it's my daddy,' I told my mother, waving the paint-wetted paper at her. We were walking home. She suddenly let go of my hand. I squinted up at her, the brightness behind her protecting me from focusing on her fierce scowl.

All my life, she only ever said one thing to me about my father and it was then, the sun flashing on our backs that September day, completely alone down the lane that led to the farm. 'You do not have a father, Julia. Never, ever speak of him again.' And she pressed her forefinger to her lips and whispered a firm *shhh*, silencing me eternally.

Now, grown up and with children of my own – a fresh generation of emotional wounds to deal with – I am left wondering, from that brisk walk home with my mother all those years ago, how can you speak of something you've never had? How do you know which words to use when they simply aren't there?

It's the very nature of language, the shape of the syllables, how they slide off the tongue, linger in the air like pollution or sunshine, that makes each of us unique.

But it's when those words take on a life of their own that the real story begins to unfold. When the unspoken past collides with the present.

JULIA

I discovered her completely by accident and really, with so much to think about, I could easily have missed her. She was lying in the field, twisted on her side in the brittle iced grass. Her lips were violet and her eyes drilled holes in the winter sky.

She lay perfectly still, her pale skin sparkling from frost and her red nails spread like a broken string of beads.

'Grace!' I fell to my knees. If I touched her, I could be tampering with evidence. If I touched her, I might find out she was dead.

I fumbled my mobile phone from my pocket. Grace blinked, cracking the connection she had made with whatever lay behind the skim of clouds.

'Grace . . .' I leaned forward, my pink wind-seared cheeks a breath from hers. I tore my jacket off my back and made her into a parcel. Her bare legs protruded, askew of their natural position.

'Grace, what happened to you?' I still wasn't sure that she was alive. The weight of her was corpse-like in my shaking arms. Perhaps her soul, the heaviest part of anyone, had already taken leave.

She turned her head and a tendon in her neck snapped against my wrist. Her mouth opened, revealing a crust on her lips like salt on a Margarita glass.

'What *happened*, Grace?'

Last time I saw her she had dropped her English essay on my desk and left the classroom in a flurry of teenage urgency. It was the end of term and everyone was full of Christmas excitement. With all that was going on in my life, with Mum, with Murray, I'd not even marked her work yet.

'Doc . . . tor,' she rasped without breath to force out the word. I think she said doctor.

'I've called for an ambulance, Grace. Sit tight.' I pulled her broken body closer and encased her in my arms, my legs, my hair. Milo bounded across the field and instinctively slumped on her legs, panting, his breath falling in bursts of steam on her knees. Warming the life back into Grace.

It was twenty minutes before the paramedics crowned the rise that splayed from the end of the footpath. Everyone walked their dog down Lightning Lane but not everyone got as far as the unnatural quarry bowl of amphitheatre-like proportions beyond. As a kid, I used to run down, my knees buckling, my hair a mess, our dog barking at my madness as we descended into the manmade hole. That was years ago.

'Can you hear me, sweetheart?'

Grace was levered from me by a paramedic. There were three of them, two men and a woman, while two police officers marched behind across the white-green grass – their footsteps recorded in staccato prints until the sun dissolved the frost.

'I just found her like this,' I said. 'I was walking my mother's dog.' I wasn't shivering even though Grace had my coat; even though the breath fell from my mouth in icy clouds. 'I thought she was plastic.' A mannequin, dumped. A useless shop dummy, fly-tipped. That's what I'd thought when I saw Grace on the ground.

'What's your name, love?' the female paramedic asked.

'Grace. Grace Covatta. Her father's Italian,' I said when Grace didn't reply.

'Grace, can you hear me, sweetheart?' While the woman coaxed her to talk, the other paramedic wrapped her in foil blankets and opened a small case containing portable monitors. She was hooked up to a mini oxygen canister and a machine beeped, registering her barely alive.

'Has she said anything about what happened?'

I shook my head. 'I was walking my mother's dog. He started to chase a rabbit and I turned to call him off and that's when . . .' That's when my eyes blurred and I'd squinted through the morning mist, disbelieving. 'That's when I saw Grace. Will you take a look at her feet? They're hurt.'

'When she's safely in hospital and warmed up. She's not bleeding now.' The paramedic turned to Grace and spoke to her as if she was deaf. I should know. People do it to Flora all the time, as if she's stupid. 'We're going to put you on a stretcher, Grace. We're taking you to hospital.' His mouth was big and wide, a goldfish trying to get through to her.

Grace said nothing. She stared. Her tongue, swollen and dry, tried to lick her lips as if she was preparing to speak.

'Oh God,' I cried and turned away, yanking on Milo's collar. It was something familiar, purposeful, reminding me of the reason I was out in the fields at eight-thirty on a freezing December morning. 'If I'd not found her . . .'

The crew moved fast. Did this mean they'd done it before? Was Grace just another name on their everyday job list? The police cordoned off the area and alerted their superiors to the situation.

Grace was loaded on to a fold-up stretcher and I followed beside as she was carried down the footpath. She said nothing, just jolted in time with the steps of the ambulance crew, her tongue caught between the roof of her mouth and her dry lips.

'Grace, your English essay was fabulous. I gave you an A.' I touched her foil shoulder, hoping I might register a link of normality with her. I'd got the class to write a two thousand word essay on evil. It was a broad spectrum assignment, to see what they came up with. I hadn't marked any of them yet but I wanted Grace to have an A. I hadn't reckoned earlier that she would be able to write about the subject from first-hand experience. 'Do you know what's happened to her?' I asked the paramedic as we headed back to the village. 'Is there any evidence of . . . ?' I couldn't say it. I panted from the half run necessary to keep up with their pace and pulled hard on Milo's lead so that every breath rasped in his throat. I wanted him close.

'The doctors will examine her. Are you a relation?'

'I'm her English teacher.' I might as well be related, I thought. They all jot down their hearts instead of doing their homework.

Lightning Lane eventually dissolved into the road at the edge of the village in an estuary of mud and frozen leaves. It's always been called that, since way back when I was a child and beyond. Mum said it was because for three winters on the trot an oak, a beech and a chestnut were taken down by storms. Mum also once said that bad things come in threes. Neat triangles of trouble. In all this mess, I was reminded of her, of Murray, too. Our own triangle of pain.

An ambulance and a police car barricaded the lane, their blue lights ticking through the murk and suggesting trouble. The sight had drawn quite a crowd of curious onlookers and I knew that the ripple of news would already be reaching neighbouring villages, towns, journalists, front pages. Within hours the presses would be rolling, Grace's name at the top.

We marched up to the vehicles like a team of arctic explorers and just the very faces that I would have expected to be there came hustling forward for news. They reminded me why I had moved from the village with its tittle-tattle and messaging system faster than email. Had Grace not been on the stretcher, I would have smiled and walked on, thankful not to be a part of it any more. Eight miles wasn't much, but Ely provided a level of anonymity that suited me.

I ushered the onlookers back – I was a storm wall against the tide, protecting Grace from their invasion – but because of this, I didn't see the medics get her into the ambulance. I didn't wish her well or bon voyage or let her know I hoped to see her at school soon. Just what *are* you supposed to say when someone's like Grace?

Within seconds, the vehicle was pulling off down the lane with a single blast of siren to clear the gathering. Extra police had arrived and that's where I came in. As I slumped onto the frozen grass, they asked me to make a statement. They asked me what Grace had said.

That was Friday and I'm still here, staying at Mum's farm. It's what you do, isn't it? Walk the Labrador, discover the victim of a brutal attack, come home and read the paper. I'm not sure how much more I can shoulder.

'Mum,' I say gently. I'm getting used to it being pointless. 'Grace is still in hospital.' Four days she's been there. She can't walk or talk. The tendons in her feet were cut and they don't know how long it will be before they're healed. No one likes to hazard a guess about Grace.

Mum stares and I wonder if there was a slight turn of her head, a glimmer of interest. She doesn't know Grace but I've told her that she's one of my pupils. Over the last week, I've told Mum lots of things – mostly light-hearted babble and stuff about the kids. I thought perhaps the shock of finding Grace down Lightning Lane would elicit a reaction but there's simply nothing in her. Mum is empty. Her eyes are drained and her lips thin and unwilling. Only when I pass her a cup of tea or slide a plate of food in front of her does she bother to move. I'm sure I hear her bones creak while she's eating, as though they are whispering behind her back.

'They say poor Grace will be in a wheelchair for ages and have months of physiotherapy.' I sigh and wonder if that is a mini-sigh in Mum's chest, an echo of mine. A tiny heave of sadness beneath her brittle breastbone. 'I'm going to visit her soon.'

I put the children's sandwiches on the table just as they come bowling into the kitchen, saving me from calling them down. Alex curls his mouth around the soft bread before he is even seated. I trail my fingers through Flora's hair and tuck her chair under the table.

Orange juice? My hands form the words for Flora. She nods and smiles, cheese poking from her mouth.

Nothing much has changed in this house over the years. The window still rattles from the wind and if the rain comes from the north, a bowl is still needed to catch the water on the window ledge. Old pine cupboards and dressers line the room, insulating the walls with a vast stash of family crockery, glassware, chipped dinner sets, children's paintings, lace table cloths, drawers full of string, glue, tape, broken pens and ancient bills. The flagstones are perhaps a shade darker than I remember, the walls more yellowed, but the whole place smells the same: of wood smoke, cooking and love.

'Why don't you wrap up warm and take Flora down to the rope swing after lunch?' I say to Alex but then I stop, halfway to the sink. 'Actually, it's probably too cold. Why not watch a movie?' Someone did that to Grace. Someone bent and cut her body and left her naked in the field. I kiss each of my children. They will not be playing outside while we are at Grandma's house.

'No, we want to play in the fields. It's not cold.' Alex doesn't whine but rather states his case. He knows it won't do any good. I shoot him a look.

'Mum,' I say wearily. 'Cheese for you, too?'

She doesn't answer, of course, so I give her cheese anyway. What would she say if she did start speaking again? I'm finding it hard to remember her voice, even though it's only been a week since she fell silent. No one knows why her words stopped.

I put the sandwich on a tray and rest it on her knee. 'If you sit any closer to that fire, you'll turn into toast.' I'm talking to her in a voice fit for a kindergarten class. Is it all a big tantrum, I wonder? 'Anyway, Alex, your Dad's taking you out later.' I say it like it's good reason for them not to play outside. 'He's coming at five.'

Alex grins and immediately turns into a little Murray, his face broad and alert, his eyes filled with more anticipation than the situation warrants. Flora pulls at my arm and signs, What? Her finger is an annoyed scribble in the air, her eyebrows tucked together.

Dad, I tell her. He's coming to fetch you at five. That's when Flora abandons her sandwich and runs to nestle on her grandma's lap, competing with the tray for space. It seems she doesn't want to go.

I sigh and snap on rubber gloves to tackle the dishes. Mum doesn't have a dishwasher. Neither does she have a washing machine, a dryer, a television or even an electric kettle. When we visit Grandma's house, we put on an extra sweater and the children bring their portable DVD player.

'Where's he taking us?' Alex asks, chomping on the last of his sandwich. He drains his milk. 'Dad, I mean.'

'I hope to God not anywhere on that boat. Not in the dark.' I plunge my hands into the soapy water and see Flora slipping off the side of the narrow boat, her mouth unable to do anything but drink the River Cam. 'Probably bowling or to that nice pizza place.' I comfort myself with the thought of them having an evening in the city.

'Or to his friend's house,' Alex chips in.

'His friend?' I know I said it too quickly, although an eleven year old would hardly notice, but it's not like Murray to have friends.

Alex shrugs and I don't press him because there is suddenly the sound of breaking china. Flora has knocked Mum's plate on to the floor.

Don't worry, I tell her with my wet, yellow hands. She tries to hide the smile and pushes her face into Mum's shoulder, who vaguely curls an arm around Flora's waist. It is the most animated I have seen her in days.

Murray is an hour late. He stands in the doorway and I throw my keys at him. I am hoping that the use of my car will discourage him from taking the children on the boat.

'Sorry. I was—'

'Kids!' I call. I don't want to hear why he was late or, indeed, why he is only wearing a T-shirt when a frost has already set a glaze on the courtyard beyond. 'Come in and shut the door. You'll freeze.' Come and join my kindergarten class, I think, yet I still find myself wanting to wrap a blanket around him.

'Tea?' I offer then wish I hadn't. It'll take the kettle an age to boil and I don't want the children back late.

'Yeah, why not,' he replies and goes to stand with his back to the fire. He only notices Mum after a moment or two. 'Mary,' he acknowledges. He doesn't know what to say to her. 'How are you?'

Mum happens to be staring at Murray's knees now he is beside the fire. She doesn't reply, just a swallow and a blink. I ease between them and put the kettle on the hotplate.

'She's the same,' I say. I realise that it's the wrong thing to do, talking for her, but Dr Carlyle said to include her in conversation as if everything's normal. 'Dr Carlyle comes to visit her often.'

'I didn't think doctors could afford to make house calls these days.' Murray rubs at the stubble on his chin.

'Are you growing a beard?'

'How often does he come?' Murray presses on.

'He came yesterday and will be here tomorrow.' I spoon tea into the pot. No quick-fix teabags here at Cold Comfort Farm. 'I think Mum appreciates his visits.'

'And you?'

I stop, sigh and make my face into a picture of weariness. 'I'm not sick, Murray. I don't need a doctor.' Deep down, I know this is not true.

'Do you appreciate his visits, I mean?' His voice is dry and determined.

'Murray, for God's sake!' But Alex hears that his dad has arrived and runs into the kitchen, begging him to take a turn on his Nintendo.

'Why not wait until you're in the restaurant to show Dad your new game?'

'We're going to a restaurant, are we? My four hours of time with my children has already been planned. That's nice.'

'Well, you wasted one of them by being late,' I mutter.

Swiftly, Murray unhooks Alex's coat from the over-burdened stand and tucks our boy inside. Then, the timing perfect, Flora spills into the room – delighted to see her father even though she hates the upset of being taken from me for even an hour – and she too is padded in coat.

I am struck by a slice of freezing air as they leave. 'I'll have them back by ten,' Murray commands in a voice I recognise from way back.

'*Nine*!' I call out but the word gets caught in my throat. For the rest of the evening I sit in silence with my mother and wonder what happened to my family.

The Take

Martina Cole

If you want it badly enough, take it . . .

Freddie Jackson is just out of prison. He's done his time, made the right connections, and now he's ready to use them. His wife Jackie dreams of having her husband home, but she's forgotten the rows, the violence and the girls Freddie can't leave alone.

Bitter, resentful and increasingly unstable, Jackie sees her life crumble while her little sister Maggie's star rises. In love with Freddie's cousin Jimmy, Maggie is determined not to end up like her sister.

Families should stick together, but behind closed doors, jealousy and betrayal fester until everyone's life is infected. For the Jacksons, loyalty cannot win out. In their world you can trust no one. In their world everyone is on the take.

Praise for Martina Cole's phenomenal bestsellers:

'A blinding good read' Ray Winstone

'Distinctive and powerfully written' *The Times*

'The stuff of legend . . . utterly compelling' *Mirror*

'Her gripping plots pack a mean emotional punch' *Mail on Sunday*

'Martina Cole again explores the shady criminal underworld, a setting she is fast making her own' *Sunday Express*

978 0 7472 6767 6

headline

Now you can buy any of these other bestselling
Headline books from your bookshop or
direct from the publisher.